GW00643444

DRAGON'S KISS

THE BLOOD & FLAME SAGA
BOOK ONE

E.A. WINTERS

DRAGONLEAFPRESS

To anyone who has ever believed the lies they were told.

SOCIAL MEDIA

Connect with me on social media! [1]

- Website and newsletter: https://www. eawinters.com
- Facebook: https://www.facebook.com/ eawintersnovels
- TikTok: @eawinters
- Instagram: @e.a.winters

---

1. Warning: connecting on social media may lead to exclusive content, behind the scenes snapshots, and joining a community that is way more fun than your daily to-do list. Engage with caution.

ALSO IN SERIES

The Blood and Flame Saga
Dragon's Kiss
Broken Bonds
Noble Claims
Crimson Queen

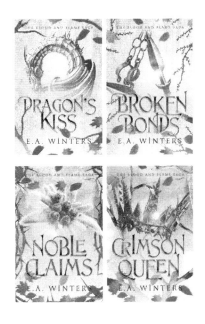

1

Any minute now, Governor Mallen would walk Governor Reza and his aide out of the building, which meant three minutes from now, Governor Mallen would be dead. Semra shifted uncomfortably under the servant's garments, wondering how the women serving here got anything done with such long skirts. She'd trained in all manner of clothing, of course, but missions requiring dresses for disguise were never her favorite. She preferred never being seen at all and wearing loose pants for ease of motion.

The great double doors of the meeting room opened, and three men stepped out onto the hallway's marble floor. Semra recognized Governor Mallen at once as the tall, over-weight, middle-aged man with a booming voice and bois-terous laugh. Semra wondered how many people's lives he'd squandered to afford the rich linens he wore. The Framatar had told them Mallen was corrupt through and through, and Semra had seen the exorbitant lifestyle herself—a stark contrast to the poor villages just four leagues from this grand house of legislature.

The second man was also tall and richly dressed, though more slender, soft spoken, and solemn. This must be Governor Reza. Reza's aide trailed him, carrying an assortment of papers and ink pens. Though young, only a couple years older than Semra's seventeen years, he wore a confident demeanor.

Mallen laughed again, loudly, and Semra thought perhaps his political practices weren't the only things the world would miss about him when he was gone. The man clapped Reza on the back and dipped his head at the aide, gesturing them to walk with him out to the outer courtyard that spilled down the steps and off the property.

As the men receded from sight, Semra assessed the two guards outside the meeting room. She'd been working here for two weeks in preparation for the job, and a pang of envy turned her belly again. Brens and Behruz never had to enter the building at all. They perched sixty yards from the courtyard steps with a longbow. They hadn't had to endure the rudeness of the guard to the right or the long glances from the guard to the left. The first guard, Bratar's, rudeness meant he didn't care about her, which served her well. The attention from Javed, however, could be problematic. In her line of work, she didn't like anyone taking particular notice of her. Still, it had its uses.

Semra dipped her head at the guards and smiled at Javed. He smiled back at her.

"Awfully late for you to be here, wouldn't you say?" he asked.

Semra tossed her hands up. "I know, I know! But I think I left my sash under the table when I was cleaning earlier. I thought I could slip in and grab it...? Please, don't tell the governor. I need the money, and I know he doesn't take easily to new servants."

Bratar scoffed, but Javed peeked into the meeting room and then nodded. "All right. Make it quick, pretty girl. I won't let Bratar tell on you."

Dipping her head gratefully, Semra ducked into the meeting room. The city key, five inches long and made of ornate gold, sat on a mount in the center of the table. Mallen customarily kept it on display as a symbol of his authority during meetings, but he carried it on his person at all other times.

Semra examined the key's mount. She'd spent the past two weeks snatching a few secret minutes here and there to study its intricate security measures. Semra lifted her skirts to pull out the sash she supposedly lost and climbed under the table. She turned on her back beneath the mounting system and saw a square panel with nail heads on its four corners. Except they weren't just nail heads. Semra pressed them in the sequence she'd learned—left, left, top, right, left. A soft click rewarded her, and the panel slid forward to a combination lock made entirely of wood inside the thick tabletop.

Shouts erupted outside, and she heard Bratar and Javed's heavy footsteps running toward the grand steps, followed by another six guards running from various directions. Brens had taken her shot. Governor Mallen would be dead, and the incident would draw the guards away to open her escape path out of the legislature and into the residence portion of the building. She had less than a minute.

Nimble fingers flying, Semra moved the mechanism clockwise eight clicks, paused, then rotated it left. The lock cycled through a five-number series, then the last number swung the bottom three inches of the compartment, housing the gears, toward her. Semra reached up and turned the knob, loosening the tension and releasing the key on top of the table. A quiet click sounded above her, and she shut the compartment, locked it, and slid the panel back into its place. Semra scurried out from underneath the table, snatched the key, stowed it in her sash, and ran to the doorway.

Toward the front of the building, to her right, there was a hall with rooms on either side and a fountain in the middle. To her left, the hall extended to the governor's study and court before branching off to the residence.

Semra darted around the corner to the left and opened the heavy brass door into the atrium. A pool, flush to the ground, graced the center of the large, long room. At one end, a fountain splashed water in graceful arcs. Pillars reinforced the ceiling at its four corners, and evening light illuminated the room through a rectangular opening above the pool. Nothing else filled the room except for murals on the walls and an archway on the far end, where any one of the governor's family members might pass by. The open ceiling stood an impressive twenty feet over her, too high to be of any use. It was a beautiful room, she supposed, but all she could feel was the nakedness of having nowhere to hide.

Semra took a breath and walked across the room toward the archway. The rattle of the large brass door behind her and a great booming voice stopped her in her tracks.

"I want her found; do you hear me? If she doesn't talk, she dies. This was a targeted attack on a Jannemar official, and I won't have it!"

Governor Mallen. He was alive!

Frantically, Semra stuffed her sash with the key into the bottom of the potted plant by the fountain. Forcing herself to move slowly, she eased into the pool, making only a few soft ripples as she slid under the fountain just before the doors swung wide.

"Respect, my liege, but she was not close enough to be the killer. How can we know it was her?" Javed's voice.

"Do I look like an idiot to you?" Mallen demanded. "The key is gone, and she took it. She took it at the precise moment Governor Reza was murdered! She knows something. Keep Reza's aide safe in my quarters until she is found, and guard Reza's body. I want it examined. Conspirators to eliminate officials of the king shall not be tolerated!"

The footsteps stormed through the atrium, and Semra took a breath and ducked down beneath the surface of the pool. She hoped the fading light and brazenness of her hiding place would be enough to conceal her, but getting out of the centrally located pool would be a major problem. The room contained nothing that could hide her. One side opened up into the main hallway and the other lead to the residence.

Semra remained under the surface of the water, her mind reeling. Mallen was alive, and Reza was dead. Brens had missed? She couldn't possibly be that miserable of a shot. Conditions were favorable, and only sixty yards separated Brens from the target at the wide-open top of the grand stairs. It was an easy task for any of the Framatar's children.

Still, Brens' last assignment should have been easy too. Brens' sloppy preparedness caused her to get nervous and rush through the job; she broke a vase and it cost her the mission. Most recently, she'd hit her target but got herself seen, which ruined the frame job. Commander Ramas decided then that it would be a good idea to let Brens see how Semra operated in the field on entry and exit. No longer trusting Brens on her own, he'd sent Behruz along to supervise Brens' work. How could he have let this happen? Brens would be in big trouble when they returned to the mountain.

Semra waited several beats after she heard the footsteps fade away before coming up for air. The longer she stayed here, the greater her risk … but getting out now would be the highest risk of all. The guards would search the entire legislature and residence portions of the building, including the courtyard through which she'd planned to escape. Then they would focus their efforts on the surrounding area. Located as centrally as she was, staying put and waiting it out until she had a safe window to escape was her best option. After all, a dripping-wet servant girl would draw attention even at a distance.

Goosebumps ran up her arms. Even if she did get out, the target was still alive—unacceptable. Best case scenario, Brens would get a beating. Semra wanted to help her friend avoid that, but the Framatar would tell her that thinking that way meant she was too sensitive and selfish, because their purpose was bigger than them—children of the mountain purged the world of evil. Semra knew the beatings sharpened their minds and bodies to ready them for missions. When they failed, they earned a beating, to make sure they stayed strong enough to protect themselves and others. It wasn't the Framatar's fault. Still, maybe … maybe if Semra found a way to take out the target, the damage would be minimized, and the Framatar wouldn't have to know how bad Brens messed up.

A crash rang out through the archway to the residence, and Mallen yelled, "I don't care! Find them! Find them all! And I want guards in every room; all night!"

DARKNESS FELL QUICKLY in the atrium, and the flickering of torches on the walls cast orange glow onto the wall on either side of the pool. The guards were spread thin, but as the governor had commanded, one guard stood faithfully by the brass doors all night.

Semra's stomach growled, and she was grateful the soft gurgle of the fountain stifled the sound. She slowly rotated her ankles under the water, working out the kinks in her stiff muscles, then glanced at the guard again. The first several hours of the night had been frenzied, as the governor barked orders, his wife and daughters screamed at sleepy servants, and guards tore the place apart. As the night wore on, the palace grew silent. Even the governor grew weary, and their efforts had been fruitless.

After they'd completed a thorough search of the grounds for the tenth time, most believed she'd somehow made her escape. Though well connected, the governor still had limited resources, and Semra had heard him order reinforcements to scout the surrounding area. His captain of the guard argued that no good would come of it during the night, and the search would have to continue at first light.

Semra guessed it was only an hour or so until sunrise, and when morning light filled the atrium, the clear pool water would betray her. She glanced again at the guard. He'd been nodding off for the last fifteen minutes, and though still standing, his helmet was askew and his chin dropped forward.

Semra slowly drew her hand out of the water and reached into the potted plant by the fountain. She raked her fingers through the dirt until she found the sash she'd stashed there, then she pulled it out and laid it on the ground. No movement from the guard. She waited three, four, five beats of her heart, then reached under her skirt to retrieve one of the two knives strapped to her thighs. Semra kicked off her shoes, abandoning them at the bottom of the pool, and slithered up and out onto the floor, one hand on her knife, the other wrangling her skirts.

The floor felt cold against the balls of her feet as she crouched in the pitch-black shadows next to the fountain and away from the dying torches' light. She couldn't afford a trail of dripping water, so she dried herself off as best she could with her sash. She needed to get to the residence on the opposite side of the room, but if the guard woke and saw her, he would raise the alarm and be too far for her to silence. On the other hand, if she got too close, he might rouse and attack her then and there.

Semra considered simply throwing the knife into the man's throat, but she only had two knives with her. Best to use them wisely. Instead, she crept low and quiet along the ground until she was only ten feet away, then in three bounds she rushed him and hit him, hard, in the sweet spot just beneath the jawline and unprotected by his helmet.

The man crumpled. Semra caught him with some effort and lowered him quietly to the ground. She stripped him of his helmet and purple guard's cape, wrapped the cape around her shoulders and placed the helmet on her head, then ran to the archway, knife in hand. Back against the wall, she peered into the room beyond. A large room for entertaining and dining, two long tables and chairs lined the wall on one side, and couches lined the other. Doors lead to the rooms encircling it. Bratar stood to her left, guarding the room. Semra adjusted the grip on her knife.

Semra crept closer, but not quietly enough. Bratar swung toward her. She blocked his arm as he moved to hit her, then darted in and slashed his throat in one clean, swift motion.

She lowered him to the ground and wiped the blood from her blade on his clothes.

Governor Mallen would be through the first door on the right. His bedroom looked out over the courtyard. Without giving herself time to think, Semra opened the door, rolled to the other side of the room, slid open the window, and perched in its open frame. Looking back into the room, she saw a vanity and couch on one end and a large bed with exquisite purple fabric on the other. Governor Mallen and his wife slept soundly. Mallen lay face down into his pillow on the side closest to Semra.

It was now or never. The mission must always come first, Semra thought to herself, and sighed deeply. After all, he was a wicked man. They all were. With a flick of her wrist, Semra sent her knife soaring into the pulsing artery of his oversized neck and then dropped to the courtyard below.

2

Semra rolled on impact, sprung to her feet, and walked confidently toward the servants' quarters. The plants in the courtyard had concealed her descent, and if she walked quickly enough, she might make it to the door without being caught. A casual glance at her from behind would reveal only the distinctive purple cape and helmet of a guard. A closer look would show skirts and bare feet below the cape. A guard stood on the other side of the courtyard, and she angled herself away from him, wishing she had her other knife in hand rather than on her thigh. Maybe he wouldn't notice her, and she wouldn't have to kill him.

Semra walked past the four columns on one side and ducked into the servants' quarters. To her immediate right was a hall to the kitchen, and after that the laundry, which had a backdoor onto the street. Four bedrooms lined her left, housing the governor's full-time servant staff. The third was her own room, but she'd been careful not to leave anything behind, and her fellow servant roommate would be inside.

Down the hall to the kitchen, she heard the sounds of morning—Corithia arranging pots and pans in preparation for the day. Semra walked into the laundry room—by now Betha would surely be off warming water for the ladies' morning baths. The rest of the servants didn't wake until sunrise, still half an hour away. Semra took off her helmet and cape and dropped them into the large basin of sudsy water on her left. She snatched one of the governor's daughters' dry dresses off the line, grabbed a pair of rejected unshined shoes from the corner, changed, and slipped the city key up her sleeve. Just like that, as if nothing out of the ordinary had occurred, she let herself out the back door.

Once she got away from the governor's property, she found it easy enough to weave through the streets and head to the rendezvous point. She knew how to change her appearance on the go, double back, and look for a tail, and by the time she finally climbed the hill outside the city, it was afternoon and Semra wore the simple tunic and apprentice boy's trousers she had swiped. Some lucky woman would find the rich dress Semra had dumped through an open window. For her part, Semra felt grateful to have more practical clothes again for running, tumbling, and fighting. She'd piled her hair underneath a cap, but as she got away from any prying eyes and finally reached the top of the little knoll on which they'd planned to meet, she yanked it off and let her dark-brown hair fall free about her shoulders.

The trees provided cover, and the wind rustling the leaves and playing with Semra's hair brought a soothing hope. Whatever had happened, the target was eliminated. They were safe, and the mission was ... well, it was botched, but the outcome was less horrendous than it had been.

"Come out, come out," Semra called softly.

The tree to her left shook, startling her, and from its

branches dropped a teenage girl. She wore a light-green tunic and dark pants belted with bands of cloth wrapped around the waist, typical of any townsperson of lower class. A quiver and bow were slung across her back. She had small features, straight brown hair, brown eyes, and a sheepish smile.

"Hey."

"Brens. Where's Behruz?"

"He should be back any minute now. Told me he had to see how much of ... how much of my mess he would have to clean up. Told me to stay here and not do anything stupid." Brens looked down at her feet.

"What happened? This mission was supposed to be your saving grace! It was simple; it was easy!"

"The governor showed up with the young one, and the young one turned to leave, and so I figured maybe the visiting governor was the young man, and he just wasn't dressed as nicely for some reason! The governor was dressed up all fancy like Mallen, and he was tall, and he started to turn back ... "

"Brens, Mallen is fat! Reza is the slender one! How could you miss this? There were two governors and an aide— wasn't it obvious?"

"Mallen didn't show!" Brens blurted out, voice rising in defense of herself. "He was supposed to walk them all the way out, like he always does, and say his goodbyes on the steps. Well, I saw two men, and I thought it was him!"

Semra ran her hand over her face. This was bad. "Rats and rot. And you thought ... you thought the aide was Reza?! How could you not know he was an aide?"

"I ... " Brens' voice trailed off, and she clenched her jaw.

"She's an imbecile, that's how," called a low voice from behind them.

Semra jumped and turned to see Behruz sauntering toward them. He was also dressed simply, and though no weapons were visible, Semra guessed he carried at least five. Behruz had almost the same honey-bronze skin tone as Semra, but his was more suntanned than natural, and he had sandy hair. His lip curled as he looked at Brens.

"I told her not to screw it up like last time and that she couldn't wait around to take her shot. But I didn't mean to shoot so fast you don't even wait for your target to show up." He glanced at Semra. "Nice of you to join us, by the way. Where were you?"

"What do you think? I was trapped inside with the key and a paranoid target, waiting for a clean exit."

Behruz sighed. "Framatar is not going to be happy with this one." He jerked his head toward Brens.

Semra glanced at her. Brens was angry, but fear simmered in her eyes. He was right.

"What do I do?" Brens asked.

"Do? What do you do?" Behruz scoffed. "Earn your name as a Bandaka. How on earth did you make it to your naming ceremony? Maybe he'll reassign you. Cooking or something. That way anything that needs killing is already dead."

"Hey, now," Semra broke in, seeing Brens' stricken expression. "Okay, so it's not great. That much is obvious. But the way I see it, the Framatar handpicked you to watch over Brens and make sure she carried out the mission successfully. You were in charge. How will that go for you? Hmm?"

"Me? I did what I was supposed to do. I told her everything. She's just too stupid."

"Sure, sure, and other people's stupidity is an acceptable excuse for failing your own responsibilities. Pass them off to other people; that looks fantastic."

"But it's true!"

"I'm not an idiot!" Brens ran her fingers through her hair and started pacing. "He didn't show; something went wrong, I know what I'm doing! I need another chance!"

Semra felt a tug on her heart for Brens. They'd been the same year in the program, training together. Even in the dark days, they were there for each other. She hated seeing her friend like this.

Semra turned to Behruz. "Listen, I took out the target before I got out. Maybe the Framatar doesn't have to know everything. The bad guy is dead, and that's what matters. Behruz, you were mission ready a year before Brens was. You really think blaming her is going to make you look good to the Framatar? No. So maybe ... maybe we tell him she shot Mallen, but Reza saw where the shot came from, and she took him out too? That way, she still did something stupid, but taking the shot wasn't the problem. Maybe she'll get recycled back to practicum, instead of repurposed."

Brens' shoulders sagged. "You think I'll get sent back to practicum? I'll be a fresher again after a year in the field?"

"Better than not being in the field at all," Semra said.

"How does that make me look any better?" Behruz demanded.

"Well, she did just what you told her the first time. She knew her target, she timed it right, everything you coached her on was precise."

"Except for basic concealment," he grumbled. "To make things worse, I was supposed to plant the key on Reza after he left and you got out."

Semra's jaw dropped open. This couldn't have gone more poorly.

Behruz sighed. "The meet was perfect timing. It was all set up. Now I'm going to have to do a quick patch-up job instead of the framing masterpiece I worked on for the last three months."

"I ... err ... hmm." Semra crossed her arms.

Brens tapped her foot anxiously.

Behruz rolled his eyes.

"Okay, so the situation isn't exactly ideal," Semra stated. "But you are a phenomenal framer. It's your specialty. And you will do such clean work, I will sing your praises when we get to the Framatar."

Behruz stepped forward and pointed his finger in Semra's face. "I am a phenomenal framer. And you will make it clear that this mission succeeded because of me."

"Yes, because of you. You're brilliant, genius, whatever."

"Except, she'll be more convincing in person," Brens put in.

"Fine. Where's the key?" Behruz asked.

Semra reached into her pocket and pulled out the city key. "We'll see you back at the mountain."

Behruz grabbed the key and turned on his heel, muttering under his breath. Semra breathed a sigh of relief and hoped Behruz would hold up his end of the bargain. Brens and Semra stood in silence as they waited for Behruz to disappear from sight. When he dropped out of view, Brens let out a breath.

"Ugh, thank you for that."

Semra pursed her lips and gave a curt nod before turning round and striding northwest, away from the city and toward home in the mountain above Kalma.

Brens scrambled to follow. "Semra, wait! Slow down. You're walking too fast."

"No, I'm walking just the right amount of fast considering we're hours behind schedule."

"The best missions are successful missions, not fast or

slow missions. And the target is dead, right? So it's success-ful. We had a ... a hiccup, but we got it sorted out."

Semra wheeled back to Brens. "We? We got it sorted out? Successful mission? You killed the wrong person! Who even does that? We've trained for this since we were four."

"You don't understand. You don't know what it's like."

"I admired you from Egg class, when you welcomed me into the mountain, all the way up to Arrow. You were so good at the medical and hunting classes; the dragon feedings didn't terrify you as much as they did me, and you were a great philosophy student in the doctrines. We were the same year, the same age, the same classes. What do I not understand?"

Brens put her hands on her hips and bit her lip. "You are a record breaker, Semra. From Egg class to Arrow, is that it? That's where the admiration ended, right, because once you were in the field doing mission support and practicum, you took off. You weren't just top in our class, you were the first ever to graduate at fifteen-years old, instead of sixteen. You were mission ready a year before the rest of us. The Framatar's favorite.

"So what if I was great at philosophy? I'm a good learner. I can memorize things. But you blew everyone out of the water, and you were always good in the program. You've never really struggled like I have. Not all of us catch on as easily as you, and you've never had to be afraid you'll be repurposed. Only one from our class was so bad he needed to be repurposed before even reaching practicum. Pintin worked as hard as any of us, but he just didn't have a knack for it. And now what does he do? He teaches the Hatchling philosophy class six-to-eight-year olds. I hate kids, Semra. I don't get them. I can't do it."

Semra sighed, guilt flooding through her. "I don't know

what to say. What do you want me to say, that I'm sorry I was good at it?"

"No. But don't pretend you know everything there is to know about me and how I do things."

"Okay, I won't. I'm sorry this happened. But I can't pretend you didn't make a stupid mistake, Brens. Because that's what it was. It should have been a simple job. I'll do what I can to help you, but I don't know what else to say, because you can't undo killing Reza."

"I know I can't."

"If only I had just done the job on my own, none of this would have happened."

"That's your best solution?" Brens demanded. "Just doing everything alone?"

Semra shrugged. "It's what we're trained for. We only cooperate for the more complicated jobs. It would have been simpler and cleaner if I took the key and took out the target. That's what I ended up doing anyway, and if I'd been allowed to do it myself from the get-go, nobody would have gotten hurt."

"Except Mallen, of course."

Semra rolled her eyes. "Nobody good, dummy. Obviously Mallen, but you wouldn't have gotten hurt." She let her shoulders sag as she started walking forward again, slower this time. Brens walked alongside her.

"You've always had my back," Semra said. "Remember when we were in Arrow class ... what were we, ten years old? And we were responsible for hunting and preparing our own meals that day, and I couldn't catch anything, and Captain said I'd go hungry? He said I needed to learn that urgency doesn't mean we need to be impatient, but more patient. If I'm hungry, I need to be more careful in my approach, not less. He was right, and it was a good lesson, but I was starving."

Brens smiled. "You were so mad."

"I was. But you split your squirrel with me. You would've been in such trouble if he found out!"

"Ramas and Captain would say it makes me too sensitive. That I'm weak."

"Yes," Semra said, "But if that makes you sensitive, I must be too, for trying to convince Behruz to sell the story to the Framatar. We'll have to hope he holds up his end. I owe you for back then, and I'll do what I can to help."

3

It had taken five days on foot to reach the mountain, and Semra felt anxious butterflies in her stomach as she took the narrow stairway down into the cavern. She always had mixed feelings when coming home. It was familiar, it was family, and it was only here that other people knew her for what she really was. Still, the mountain caverns were dark and cold, and her heart reserved a bitterness toward how much she needed this place. But as the Framatar so often reminded them, although family wasn't perfect, they would always be there. And that loyalty demanded reciprocity.

Semra was grateful to come home when it was light out, when the large fissure high above combined with two main entrances into the common area ensured some natural light still made it to the dim floor below. Lanterns lined the walls down the corridors and into larger caverns deeper into the cave system, but the common-area lanterns wouldn't need to be lit until nightfall.

The rocky way opened up into a large, open space

sprawling fifty feet below the cave ceiling. A second entrance wound around the side of the mountain into a wide-open cleft out of sight from the main cavern. Semra watched five Bow class students, ranging from eight-to-ten-years old, trudge in from this entrance carrying a variety of dinner items they'd either gathered or caught earlier that day. Each student ran up to their class leader and presented themselves for inspection, proudly offering a rabbit, two squirrels, and an assortment of berries and roots.

Here and there older children and adults went to and fro about their duties, and when Semra and Brens arrived, only a middle-aged man passing by one of the corridors paused to take notice.

"Good, you've returned," he called to them in a gravelly voice.

"Only just," Semra answered as they crossed the large space. "We could use a rest."

He waved a hand dismissively. "Sure, sure, I'm sure you could. And your … your target?" Dark eyes bored into Brens.

"Eliminated, Commander Ramas," she answered, leveling her stare back at him but dipping her head in respect.

Ramas nodded. "Very good. I knew you had it in you. All my oversight couldn't have been for nothing. Report to the Framatar at once. You must have practically crawled here!"

Semra gritted her teeth but turned and walked with Brens down a wide corridor of rough sandstone. They passed a Saber class of thirteen-and-fourteen-year-olds discussing their mission-support duties, and a lieutenant, or practicum student, walking with his close-range captain to discuss tactics for infiltrating a corrupt noble's villa.

The further they went into the mountain, the darker it became around them, and they navigated the well-known paths by lantern light. After three turns passing various openings, they passed into an enormous cavern crisscrossed with a web of footbridges and filled with the distant sound of running water, which flowed seventy feet beneath their feet. Stalactites reached down like long pointed fingers from a ceiling one-hundred feet above them, and stalagmites mirrored them from the rocky floor. The two girls crossed to a platform in the center, where a large bonfire illuminated the chamber.

Semra stopped cold when she noticed two men on the far side across another chasm. The first was on his knees, and Semra didn't recognize him. A weasel of a man, he had a long, lanky frame and beady eyes. Before him stood the glowering figure of the Framatar clad in black from his hooded cloak to his heavy boots. Long dark hair framed his face, and a gem-studded, gilded collar sparkled on his chest in the light of the flames. As he turned his face to the weasel on the floor, the birthright of the gods shone from his forehead.

Semra had always thought it looked nearly like a scar, curving in a half-moon shape from the corner of his right eye to just above the temple, except for its resemblance to a rock-hard white stone. Perhaps most like opal, it refracted many colors off its surface. They'd always been told he was blessed by the gods and destined for greatness.

"You thought you could steal from me, and I wouldn't notice? You thought your dreams of being some powerful statesman would be better off without me? You ... are ... nothing without me!"

"Please, my lord, I would never—"

"Never what? Never expect to get caught? I promised you riches, status. Have my blessings not been enough for you? Ungrateful swine!"

The Framatar reached down and hoisted the man up by the throat, his eyes wild. "I could have made your dreams come true. I could have been your savior. But now ... now I will be your nightmare." The Framatar released the man and let out a low whistle, then called in a sickly sweet voice, "Oh, Rotokas! You are ever patient ... come and have your reward. Would you like to play?"

Semra sucked in her breath and gripped Brens' arm. A puff of fire from the dark recesses of the cave suddenly revealed a flash of pale-green eyes. From the blackness a great shadow stalked into the firelight. Spikes accented its serpentine head, framed its face, and continued down its long neck. It stood on massive hind legs and, in lieu of forelegs, bore weight on the claw of wing-hands, like those of a bat. Eyes gleaming with delight, the great black wyvern stalked into the light, dragging its full fifty feet from head to barbed tail into view. Its great wings lay folded above and behind it.

"My lord, no! I swear to you, I didn't take it!" The man backed up until his heels were at the edge of the abyss, eyes wide in terror.

The wyvern snapped its jaws and breathed out a blue-hot flame, engulfing its victim. The weasel man screamed and leaped from the landing in hopes of a more pleasant death down below. He would never be so lucky. The wyvern roared and dove down after its prey. Semra flinched as the snapping sounds of its voracious attack met her ears.

Semra and Brens stood frozen at the center platform.

The Framatar looked up, saw them and smiled. He clapped his hands. "Excellent! My children are returned to me. Come, tell me what happened."

Brens gulped beside her, and Semra glanced anxiously over the chasm after the wyvern. Everything was blackness.

Rotokas was always with the Framatar. That was why the Framatar was so titled, after all—Lord of Dragons, Lord of the Mountain. But she'd always hated Rotokas. Sinister and evil, he served only the Framatar, and though Semra knew they were safe as long as the Framatar was with them, he terrified her just the same.

"Come now, children," the Framatar called again, this time with a warning in his tone.

Semra took a deep breath and stepped out onto the narrow footbridge over the abyss. Just as she did, Rotokas swept up from below, the wind from his wake cutting across her face and knocking her backward. He alighted on the long shelf on which the Framatar stood, tilted his head to the sky and choked down the remains of some body part or other.

"My, your faces," the Framatar chortled. "He likes his meals lightly roasted. Don't we all? Now, you have dawdled long enough."

Semra and Brens crossed quickly to the other side, taking care to place themselves on the opposite side from the wyvern.

"What ... um ... who was that man?" Semra asked.

The Framatar waved the question off. "Someone who lied to me. No one to concern yourselves with. Now tell me about the mission. Brens, how did it go?"

"I did it. I shot Governor Mallen."

"Wonderful. I'm so proud of you! You," he said, touching her face, "may just be getting back on track. Any complications?"

"Only one," said Semra.

The Framatar raised an eyebrow. Semra nodded at Brens. It had to come from her.

Brens tapped her foot. "The shot was clean, but they

didn't walk far enough over, and Reza saw our position ... so ... I took him out, to keep him quiet."

"You ... gave away your position from a carefully scouted concealment sixty yards out?"

"It was the best option, but ... the ... wind knocked my gear down the hill. He saw it before I could get to it."

The Framatar leaned into Brens' face. "And what, pray tell, drove your impulsive decision?"

Brens' eyes grew wide, and she swallowed.

Semra's mouth went dry. She took in her friend's stricken face, and cleared her throat. "Her timing was perfect. The hit was clean. It's just two hits instead of one. Behruz is a master framer, and he already has a spectacular plan in motion. He said this way could even be better than Mallen on his own. Brens didn't hesitate."

"Pardon, but please ... when did I ask you for your opinion?" The Framatar glared at her, and Semra's veins turned to ice under his gaze. "Even better, you say? I look forward to hearing this plan. But you, Brens, I asked you a question. What drove you to shoot on impulse rather than according to the mission?"

Brens took in ragged breaths and shook her head.

"I'll give you a hint, child. You're feeling it right now."

"F - f - fear," she stuttered.

"Fear! Fear! You know nothing outside this mountain is deserving of your fear." The Framatar struck her across the face and she stumbled back. Semra stood rooted to the spot, afraid her intervention would make things worse. "Are you a coward, or a moron? Which is it? You leave your pack in a precarious position, and when your own mistakes find you out, you destroy months of work on a whim? Could your training not have given you any saving grace? Were your legs broken, such that you could not move fast enough to escape if he sent his dimwitted guards after you?"

The Framatar licked his lips and curled them back in a disgusted snarl, then hit her again. "No wonder everyone hates you. No wonder you were abandoned in Kalma! Both cowardly and stupid, aren't you? What's wrong with you? I took you in when no one else would. I clothed you, fed you, raised you, taught you how to save others from the fate you were once doomed to die, and this is how you repay me?"

Brens shook her head again. "It won't happen again. I can do better; I can be better. I won't let you down."

"You're weak. Pathetic. And you held such promise. You were such a lovely child ... not on the outside, of course, but I saw through all of that. I believed in you."

A tear slipped down her cheek, and she brushed it away angrily.

Semra stepped forward, a weight on her chest, but was powerless to stop the diatribe.

Rotokas huffed and skittered his barbed tail across the limestone floor.

The Framatar sighed and passed a hand over his face. "And here you are, manipulating me with tears. They don't work on me. You will need to earn my trust back. This hurts me more than it hurts you ... why, why do you make me do this to you?" He clucked his tongue and shook his head sadly. "There is nothing I can do. I will save you from the worst of it, but you know what must happen. We shall purge this fear from within you, and your— "

"No!" Semra cried out, throwing herself in front of Brens. "Framatar, my lord. Please. Her loyalty is to you, forever yours. Her fear was only of disappointing you ... not of Reza or the guards. Only of you."

The Framatar paused and looked at Semra with interest.

Though twice her age, in his midthirties, he had the energy of a younger man, yet carried the confidence and authority of one much older. "Only of me, you say? Is this true, Brens?" He directed the question at Brens, but kept his eyes locked on Semra.

"Only of you, my lord. It's true. I was afraid ... to let you down. That you wouldn't want me anymore."

"My dear, my dear ... you know I'm the only one who has never left you."

Semra suddenly found it hard to breathe under his piercing eyes. They searched her soul; they found her out. She could have sworn he knew their lie already. The fire crackled behind them, and the red-orange light highlighted his sharp jawline and the golden flecks in his irises, mixed with a deeper, amber color. She jumped as Rotokas coughed and let out a blue-hot flame to warm the stone beneath him. He yawned, curled in a massive ball, and eyed them suspiciously from the dark corner.

The Framatar took hold of Semra and moved her firmly to the side, then turned his attention to Brens and pulled her to her feet. "Loyalty," he said slowly, "is the greatest attribute one can have. Precision, art, success ... these are all critical, but it is loyalty that makes any of them worth anything. And what could loyalty be better suited for than supporting a love for all that is good in the world, and a willingness to sacrifice to save it?

"It's not easy, living here. Your tasks are not simple tasks. What I require of you—what the future of this world requires of you—is a heavy burden. Do not take it lightly. If I didn't care so much about you, I would not have to use such a heavy hand with you. Alas, the times are hard. But never fear. The time is coming, and soon, when all of this will be a distant memory. You will not serve me from a pit in a mountain but from glorious places of leisure. Those that have served me well will be richly rewarded, and those that do not ... well, Rotokas deserves his rewards also."

Semra shuddered.

The Framatar continued. "This mistake is grave. Brens, you must show me your loyalty and eradicate all fear within you. Loyalty to one another as sibling children is admirable, but letting your emotions get in the way of the cause is to betray the highest loyalty. Please, my dear, don't make me do anything I will regret. Show me I can trust you. Do not fail me again."

Brens knelt before him and kissed his hand. "I swear it. I will prove my loyalty, my lord."

He nodded. "Yes, you will. Go."

Brens stood, glanced at Semra, and fled back across the footpaths and into the labyrinth of corridors. Semra felt her stomach tighten into impossible knots. Why hadn't he dismissed her?

The Framatar clasped his arms behind his back and paced in front of her. "The story you told me today ... is it true?"

"My lord, how could you ask me such a thing? I would not lie."

"Deceit is cowardly, to be sure, and you are far from cowardly. But I would hear it just the same. Is the story you told me true?"

Semra swallowed but kept her face calm and collected. "Yes, my lord."

"Mmm." He stopped and turned toward her again. "You know, defending a friend against evil is good. But you have no friends, not really. Only allies. None of them have saved you from certain destruction, seen you for who you really are and taken you in anyway, cleaned you up when you were malodorous and filthy. When I found you, your family had abandoned you, a defenseless four-year-old child, and left you to die. You caused such pain, such trouble to them that they were begging to part with their own flesh and blood. Say it isn't so."

A lump rose in her throat. "It is so, my lord."

"I do not accept these evil practices! I brought you in and built you up. I taught you to be strong, to take care of yourself so no one could mistreat you or see you as weak again! I gave you a place here, a purpose, a name. And what is your name?"

"Bandaka. Semra Bandaka."

The Framatar stepped forward until they were nearly nose to nose. "Say it again. What is your name?"

"Semra Bandaka."

He smiled, took her head in his hands, and leaned down to kiss her forehead. She dropped to her knees and kissed his hand. As he raised her up, he held her close and whispered in her ear.

"We are family, Semra. And we don't lie to family. You may go."

4

Semra wound her way through the corridors and open caves toward the barracks, heart beating wildly in her chest. He knew. She couldn't call him on it, of course, but he knew she'd lied about something, and not only had she lied, but she'd stopped him from making Brens stronger through discipline.

Would beating her or having Rotokas breathe third-degree burns on her really make her stronger? What would the Framatar do to Semra if he decided to punish her for lying? Behruz had to sell the story. And now that Semra had said so, he would have to make it sound as though killing Reza along with Mallen really should have been the plan from the beginning.

Semra walked into the barracks, an open, naturally occurring oval room with bunks lining the walls on three sides. The third on the left was hers, top bunk, and she reached up to retrieve her pack and longsword. Everyone in the mountain, child or graduate, had one simple pack for belongings. It usually included a small pan, whetting stone, cloth, change of clothes, medical kit, and additional weaponry and accessories.

With one-hundred-and-fifty people living in the mountain, privacy was hard to come by. Rotokas brought one new child in on the first of every month, mostly from the village Kalma at the base of the mountain and surrounding areas. Semra herself had been saved from the people of Kalma, who had abandoned her there. The mountain held a dozen children of each age starting at age four all the way up through mission ready. There had been a dozen in her own class, and a dozen in the class before her.

Semra was in the fourth class the Framatar had taken in. The first year there were twenty, the second, fifteen, and ever since then, he'd settled on saving and investing in twelve children every year. Some of the children were unsuited for assassin work, and when this was determined, they were repurposed into other positions such as cooking, hunting and gathering, doctrine leaders for the classes of children, and tactical trainer and survival guide. There were also five dragon wranglers, working to capture and train dragons, but they had nowhere near the control over the smaller species they were able to bring in as the Framatar had over Rotokas. Semra stayed as far away from the dragon cages as she could.

Semra took the bag and descended into the lower levels of the cave system, grateful for a few minutes to herself to dip into one of the pools, clean up, and change out of her dirty travel clothes. Except for the Framatar and his generals, everyone serving in the mountain wore basic clothing in earth-tone colors. An assassin needed to be practical in all things, and fancy clothes were reserved for missions that required them to blend in.

By and large, it was best to be simple, poor, and easily forgotten. On the mountain, concealing weapons was less important, and she didn't have to bother with wearing the skirts that typical townswomen generally wore. When she did have to go to towns for missions, she wore pants and a leg rig holding a dagger close to her outer leg, carried extra knives sheathed on each leg, and wrapped a custom skirt overtop to conceal them. Slits hidden in the skirt allowed her unique access to her weapons while appearing all too ordinary to the casual observer. Wraps on her arms underneath loose long sleeves were also effective in hiding essential small items, and adding a belt and boots provided further options still.

Semra washed off the dirt of the road and came up onto the bank. Grateful she didn't have to bother with the extras for a while, Semra left the skirt in her pack, pulled on her black pants, and sheathed her dagger and knives. She shrugged into an olive tunic, slung her sword across her back, and picked up her pack. She needed to think.

The Framatar's words to Brens rang in her mind. *What I require of you—what the future of this world requires of you—is a heavy burden.* It was true. Their cause was to remove evil from the world, and only the strongest of mind and body were fit for this noble purpose. Without the program, as brutal as it was, malice would reign in the world unchecked.

Semra climbed the slope up and away from the water, grateful for the time alone but anxious to be out of the deep dark and sitting somewhere warmer. After several minutes she entered a common area with a small fire pit in the center. A Hatchling class, ages six through eight, sat in a circle to her right with their survival guide, learning to dress small game for dinner. All of the children wore normal clothes and purple armbands signifying their class, but their leader wore a distinguishing top with a short, stiff collar and purple epaulets on the shoulder. To her left, three mission readies played jacks with small pebbles and a circle drawn in the dirt.

Semra seated herself cross-legged by the fire and closed her eyes. She listened to the soft crackling sound, the shifting of the kindling as the sticks gave way, and watched the dance of light across her closed eyelids. The warmth on her face and neck, contrasted with the coolness of the stone beneath her, brought her solace. This was home.

The same home that threatened Brens and frightened Semra, that hurt her, saved her, trampled her, and saved her again. Semra reached into her pack and laid out several of her knives, a cloth, and two small bottles. The first bottle was alcohol, and she poured some on the cloth. She took the knife gingerly in her hands and carefully wiped down the blades, taking extra care around the handle to ensure every piece of the steel was treated.

"Bothered by something?" a gravelly voice asked.

Semra glanced up to see Commander Ramas peering down at her. Like the Hatchling leader, he wore a top with a short, stiff collar, but the epaulets on his shoulders were red and depicted a black dragon. He oversaw all mission-ready program graduates, though arm bands were no longer required after graduation.

Semra looked back down at her work. "Why would you assume I am bothered by something?"

Ramas laughed and took a seat beside her. "Because your blades are already clean. You wipe them down when you're worked up."

"I just got back from a long mission and spent a week on the road coming home, using them for everything."

Ramas picked up one of her knives, wiped his finger across the sparkling blade, and arched an eyebrow.

Semra glared at him. Why wouldn't he just leave her alone?

"I heard you hit a snag." He set the knife back down.

"Word travels fast."

"Not as fast as you might think. I see no reason to spread news of it. But what do I know ... I saw no reason for you to mislead me when you returned saying the target was eliminated, and here we are."

"The target was eliminated," Semra answered, opening the second bottle and pouring a drop of oil onto the cloth.

"Yes. By you."

Semra's blood ran cold. How could he possibly know ... Behruz. Had he made it back early somehow? No, it was too soon. Was he guessing? If he was guessing, and she confirmed it, Brens was in deep trouble. But if he wasn't guessing, and she denied it ... Semra shuddered.

"What does it matter who did it? The point of cooperative missions is cooperation, isn't it? Getting the job done. The job is done." Semra felt her defenses rising, and she tried to focus on oiling the blades and keeping her voice low.

"The point of this mission was testing Brens, and you know it. Mallen needed to die, and Brens needed to be the one to do it."

"She took the shot."

"And?"

"No 'and!' Commander, sir, what are you getting at?"

Ramas sighed and thumbed the emerald-green, snake-shaped amulet at his wrist. He often played with it when he was in thought. He leaned in, speaking quietly, "You questioned the Framatar. Lord of dragons, Lord of the Mountain, blessed by the gods, and you—absolutely no one—think you know better? Is it because you are so brilliant, and the rest of us so dim?"

Semra's heart began to pound in her ears. She would rather he hit her than accuse her in such dulcet tones. For a moment Semra wondered if the weasel man wouldn't be Rotokas' only dinner tonight.

"I ... I was wrong. It just seemed so ... she can do it. I know she can. And the mission was complete. It seemed needless harm."

"There is much evil in this world, Semra. You know this. Evil parents abandon a helpless child, evil kings and statesmen abuse their power, evil in every corner where man takes breath. The world needs saving, but not by the weak. Great evil requires a great strength to conquer it. Discipline is not evil. It is kind. Discipline creates strength.

"You are strong of mind and strong of body, full of skill, and yet, you struggled greatly in your Egg and Hatchling classes. Your failures made you strong, yes? Tell me, when a bone breaks, does it heal stronger or weaker than before?"

Semra swallowed. "Stronger."

Ramas nodded. "Stronger. Good. And when skin is burned, does it grow back more or less sensitive than it was before?"

"First more ... and then less."

"Tenderness. Tenderness lasts for a moment, but protection lasts forever. Your loyalty is misplaced. If you truly cared for Brens, you would want her to be strengthened. At whatever cost, because the world is dark and cold. Emotion is weakness. You are strong of mind, but today I see you weak of heart. It is not a good color on you. What must we break to ensure you become strong again?"

Semra's fingers froze on the dagger she was oiling, and she looked up from her work. She watched the Hatchling class across the room—a little boy skinned his rabbit expertly while the girl beside him frowned down at her

mangled squirrel. Semra remembered feeling so lost and
confused, not fully grasping the ways of the mountain or
why the training had to be so vigorous. She had been too
young to understand. Later she would come to appreciate
the sense of accomplishment and belonging these small
victories brought with them.

"Emotion is weakness," she repeated. "Forgive me,
Commander. I did not forget. It was a momentary lapse in
judgment, and it will not happen again."

Semra met his eyes and he looked at her intently.

"I should hope not. Everything you are is because of the
Framatar's favor. Don't forget it." With that he stood and
walked away, leaving Semra alone with her oils and blades.

Ramas was right. The Framatar and the leaders had
taught her everything she knew, taken her in when no one
else would, showed her a way in the world when she felt lost.
What had they asked from her in return except to improve
this harsh world? And still she had doubted. Guilt swept
through her.

Semra sheathed her knives and daggers, placed the
cleaning alcohol and oil back in her pack, and stood. She
scanned the room out of habit, then jumped as she noticed a
lone figure watching her. He had gray eyes, disheveled brown
hair, and was made of lean muscle and moody energy. Siler.

Did he know she felt unsure of herself? Could he tell
she'd been so conflicted, so guilty? Semra shifted her weight
uncomfortably under Siler's unflinching gaze and stared
back at him evenly. He looked away, seemingly unconcerned,
but Semra carried an uneasy feeling with her as she left the
room.

She knew what she must do. First thing in the morning,
Semra would go to the Framatar, ask for forgiveness, and
reaffirm her allegiance.

5

The next morning Semra got up early and went to the chow hall, another tall cavern in the cave system with stalactites serving as chandeliers. It was probably dawn outside, but lanterns set on several long tables remained the only light in the large room. Semra moved quietly among several of her colleagues, scattered here and there, to grab some fruit and roasted rabbit.

She exited the chow hall, lit her own lantern, and took the corridor to the left toward the Framatar's personal chambers. His chambers were all connected to the receiving room she and Brens had met him in the day before. Semra crossed a larger cavern on the way, and came to a fork on the other side. A medium-sized cavern was tucked away to the right, and two passageways branched off from there in separate directions. The passage ahead and to the left was narrow, only wide enough for two people to walk side by side, while the passage ahead and to the right continued on wide open, the ceiling rising high overhead.

Voices drifted out of the cavern to the right, one low and

gravelly and the other smooth as butter. Ramas and the Framatar. Semra paused, unsure what to do, and then hugged the wall and crept forward.

" ... always been one of our strongest," Ramas was saying. "But deftness with a blade or quick thinking on one's feet is a blessing only while loyalties are certain. If she were to change her mind, the very things that we encouraged would become dangerous."

"Did she admit it?" the Framatar asked.

"No, but I could see it was true. And you were right, Brens cracked like an egg. She is terrified and lied to cover up her failures."

The Framatar sighed. "If only we could mix the two of them. Brens' unwavering insecurity-fueled loyalty and Semra's reliable skill. But she is an investment years in the making, and I'm not quite ready to waste it. Questioning my methods is acceptable, as long as a stronger allegiance is brought about on the other side. Doubt is natural, and if resolved correctly, that devotion will be greater still than it could ever have been without."

Semra gasped and reached into her lantern, turning the wick down and extinguishing its flame in the oil.

"My lord, perhaps she has it in her blood. Her parents were fighters."

Semra felt a tremble in her bones at the mention of her parents. She had only vague memories of them, but even those were untrustworthy, because her parents were master manipulators. Everyone in Kalma was.

"Dead fighters. And though it was certainly a surprise when they left their pathetic little village to actually climb the mountain, I favored her all the more. It takes great courage to leave everything one knows and risk life and limb for the ones you love. What tremendous loyalty, Ramas! And

loyalty is admirable. They were loyal to their child, and
though they believed Rotokas was simply snatching children
to eat them, they were willing to take on a wyvern. Totally
unprepared, untrained, but when they were afraid, they took
action.

"It is a pity such loyalty and courage needed to be
snuffed out. Well, it served our purposes. But to your point,
Ramas, traits like these are good ones, and I knew that as
long as that fierce loyalty was bound to me, she could be my
greatest asset. With the proper training, her potential would
be unmatched. Do you remember how angry she was that
day when Rotokas brought her to us?"

Semra's head swam. It couldn't be. Her whole body
began to shake. She clutched the lantern in her left hand and
reached out to steady herself with her right. Her parents
hadn't abandoned her. They hadn't hated her; they had
loved her! She wasn't saved; she was stolen! And the
Framatar had murdered her parents when they tried to get
her back.

Ramas was speaking now. " ... and refused to believe
anything they had to say. Stubborn little thing! I did not envy
her doctrine leader in Egg class. But what will you do now?
Brens wants nothing more than to please you but is losing
her usefulness in the field. And Semra ... well, if the outcome
of her doubt doesn't bring her closer, she will be dangerous.
How severe are you planning the ... solution to be?"

"My children are not loyal to me because they fear me.
They do, and they should, but they are loyal to me because
they fear everything else. We will increase their fear of everything else, and as ever, I will be their constant and safety. If
she doesn't come around, we can dispatch her later ...
quietly."

Down the passage behind her, Semra heard footsteps

echoing off the rock walls, growing nearer. Someone was coming, and if the Framatar was threatening to kill her now, he would not hesitate if he found her listening. Semra shrank back into the corridor, crossed to the other side, and fled across the opening in the shadows. She saw the silhouettes of Ramas and the Framatar in the dim lights of lanterns in the cavern meeting room as she passed, and slipped into the narrow passage branching off to the left. Semra carefully edged backward several feet but stopped herself from moving too much once the footsteps approached.

The broad-shouldered frame of General Gresvig swept into view. He called to the Framatar, "My lord, a word." He touched his right fist to his left shoulder in a sign of respect.

"Thank you, Ramas. That will be all." The Framatar dismissed the commander and turned to the general.

Ramas dipped his head, placed his own fist to his left shoulder briefly, then turned to leave. As the sound of his footsteps disappeared, the Framatar spoke again.

"What news do you bring me?"

"Excellent news, my lord. The lord and lady of Camar have listened to the wise counsel of your friend Voldar. They will support you when the time comes. And all is prepared for the mission one week from today."

"Well done! I knew you would not fail me. Now tell me of Zephan."

"He is ... still in the wind, my lord. But as Turian's only son, Prince Zephan will most assuredly be present at the gala. Any event as significant as Belvidore offering a political alliance with Jannemar through a union between the Belvidorian Prince Axis and Jannemar's Princess Avaya is too great an opportunity to miss. After all, Zephan and Axis would presumably be the future kings one day, and establishing strong relationships now with both kings and heirs apparent is wise."

Semra watched, wide eyed, from her hiding place in the dark. What could he want with the royals? He was planning something big and must've been working on it for months already.

"Tell me, Gresvig, how has the prince escaped your capable hands?"

"His location is top secret. He's supposedly away on business, but I suspect the king pays homage to his mother's unorthodox theories of preparing a prince for the throne. Although, if indeed that is his intention, his approach is far more temperate. The prince has disappeared for several months at a time during the past several years. Never fear, my lord, no excuse could keep the prince from either the gala or the New Year's celebration."

"Once the mission is carried out at the gala, King Turian will be so devastated by his loss that he will be desperate to keep safe the rest of his family. He is not like you. He is weak, and his emotions will make him vulnerable to manipulation and believing the stories he's told."

"Not like me indeed!" The Framatar snorted. "Turian Shamaran is nothing but an entitled, conniving princeling in a costume. Pretender! The Jannemar kingdom will be mine soon enough, and its people will see him for who he really is. Ha!"

Semra gasped. He was after the kingdom!

"By this time next week, only one step will remain between you and your rightful place on the Shamaran throne."

"I trust my uncle has been found and killed? I must be the only male Shamaran left after Prince Zephan is dead."

The Framatar exited the chamber with General Gresvig

and turned down the wider passage on the other side of the fork. Semra shrank back into the crevice as they passed.

"As we speak, surely," the general answered.

"Good. Please ensure for me that negotiations on the union do not go well."

Semra's heart pounded in her ears, and her hands shook as Gresvig and the Framatar disappeared down the corridor. It was too much to process. If Semra didn't prove her loyalty, they were going to kill her, just like they had her parents. The Framatar wasn't purging evil from the earth, he was using the program he had built to pick off obstacles to his own agenda! And he was going to kill the prince and the king and take over Jannemar.

Semra wasn't sure how long she stood there in the dark, mind whirling with a thousand thoughts. He had lied, all this time! Everything she thought she knew was turned on end. She had to do something.

Slowly she eased out from the narrow pass and stuck her hand out in the pitch blackness. Her hand touched cold, damp stone, and she kept one hand on the wall and the other on the lantern as she made her way as quickly and quietly as she could back toward the common areas. She wouldn't light the lantern until she was in the main corridors.

Semra padded down the long passageway, back through the large cavern, and stopped to try and force her breathing to slow before entering the common halls. But her efforts were of no use. Even after five minutes trying, her palms remained sweaty, her heart beat wildly in her chest, and her fingers still trembled. She wiped her hands on her pants and steeled herself to move slowly and confidently, but it was no use. She had to keep moving as she was.

Semra kept her lantern dark, and as she walked by the chow hall, deposited it by the door. She would need to return without it in an hour or so, when more people would be around to see her. Hopefully the few people awake as early as she was that morning hadn't taken notice of her, and if they had, she'd concoct a story. It would be best to show her face where the most people could observe her acting normally. Of course, that required Semra keeping it together.

It was daylight now. The two main openings to the cave were large enough to allow natural light to fill the outermost areas, and fissures from above let down light. She walked as nonchalantly as she could past an Arrow class on their way to morning doctrine and three Saber class students heading to mission-support assignments.

Semra strode into an open common area and paused, unsure of what to do. Three classrooms branched off from the common area. A Bow class doctrine leader stood at the doorway of her class while her young charges marched in single file to present themselves. The doctrine leader clicked her tongue as the last child, a boy of about nine, presented himself.

"Where is your knife? You know you have to have it on you at all times! That's the second time this week!"

The boy looked down at his belt in shock, mouth agape, then looked back up at the leader. "Please ..."

The leader shook her head. "Get it and be back here in two minutes, and you will only owe me twenty pushups. Don't let the captain catch you without it!"

Semra watched as the little boy breathed a sigh of relief and took off back around the bend toward his bunk to retrieve his knife. The doctrine leader retreated into her classroom with her students.

A soft sob startled Semra, and she turned to see a little girl sitting against the wall behind her. She sat with her knees pulled up to her chest and her arms wrapped about her legs, head down as she cried to herself. Semra cautiously crossed to the other side of the little girl and leaned down to tap her on the shoulder.

"Hey, are you okay?"

The little girl jerked her head up, and big blue eyes looked up at Semra. Her hair was dark and tangled, and her tears had made trails through the dirt on her face. Thin lips quivered as she stared hopelessly back at Semra. She looked to be around four, which is the age just about all the children were when Rotokas brought them into the mountain. It wasn't unusual for newcomers to have a hard time adjusting at first.

The induction specialist, Adis, spent an entire month taking care of the new kids one on one, explaining life in the mountain and making them feel important. The trip from Kalma and the other villages at the base of the mountain was always traumatic. Semra remembered all too well the fear she felt as the huge black shadow swooped down from the sky. She'd been playing outside right before dinner and had started running and screaming, but to no avail. Rotokas snatched her up with his massive claws and the earth rapidly dropped away below her. It was natural for children to be afraid at first. They felt they'd been ripped from their family, and it took time to realize they had in fact been saved from deceptive and cruel oppressors.

Semra felt her own eyes prick with tears as she saw in those big blue eyes her own experience back then. Terror. Helplessness. Despair. Semra had found it comforting to know they'd been saved for their own good. Knowing the truth about their abandonment set them free. It allowed them to join the cause to purge the world of evil, preventing such pain in others. Now though, Semra knew it was all wrong. Work spared no one their pain. They were all nothing but pawns. Part of Semra still wondered, however, if perhaps they at least only took children from bad homes. Maybe Semra's parents had been a mistake.

"Who ... who are you?" the girl asked.

Semra realized that they'd been staring at each other for several minutes. She sat down next to the little girl and said, "My name's Semra. What's your name?"

"Lesala," she answered, wiping her face with her sleeve.

"Hi." Semra paused. Why was she sitting here with this kid instead of trying to figure out what to do with the monumental information she'd just learned? She cleared her throat. "So, um ... what are you doing here, all alone? Where's Adis?"

Lesala sniffed. "She said my family didn't want me. I said she was lying and ran away from her." Her voice broke as she spoke again. "My mommy and daddy love me. I want to go home."

Semra's heart ached, and a lump rose in her throat. She thought about growing up in the mountain. Over time, her doctrine leaders and survival guides came to feel like family, and she learned that her own family wasn't worth hoping for. No one ever went down to Kalma. Why would they want to, except for revenge? Kalma was full of the scum of the earth, master manipulators—or so they'd been told.

"Were you taken too? When you were little like me?"

Semra was dumbstruck. What could she say? A tear slipped down her cheek, and she wiped it away. "Yes," she answered simply. Somehow, here on the floor of this cold cave, after all the years of training and lives she had ended, the person who most understood her in that moment was a four-year-old child. She was the only one in the mountain who knew, as Semra now did, that her family was good and the program was a sham.

"Lesala!"

Lesala and Semra both jumped at the sound and twisted around to see a slight woman in her sixties standing nervously at the cavern opening, wringing her hands. She had small features and gray-streaked hair pulled back neatly in a tight bun. Adis smoothed the skirt of her lilac frock and stepped forward to stroke Lesala's hair comfortingly.

"Lesala, there you are; oh, goodness me! Now, now, I know it's hard to take, of course it is, of course, but you'll feel better once we've had some tea and gotten you all cleaned up. You've refused to bathe for days now, and I think it's time you did. You'll feel ever so much better. You just can't run off on me like that, now, you have my nerves all a-jitter and set me to worry!"

Semra took a moment to take in her flighty movements and earnest tone, wondering if this too was all a facade. She remembered Adis being her only safe place when she first came to the mountain, before she came to know the Framatar. Adis was always nurturing, a mother figure to new children. When Semra first saw Rotokas again after getting to the mountain, she'd been paralyzed with fear and had run to Adis as soon as she could move her feet. Adis filled a need, and the Framatar had been kind to her back then.

He showed her a magic trick, pressing his hand on the opal-looking mark on his temple until it glowed bright. He'd told her the gods had gifted him with a special light just for her to see. Whenever she was afraid or the big black dragon scared her, she could ask for the magic trick, and he would give her something bright and beautiful to look at to take her mind off the dark, sinister wyvern at his side.

How much of it was a lie? Was Adis wicked too? As Adis' anxious gaze fell on Semra, Semra felt sure the earnestness she found there was real. Did Adis even know the truth? Was she being forced to work in the mountain?

"Semra, dear," Adis said with a sigh of relief. "Thank you for keeping this little one company for me. What … what have you been talking about?"

"Nothing," Semra answered cautiously. "She just said she was sad and scared, so I thought I would sit with her until you came looking. And I told her about how helpful you were to me when I first came." Semra looked at Lesala, who blinked back at her in confusion, then looked back at Adis.

Adis' face relaxed and she pulled Lesala to her feet. "Thank you, dear, thank you. You had a hard time too when you first came, didn't you? And look at you now, top of your class, doing so well! I'm very proud of you, very proud. Well, now, goodness me, we have to get you fixed up, little one. Let's get you cleaned up, and we'll warm ourselves with some tea, hmm? Won't that be nice?"

Lesala glanced back at Semra, uncertain, and Semra nodded. No one could know anything was amiss with Semra, and getting in the way of a new recruit to the program would certainly call attention to herself. Lesala seemed to take some solace from Semra's encouragement and nodded her somber acceptance of the offer.

Adis patted the girl's shoulder and smiled. "There, now, good girl. Come along …" Adis mouthed a thank you back at Semra as she turned her little charge around, and they moved out of the chamber.

Semra felt a pang of guilt in her gut, first for betraying Lesala by encouraging her to accept her fate and second for lying to Adis. After all, she was a sweet woman, and Semra could do nothing about Lesala's position.

Four-year-old Lesala fought with the older woman and screamed her hatred, and Semra suddenly saw a flash of her own induction with Adis. Had her real parents come up the mountain to find her and been slaughtered on her doorstep as she'd cried herself to sleep that first night. A wave of emotion hit her, and she stood and ran toward the barracks. She had to talk to Brens.

Semra arrived at the barracks and poked her head in. Several of her colleagues still lay on their bunks, but Brens' bunk was empty. Semra searched the surrounding rooms and finally headed for the exercise room. The work of an assassin didn't always require additional exercise, but that didn't keep them from pushing their physical limits on a regular basis.

The exercise room held several large stones, ropes attached to the rock wall, and space for brawling and sword-play. Brens was there, alone, swinging her sword in the various flows they had learned for practice. Semra drew her sword from the sheath at her back and jumped in to meet Brens in a good-natured duel. Brens heard her unsheathe her weapon and swung her sword around with all her strength, meeting Semra with a mighty force. Semra stepped back in surprise, lowering her sword and assessing her friend. Brens' angry eyes softened as she recognized Semra, but it wasn't just the intensity that took Semra by surprise. It was the bruises around her eye.

"Are you okay?"

Brens wiped her nose with the back of her sleeve and turned away. "I'm fine."

"Really? Because you don't seem fine."

"You wouldn't understand."

"What do you mean I wouldn't't understand? We're the same."

Brens shook her head and walked over to sit on one of the large stones to the side of the room. "No. We trained together, live together and were saved from the same village. We're the same age, but we are not the same. You've always been good at everything, like I told you after the last mission. You're so ... focused, so unbothered by emotion."

Semra walked over and sat on another of the stones, leaning forward to touch her friend on the arm. Brens flinched and pulled away.

Semra looked at her. "Let me see."

"No."

"Brens, it must be bad if it hurts that much to touch. You're tough. What did he do to you?"

"He knew. He knew I was lying, and I had to tell; I had to. I couldn't keep it in anymore. He ... he had to make me stronger. He did it for me. I deserved it. He did it to make me better. If I could only have gotten it right the first time, he wouldn't have had to ... " Brens shrugged hopelessly.

Anger burned in Semra's chest. Up until now, this exchange would seem normal. After all, discipline was out of love. But somewhere deep within her Semra began to wonder if love should hurt quite so much. Could Brens' failure really have earned being beaten and bruised?

"Semra! Did you even hear me? I said the Framatar doesn't trust me, and what will he do if I fail him again? He questions my loyalty. Are you listening? Do you even have emotion at all?"

Semra's mouth dropped open as Brens' accusation pulled her out of her troubled thoughts. Did she have emotion? It was to sort out her emotions that she went quiet just then!

Brens wasn't finished. "When you killed Mallen, did you feel it? I'll bet you didn't even feel it. It's what makes you so good. And if you did, you'd never tell me. You wish you could do everything alone! Why do I bother?"

Semra stared back at Brens in shock. Of course she felt

something. Semra remembered for a moment how it felt the first time she took a life: the way Commander Ramas had congratulated her and she'd smiled and accepted his praise before sobbing alone for hours until she fell asleep, even though she knew taking the life of the wicked was the right thing to do. It had to be. Ramas had said it was.

Ramas. She had always held the utmost respect for him. He was brilliant as a strategist and an astute observer, always able to cut to the chase with Semra's own insecurities. But now?

It was true; Semra was good at what she did. There was an art to her trade—if indeed it could be called a trade. She enjoyed the craftsmanship, the knowledge of a blade, the feel of its smooth motions in her capable hands. She loved the confidence it gave her to do something and do it well. But she did not enjoy the killing.

Suddenly Semra reached forward and gripped Brens by the wrists. "Is this all you want for your life?" she asked, her voice low and insistent.

Semra felt a shadow cross the doorway, and she twisted around just in time to see Siler turn away from the opening and head down the passageway. Semra's stomach turned. Had he heard? Would he think she'd been speaking treason?

"What are you talking about?"

Semra tried to focus on Brens' voice, but she had to know where Siler was going.

"Semra? What do you mean?"

"I ... nothing," she answered absentmindedly. "I have to go." Semra rose from her seat and patted Brens' hand. "It'll be okay."

Without another word, she left Brens behind and followed Siler down the corridor, knowing very well that she'd just lied to her friend. It wasn't going to be okay. It might never be.

In that moment, Semra knew in her heart she couldn't go on this way, pretending everything was fine when she knew the truth. The Framatar would find her out, one way or another, as they had Brens. Brens was dangerous now, both to herself and to Semra, because she was desperate. Semra would have to watch what she said around her.

It was true that Semra liked to work alone. She knew her work was good quality, and with less people to rely on, there were less variables to go wrong. But while she was independent in her work, she didn't know the way of the world. The Framatar had always told her so, and he was right—she would be lost without him.

Still, she didn't want to be under his thumb anymore. He kidnapped her and murdered her parents, and he would go on doing the same to others. A burning rage roiled in her chest as she remembered her parents' fate, and her fingertips tingled with the itch to return the favor. No, not yet. He was untouchable—any direct assault would be fruitless.

But Semra knew what he wanted next. In one week, the Framatar would be killing the prince of Jannemar, destroying yet another family and turning the political sphere on its end. Even so, what could she do? She was only one small girl in an army of trained assassins and powerful political players loyal to the Framatar, who was the most dangerous man she had ever met. Not to mention Rotokas. He would feast on her flesh at the snap of the Framatar's fingers ... maybe roast her a bit first so she was more tender. A chill ran up Semra's spine. For the first time in her life, she felt truly alone.

6

Semra only saw the edge of a cloak whisking around the bend by the time she got to the corridor, and she picked up her pace. She needed to be fast, but not too fast. The passage turned again, into a long hall, and she'd lost Siler. She jogged past the barracks and glanced around the large room, but he wasn't there, so she crossed into the chow hall and scanned the room.

Semra caught sight of him on the other side of the hall, laughing about something with Behruz and clapping him on the back. That was quick, Semra thought, surprised to see Behruz returned to the mountain so fast. Maybe he really is as brilliant a framer as he says. Or maybe his impatience led to shoddy work. Semra was yet again grateful she didn't have to be responsible for that outcome. She'd completed her portion of the mission in full.

Siler laughed again, and Semra gritted her teeth. The man looked like he had nothing on his mind but roast rabbit and Behruz' tales of adventure. Which was interesting, since he was more of a loner than anything. Perhaps that was his tell. For a moment their eyes met, and something in Siler's deep-gray eyes held her, solemn and knowing. Her mouth went dry, and she stared back at him across the room, unsure of what to do. If he'd found her out, that was it. Her life was forfeit.

"Semra! There you are. Been looking for you, little lady, but couldn't find you anywhere."

Semra spun to find Colonel Nepraunik ambling toward her. Middle aged, average in height and with a muscular build, he had a definitive scar running from below his left ear to halfway around the front of his neck. Someone had obviously tried to kill him, but Nepraunik didn't talk about it much except to say the "other guy" got what he deserved. Nepraunik was in charge of the entire program in the mountain and had a soft spot for Semra.

"Colonel," she answered. "What can I do for you?"

"Not for me, I'm afraid. No, but it's a good thing, really." He spoke more to himself than to her, she thought. He drew her aside and spoke quietly so that only she could hear. "You've been temporarily reassigned."

"Re ... reassigned?" Semra stammered, taken aback.

"Don't look so grim; you've not been repurposed, girl. Reassigned. Temporary, I'm sure, but you're grounded from all missions until further notice."

Semra glanced back toward Siler and saw him cast a nonchalant look in her direction. Could he have ratted her out so fast? Was she being punished for being disloyal? Semra thought about Brens' bruises and wondered what they'd do to Semra if she failed any test from here on out.

"I ... would be honored."

Nepraunik laughed, and it grated her nerves. "No you

wouldn't. You're perfect in the field, and that's a fact. So whatever you did to fall out of good graces, fix it and fix it fast. Keep your head down and do a good job, and I'll see if we can get you a better gig once you're through. Maybe a sleeper, hmm? You could work outside the mountain, be on your own, get your missions that way. You'd like that. Of course you would, so would everyone! There's only five sleepers out right now, anyway. Now, about your assignment. You'll be working under Vix."

Semra blinked. "I can't work with dragons!"

Everyone knew Vix was head of the dragon-training program. He was the primary authority over the other four dragon wranglers and anyone involved in their care. The Arrow class, ten to twelve-year-olds, were responsible for feeding and cleaning up after them, but only the dragon wranglers were permitted to truly interact with the beasts. The dragon training was the Framatar's pet project. Semra wondered what he'd want with a dragon fleet if he had one.

Thus far results were less than promising, as the only dragons they had managed to capture were small, cunning, and unmotivated to acquiesce to any human handler. In reality they were drakes rather than true dragons, just as Rotokas was technically a wyvern, though the word dragon was often used as an umbrella category term. Two hind legs and no real forelegs distinguished the wyverns—their arms were part of their wings, like a bat. Drakes had similar anatomy but were smaller, ranging from only two-to-three feet in length on up to ten-or-twelve feet. They were significantly more manageable than a beast of Rotokas' size, but still formidable fighters.

Nepraunik chuckled. "You'll do fine; you'll do fine. You've dealt with worse, I'm sure. They're drakes, it's not like you have to take on Rotokas. And Vix certainly isn't ready to have you as one of his dragon wranglers, so just do as he says. You'll probably just be on clean-up crew."

"I'll die trying to scoop poop then. Fantastic."

"That's the spirit; there you are. Come on, Vix is over there by Behruz. Let's take you on over and get you started. Remember, you have it good in the field. Do right by Vix and show the Framatar you belong out there, not stuck in the cages in here."

Semra sighed. Not only did she hate dragons, but working with them was often a cooperative endeavor, and Semra didn't love working in groups. She walked resignedly with Nepraunik as he led her over to where Behruz, Vix, and Siler stood. Semra glanced at Siler, but the knowing look had gone. All she saw now was nonchalance. What was he thinking?

"Gentlemen, good morning. Vix, Semra is going to be working for you in the dragon program for a while. Heard you needed an extra set of hands."

Vix turned to look her over. He was one of the oldest graduates, in his early twenties, and he bore a deep scar across his left bicep from an unpleasant encounter with one of the drakes several years prior. "Know anything about dragons?" he asked her.

"Just that they hate you. And us. And being in cages."

Vix laughed. "They don't hate us. They hate uncertainty. If we can remove any uncertainty about who's in charge and whether or not serving our purposes is beneficial to them, then they know what to expect. We're making some headway. If you bring an attitude though, they'll pick up on it."

"Imagine that; a killer with an attitude! A killer attitude, she has, doesn't she?" Nepraunik roared, slapping his thigh.

"Can't expect much else, I'd wager. She's a fire. Keep her burning, but channel it. Good luck with that," he added, and nodded at Siler and Behruz before turning to leave.

"His jokes are terrible," Behruz commented, shaking his head good-naturedly.

"You wrapped up your mission pretty quickly," Semra said, looking at him. "Was it successful?"

"As well as could be expected, I think," he answered, sobering as he met Semra's gaze. "I'm giving a full report to the Framatar this afternoon. Heading out with the wranglers for the day to solve a dragon problem on the plateau first."

Semra's eyes widened. "The plateau? That's too close for them to be coming in. Doesn't Rotokas' scent stave them off?"

"Usually," Behruz said. "But there's a Rangchanj dragon on their usual haunt."

Vix shook his head. "It can't be. Rangchanj dragons are even more rare than Rotokas' species, the Atas Mountain Wyvern. Real dragons in general haven't been seen around here for decades ... just the common drakes."

"I'm telling you, I saw it on my way in. Four legs and huge wings. Looked blue when I first saw it, and then it looked gray. A few of us are going back out to try and kill it. I'm thinking it'll be near impossible to catch, but we'll try that first. If we can kill it, I'm taking the scales and teeth for armor and weapons."

Siler spoke for the first time. "The Framatar know about this?"

"He gave me the go ahead. Rotokas already got into a scuffle with it earlier this week, and it's injured. The two might actually be about the same size."

Siler snorted. "Because you would dare go after Rotokas."

"Of course not, but this dragon is worth a try. Can you imagine, having real dragon skin for mail? The Framatar doesn't want to risk the whole horde of drakes trying to come into the mountain, so he said to get rid of it."

"There's no way it was a Rangchanj," Vix said again, unable to shake the topic. "They use color for social cues, mating, and camouflage. You're saying that you actually saw it change colors? I bet you my dinner that your eyes played tricks on you."

"Ha! Come on out then. I'm telling you; I know what I saw. And if we kill it, we'll split the teeth among us. We're leaving in just a few minutes."

"So," Semra began, "I'm assuming the suicide mission is volunteer only, and I'm not volunteering for that. What am I supposed to do?"

"I wouldn't trust you with any direct dragon catching or training," Vix replied. "You haven't studied their behavior nearly as long as we have, and you don't know what you're doing with the drakes. While we're out, you can feed and clean up after them ... we could use an extra pair of hands there. I'll get you started and head out to the plateau, and Kiar should be back after lunch to show you the ropes. Siler, good chatting with you. You got a mission coming up?"

"Planning stages," he answered. "But I have a feeling I'll be leaving the mountain soon." Siler glanced at Semra, and something in her stomach felt uneasy.

"Right, well, I'm headed to the plateau," Behruz said. "Vix, see you there in a bit. Bring every weapon you've got, and don't dawdle."

Semra snatched some dried fruit off the table on her way out and followed Vix back through the main common area and down the wide passage on the other side. After one smaller passage that shot directly off from the common area, the ceilings became at least twenty feet high, making it more ideal for the drakes. Further along, the corridor opened up even more, about forty feet wide and thirty feet high.

Grating sounds mixed with screeches and warbling calls rose to meet them as they descended further down. As they drew closer, the sounds grew louder, and a putrid smell assaulted her nostrils. Semra wrinkled her nose in disgust as they turned the corner into a large cavern. Tall steel bars cordoned off ten spaces around the edge where the ceiling was only twenty feet off the ground. Each cell contained only one drake, but two stood empty. She counted eight drakes either flying against the bars or curled up in the corners of their cells.

The smallest drake, only five feet long, had a bright-green back, a matching crest on its head, and a blue belly with yellow spots. As they approached, it walked up to the edge of its enclosure and bobbed its head up and down.

"See that?" Vix asked, gesturing to the drake's body language. "The crest shows it's a male, and that motion he's doing with his head is a warning sign. He's the newest to the group, and he's telling us to stay back or he'll get aggressive."

"Great," she said. "You've never had one break through those bars, have you?"

"No, these guys are too small. But we have had a drake small enough to fit through them. Had to add bars closer together. Maybe one day we can get eggs ... that could be the breakthrough we need, to train them right from the beginning."

Vix pulled a wheelbarrow overflowing with fresh meat out from the shadows to their left. Large chunks of meat had been rudely cut and tossed into the wheelbarrow, and a short wooden spike stuck out the top, spearing the top piece.

"Use the short spear to give them these. The dividers

between each cell have a door that opens by the lever in between them, so when they're done, you can open the door and let them go one cell over. Don't pull the top lever—that opens the front door out here with us. Only the bottom lever, between the cells. When the cell is clear, go in and clean up any extra bones and shovel the poop out. The Arrow class that usually does it has been training off-site for the past few days, so they've gotten pretty bad. You remember where to dump the wheelbarrows after?"

Every Arrow class spent time on menial tasks with the drakes. Semra nodded. It had been her least favorite part of her training years.

"Good. Get lunch whenever, and I'll give you some new assignments when I get back." Vix turned and headed out of the cavern, no doubt dreaming of dragon-tooth necklaces and dragon-scale armor.

Semra took a deep breath and sighed. She glanced over at the drakes, and saw the little one peering at her inquisitively through the bars. Two of the eight lay curled in tight balls in their cells, fast asleep, and the other five either stared at her or fluttered up to the ceiling of their small space. Fifteen feet wide and twenty feet tall was hardly spacious for a creature fit for the wide-open skies. One started gnawing on the steel bars, and Semra wondered for the first time if it was aggression or boredom that caused the behavior.

Perhaps they had more in common with her than she'd thought, trapped here against their will to bend or to break under a thousand new training attempts. They wouldn't stop until the Framatar had found success in training dragons to do his bidding. Semra couldn't help but wonder how he'd been able to bring Rotokas so perfectly under his control, and why he didn't simply duplicate that process with other drakes and wyverns.

Semra brought the wheelbarrow over to the cell that housed the littlest drake and tossed a chunk of meat through the bars. The drake reared up and caught it, shaking it side to side before choking it down. The two sleeping drakes woke at the sound of the wheelbarrow, and gnashed their teeth as she drew closer. Semra stared at the strong musculature, wiry frames, and cunning eyes. Their claws could tear her apart, and if one of the longer drakes hit her hard enough with that tail, it might break bones. Semra was grateful she hadn't been charged with bringing them into the mountain.

She speared another chunk of raw meat and tossed it into the next cell. The beast attacked it viciously, devouring it in an instant, and goosebumps ran up her arms as the last shred of flesh disappeared. The drake returned to the bars, watching her anxiously as she moved on to the next cell. If these smaller versions terrified her so, what hope did she have of facing Rotokas?

Was there a way out of the mountain without facing the Framatar or Rotokas himself? Swarms of assassins came in and out of the mountain all day, and now that she was banished to spend most of her days with the dragons, she'd have limited excuses to leave the mountain. Meals and evenings would be her only time to plan an escape, but even if she got out, they could always track her down and kill her then. The faster she left, the harder it would be to cover her tracks.

Semra wondered how much time she could buy for herself by waiting until Rotokas went out to hunt. He followed the Framatar's commands with precision but was more than capable of taking care of his own meals. If she managed to survive long enough to blend into the villages or larger cities, where would she go? What kind of life would she be equipped for?

Perhaps Colonel Nepraunik was right, and she should keep her head down and prove she was still trustworthy and most useful out in the field. The independence of the assassin assignment was absolutely necessary for getting any distance from the mountain unheeded, and if Nepraunik was right and she could get assigned somewhere as a sleeper … that would be perfect. She'd be strategically inserted into a life somewhere with a cover story prepared, ready and waiting for instructions to rise up whenever and wherever the Framatar might need. If she threw herself into it, maybe she could convince them to put her back in the field sooner rather than later. It would be her final long con before escaping for good.

Semra emptied the wheelbarrow, feeding all the drakes, and pulled the large lever on the end of the filled cells. The great steel door lifted up between the empty cell and the first occupied cell, and a dark-rust-colored drake about seven feet long screeched at her through the bars. Semra tapped the bars with the spoke.

"Come on, get going. Into the next one, so I can come clean out yours. Ugh, these smell so bad."

The drake cocked its head and screeched again.

Semra glared back at it. "What are you looking at?"

She stepped forward tentatively and poked it through the bars with the spoke, hoping to urge it into the next cell. The drake whipped its head around, snatched the spoke right out of her hands with its teeth, and tossed it backward, flapping its wings. Suddenly the drake lunged forward against the cage, and its narrow head just managed to slip between the bars and snap its jaws two inches from her face.

Semra yelped and leaped back. "Fine! Stay there! I'm going back up, and you can move when you want to. I'll be back in an hour."

She deposited the empty wheelbarrow back in the corner and stalked out of the drakes' dungeon and back up into the common area. Semra went to chow, needing an excuse to be away from dragon duty and not particularly in the mood to be in larger groups of people when lunch came around. She stashed dried meats and fruits in her pack for later, slung it over her shoulder and turned to leave, but a commotion coming from the main-entrance common area drew her to it. Semra followed the sound and poked her head around the opening into the large room.

The little girl from earlier, Lesala, was kicking and screaming as an Egg class doctrine apprentice dragged her away from the entrance to the mountain. Lesala's dark-brown hair was a disheveled mess, and Semra recognized the fourteen-year-old girl who held her in a firm grasp as Conet. Semra didn't know Conet well, but knew she'd been unsuited to field work and assigned doctrine leader apprentice a year ago. Conet, straining to keep a hold of the four-year-old, yanked her backward again.

"Get it through your head; your family left you to die! Do you know what Kalma thinks of Rotokas? They think he eats children, and they deposit their undesirables outside for him. You were manipulated and abused down there. There is nothing for you in Kalma!"

"Liar!" Lesala screamed, her flashing blue eyes cutting through Conet. "Maybe your family hated you, but mine loves me! Let me go!"

"We are your family now, idiot! And you're doing a terrible job being part of it so far. Ungrateful! How did you get away from Adis again?"

Semra's heart lurched into her throat as she watched. Conet had it perfectly backward. The manipulation happened here, in the mountain, and Semra and Lesala were the only ones who knew the truth. Semra wondered how many students in the program were "dispatched" for rebellion, like the Framatar had threatened doing to Semra if she didn't get on board. With this girls' fiery spirit, they might kill her rather than let her live unturned.

Conet struggled to drag Lesala across the stony floor, and Lesala screamed again and bit her hard on the arm. Conet yowled and slapped her across the face. Semra stiffened, and as she watched, Lesala's blue eyes looked up at her and pierced her through. With that moment of eye contact, Semra knew deep in her soul that she couldn't abandon this little child to the harshness of the mountain.

Semra waited for them to pass by her and make their way down the corridor toward Adis' rooms, then she took a less common route through several more caverns and passages and looped back around to Adis' rooms. She felt along the familiar walls in the dark with her hands, noticing that the cold stone alternated between dry and damp.

At last, as she rounded the last corner, natural light warmed the stone beneath her fingers. Forty feet above her, an opening several feet wide allowed light to pour into the room ahead, and it filled the cavern and surrounding nooks and crannies. She assumed these rooms had likely been selected for their natural light, paired with being further into the mountain and separated from the rest of the program. The smallest children needed to feel safe, and pitch blackness didn't lend itself well to that endeavor. The children also needed to be unable to navigate the halls or escape easily.

Semra knelt close to the ground and peered through a large grouping of stalagmites that obscured her from view. The cavern was a near perfect circle with open space in the middle. Two cots stood at one end, and blankets lay on the floor beneath straw dolls, an assortment of colorful rocks and fresh cut flowers, and a plate of food. Adis hovered over Lesala stroking her hair, while the girl sat resignedly on the floor, arms wrapped around her knees as she had been when Semra first saw her. Conet stood tapping her foot, arms crossed.

"Goodness me, poor thing," Adis said. "Of course, of course she wants to go home. It's familiar; it's comforting. She isn't used to us yet, don't you know? Conet, remember even you were afraid when you first came to us. You didn't know the evils of the Kalmian villagers yet, because they'd brainwashed you, like the rest of them!"

"You've never had this much trouble with a recruit before," Conet snapped. "Maybe you're losing your touch."

Adis pursed her lips and released Lesala's hair, gesturing for her to go play with the items on the floor. She drew Conet to the side of the room nearer to Semra and, lowering her voice, said, "My touch is just the same as always, thank you very much. She is perhaps the most difficult child we have had ... few children in this stage have actually made it out of the mountain, and none have made it out three times! Her potential is incredible, and her strength is good for us. But only if it can be appropriately channeled. Similar to your passion, I might add."

"What are you going to do with her?"

"If she makes it out of the mountain again, the Framatar will have our heads—"

"Your head," Conet corrected grimly.

"Goodness, what an ungrateful sprite you are! Now, now, you're the one that let her get so far, and you're on loan to me all this week. Don't for one second think I'll take all the blame for this. It may be time to speak to the Framatar about removing her from the program."

"She won't be any good to us anywhere, even if she is repurposed to cook or hunt or something. She'll keep trying to leave."

"I didn't say repurpose. I said remove."

"Remove? She ... she can't leave the mountain."

Adis shook her head sadly. "No. No, she can't."

Conet's eyes widened, and she glanced at Lesala, who fiddled absentmindedly with a straw doll. "Is that really necessary?"

"Conet, we're here to save children from evil. And we have saved her, but if she refuses to be saved, death is a sweeter end than living in Kalma. No one is forced to live in the mountain. They choose it, as you did. But if they don't choose it ... we ... we help them reach their peace. Tell the Framatar we'll bring her to him this afternoon."

The hairs on the back of Semra's neck stood up and gooseflesh sprang up all over her body. She felt as if fire seared her heart and white-hot flame shot through her muscles. Shock and anger warred for prominence within her. If Lesala didn't get on board, they were going to kill her. And it looked very much like Lesala had no plans to get on board.

Semra could stay silent no longer. She turned and fled down the corridor, thoughts whirring as she tried to think of a plan to save the girl. Her soft footwear sounded lightly on the limestone floor as she flew across it, dodging left and right through the abandoned passageways. Once, she stumbled and fell, the sound echoing deep into the recesses of the mountain. She held her breath ... but no one heard.

Afraid a misstep would cost her her life, Semra slowed, panting, to a brisk walk. Suddenly she heard the unmistakable voice of General Gresvig coming toward her. She froze. The passage didn't split for another thirty feet, and the general and his companion were nearly upon her. Behind, nothing branched off for a quarter mile. The flickering light of their lantern swaying back and forth grew brighter as they neared the bend.

Semra dashed back until the pass opened up wider, frantically looking for something to help her. Stalagmites melted into a small crevice to one side, and she wedged herself between them and the rocky wall just in time for the lantern light to expose the walkway. It was dim in the shadows, but if they looked in her direction, they'd see her.

"The prince is devoted to his father and the Jannemar people," Gresvig said. "He'll not risk the king's reputation or the strained relations between Jannemar and Belvidore. He'll be brought out of hiding, and you'll not lose him again."

"He's soft, like his father. Whines all the time about how the people are struggling; they need more support; the nobles need to understand them. Ha! He may yet be a tool against the marriage between Avaya and Axis. Acts as though marriage to someone you don't like is the end of the world. Royal marriage is a political assignment, and his idealistic views have kept him from accepting proposals so far and may very well impede this one."

Semra recognized the second speaker as Tymetin, a nineteen-year-old who'd graduated one year before she did. He'd been two classes above her before she graduated early. He was another one of the Framatar's favorites and one of his most reliable assets.

Gresvig laughed. "Turian was heartless as a young lad, and now he's nothing *but* heart. He'll be putty in your hands. There are many he loves. Use them to your advantage, but do not underestimate his skill with a blade."

"Perfect. More time to enjoy it! You know the last one was hardly worth my time. Ran him through like a pig on a spit, and he was about as difficult to kill!"

"My favorite story was that rich, entitled snob from a year ago. Remember?"

"Ah! Top three memories. We blew him to high heaven, and there were too many pieces to count!"

Semra pressed herself further into the crevice as they walked by, only three feet from her hiding place. She felt slightly nauseous hearing them speak so glibly, especially now knowing the targets were likely undeserving.

"Explosions are fun to watch, but so inelegant," Gresvig commented casually. "There are so many more artful ways to go about it."

"General! I'm disappointed. Explosions are beautiful pieces of art, with a side of guts tossed around like confetti."

"Nevermind, nevermind. Regardless, Prince Zephan is beloved by the king and by all of Jannemar. He has lofty goals and high support, representing the hope of a nation. We need to eliminate that hope."

Gresvig and Tymetin continued down the pass, and Semra didn't stop to think. On her preoccupation with her own situation, she'd nearly forgotten about the prince's fate. But now, the fresh knowledge of her parents' murder, the threats on her life and on the life of innocent four-year-old Lesala, and the impending slaughter of the royal family all rose in a great jumble to the forefront of her mind.

One-hundred-and-fifty people resided in the mountain, and the Framatar had enslaved them all. At four years old the "choice" to live in the mountain was no choice at all, and the naming ceremony merely celebrated joining a sick family of killers. It was a calculated deception built to foster obligation and blind allegiance, and the Framatar was about to bring the full force of his wickedness down on an entire kingdom of innocent people.

Semra took off through the passageways, passed the

chow hall, raced through the common area, and back down to the drakes' dungeon. She resolved in that moment that she would expose the Framatar's true nature and save the world from his victimization ... or she would die trying. And she was going to start with Lesala.

7

Semra's plan to save the world was rather half-baked at this point. It had something to do with getting to the prince and saving his life, getting the king to believe and trust her, and using the kingdom of Jannemar to help protect her while she exposed the Framatar's lies. The plan to save Lesala was built on a whisper of hope, a sizable amount of impulsivity, and drakes running amuck.

Semra burst into the dragons' room and observed with some small satisfaction that the rust-colored drake had finally made it to the empty cell. She closed the side gate with the bottom lever between the cells, reached for the top lever, and pulled down hard before she had the chance to talk herself out of it. The front gate swung open, and the rust-colored drake screeched at her and backed away from the open door.

Semra couldn't pause to think. She ran to the next cell and pulled down its lever, then proceeded through all eight cells until the last little green drake with the blue belly was free. After hurrying through the motions, she stepped back away from the cages, breathing fast. A ruddy-brown drake escaped first. It plunged through the open door at a run, then came to an abrupt halt and sniffed at the air before letting out a high-pitched screech that grated her ears and quickened her heart. Then it took off at a run down the open passageway toward the main common area and cavern entrance.

The clock was ticking now, and with the drakes released, there was no turning back. Six other drakes pounded out of their cells, beating their wings, some taking to the air for a few low circles inside the cavern before being forced to the ground again to fit through the smaller passage. The little green drake swept out of his cell and bobbed his head up and down toward Semra.

Slowly she reached for the sword at her back, suddenly aware of the oversight she'd made in releasing eight small dragons in the same room as her. The green drake roared a sputter of hot smoke in her face, flapped its wings, and ran as fast as its legs could carry it after the others down the corridor. Semra exhaled in relief, but her reprieve wouldn't last. A cacophony of screeches and screams rang down the passage.

She couldn't be found there when someone came to investigate, so she dashed up the corridor after the drakes, praying the chaos was big enough that no one would notice her, but not so big that she couldn't make it to Adis' induction rooms. She'd almost made it out, when a figure charged toward her, sword in hand. Semra skidded to a halt, unsure of what to do. She recognized Siler, his face as hard as flint. He was going to kill her.

"What did you do?" he yelled, coming to a stop three feet from her.

"I ... I pulled the wrong lever, and they got out!"

Siler drilled her with a pointed stare. "You accidentally

pulled the wrong lever ... eight times?" He whirled his sword in a wide arc.

They stood there in a silent stand off for a moment, each waiting for the other to make a move. A loud crash sounded above the din in the common area, jolting Siler into action.

"Well, come on," he said. "You just endangered a bunch of kids." He jerked his head up the passage and waited for Semra to move before breaking into a light jog beside her.

What was he doing?

They reached the common area and Semra gaped at the sight. Two of the drakes were engaged in battle with a sea of mission readies and doctrine leaders who had positioned themselves in the doors of classrooms between the dragons and the children. Semra felt a whoosh of air as a drake plummeted down on them from above. Siler sliced at it with his sword just in time, and it pulled up sharply.

Semra glanced up and saw a fourth drake circling the high cavern and angling down for a dive. Semra ducked under its wing as it plunged, dodging Siler and the mass of twenty fighters thronged together in that space. She heard him shout behind her, but in a flash she melted away through the crowd, snatched a lantern from outside the chow hall, and took off down the maze of halls toward Adis and Lesala.

She took the direct route this time, which was much shorter, and stopped, breathing hard, at the entrance to the induction rooms where Adis and Lesala sat together on the blankets. They both looked up, startled.

"The ... drag ... the drag ... " Semra managed between breaths, gasping for air.

"Semra? What is it?" Adis stood, concerned.

"The dragons ... the drakes are loose. Conet was attacked," Semra lied, "so the Framatar asked me to escort you both to his chambers immediately and keep you safe until they recapture them all."

Adis' eyes widened. "Attacked! Is she okay? How did they escape?"

"No time, no time! She's with medical now. I'm sure she'll be fine, but we might not be if I don't follow orders. Let's go; let's go."

"Goodness me, goodness!" Adis wrung her hands nervously and smoothed her skirts. "All right; my, my, we'll do as you say. You'll watch over us, won't you?"

Adis had never learned to fight. She was one of the few in the mountain with roles that didn't require it, and one of only a handful that were older than early twenties. She'd not been a student of the program but had come to the mountain with the Framatar when he founded it.

"Yes, of course, but we have to move now. One is trapped in the back corridor and could be here any moment." Semra pulled Lesala to her feet, and she jumped up willingly, saying nothing, face full of terror.

Adis twirled a wisp of gray hair behind her ear and nodded. Semra patted the older woman reassuringly on the shoulder, then swiftly hit her in that same sweet spot beneath the jaw that had crumpled Governor Mallen's guard. Semra caught her as she fell and dragged her unconscious form behind the large grouping of stalagmites Semra herself had hidden behind just that morning. Lesala's eyes seemed to just about pop out of her head, but her feet stayed rooted to the floor.

Semra lowered Adis carefully to the ground and touched her face gingerly. She had always felt a genuine care from this woman. She hoped it was real, at least a little bit. Semra whirled back to Lesala. "She's okay; I didn't hurt her. I just couldn't have her following us, you hear? There is no dragon in the back corridor, and we have to take it, now."

Lesala's lips parted and started to quiver. Semra rushed over and knelt in front of the small girl. They couldn't afford any delays. "Lesala, I'm here to help you. If you want to get out of this mountain, if you ever want to see your family again, you'll do everything I tell you; you'll stay close, and you'll run as fast as you can. Do you understand?"

Lesala nodded. "Yes."

"Good. Take my hand. Let's go."

Lesala grabbed Semra's hand and they ran through the back corridor, which Semra knew would empty out near the exercise room and chow hall. A shorter passage just before the exercise room lead to the main entrance of the mountain. Using it would keep them from having to go through the common room again. Though far too close for comfort, it was their only option.

They made it down the back halls without incident and were in view of the short passage they needed when one of the drakes dashed across the corridor and into the exercise room ahead of them. Rotokas' huge head came into view, and Semra pushed Lesala behind her and against the wall. The great black wyvern eyed her distrustfully, but turned its head into the exercise room. The huge black wings expanded and filled the passage as he let out a torrent of blue-hot flame after the smaller drake. Semra ducked and shielded Lesala with her body as Rotokas' wing extended over their heads.

"No damage to the cages means this was intentional, and heads will roll when I find out who is responsible!" The Framatar's voice coming from the other side of the dragon curdled her blood.

"My lord, perhaps there is something we don't understand, and it was yet an accident. Perhaps death isn't necessary." Colonel Nepraunik. The voices were only fifteen feet away, obscured only by Rotokas' body filling the corridor.

A horrible gnashing of teeth and screeching mixed with the sound of Rotokas' deeper roar. Semra yanked Lesala after her into the short passage to the right, just in time as Rotokas moved to fit more of himself into the exercise room after the drake.

The Framatar spoke again. "The thing about dead people, Nepraunik, is that they don't cause problems. To do something like this, one is either a blithering idiot or a traitor. I have no room for either on my mountain."

Semra waited for another loud sound to cover their escape, and only a moment later she heard the agonized cry of the drake as Rotokas filled the room with fire and ripped it to shreds. She ran, half dragging, half carrying Lesala behind her.

The passage to the entrance wasn't far, and as they followed the path around two lefts and a right, bright light poured down from a wide-open flat before them. The ground rose up to a ledge, meeting a second corridor that pulled away and wound back down into the common area, but beyond this joining, the ledge dropped away down the rocky mountain to the plateaus. Only thirty feet stood between them and open air.

A breeze wafted over them, and Semra rushed forward with Lesala close behind, reinvigorated by the hope of outside air. In seconds they reached the top of the fork, but a great force collided into her and sent her tumbling to the ground. An instant after impact, Semra had a knife in her left hand, but the form on top of her rolled away and sprang to its feet. Semra leaped up and turned to face her attacker, hearing the familiar ring of steel as her adversary drew her weapon.

"Brens!" Semra cried out in surprise.

Her friend stood in an engagement stance between her and freedom, eyes dark as pitch, mouth pressed in a firm line. "Hello, Semra."

"What are you doing?"

"What am *I* doing? Why, I believe I'm stopping a dangerous traitor from leaving with the troublesome new induction girl."

"Traitor?!" Semra gasped. "Brens, you don't understand!"

"I understand you were banished to dragon duty, you lied to the Framatar, and here you are with your pack and your weapons and a four-year-old you have no business being with."

"Brens, I don't have time for this! I lied to the Framatar for *you*, and we always carry our weapons! But it doesn't matter, Brens, because the Framatar has been lying to us. All this time. Our parents didn't abandon us; we were kidnapped! He murdered my parents; they really did want me. It's all wrong!"

"You're lying!" Brens lunged forward.

Semra ducked, drew her sword with her right hand and swung it round to meet Brens' blade, being careful to stay between Brens and Lesala. "I'm not! I swear it!" Their swords met again, and Semra deflected a mighty blow to the head. "Brens! Stop! You're going to kill me!"

"I'm dead if I let you go! The Framatar already killed Kiar over the drake incident. He was a suspect, but he arrived back in the mountain after they were let out. By you. Don't you see? This is the only way to prove my loyalty!"

Semra parried another blow, and another, then faked right and danced in close to slice Brens in the torso. Brens cried out and rushed at Semra again, but Semra sheathed her knife and brought her sword straight down from above with both hands. Brens met her blade over her head and angled in toward Semra, but in a swift motion Semra slid her blade down to Brens' hilt with her right hand, gripped Brens' blade toward its tip with her left hand, and stepped in to wrench it downward with her sword arm. Holding her own sword by the hilt in her right hand, and Brens' sword by the blade in her left, Semra tossed Brens' sword aside. She now had the mouth of the cave to her back and Brens before her.

"Lesala, behind me!" Semra called, and the girl ran dutifully to stand behind Semra. Still facing off with Brens, Semra took out one of the knives on her legs and passed it behind her to the little girl. "Take this with you. Get out of the cave and hide in the rocks. Don't come out until you see me."

"Semra?"

"Go!"

Lesala went, and as Semra glanced after her Brens knocked her sword from her hand and pinned her to the ground. Semra blocked her face, bucking her hips up in the air to throw Brens off balance and rolling until their positions were exchanged and Semra was on top. Semra hit Brens in the face again and again, then she pulled away, jumped to her feet, and reclaimed her sword.

Brens moaned and spat blood to the side, glaring up at Semra. She rolled twice to reach her own sword before regaining her footing. "You think you're so much better than me," she snarled. "Best of your class, everybody's favorite, and now you have to have parents that love you too? You're so perfect!"

With a flick of her wrist, Brens flung a knife at Semra, who hadn't registered that Brens had held it. Semra turned just in time to evade the hit, but the blade grazed her left arm and slit her sleeve. On instinct Semra sent one of her own knives flying back at Brens, and it lodged itself in the palm of Brens' throwing hand. Semra let out an involuntary roar and surged forward, barreling into Brens. Brens stumbled backward, delivering elbows to Semra's back and neck as they went.

Semra pushed down on the back of Brens' neck and up on her right shoulder so that she spun and flopped on the floor in front of Semra, facing the wall, then Semra wrapped her elbow around her friend's throat and cinched it tight. Brens' hands clutched at her arm in a desperate attempt to regain her air supply.

Semra whispered in her ear, "Don't fight it. I won't kill you. But I can't let you follow me, either."

Brens writhed in her arms for a few moments more before blacking out and going limp. Semra re-sheathed her sword and wiped her knife off on Brens' pants before noticing the blood dripping from Brens' hand. With a grunt, Semra hoisted Brens onto her shoulders so that she bled onto Semra's back instead of the floor, and carried her out of the mountain. She deposited her friend behind a large outcropping to one side of the cave mouth. Though blood dripped onto the ground now, they'd left no trail.

Semra wished Brens had been able to come with her and escape the mountain. But the hardness in Brens' eyes had been so resolved, she knew it wouldn't have done any good. Semra wouldn't have been able to trust Brens not to turn her in or kill her in her sleep. Desperation made people do things they wouldn't normally do, and Brens was most certainly desperate. Semra hoped the bruises and injuries Brens had sustained would prove her loyalty rather than her uselessness to the Framatar's cause, and so keep her safe.

Time was running out. The drakes would keep them busy a while longer, but after Siler saw her coming up from the dungeon it wouldn't be long before the Framatar had his answer.

Semra stepped around the outcropping and called softly, "Lesala!"

The little girl appeared from behind another large rock, holding Semra's knife delicately with both hands.

Semra let out a sigh of relief and motioned for her to follow. "We have to move quickly now. Follow me."

"But home is the other way, around the other side of the mountain." Her voice was small, frightened, but resolute.

Semra shook her head. "Kalma is the first place they'll look, and they'll probably send Rotokas. We need to get somewhere safe and sort things out, or you won't have a family to go back to."

The little girl's lip quivered, and Semra suddenly realized how harsh she'd sounded. Guilt washed over her, but she didn't have time to mince words. And everything she'd said was true. Semra motioned her forward, and they both took off in a run down the mountain toward the plateaus, large flats of land further down the mountain on one side.

The mountain they called home was actually one in a ring of mountains encircling a lake, with Kalma in the foothills at their base. The plateaus stuck out halfway down the Framatar's mountain. Drakes liked to sun themselves there when they felt gutsy enough to encroach on Rotokas' territory. Trees cropped up around the plateaus at the bottom and so offered the best way down, but to get there, they'd have to move slowly due to the severity of the slope, and they could be seen and picked off instantly at a distance.

Semra led the way, careful to make sure Lesala was right behind. They raced down the rocky way as quickly as they could without tumbling down the steeper portions. Semra fell into a rhythm, feeling the air pulled into her lungs and expanding her rib cage, then expelled out with a whoosh as she ran. With her boots thudding on the ground, her legs carrying her like lightning, even the urgency itself felt calming. Finally, she was doing something again! No pretense, no long con, and no longer under the control of anyone but herself ... for however short a time.

A small cry sounded behind her. Semra spun around and saw Lesala skidding down a steep bank. She raced back, reached down to grip the little girl's wrists, and as she pulled her up and into her arms, she saw a lithe shadow disappear behind the rocks. Someone had followed them.

Semra put a finger to her lips and motioned Lesala to run ahead, then she crouched low, silently drawing a throwing knife. In a moment the figure appeared again, around the side of the rock. Semra let fly her blade, but a sword deflected it. As the figure came into full view, Semra saw the same brown hair, gray eyes, and full height that had haunted her the past two days. Siler.

8

Semra launched herself forward and struck Siler in the jaw, but he turned into her movement and flipped her on her back as she propelled past him. She hooked his leg on the way down and brought him crashing on top of her, then wormed her foot up onto his hip socket to shove him away. Siler dragged her forward by the ankle and drew his dagger, dropped his knee on her chest, and placed his dagger against her neck before she could reach her knife.

Semra stiffened.

"Stop it! I'm not here to fight," he said, tapping the dagger against her carotid. "I could have killed you already. You weren't nearly careful enough thus far, and the girl slowed you down."

"You ... what do you mean, you're not here to fight?" Semra stammered, glowering at him skeptically.

"You let out the drakes to save the girl and escape. You must know something."

"I don't know what you're talking about," she insisted,

squirming beneath his bodyweight bearing down on her chest.

He leaned into it, increasing the pressure. "You're not as practiced a liar as he is."

Semra's eyes flashed. "Now you insult me?" *He knows the Framatar is a liar?* Semra looked at him again, this time more curious than angry.

"I've wanted to get out, too, but didn't know how to go about it. Figured now was my chance. I'm coming with you, and you don't have time to argue."

"You think I'm an idiot?"

"No, I think you're the girl with a knife at her neck and a four-year-old standing in the open staring at us from forty feet away. I think we'll all die if we stay here chatting, and she'll be the first target they pick off." Siler stood and flipped his blade around, extending the hilt to Semra. "And I think you know I could have turned you in at the drake dungeon, and I could have killed you just now, and I've done neither."

Semra narrowed her eyes at him, then turned to look down the slope. Lesala stood there, looking back at them—a tasty morsel for any dragon and easy pickings for any archer. She took Siler's dagger and stood up, also retrieving and sheathing the knife she'd thrown at him earlier. "Fine, but I'm watching you."

"Of course," he nodded somberly. "I would expect nothing less. You have to compensate for not noticing me the whole way down so far."

Semra glared at him but turned and ran down the slope to Lesala. She repositioned the knife in Lesala's hands. "Here, hold it like this. Come on, time to go. Siler, this is Lesala. Lesala, this is Siler. It's possible he will decide to kill you soon, so stay close to me, okay?"

Semra kept walking, at a pace so brisk that Lesala had to run to catch up with her. Siler kept up with long, easy strides.

"Why would he kill me?" Lesala asked, wide eyed.

"Because you have a mind of your own, and the Framatar hates people like that."

Siler shook his head at Lesala and rolled his eyes at Semra. "Really? Great way to calm her down."

"I wasn't trying to calm her down. I'm trying to keep her alive. Sometimes being calm gets you killed, and handing me your dagger when you're still strapped with multiple weapons is hardly cause for me to trust you. As a matter of fact, I have my own weapons and don't need to be your packing mule. Take your dagger back."

"Well, aren't you a ray of sunshine."

"So sorry. What is the appropriate response to being stalked and then attacked?"

"I think you meant saved and then helped. Because not only did I keep quiet about your little stunt with the drakes, but I deflected blame to Kiar to cover for you. And I'm pretty sure you attacked first. So I think what you meant to say was thank you."

Semra whipped her head toward him. "You got him killed!"

Siler shrugged. "Better him than us."

Semra shook her head and gritted her teeth, redoubling her focus on picking up the pace once again. Siler swept up behind Lesala and swung her up on his back over his sword and bow and arrow. She protested for a moment, then decided he was safe enough, and settled in.

"Gee, thanks, Siler," Siler said in a mocking, mimicking voice. "You saved me. My terrible decision to escape with the slowest and least-skilled human in the mountain would have surely killed me if it weren't for you. How could I ever thank you?"

"Shut up. You've said hardly a word to me before now, and all of a sudden you're some chatterbox?" Semra glanced at him incredulously and saw the corner of his mouth twitch.

They clambered down to the first plateau, and as they approached the edge, they saw down to the second where a group of fifteen drakes moved into view from behind a large rock formation, screeching and flapping their wings.

"Vix is down there," Siler said. "There's no other way down. But they won't know about the ruckus you've caused yet."

Semra's heart sank. She'd entirely forgotten about the Rangchanj dragon venture.

Siler spoke again. "The best way down is either two plateaus over or, if you're not worried about anyone chasing you, right down the mountain itself back where we came from. It's too sheer here."

"I've done it," Semra said, lifting her chin. She glanced at Lesala. "But only with just me. What are we going to do?"

"I'll go tell Vix I came to help and draw the dragon out so you can sneak behind the formation and down to the next level. If it doesn't work, we'll have to fight them all off."

Semra nodded. It was a terrible plan, but it was the best one they had. "If we get to the base, we can't wait for you. If you catch up, you catch up, but we need to gain some distance between us and the mountain."

Siler gave a nod of acknowledgment and they split up, Siler veering left toward the drakes, and Semra and Lesala to the right to be shielded by the rock formation. The semicircle formation bent away from them, and fifteen feet of open space separated it from another formation on the other side.

If they could get across the gap, they just might be able to make it to the next drop down.

Semra and Lesala crept to the other side of the rock formation. They could hear Siler calling to the dragon wranglers.

"You took on a dragon with only five of you?"

"Rotokas ripped her wing pretty good last week," Behruz replied. "She's been licking her wounds up here and unable to fly, so now's the time. The drakes have been picking on her too since she's been down and out. Hey, watch it! She may be injured, but she nearly killed Vix!"

A terrible roar rocked the air, and Lesala squealed in fear. Semra covered the child's mouth with her hand.

Siler spoke again. "Sportsmanlike, since you wouldn't have a chance against her when she is all healed up."

"Since when did you grow such a conscience? Are you going to help, or what? We need her head real low. Our best shot with the weapons we have is to drive one of our spears straight through one of her eyes and into her brain. We have to be fast and precise. Want to serve as bait?"

"No thanks. I'll volunteer one of you idiots for that pleasure."

Semra and Lesala crept to the edge of the formation. They heard a scuffle on the other side, followed by a roar and a thud that shook the ground. A large tail swept around the formation and Semra jumped back to avoid touching it. Its deep-violet scales fitted perfectly together like a snake's, supple and smooth, and spikes stood on end down the length of the tail. They flexed upward as another roar emanated from the dragon, and Semra realized they were like a muscle the dragon could control. It reminded her of the hackles on a cat.

The tail swished and then vanished as the dragon leaped

forward, and Semra couldn't help but peer through a crevice in the rock to see what was happening. Siler would be working to get them back toward the drakes, distracting the wranglers long enough to let them escape. Semra gasped at the sight of the deep purple dragon spewing fire from its mouth on the five young men before her. The sixth, Vix, was climbing up the formation on the opposite side from Semra.

The dragon was roughly the same size as the Framatar's wyvern, about fifty feet from nose to tail, and on all fours, it still towered over its human adversaries. In an instant it reared, unfurled its wings, and flashed a bright red color, then back to deep violet and into royal blue. The humans leaped away from it, except for Behruz. He stood his ground and yelled at the dragon, banging his sword and spear together to make more noise.

The dragon's wings remained unfurled, and Semra noticed a small tear and several long, nearly healed claw marks on the dragon's right wing—presumably from whatever scuffle the dragon had with Rotokas. Semra glanced back up to the formation. Vix was nearly to the top. She had no chance of getting to the other side now, not with the dragon still in this direction, but once Vix was at the top he would see her on the other side.

She turned back to the dragon just in time to see two of the dragon wranglers rush it. The dragon smacked one backward ten feet with a foreleg, and he hit his head on a rock and went limp. The second wrangler stabbed the dragon with his spear but it glanced off the armored hide. The dragon turned and blazed fire down on him. An agonizing scream cut through the air, and the smell of burned hair made Semra draw back. The man lay on the ground, moaning in pain, one sleeve still on fire. Siler dragged him further from the dragon and helped him roll and beat out the flames. He turned back to Behruz, who was still holding his ground before the dragon.

"It's not worth it! Let Rotokas keep her away from the mountain. You're going to get us all killed!"

Behruz shook his head, glancing at Vix. "No, we've almost got her! Vix, she's coming to you."

The great dragon beat its wings again, screeched in Behruz' face, and circled back against the rock, crouching low in retreat. Semra felt her heart go out to the dragon. Beaten and worn, all it had wanted was some peace to heal its wounds. Perhaps like the drakes, the evil she'd seen in dragons was simple self-preservation rather than inherent malice.

Behruz and the last dragon wrangler, Brigg, approached the dragon to hem it in while Siler pulled the unconscious wrangler out of the way to protect both the wounded men. Semra glanced up at Vix. The dragon didn't see him. She cycled through colors now, bright blue, green, purple, yellow, dark red, purple again. Her head hung low, and she backed against the rock. Semra had never seen such a powerful creature act this way. It struck Semra that the dragon was afraid.

Vix leaped down onto the dragon's head from the tall rock and threw ends of the rope to both men down below. She wavered for a moment, and her head lowered. A moment was all Behruz needed. He pulled back his arm and stepped forward to plunge the spear into her eye and brain, but just before he landed the fatal blow, Semra darted out from her position and startled the dragon so that it whipped its head around.

The spear glanced off the dragon's impenetrable scales, the rope fell uselessly to the ground, and Vix tumbled down from its great height. Behruz let out a guttural cry and was upon her in a flash, but Semra drew her dagger and slashed across his torso before he could blink, then met his blade with a visceral snarl. Brigg jumped toward them, but Siler threw a knife into the base of his neck, and he dropped like a stone.

The dragon flared bright blue and circled them, knocking Semra and Behruz off their feet and sweeping Vix out of the way with her tail. Semra rolled to her feet, leaving her pack on the ground. Her head and arm throbbed from the impact.

Behruz lunged his knife at the dragon, but she scooped him up with one of her massive clawed front feet and threw him against the rock formation, then turned back toward Semra. Semra's eyes widened and she scrambled backward, drawing her sword and extending it to the dragon. The dragon tilted its head as it looked at her, then snatched the sword in its teeth and snapped it in two.

Behruz nodded at Vix and they split up. Vix attacked Siler and Behruz focused on Semra. He called to her from the other side of the dragon. "You're running away, aren't you?"

"At the moment, I'm a little busy trying not to be killed," Semra called back. Her heart pounded as she watched the dragon pace between her and Behruz, crushing Semra's useless shards of sword underfoot. She wished Vix had told her what pacing meant.

"How much time do you really think you have? But then, maybe you have more than you think. Traitors always die slowly." Behruz ducked under the dragon's long neck and rolled across to face her just as Vix lunged for Siler, and the sound of ringing steel met her ears.

Semra drew the dagger at her side and faced off against the spear and sword he'd regained. The dragon swung toward Siler and Semra called out to him, but her distraction came at a price. She parried the thrust of Behruz' sword too late to stop his spear. Holding it close to the spearhead, he drove it into her chest with a hideous grimace. Semra gasped and staggered back, clutching at the spear to keep it stable, feeling every jostle it made inside her chest.

Siler rolled on the ground with Vix, delivered a devastating blow to the temple, and then twisted away. The dragon swooped in and tossed Vix up in the air. She shook him from side to side and tossed him onto the pile of dead or wounded bodies from the fight ... only one now. Brigg was gone.

Eyes wide, unable to speak, Semra stared up at Behruz. Pain ripped through her body like white-hot flame. She fell to her knees, and the movement felt as though she'd torn open her chest. Behruz reached down and gripped the spear again.

"My spear is the only thing keeping you from bleeding out. You'll bleed out anyway, sure, but I can make it last longer." He twisted the spear, and Semra cried out. Her vision swam, and she saw black spots.

"You wanted me to lie to the Framatar for you and your pitiful friend Brens. My work is exquisite. I don't need to stick my neck out for anyone else, and I, unlike you, have loyalty."

Semra felt herself fading. She used every ounce of energy she had left to surreptitiously draw a knife from her leg. If she was going to die, she wasn't going to die alone. She looked up to take in her surroundings once more before sinking her knife into Behruz, and she saw Brigg drag Lesala out into the open, dagger at her throat. Siler had Vix restrained, weakened by the dragon, but the dragon itself suddenly turned back to Semra.

She had moments to act before all traces of consciousness and will were sapped from her body forever. Semra would die either by Behruz or by the dragon, but as she looked for the last time into Lesala's bright-blue, tear-filled eyes, she knew the knife she held wasn't meant for Behruz. With one final flick of her wrist, Semra sent it flying at Brigg. The blade sank into his chest, and he released his young captive as he toppled to the ground.

The dragon roared a great roar, caught Behruz in her teeth and lifted him off his feet and into the air. As she did, the grip he held on the spear ripped the spearhead from Semra's chest with a tug. She collapsed on the floor, vaguely aware of screaming somewhere in the periphery.

Life—the last of it—seemed to move like a slow dream. Semra reached up to her chest and felt a great gash where her skin should have been. She drew her hand away, dripping with blood, her blood, so much blood. Her mind raced in the dream, and her heart beat wildly. Somewhere Semra knew her heartbeat needed to slow to live, but it only made her more afraid to learn she couldn't contain her fear. She felt vaguely aware of feeling thirsty and wondered for a moment if all her miserable life was for nothing, stolen from her family and turned into a professional killer that no one could love.

It was what she deserved, after all. A fitting end to an existence of evil. The great head of the dragon swung over her body, flicking its long, forked tongue in and out. The huge head came lower and lower until its nose was inches from her face. Semra took in a ragged breath and let it out. The end had come.

9

The great dragon's head hovered over Semra as the last of her strength waned. Its tongue flicked out again and Semra felt an odd pressure against her chest over her heart where the spear had been. The dragon flushed suddenly a blazing white, the sun radiating a thousand different shades of the rainbow off its shimmering scales. Semra felt a jolt, like lightning, starting in her heart, and then emanating throughout her body. Her body jerked at the intensity of it, and she sucked in a lungful of air and sat up.

Siler and Lesala stood to one side, gaping at her. Semra glanced up at the dragon, whose color melted into an aquamarine head with royal-blue accents. The deep blue formed in a diamond pattern over the aqua background on its forehead, then transitioned into a rose gold shimmer on her legs, underbelly, and throat. The dragon stepped back and folded her wings, admiring her work, and eyed her proudly.

Semra looked down at herself, seeing her arms, hands, and tunic still covered in her own blood, but found with surprise that she felt no pain at all. On the contrary, she felt energized and a strange sense of ... was it accomplishment? Strange, since she hadn't done anything particularly noteworthy, aside from nearly dying. A warming sensation came to her heart like a pulse—odd, like nothing she'd yet experienced, but not uncomfortable. She looked up at Siler and Lesala, unsure of herself.

Lesala pointed at her chest. "Are you ... blessed by the gods now?"

Semra recoiled from the question, but looked down at her chest. The entire length of the fatal wound Behruz had dealt her—for there was certainly no good explanation as to how she was alive—was bright white, hard, and iridescent like opal. She reached up to tap the spot, and found it smooth and cool to the touch.

Semra looked up at the dragon. "Rats and rot, what did you do to me?"

The dragon swished its tail.

"That's the same mark the Framatar has," Siler said.

"Well, I don't think I've been blessed by any gods. Whatever it is, the dragon gave it to me, and Rotokas must have given his to him."

"We have to get off the plateau. Can you walk?"

Semra stood and brushed herself off, shaking her head in disbelief and eyeing the dragon. "More than walk. I feel great." She gathered her fallen knives, wiped them on her already bloodstained tunic, and sheathed them again to her pants legs. The dragon got up and followed her. Semra turned around to look at it. "What?"

"It seems to like you now," Siler said. "You did save its life."

"Is the dragon coming with us?" Lesala asked.

"No, it's not coming with us," Semra said. "Dragons are dangerous, and they do whatever they want."

The dragon nosed Semra. She jumped, but Siler laughed.

"Which means if this one wants to come with us, there isn't much we can do about it. It's obvious this dragon has decided not to kill us, and if you made some special bond with it, that's great, because we're going to need all the help we can get. You can't say no to a dragon on our side!"

"Dragons are evil," Semra replied, but even as she said it, she wasn't sure it was true. It cocked its head and bounded to the edge of the plateau, looking down the steep drop off and back at Semra. That warm pulsing sensation came over her again, and an odd excitement crept over her.

"I think she looks happy now," Lesala commented, reaching up to the huge beast. The dragon lowered her head and touched the girl's palm gently. "Nice dragon!"

Siler folded his arms and drilled Semra with a cool glare. "Listen, I've been waiting for a chance off this rock, but I didn't imagine a dragon escort in my wildest dreams. We have to move *now.*"

Suddenly the dragon rose and unfurled its wings above the little girl. A small *tink* sounded against its solid scales, and an arrow fell to the ground. Semra and Siler whipped their heads around to look up the plateau back toward the mountain. They saw no one, but at least one archer hid somewhere in the rocks.

"Dragon it is," Semra muttered. "How do we get down now? We have to be fast."

The dragon lowered itself to the ground, reached down and gingerly snatched Semra by the tunic, then swung her around and plopped her on her back.

Semra squealed, then patted the dragon awkwardly. "Okay, I guess you have some ideas of your own. But we all need to get down. Hurry, Siler, pass Lesala up here and hop on. Oh, and grab my pack!" Semra's heart beat wildly at the thought of being so fully out of control, up there in the sky, but the thought was as exhilarating as it was disconcerting.

Another arrow hit the dragon's neck as Siler handed Lesala up to Semra. She set the little girl in front of her while Siler picked up Semra's pack and climbed up behind Semra. He held tight to Semra's waist, and Semra held tight to Lesala with one hand and one of the spikes running the length of the dragon's neck with the other. She gripped tight with her thighs as she would a bareback horse. Several rows of spikes ran along the dragon's sides further down, and Semra hooked her feet behind these as best she could to wedge herself on.

The dragon unfurled its huge wings and stood, beating the air. Semra could see the hole in her injured wing, but it was mostly healed. She wondered how long the dragon had been up here recovering from Rotokas' attack, and if it would still be painful to fly. She remembered Behruz' comment that she'd refused to fly away from them to escape.

An arrow whipped past Semra's face, just as the dragon surged forward and lifted them off the ground. They leaned into the movement, and Semra's heart rate skyrocketed as the plateau dropped away. The dragon flew low, veering off and down the slope toward the trees. Her wings beat again, and again, and then she let herself glide. Semra saw five dark figures armed with swords and bows and arrows on the mountain behind her.

Before her sprawled empty rocks, a forest, and all the kingdom of Jannemar. The castle would be to her left some-where, but all Semra could see were the villages on the outskirts and the developed cities further in. Sprawling fields of farmland could be seen on the other side of the forest as they flew, and Semra was lost for a moment at how peaceful everything looked.

The dragon turned into the wind and out of range of the last of the archers' arrows, and as she did, Semra felt herself sliding. She lurched to the other side, trying to compensate, and felt Siler's strong arms cinch tightly around her. Lesala screamed and slipped off the dragon, but Semra reached out and grabbed the little girl's hand. They climbed higher still.

Terror hit Semra like a boulder, and a warm throbbing in her chest brought a new wave of anxiety rolling over her. She hugged the dragon's neck and held tight to Lesala's hand … but her palm slipped.

"Lesala!" Semra screamed, but her voice was lost to the wind as the little girl's hand broke free and she fell to the depths below.

The dragon dove sharply downward, and it was all Semra could do to hold on with both hands and grip with her thighs and feet as best she could. The dragon swooped down over Lesala and caught her with its massive hind feet. Semra could no longer see the girl, and could only hope she was safe beneath the dragon. They leveled out over the forest as they drew away from the mountain, but it wasn't long before Semra felt a shaky turbulence on her right.

She glanced back over the dragon and saw the injured wing trembling. They had to land. As if knowing her thoughts, the dragon descended lower and lower over the tree line until she skimmed the branches. She beat her wings to slow them down, but with her injury, they came in fast.

Lesala screamed again as they barreled down through the trees. At least she was still along for the ride, Semra thought with relief. The dragon released Lesala close to the ground and skidded to a stop under the cover of tall trees. At the abrupt stop, Semra toppled over the front of the dragon, rolling down its foreleg and onto the forest floor, while Siler pitched off sideways.

For a moment no one moved, each breathing hard, getting their bearings. Semra lay on her back and passed a hand over her eyes. She sat up slowly.

Siler leaped to his feet. "What a rush! Wow! I've been missing out—dragon riding is the way to go. I can't believe you have a dragon. We need to name it!"

Semra rolled her eyes and walked over to pull Lesala to her feet. "Are you okay?"

The girl nodded, keeping a wary eye on the dragon.

"Semra! What are you going to name the dragon?"

Semra turned to face Siler. "What? It's a dragon. I call it my dragon." She walked over to the dragon and patted its neck. It had turned out to be a faithful creature—so far. Semra still couldn't make head nor tail of it, or what had happened between them. But when she touched the dragon, she felt that same warm throb over her heart where the opal substance was, and an excited joy came over her. "I think ... I think I can feel its feelings," she murmured, almost to herself. She ran her hand along the dragon's neck and felt a glimmer of pleasure.

The dragon's huge head swung around to face her, nose to nose, and Semra reached up to stroke its smooth forehead. Stronger than swords, yet almost soft to the touch, like snakeskin but heavier.

"What about Banu? Yallin? Rotokas the Second?"

"She hates that one," Semra answered, laughing despite herself.

"Zez," suggested Lesala.

"Ooh! I like that. Only ... Zez ... Zezin. Zezun. Zezura."

The dragon turned three shades brighter aqua and lifted

her head, letting out a low rumble. Semra smiled. "Zezura. She likes it."

"How do you know?"

"I can tell. I can feel it. In the ... the mark."

Siler paused, glancing at her. "Interesting."

"We need to get to town. The drag ... Zezura needs something for her wing, and I can't very well traipse into the castle looking like this." She gestured to her blood-soaked tunic.

Lesala's eyes grew wide. "We're going to a castle?"

"Um ... well, no. We aren't. And we need somewhere you can stay safe."

"You're going to the castle?" Siler asked, suddenly serious.

"I want to go home," Lesala said, bottom lip in a pout.

"We'll get you home, but remember what I said. They'll kill you and your whole family if you go back now. You have to wait until the Framatar is out of the mountain."

Siler's eyes widened. "Out of the mountain? Are you out of your mind?"

Semra started walking, and Zezura, Siler, and Lesala followed her. "I have to expose him. It's the only way he'll stop. And I can't expose him on my own. He's planning on killing the prince and the king of Jannemar, so I have to start there. I'll go to the castle, warn them of the danger, and get Jannemar to back us against the Framatar. There's a gala in just a few days, so we need to do it by then if we want to save the prince. Once the rest of them in the mountain realize how the Framatar has been lying to them all this time, maybe they'll turn on him."

"That's not a plan, it's a pipe dream," Siler said. "What evidence do you have? They won't believe you. I've known he was lying for a while, but he'd have killed me if I said anything, and no one would've believed me anyway."

"You knew? And you didn't do anything?"

"Well ... I didn't do nothing, exactly. I've been squirreling away valuables from missions. A few little things here and there to get me started once I'm all set up."

"You've been skimming from the Framatar? You've got a death wish! How long?"

"A while."

"How much do you have?"

Siler clucked his tongue. "Did you know 'the Framatar' means 'lord'? He calls himself lord. dragonlord. Hmm. Maybe you need a fun nickname too. *Muntasir* means conqueror. Nope, that doesn't fit. Sounds too formal for you."

"Fine, don't tell me. How long have you known about the Framatar?"

"I graduated with the class of 4996, and was in the second batch of experimental children he ever took. He was still smoothing out his process then, and the class of '97 was the first year he started taking just twelve children a year, one per month. There were fifteen children in my year, and five of my class have died in training or on missions. One rebelled openly and was murdered for it, and I saw them do it. They said a mission went bad, but I was the only one who saw the truth. I was thirteen."

"Thirteen! You're what, nineteen now, right? You've known he was a liar for six years?"

Siler nodded. "I paid close attention and kept my eyes and ears open after that. I learned that the year before me, his first run of the program, he took twenty kids ages six to ten. The kids were too old to be properly indoctrinated, and the training wasn't as efficient. Only six survived. So he took less children with my year, revamped the program, and most of us lived. It only took three years to settle into the pattern he has now."

"What's indocinating?" Lesala asked, running to catch up to their long strides.

Semra picked her up and plopped her on Zezura's back as they walked. "Indoctrination means teaching people lies in such a way that they believe it without question," she answered. "Like when Adis and Conet tried to tell you your family abandoned you. They were lying, but you knew they were lying and called them out on it. They want to make everyone believe whatever they say, without asking any questions or causing any problems."

"Being blessed by the gods is a nice way to add credibility," Siler added. "Although that was an obvious lie. Especially now that we know those marks are somehow caused by dragons."

"He wasn't blessed by the gods?" Lesala asked.

"You believed that?" Siler scoffed.

"She's a kid. We all were when we were brought in, that's how they get away with it," Semra said.

"I thought they were angry gods," said Lesala. "I hoped there were good gods that would stop the bad gods' blessing."

Semra pursed her lips. "Sometimes a man is just a man, doing bad things for his own personal gain, no matter who he claims to be doing it for."

"Everybody does what they do for their own personal gain," said Siler.

Semra shook her head. "Not me."

"Oh, come on. Of course you do. You're running away for freedom, a better life, but definitely for you."

"Sure, I want freedom, but it's more than that. My parents wanted me, did you know that? Maybe all of our parents wanted us. They came up the mountain to find me, and he slaughtered them right under my nose. But even still, it would've been safer to stay in the mountain and work on getting assigned as a sleeper, hoard resources, prepare slowly like you have. I left when I did because Brens was beaten up and blamed herself, and because Lesala was going to be killed if she didn't get with the program."

"What?" Lesala's eyes bulged out of her head.

"Oops. Yeah, sorry."

Siler remained quiet for a moment. Semra trudged on, and all she could hear were their footsteps on the leaves, and Zezura's tail dragging behind them.

"I'm sorry about your parents," Siler said at last. "That's really special that they actually followed you up the mountain."

Semra felt a lump rise in her throat, and she swallowed. "Thanks."

"You want revenge, then. Revenge for your parents."

"I want to expose him, so he doesn't keep killing innocent people and ripping apart families. Real families with a chance at being happy. Who've we been killing all these years? What did they ever really do to deserve death? Stand in his way? He has to be stopped, because it's wrong."

"And the plot against the king ...?"

"If he takes control of Jannemar, he'll never be stopped. If we can foil his takeover, save the king and his son, and gain their support, we have a shot."

Siler shook his head. "It won't work."

"It will."

"You'll just dance into the palace and tell them you've got an affinity for murder and some security recommendations?"

Semra shook her head. "It'll be like any other mission; except this time we have to be three steps ahead. Anticipate, protect the royal family, and in so doing, earn their trust and support."

"You're crazy."

"What's your grand plan, then? Disappear into a pile of stolen money?"

Siler grinned. "Sounds grand, doesn't it? I do love a good villa."

Semra's eyes narrowed. She took a step forward. "Imagine it ... fearing every servant in your villa, wondering who's a sleeper for the Framatar and when your last moment will be. Lying awake at night on your too-comfortable mattress and dreaming of everyone you killed – who they might have been, what sin they really committed, and whether they truly deserved to die. Imagine getting sloppy after a few years of gluttonous living and becoming too prominent, drawing attention to yourself and becoming just another target in just another villa for some fresh graduate." Semra held her breath. She needed all the help she could get.

Siler regarded her with a stony expression, the corners of his mouth turned down. After a moment, he said, "Gutsy. Suicidal." His expression changed to a mischievous smirk. "I like it. The Framatar will be furious. And you'll probably get a handsome reward at the end, no? Maybe live in some cushy castle at the end of all this?"

Semra snorted. "Women in castles have to be prim and proper and wear long dresses. With trains. I could never live in a castle!"

"Ha! You're crazy ... but in a good way, so I guess I'm in. Let's go rile up a dragonlord."

10

They spent the next two days walking through the woods. The three humans split the meal Semra had packed for her lunch in the mountain and caught small game to stave off their hunger. Zezura stayed with them, and Semra wondered how often she had to eat. At the end of the two days, they came to the edge of the woods and looked out on a village of farmland.

Fields of crops, sheep and goats dotted on green pastures, and modest thatch-roofed houses spread out before them. Lines of laundry swayed in a gentle breeze by the nearest house, and smoke rose from the chimney as evidence of a fire inside. Zezura nuzzled Semra's hands and looked longingly at the sheep.

"I know, you must be hungry too. But we can't have a dragon swooping around when we're trying not to draw too much attention. Stay here and we'll get you something." Semra felt Zezura's disappointment, but she resigned herself to staying where she was. Semra wasn't sure if the dragon understood all they said, but she certainly could decipher what Semra wanted her to do. They could feel each other's emotions and were learning to understand what they meant.

"We need something off that clothesline for you," Siler said, looking her up and down. "At least a fresh tunic ... you look like a walking corpse. And you'll need to wear the skirt from your bag to blend in."

Semra grunted. Ugh, skirts. At least hers was billowy and had concealed slits in the sides to access the weapons strapped to her legs. She would wrap the long skirt on over her pants, and no one would be the wiser.

"Whose bright idea was it for women to wear skirts, anyway?" she grumbled.

"I think they're pretty," Lesala sighed, ogling the bright colors on the line. "You should wear the pink one!"

"Um, no. I need something bland, like tan or brown or forest colored."

"That's boring," Lesala said with a pout.

"Lesala, I want you to remember something. It's better to be dull than dead. You're going to have to lay low while we sort this whole thing out, and you're going to have to remember to be boring. If you don't talk at all, people will remember you as being standoffish. If you talk too much, they'll remember you as obnoxious or interesting. Participate just enough to be ignored. Right now, bright pink would not be helpful in quietly moving in and out of the woods where Zezura will be and where we'll be sleeping."

"But why can't you be a fun boring?" Lesala asked.

"Come on," said Siler, taking the little girl by the hand. "This is too small a village to go totally unnoticed. We're going to look very sad and pitiful and see if some sympathetic sap will give us a meal, and maybe information on the gala at the castle. We could also use an ointment of some sort for Zezura's wing. Semra, stay here and we'll get you a new shirt."

"Well, I could—" Semra started, but Siler cut her off.

"I'm sure you could, but when you have the numbers, use them. You know it's stupid to risk people seeing a lone crazy woman, drenched in blood, roaming the village for new clothes. Let us do this for you. Sit back and relax, and we'll show you how it's done." He winked at Lesala and slung Semra's pack over his shoulder. Lesala giggled.

Semra crossed her arms and sighed, but leaned back on Zezura. He was right, and they both knew it. Siler took off his sword and sheath and handed them to her, and she watched anxiously as he and Lesala angled for the nearest house. He spoke quietly to her as they went, and Lesala nodded. Siler walked a bit ahead of her toward the front of the house, then stepped up to the door and knocked lightly. Lesala lagged behind and veered to one side to where the laundry hung. She reached up toward a white tunic drying in the sun.

Not white, Semra thought to herself, frustrated she could do nothing to stop it. *I'm not clean enough for that. Anything but bright pink or perfect white, so I can blend in and still get away with a little dirt.* The door to the house opened, and Lesala changed her mind at the last minute and snatched a breezy lilac tunic instead of the white before scampering over to Siler. A more outdoorsy color would've been preferable, but at least it wasn't a bold purple. Siler made a fuss over finding Lesala and, while picking her up, snuck the tunic into the pack over his shoulder. If she hadn't been watching, Semra would have missed it herself. The person who opened the door ushered them inside, and Siler and Lesala disappeared from view.

Semra sat on the ground in the cover of the trees with Siler's sword across her knees and chewed on a nail. Zezura shifted colors to match the woodland surroundings and curled into one huge ball next to her. Minutes ticked by into an hour, and Semra started shredding a leaf she picked up off the ground. She felt Zezura's annoyance at the shredding noise, but she didn't care. She hated waiting and doing nothing, but late afternoon seeped into evening.

How quaint and peaceful life here seemed, Semra thought as she gazed out over the farmland. She found the bleating of the sheep comforting and wondered what it would be like to worry only about the crops and the next rain. As tranquil as it was, she wasn't sure how to have a life without adrenaline-laced, life-and-death experiences.

"Ow!" Semra hissed, releasing the leaf in her fingers. Startled, she looked down to see Zezura had sent out a single puff of hot fire to incinerate the leaf, which was now only flecks of ember and ash. She felt Zezura's satisfaction that she'd made her point. Semra rolled her eyes. "Fine, no more tearing of leaves. Sorry. Couldn't you have asked a little nicer?"

A sound from the house caught her attention, and she looked up again. Siler emerged from the house, followed by Lesala and another young man about the same age. He wore simple clothing and carried a sword on a belt, a bucket, and a bag over his shoulder. Lesala had Semra's pack and started running for the forest edge where Semra was hiding.

Semra leaped to her feet, pushing on Zezura as she did so. "Get up, get up! You have to hide. How do you hide a dragon?!"

Lesala kept running. "Mommy, Mommy! We found help for horsey!"

Great. So they were bringing help out to the horse, which they didn't have, and would instantly discover was actually a dragon? Lesala broke the tree line and ran up to Semra with her pack. Semra ripped it open and ran behind a thick tree, taking off her ruined tunic and replacing it with the fresh lilac one Lesala had snagged. She smoothed the top down over her black pants, and quickly wrapped the skirt around her waist to cover the weapons she carried. She laid Siler's sheathed sword against the thick tree behind which she hid, just as Siler and the stranger entered the woods. Zezura had scampered behind a clump of brush amid the trees and camouflaged herself. Semra could still make her out since she knew where to look, but hopefully the stranger wouldn't.

" ... they've been using pinlin for healing salves for the last three-hundred years, so we travel to surrounding areas to teach better medical skills," the stranger was saying. "Some of the outskirts are pretty outdated, but here in Ryden, everyone is well taken care of because of Shafii's skill."

Semra stepped out from behind the tree, and the young man stopped in his tracks. Shorter than Siler, but of average height for a man, he had well-kept, dirty-blonde hair and warm amber eyes with flecks of gold. Semra noted his attractive face and muscular frame, and his gaze, intent on her. Her mouth dropped open for a moment. She'd seen this man before, hadn't she?

"Do I ... know you?" she asked.

The stranger paused, taking her in. "I don't think so. I would've remembered you."

They stood there for a moment, Semra unsure what to say, before he spoke again. "I am Dahyu, apprenticed to the healer, Shafii Rinab."

"Dahyu." Semra rolled his name around her tongue. No, she hadn't heard it before.

"And you are?" he prodded gently.

"Semra. Pleased to meet you."

"He came to make our horse feel better, Mommy," Lesala said.

"You must have been very young when you had her," Dahyu mentioned softly.

"Yes, well, it was certainly a surprise to me," Semra grumbled, shooting a dark glance in Siler's direction.

"Honey, what have you done with the horse?" Siler asked her, smirking.

Semra's eyes flashed. "You ... " Her voice died away, speechless as she looked at him.

"Tell me she didn't run away again! That's twice this week, dear."

Semra glared at him. "Yes, well, she certainly did. Maybe if somebody didn't drive her so hard, she wouldn't escape as soon as you're out of sight. Never mind, I'll find her. Dahyu, so sorry to trouble you, but I'm afraid we haven't a horse on hand to heal! If you would be so kind, though, I would love to keep a portion of any ointment you may have brought her. She's a faithful old mare, but rather clumsy, I'd have to say. Stumbled in a river crossing, and was bested by some sharp rocks up her foreleg."

"I thought you said she got a gash under her foot," Dahyu said, looking at Siler.

"Well, she did. It was a nasty fall."

"Mhmm. I see."

"Our horse is rainbow colored!" Lesala blurted out, dancing around the space between them. "Here, horsey, horsey!"

"Honey, shh," Semra said. She turned to Dahyu. "Very imaginative little girl we have here."

"I can see that." His eyes narrowed.

Just then, a squirrel started chittering angrily from the tree behind them, and a large thump sounded. Semra whipped her head toward the sound just in time to see a blaze of fire envelop the squirrel, which gave a hideous screech and fell from its branch. Semra passed a hand over her eyes and slipped the other hand through the slit in her skirt to grip the handle of one of her knives. The game was up.

Zezura lifted her head from behind the thick foliage and caught the squirrel in her mouth, swallowing it whole. Dahyu set down the bucket and bag and drew the sword at his side. Semra drew her knife and held it slightly behind her and out of view.

"Zezura!" Semra yelled, and the dragon blanched, turning yellow marked with orange before settling into an anxious green. Semra could feel Zezura's embarrassment as she remembered she'd been supposed to stay discrete.

"Rainbow horsey!" Lesala laughed, clapping her hands.

"What the ... is that what I think it is?"

"Um, probably. Could you possibly be thinking it's anything other than a dragon at this point?" Siler asked.

Zezura walked up behind Semra and lowered her head protectively over her shoulder.

Dahyu sheathed his sword. "That's a Rangchanj," he said in wonder, eyes wide. "Where did you find it? And you ... how have you tamed ... a dragon ..."

"I didn't," Semra answered truthfully, turning to pat Zezura's neck.

Dahyu gasped. "You're a dragonlord. You have the mark."

Semra whipped her head around to drill him with a hard stare. "What mark? What do you know of it?"

"You mean you don't know? The mark of the dragon's kiss ... on your upper chest there, peeking out behind Tinat's freshly washed tunic that you pinched."

Semra's lips parted, but no words came. She adjusted her tunic to cover the opal mark.

"Dragon's kiss?" Siler prodded.

Dahyu motioned toward the dragon, and Zezura huffed at him. "May I? If it really is injured, I could ... apply the ointment I prepared ..."

Siler eyed Dahyu skeptically.

"Oh, come on. I'm outnumbered, and you have a dragon. What exactly could you possibly be threatened by? Also, I'm pretty sure your girl here has a knife in her hand this instant."

Semra grinned sheepishly and brought the knife from behind her, twirling it in her fingers. "True," she said calmly. Semra touched Zezura to calm her and nodded to Dahyu.

Dahyu stepped forward and glanced to the side, seeing Siler's sword against the tree. "What exactly are you preparing for?"

Siler and Lesala answered at once:

"None of your business."

"Saving a prince!" Lesala grinned.

"Lesala!" Siler and Semra hissed together.

"What?" she demanded defensively. "All of you keep talking, so why can't I?"

"Lesala ... why don't you go gather the very best sticks for a fire this evening." Semra phrased it as a question, but her tone made it a statement.

Lesala's shoulders drooped. "You won't let me do anything. I can't come to the castle or meet the prince, and you won't wear any pink!"

"Lesala. The sticks. Now." Semra gritted her teeth together as Lesala scampered off. Semra hadn't spent that much time with little kids since being one and hadn't thought of how their unfiltered speech could ruin everything. If this Dahyu character was dead by the night's end, it would be Lesala's fault.

"You're saving a prince?" Dahyu asked casually. He reached into his bag and brought out a small jar of ointment. Oddly nonchalant, considering all he'd just witnessed. Dahyu uncorked the top of the jar, dipped a clean cloth into it, and walked around Zezura to where Semra showed him the injured wing.

"Not if the kid keeps running her mouth," Semra said coolly. "How long will it take for this to heal?"

"Dragons heal much faster than other creatures. With this blend, I would say only twelve to twenty-four hours, though you never really know with dragons. There are few who could truly consider themselves experts in the field. And why would a prince need saving? Doesn't he have the king's army and such?" Dahyu began applying the ointment to the dragon's wing.

"Excuse us, but our little adventures are not exactly your concern," Siler said.

"Ah. Well, whoever this poor girl is, she isn't your daughter. Your 'rainbow horse,' as she called it, turned out to be a rare color-changing dragon that was all too real. You are distrustful of people, and when you weren't sure of my reaction, your first instinct was not negotiation or explanation but weaponry. You lied about your situation, and you stole from my master's wife. We may be simple folk, but not so simple as you might think."

Semra pursed her lips. "What is your point?"

"I thought it was perfectly clear. You have no idea what you're doing. You're a dragonlord with the mark of the drag-on's kiss, but you don't know what that means. You have the undying loyalty of a rare and beautiful creature, and don't even know they possess accelerated healing abilities. And you don't solve problems, you eliminate them.

"You've probably thought about killing me already, but you're hiding, and that might draw attention to you if you can't make a fast enough getaway. Whatever you're up to, you're up to no good. Now, I'm afraid I'm a curious sort. It may not be my business, but it certainly was our door that you knocked on. You obviously aren't who you say you are, and though I'm sure the prince is perfectly safe in a fancy castle somewhere, it's clear you're into some strange dealings. I like to know who is in my village."

"You imagine you know everything about us, so why bother asking to know more?" Semra demanded, crossing her arms. She could feel Zezura picking up on her irritation, and growing uneasy.

"I happen to know a lot about dragons. I could help you."

"We don't need your help," Siler snapped. "I think we're done here."

"Clearly. That's why you went knocking on doors." Dahyu raised an eyebrow and reached down for the bucket, which Semra now saw was filled with water, and set it in front of Zezura. "Here you go," he said gently to the dragon. "Won't be enough for you, but then, they told me you were a horse. Thank you for letting me fix you up. You're a beauty."

Semra watched Dahyu's tender demeanor and softened. "We don't mean any trouble. We may be on edge, but only because there are some bad people after us. And after the little girl. She's done nothing to deserve this."

Dahyu looked at her with a new interest. He glanced off in the distance where Lesala was carefully examining the sticks she gathered. "Her parents?"

"Still alive, I hope. But if we take her home now, they'll all be killed."

Dahyu shook his head. "And this prince business?"

"It's true," Semra replied. "We have reason to believe he's in danger. We aren't exactly sure how to get the king to trust us, but we know the prince will be dead in less than a week if we don't do something ... and maybe the king as well."

Siler crossed his arms, unhappy that Semra had opened up to this stranger.

Dahyu studied her. "What evidence do you have?"

"I heard the order given firsthand."

"Hmm." Dahyu paced for a moment, then glanced at Semra again. "No ... physical proof though?"

"Sorry, I didn't ask him to sign a confession and hand it over before fleeing for my life."

"All right, all right, no need to get up in arms. But even if these people do have a plan to hurt someone in the royal family, it's going to be difficult to get to him. He's protected. He'll probably be fine."

Siler snorted. "Elitist buffoons, all of them. They always think they're above it all, that their armies and fine clothes will protect them. They're easy pickings in their own homes."

Dahyu tilted his head. "Castles are not typically considered easy pickings."

"They are for these people," Semra put in, remembering Governor Mallen with a twang in her gut. Getting in had been a cakewalk. "You don't know who you're dealing with. We need someplace to stay the night, and we'll be on our way. If it weren't for Zezura's wing, we would've been long gone already. They'll be after us soon, and I fear for the village if we stay long."

"Don't breathe a word of this to anyone," Siler said. "As you mentioned, we do eliminate problems."

Semra shook her head. "Not this time. We won't hurt you

if you tell, but you may very well bring harm on your own head from those that follow us if you don't keep quiet."

Siler grunted his displeasure but said nothing.

Dahyu looked between them and nodded. "I'll speak to Shafii. Tinat, his wife, never had a daughter. I'm sure it would bring her joy to see Lesala, and I won't say any more than I have to. What about the dragon?"

Semra glanced at Zezura. "You'll have to stay out here, okay? No flying, and you have to hide. We'll come for you in the morning."

Zezura opened her mouth and let out a hiss and a stream of black smoke.

"I'm sorry, but I don't think having a dragon running amuck will help us lay low. Stay here."

Dahyu dipped his head. "Okay. Come on." He picked up the empty bucket and his bag, and headed back toward the house.

Semra called to Lesala, who came running with her bundle of sticks, and Siler dropped back with Semra as they walked several paces behind Dahyu.

"I don't trust him," Siler said.

"After less than a day? Good, neither should anyone," Semra replied snidely.

"I mean it. He's too interested in our business, and he knows too much. We can't spend all night here."

"First of all, we have a dragon. If he wasn't interested, he wouldn't be human. Second of all, I have no intention of spending the night here. If his master and his wife are good people, we will leave Lesala with them where she will be safe, and we'll leave in the night. I just have to warn Lesala before we do it. We'll come back to take her home when it's safe again."

11

Shafii and his wife, a couple in their fifties, were excellent hosts, and though they were sympathetic about the loss of Siler and Semra's horse, they were delighted to keep them and Lesala comfortable for the evening. Tinat promised to show Lesala two new lambs the next morning, while Shafii offered to work with Siler to find a loan horse or some other agreement. Tinat suggested they stay in Ryden, as the village was safe and quiet, and any violent, unstable relatives chasing them would certainly have a difficult time getting through the good stout people of Ryden.

Semra had smiled, a bit sadly, perhaps, and accepted their gracious kindness. If they knew who she really was, they surely wouldn't look at her so sweetly. Still, Semra took comfort in the fact that they would take good care of Lesala while Semra and Siler were gone. They didn't know that yet, of course, but it was better that way.

Night fell, and Semra climbed into bed in the guest room the Rinabs had put together for Semra, Siler, and Lesala.

Dahyu looked darkly at Siler as he followed Semra into the room, but Siler quickly made himself a place on the floor while Semra and Lesala took the bed. Semra brushed Lesala's hair back from her face and spoke quietly to her. She told her about their plans to leave that night, and that Lesala would have to be brave and stay with Shafii and Tinat until they returned. After tears and protests, Lesala eventually calmed down enough to be soothed to sleep as Semra stroked her hair and bid her dream of being home with her parents in Kalma again.

A shadow fell across the window, and Semra felt a warmth as she realized Zezura had decided against staying in the woods and had come to sleep just outside. Semra looked out the window and heard a sickening crunch as the last of one of Shafii's sheep disappeared down the dragon's throat. Zezura curled in a tight ball, camouflaged herself under the night sky, and fell asleep.

SOMEONE WAS SHAKING HER. Semra woke up coughing, eyes stinging, voices shouting. She still felt groggy, but heard a distant crackling sound all around her. Siler slapped her face, and Semra sat up.

"The house is on fire! We have to get out! Go, go, go!"

Semra snapped awake and saw the room lit with orange and red flame. A glance out the window showed her nothing but darkness—no dragon and no daylight. Siler ripped the thick blanket off the bed and threw it over the windowsill to beat down the flames, then he pushed Lesala through the window. Siler climbed out after her and reached a hand back toward Semra. Semra got up to follow, but the ceiling collapsed, crushing her exit and walling her inside.

"Semra!" she heard Siler scream from the other side.

"I'll come around!" she yelled. "Go!"

Flame engulfed the small room she occupied, so she dropped to her belly and crawled through the doorway into the main house. The bedroom opened into the living room, with another bedroom to her right. Dahyu and the Rinabs!

Smoke swirled around her. She heard a crack from above and rolled to one side just as a fiery timber crashed to the floor where her head had been. Dahyu flew from the bedroom, carrying Tinat in his arms.

"Dahyu!" Semra called, screaming above the din of the raging fire.

Dahyu looked frantically about to locate the sound. He saw her and ran forward. Semra stood to meet him.

"Take her; I have to get Shafii out!" he yelled, placing Tinat's feet on the ground.

Semra pulled Tinat's arm around her shoulders, wrapped her other arm around the woman's waist, and half pulled, half dragged her out of the house. Tinat's eyelids fluttered and she wheezed out slow breaths, sluggish from the fumes. Semra dodged falling logs and brought her out of the house and onto the grass just as Siler and Lesala ran around the side of the house.

Semra coughed and turned back. Where were Dahyu and Shafii? She turned and ran back inside, hardly registering Siler's voice yelling behind her.

"Stop! You've been in there too long!"

From the doorframe, Semra saw that a beam had fallen on Shafii's leg and was pinning him to the ground. Semra ran to help Dahyu try to lift it, but it was long and heavy, and one side was on fire. It wouldn't move.

"Get out," wheezed the older man. "There's no time!"

"I'm not leaving you here!" Dahyu insisted, tugging uselessly at the log.

Siler ran through the doorway and pulled with Semra and Dahyu with all his might, but the beam would not budge. "It's no use," Siler said to her. "We have to go."

"He'll die!" Semra protested.

"Yes, he will, but there's nothing left you can do about it!" Siler replied, and with that he grabbed her around the waist and dragged her backward to the door. Just before they crossed the threshold, the roof caved in and shut them off from escape. Semra screamed, but no sound came out. Sputtering and coughing, she stared helplessly at the scene before her. A burning panic rose in her, localized in the mark on her chest.

"I will not let you die here, son," Shafii wheezed at Dahyu from behind them. "I am just a man. You have greater responsibilities."

"I am exactly where I should be," Dahyu said.

A massive crash sounded above them, and the shape of a huge dragon descended, scattering debris all around them. Zezura lifted the end of the flaming beam pinning Shafii and shoved it aside, then swung her head this way and that, searching for something.

Siler yelled at Zezura. "Hey! She's over here!"

Zezura turned her huge head and spied Semra, then lunged forward and plucked Semra and Siler off the ground, up over the wreckage of the house, and onto the grass outside beside Lesala and Tinat. Semra collapsed on the ground, still coughing, breath short, and felt her world swim around her. Vaguely she was aware of Zezura depositing Dahyu and Shafii next to her on the ground moments later. Lesala came to console her, but she couldn't process the words being spoken around her.

Dahyu and Siler spoke together. Tinat came out of her fog and checked her husband's leg, and they spoke in low, urgent tones, occasionally glancing at Semra and Lesala. Dahyu and Siler ran to the stable behind the house and reappeared with two horses and a coil of rope. The two young men helped Tinat and Lesala up on one and Shafii on the other, then the trio took off at a full gallop to the east, disappearing from view.

Siler and Dahyu arrived back at her side and pulled her to her feet. Zezura crouched beside her, and Dahyu climbed onto Zezura's back and tied the rope around the dragon's neck and body like a makeshift harness. They were saying something about trying to keep Semra from falling off, and she felt herself being lifted up onto Zezura's back right behind Dahyu. She shook her head, trying to clear it, and reached around him to hold on while Siler pulled himself up behind her so that she was sandwiched between them.

Zezura started a low run across the ground, unfurled her great wings, and lifted off into the air. As the air hit her face, Semra gasped and instinctively tightened her arms around Dahyu's waist. She felt Siler do the same around her. Her mind jostled awake by the night air, Semra looked down below to see the entire village of Ryden on fire. Sinister figures ran through the village with flaming torches and swords that glinted in the red-orange light.

What had they done?

The flight was long, and Semra came in and out of consciousness as they glided across the sky. When she finally awoke, she saw that Zezura had painted herself the color of the sky and would be nearly impossible to pick out from the ground. The sun was just coming up over the horizon, shining on the scene below: the capital of Jannemar, the bustling city of Qalea, where merchants were already preparing their wares, and fishermen were bringing in the morning's catch.

The Dezapi River ran to the east of the city, running north up the hill and spilling over the edge of a sixty-foot cliff. There, the river created a waterfall that dumped into the larger Shalladin River down below. A smaller branch of the Dezapi ran underground south of Qalea, creating a smaller waterfall directly beneath the castle as it made its exit spilling out partway down the cliff. The breathtaking Shamaran Castle nestled at the top of the hill against the cliff on the north and northwest, the river to the east, and the rest of Qalea to the south and southwest.

The fortress rose up over Qalea with glistening light-sandstone walls accented by blue slated roofs and turrets. From above, Semra could see three elegant loops out front, two for the carriage roads through the main gate as they wound up levels to the carriage yard, and the third loop, its own second entrance leading to a lower level in the hill beneath the castle. The carriage road led to the castle grounds' main ward, past the outer walls and to the outer courtyard. Its inner walls rose above it all, protecting the inner courtyard and the keep, which ran up against the cliff behind.

"How are we going to get in?" Semra said aloud as they flew, but her voice was carried away in the wind, and she knew neither of her companions could hear her.

Though the city of Qalea ran right up to the front of the castle and wrapped around the lower levels below the outer wall, the Dezapi River cut it off from the right side. On the left, the city stopped short as it ran into forest and uneven ground to the west. The castle seemed to be the northern tip of a star, with the city sprawling out beneath it. Dahyu pointed to the trees southwest of the castle and tapped on the side of Zezura's neck to signal her that direction. She peeled off left and tucked her wings in a short dive that took Semra's breath away, then she leveled off in an arc and came into the woods from the west. Zezura shifted her color from sky blue to green as they dropped beneath the tree line and out of sight.

Zezura came to a stop, and Dahyu, Semra, and Siler slid to the ground.

"How are we going to get in? We need more time," Semra said as she hit the forest floor.

"Good morning. Glad you're alive. Are you okay?" Siler asked cynically.

"I'm fine. I'm feeling much better, thanks. And I do mean it ... thanks." She felt awkward suddenly and wrinkled her nose. "Wait ... what's the plan for Shafii and Tinat and Lesala? Are they going to be okay?"

Dahyu nodded sadly. "They're riding as fast as they can to Camar. They should be safe there until we can sort all this out, but it looked like those ... thugs were ransacking the entire village."

"The lord and lady of Camar are not loyal to the crown. A noble named Voldar has turned them against the king," Semra said.

"Voldar! He's a close friend of the king!" Dahyu exclaimed.

"Not so close as some might think, it seems," Siler said. "And those were no thugs you saw in Ryden. They are highly trained assassins."

Dahyu's eyes widened. "Assassins? Why, they were little older than I am!"

"You have no idea who you're dealing with here," Siler said. "They start missions at sixteen years old. By the time they're nineteen like me, they've been working professionals for several years."

"Who did you see?" Semra asked. "Was Brens there?"

Siler shook his head. "No, but Isra and Pinji were. We had a scuffle with Pinji in the stables, and I only saw Isra from afar. There were more, but they were only shadows at that distance."

Dahyu held up his hand. "Um, so can we talk about how you are on a first name basis with a whole slew of assassins? And don't assassins work alone? How do you know about disloyalty to the king in the heart of his court?"

"I told you," Semra began, "I heard it directly. We um ... " She glanced at Siler. He shrugged and sighed. Semra took a breath. "We grew up together, in a mountain west of here. He never called it by any particular name, so we just called it 'the mountain,' but it's part of a ring of mountains around a lake. There are small townships and villages in the foothills to the west and north, and we were taken as children and brought up in the mountain."

Dahyu shook his head. "That can't be true. No one lives there. Anyone passing the wasteland to Mount Hara disappears ... they say a great black dragon lives there, though I'm not sure I believe it."

"That's true," Siler said. "It's an Atas Mountain Wyvern, evil beast, named Rotokas. But more wicked still is the dragonlord controlling the thing. He calls himself the Framatar and fancies himself a great lord. I've never heard his real name. He sends Rotokas out to kidnap children and takes them into the mountain to train."

Dahyu looked between them. "He's a dragonlord? Does he have the mark of the dragon's kiss also? Wait ... so you're telling me you are assassins?"

"Precisely," Semra replied impatiently. "But he told us we

were purging the earth of evil, and now that we know better, he's going to purge the earth of us. Now tell me what you know of this dragon's kiss."

Dahyu's lips parted as he took in this information.

Siler crossed his arms. "Come now, you knew we weren't exactly run-of-the-mill travelers when you met us."

"Well, that's certainly the truth," Dahyu admitted. He sighed, then turned to Semra. "You saved the life of your dragon, yes?"

Semra pulled back, surprised. "I … was bleeding out, and she … the mark closed my wound and healed me."

"Hmm. Interesting, I've never heard of that before. But you saved her life, before that. You must have."

"She did." Siler nodded. "Remember? Zezura was healing from Rotokas' attack; Vix jumped on her from above, and Behruz was ready to pierce her brain through her eye socket. If you hadn't jumped in when you did, I think they would've succeeded."

"Yes, I suppose I did," Semra said. "She stayed pretty close to me after that. I didn't know she was trying to protect me right away, but it didn't take long to know she meant me no harm. What does that mean?" Semra glanced at Zezura and felt a warmth emanating from the dragon to Semra's mark.

Zezura shook her head and let her royal-blue and aqua colors settle in again.

"The mark of the dragon's kiss is an honor bestowed by a dragon when a person saves its life," Dahyu explained. "The dragon binds itself to its savior for as long as they live, and the magic of the mark keeps the two connected in a unique bond that can never be broken. The dragon will always know where you are and sense your distress, and can find you when you need her most. Mention of the dragon's kiss is hardly ever found, even in legend; but it's rare to find oneself in the position to save a dragon."

"How do you know of it?" Semra asked.

Dahyu shrugged. "I like to read."

Semra raised an eyebrow. "How does a healer's apprentice in a tiny outskirts village have access to that kind of reading?"

"My father works in the castle. I can get in because of him, and I work in the stables in the summers when I'm home from apprenticeship. The library in the castle is pretty exhaustive."

"You work in the castle and are just now telling us this?" Siler exclaimed.

"They let you read in the royal family's library?" Semra asked skeptically.

"My dad would sometimes bring me a book. The family didn't mind."

Semra frowned. "The family. The royal family? What on earth does your dad do in the castle?"

"He ... he's the king's attendant."

"What!" Semra and Siler exclaimed at once.

Siler stepped forward. "You're telling me that your dad has access to the king ... King Turian Shamaran, the king of Jannemar ... every day? As his personal valet?"

"Yes."

Semra's mouth dropped open. She couldn't believe their good fortune. "Well, what are we waiting for? All we have to do is have you waltz into the castle, have your dad tell the king his son is going to be murdered, and possibly the king himself, and call off the gala!"

"The gala? The target is at the gala? He'll never call it off. Every important royalty and official of Belvidore will be hosted in Jannemar! For the first time since the strain between our kingdoms hit its highest point. It's been almost eighteen years ... the last gathering was in the year 4982. The conflict between us has been growing steadier in the last few years, so this opportunity cannot be missed."

"The Framatar doesn't know where Prince Zephan is, but he seems convinced he'll show for the gala. If the king won't cancel, maybe he can come up with a reason for the prince to be absent. The king and the prince are both targets, but I think he needs Turian for something ... he won't kill him yet."

Dahyu shook his head. "No, the prince has to be there. As the heir apparent of Jannemar, with the king of Belvidore and Prince Axis, the heir apparent of Belvidore, at the event, it is critical that positive relationships are formed. Perhaps we can increase security."

Siler laughed. "Increase security! Your enemies will not look like enemies. You do not know who you can trust. You didn't know Voldar was against the king, or the lord and lady of Camar. Who else might you not know about? Maybe the king is aware of something you're not—after all, you're just a part-time stable boy—but my guess is his enemies are closer than he thinks. These hits are not haphazard violence, but intricate works of art."

"We need new clothes, clothes that don't look so out of place," Semra said, ready to get on with the practical plans. She looked down at her singed skirts and tunic and stripped off her wrap skirt to reveal her black pants and the multiple knives and dagger she had strapped on underneath. Dahyu's eyes went wide when he saw them, and Semra smiled to herself at his surprise. She was glad to lose the cumbersome skirts for a time.

"I can get you new clothes," Dahyu said. "Something that will make you fit in. I'll get inside the castle and talk to my father, but I'm not sure it will do any good. This is third-hand information through my father, and he might not want to risk telling the king of an unlikely plot that would, if false, ruin perhaps forever the trust of a powerful neighboring kingdom."

"We only have three days left before the gala," Semra said. "Be quick. We'll need to come up with a backup plan if the king won't take the threat seriously. The ransacking of Ryden was for our benefit ... Siler and mine. The dragonlord is saying, in no uncertain terms, that he's after us. And it's child's play compared to what's coming."

12

They decided that Dahyu would go inside the castle to talk to his father, and Siler and Semra would stay behind. Semra wanted to go to the city but knew she had to be patient. If Dahyu could get them clothes to blend in, they wouldn't risk attracting attention to themselves by walking into the city wearing clothes smelling of ash and looking like rags. Semra left Zezura to hunt in the forest and walked with Siler and Dahyu as they escorted him to the forest's edge.

"Tonight, when it's too dark to see her, I'm taking Zezura to scout out the best ways into the castle," Semra said. "If you don't find clothes for us, Siler can pinch some from town after dark."

"Get as much information on the gala as you can," Siler added. "What positions will get us best access inside? Scullery maid? Food servers? Entertainers? How many people are expected and is there an order of events planned? We'll need to know all of it."

"And maybe see if you can find out if the prince is in the

castle yet. If he is, he has to lay low. The biggest advantage we have is that the dragonlord's goons can't find him yet."

Dahyu nodded. "I'll do the best I can. I'll be back tonight."

"Also, anything baggy I can wear to hide my gear would be great," Semra added.

Dahyu frowned. "Skirts I can do, but there are few positions in the castle where women wear particularly baggy clothes. Certainly nothing you can wear a sword with, if that's what you're going for."

"No, no, not a sword. But my dagger, at least ... and my knives. I'll keep my pants on underneath so I can sheath them all. I just need something bulky enough to conceal it."

"But also a disguise that would get her close to the gala," Siler reminded him.

"Something we can use tomorrow too. We need to get inside and see the lay of the land before the gala."

"I'll do my best."

The trio walked around the southwesterly side of the castle until the trees dropped away to their right, thirty feet from the outer wall, and ran up to the edge of the cliff on the left. From this vantage point, nothing but wall could be seen before them, with spires in the distance. To their right, the wall extended, and the Jannemar banner waved high above the main gates. The flag depicted a spear pointed downward, like a stem, with a flower head at its hilt. A pair of dragon's wings spread on either side of the flag's design, and the wind rippled through it giving the wings almost a life of their own.

"Beautiful, isn't it?" Dahyu said, taking in the sight. "The main gate is the Nezzi Gate; the Dragon Gate is to the left of that, and the Spearhead Gate is along the east side, by the river. Each part represented."

"The Nezzi Gate?" Semra asked.

"You don't know? You really aren't from around here," Dahyu said, shaking his head. "The Nezil Myansara flower? You've never heard of it?"

"Isn't it that flower that only grows eight-thousand feet up or something?" Siler asked.

"Six-to-ten thousand, but yes. It grows in rocky ground, and although it looks lovely and delicate, it's a hardy little thing able to withstand great pressure. It was adopted as a symbol of Jannemar generations ago, and the same poetic verses have been passed down by oral tradition all that time:

> Nezil Myansara lives ten-thousand feet
> > at tops.
> The wind and rain may batter, but its
> > beauty never stops.
> Resilient is the flame within the shoot
> > that sprung of stone.
> Harshness is her home, yet wise would
> > make her friend of throne.

"So you see, with a verse like that, we had no choice but to befriend this flower and put her on our flag! Nezzi is just a nickname."

Something in Semra's stomach flipped uneasily. How was he so open and comfortable? She could hardly ask that. Instead, she said, "You spent your childhood learning poems about flowers?"

"Just one of those things you learn. Lovely, isn't it?"

Semra raised an eyebrow. "Mhmm."

"Where's the door you mentioned?" asked Siler, growing bored. "I don't see anything."

"It's around the bend there. There's two-to-three feet of ground between the wall and the cliff for the first forty feet or so, and a small door stands twenty feet in. It's every guard's least favorite post, but I know the guard, so he'll let me in to see my father. He'll want to know why I'm not coming through the main gate, but I'll come up with something."

Siler nodded. "We'll see you tonight then. Good luck."

Dahyu dipped his head and ran across the open space to the wall, disappearing around the bend. As soon as he was out of sight, Siler turned to Semra.

"It's not too late to back out. We escaped the mountain. We've meddled in the lives of rich politicians long enough, don't you think?"

Anger simmered in Semra's gut. "We are the ones that put this family in danger in the first place. We have an obligation to stop the Framatar from stealing more children like us and turning them into murderers."

"It's not our fault. *We* didn't build the program."

"No, but we're the only ones with the skill and the knowledge to stop this plague from taking over the whole country. It's not like we're unfamiliar with risk. We end this now, or we flee Jannemar forever ... and I couldn't live with myself knowing a hundred more Lesalas were going to be kidnapped, broken, and molded into his killing machines. He would have full control."

Siler stepped to her and ran his hands up her upper arms, his eyes suddenly soft. "Semra, you take on everyone else's problems. What if this is bigger than you?"

Semra swallowed and looked away from his gaze. "So much blood is already on my head. Please don't ask me to add the weight of an entire kingdom under his control. It would make me ... It might make me irredeemable."

She shifted her weight in the uncomfortable silence, then glanced back up at Siler. She couldn't read his face.

"If he's not back by tonight, I'll go to town for clothes for us, and we'll find a way into the castle ourselves," Siler said.

Semra let out a breath. He was going to stay and help. "Sure. Or, you know, *I'll* go to town and get clothes for us, and we'll find a way into the castle."

"Why wouldn't I go?"

"Well, last time I let someone else get clothes for me, you let a four-year-old take charge."

Siler shrugged. "And she did great. It was fine. Besides, don't you need to take Zezura out? I think you should go at dusk, not true night. Zezura can turn herself black, or navy, or whatever to blend in better, but you won't scope out much if you can't see anything."

"Tell you what. Why don't we go catch something to eat, and you can go to town tonight while I fly with Zezura. If you mess it up, I'll go to town myself when I get back. We'll have to take turns though, to wait up for Dahyu."

Siler agreed, and they spent the next few hours catching a rabbit, two squirrels, and digging up roots to eat. Zezura found them again by late afternoon when Siler was starting a fire and Semra was dressing their catch. Siler rubbed sticks together, but Zezura huffed on the kindling and it caught alight.

"Wow, you're nice to have around," he commented, rocking back on his heels. He turned to Semra, pausing to watch her nimble fingers prepare the meal. "What if we only exchange one tyrant for another? Have you thought about that?"

"I don't think keeping the Framatar from murdering the king and the prince is really much of an exchange," Semra said, not bothering to look up from her work.

"Kings are all the same. Living in their palaces, corrupted by power. Don't you see that? Even if Dahyu gets in and talks to his father, and his father talks to the king, and even if the king actually takes him seriously and invites two teenage strangers—who are self-proclaimed assassins—to explain this whole crazy situation ... maybe he'll believe us, maybe not, but what are the odds he'd actually defeat the Framatar?"

Semra handed him the squirrels on a spit to roast. "Not great. But if I can get the others to see him for who he really is, and turn them, it'll be him and Rotokas against ... how many mission readies does he have? Twenty?"

Siler nodded. "That sounds about right. But the new year is almost here, and the current class will be graduating. That will make seven more, and this doesn't include the five sleepers he has who-knows-where. Even if you turned some, you won't turn them all."

"I don't need to turn them all. I just need to create chaos and turn enough of them. Ruining his plan, exposing his coup, that will help."

"Even if you get all you want, the king agrees, he magically finds a way to not only stay alive but hunt down and catch the dragonlord and the multitude of trained killers at his disposal, what will you do when it's all over?"

Semra shrugged. "I don't know. Start over somewhere. Get the kids back to their families. Maybe I'll get a house."

Siler laughed. "A house? You want a house? Our kind can't stay in houses, Semra. We get too antsy staying in one predictable place all the time. You wouldn't last six months."

"Maybe not, but if I left, it would be because I wanted to, not because I was told I had to."

A crunch of leaves alerted them to someone's approach. They turned to see Dahyu walking toward them with a large bag over his shoulder. "You made dinner," he noted as he laid the bag down, then opened the top.

Siler turned the squirrel meat over the flame and set up the rabbit. "Show me what you brought us, and I'll let you know if you can have any."

"Saeb, the head of household staff, meets every new employee before they start. She delegates the hiring, but she approves each one, so Semra, you'll have to know her and avoid her. The kitchens will be a madhouse two days out from the gala, and they brought on everyone they needed months ago, so that option is out. Scullery maids steer clear of large gatherings, working almost exclusively behind the scenes. That would give you anonymity but not access. The king is only using entertainers he has used before for this event, so that option is out, and of course entertainers won't be coming until the day of the gala anyway. So, all things considered, for a position easily ignored but with access throughout the castle, I landed you a spot in candle service."

"There's an entire position for candle service?" Semra asked skeptically.

"Mhmm. Several actually."

Dahyu pulled out a servant's dress, grey-green with long, loose sleeves that closed at the wrist, and a white, sleeveless apron comprised of a long strip of cloth that ran down the front of the dress, down the back, and was cross-laced together on the sides.

Semra wrinkled her nose, and Siler clapped his hands. "Perfect! Now if only we had a girl around who could wear it!"

"Does it have a tight bodice?" Semra asked in resignation. She had to admit, he'd really thought it through.

"No, the household servants don't wear that sort of thing," Dahyu assured her. "The apron overtop would hide it anyway. And this is the same sort of clothing the cleaning staff wears, so in a pinch you can pretend to be dusting or straightening or something. It's loose, and I assume pretty comfortable, as far as women's clothing goes."

Semra nodded. "Okay. What do you have for Siler?"

"With Semra inside, I thought being a gardener would get you a good look at the outer wards and grounds, and you'd still be able to come inside to bring in flower arrangements and such. It's the best of both worlds."

Dahyu reached back into the bag and brought out trousers, a long-sleeved tunic, and a corded belt.

"Oh good, he'll have an excuse for looking so disheveled and grubby," Semra noted with a grin.

"I recently survived a house fire and multiple assailants," Siler said.

"So what's your normal excuse?" Semra laughed, and the corners of Siler's lips turned up.

"Okay, so we have covers. Good," Siler said. "Did your dad hear you out?"

"I'm afraid it took quite some doing getting even a few minutes with my father, as busy as the castle is right now. When I finally did and tried to tell him about the threat, he said threats were made against the royal family all the time. Most are unfounded, and the guards and the king's specialized security detail stop those that are real. He said there was no way the king would respond favorably to such a thing, not to worry about it, and that I really shouldn't be in the castle at all right now."

Semra sighed. "Any other news you were able to get?"

"Not good, I'm afraid. Two governors are dead, and one is missing. The king's uncle is dead. Two wealthy and very supportive nobles are dead, and a third had his cargo attacked and is scrambling to stay afloat."

"So many! What do you know of the deaths?" Siler asked.

"One of the nobles died of food poisoning, and one

became slobbering drunk and died in the night, choking on his own vomit. It looks like the missing governor, Stauv, killed both Mallen and Reza ... but that doesn't make any sense. There was rivalry between Stauv and Reza, sure, but I knew them both to be reasonable men.

"Stauv was strongly in favor of a union between Belvidore and Jannemar, and Mallen was staunchly against it, but again nothing to kill over. One of the governors, Governor Mallen, was working on a means to increase productivity in his province and decrease the tax burden on the people, and he met with Reza to go over his locality's results. He spent the past three months experimenting with certain changes. Both were killed at the end of the meeting."

Realization dawned on Semra. She leaped to her feet. "I knew you looked familiar! You're Reza's aide!"

"That's impossible," Siler said beside her.

"It's him. I know it is. Something didn't add up here, and I knew it. Why is a part-time stable boy apprenticing under a healer in a far corner of Jannemar? Anyone trying to make money would at least work under someone with a little more clout in a busy city. Not to mention how many details he has on the relationships and agendas of the land's governors."

"When would you have seen Reza's aide?" Dahyu asked.

Siler and Semra exchanged glances, and Dahyu gasped. "It was you. You ... you killed them."

"Actually, technically no. I didn't. I only killed one of them. And Reza was never supposed to die," Semra said defensively.

Dahyu's face flashed a look of repulsion, and though he covered it quickly, Semra squirmed under his gaze.

Dahyu frowned. "He ... wait, he wasn't? What do you mean?"

"Mallen was the target. Reza was meant to take the fall."

"You missed?"

Semra balked. "No. I'm good at what I do. It was an easy shot, and any fool should have been able to pull it off, but I had another job, from inside the building. My colleague took out Reza instead of Mallen, so I had to clean up the mess before the Framatar destroyed my friend for her idiotic mistake."

"Which was risky," Siler put in, "considering Behruz was there too. He had to pull off a whole new frame job in no time. And spinning the situation in a more positive light is dangerous. Lying is disloyal, and disloyalty is unacceptable."

Dahyu blinked. For a moment no one spoke, and all that could be heard was the rustling of leaves overhead as a soft breeze wafted by.

Semra tapped her foot. "It's not like I enjoy it, okay?" she said, breaking the silence.

"I don't mind it," Siler commented casually. "I mean, there are pros and cons to it, but there are few things in life more satisfying than an elegantly executed hit." He lifted one of the squirrels off the fire and spun the spit in his hands.

"Mallen was murdered in his sleep," Dahyu said flatly. "That's not very ... sportsmanlike."

"It's not a sport. It's a job," Semra spat. "Like it or not, we are who we are, and we've done what we've done. If you want to scamper away and raise the alarm now, fine, but know that we're the only people who know the faces of almost any assassin the dragonlord will use against the royal family. And if you go now, when the prince and later the king are both assassinated, remember their blood is on your head."

Siler narrowed his eyes at Dahyu. "We need to know everything you know, which means if you stay, you need to fess up about being Reza's aide and be helpful. Are you in or out?"

Semra lowered herself back into her seated position next to Siler and looked back at Dahyu expectantly.

Dahyu crossed his arms and took in a long breath. He glanced between Siler and Semra again, then slowly sat down cross-legged on the ground. "Very well. It's true. I was Governor Reza's aide."

"Obviously. So why did we find you in Ryden?"

"People were dropping like flies, and I had important results from the meeting that I needed to protect. Hiding out in the middle of nowhere while I got word to Shamaran Castle was the best thing I could do. I sent word and laid low. I'd been planning on returning to the castle to meet with a number of nobles and other governors, since many would be in the same place for the gala anyway. Normally, an aide doesn't get invited to such things, but under the circumstances ... " His voice trailed off.

Semra regarded him coolly. "If you are Reza's aide, then what exactly did you do in the castle today? How did you really get in?"

"What I told you about my father working in the castle was true. I really do know that guard, and I do have a grasp of the stables, from when I was a boy. My father has worked there for as long as I can remember, and the stables being in the outer ward, it was a good cover for me. I'm sorry I couldn't be more forthright before, but I really didn't know if I could trust you."

"Nor we you," Siler said dryly.

Semra picked up a leaf and twirled it in her fingers thoughtfully. "I'm inclined to believe you. When the house was on fire, your natural instinct was to protect, and that's a good quality. You were loyal to them—I respect that. But, though we're working together now, you should know: trust is not easily gained. I've got my eye on you."

Dahyu nodded. "Trust easily gained is easily lost. Anything worth having is worth earning. And you, also ... in the fire. You saved Tinat, but you came back for Shafii also, and watched over the little girl in your care. I think"—he stroked his chin and leaned forward— "perhaps your job, as you call it, is death, but your inclination is life."

Semra felt a burning in her chest at his words, a stirring of something inside her that she never knew had been dormant. She looked into his eyes, quizzically, doubtingly, for any sign of mockery or derision. But as she searched the depths of his deep-amber eyes, she found something that surprised her. Compassion.

It didn't make sense to her, and it felt all wrong—uncomfortable—despite the warmth it offered. Semra pushed away the warmth and glanced away, focusing instead on shredding the leaf into a thousand pieces. She chewed her lip.

Siler cleared his throat. "So ... the gala. How many people are going to be there?"

"A large portion of the court, plus Belvidorian court members. Even with a relatively exclusive list, there will be maybe six hundred? I'm not sure what the final count is."

"Wow. And the order of operations?" Siler asked.

"It's going to be a week of festivities, but the opening gala will invite everyone in, members of state will be introduced as they arrive, and the king will formally welcome the Belvidorian royal family and dignitaries to Jannemar. There will be drinks, plates of food passed around, dancing, and entertainment. Feasts and joust tournaments will start the day after."

Semra pulled the last strip of leaf off the stem and

dropped it to the ground. She lifted the other squirrel off the fire, looked up at Dahyu, and nodded at the rabbit. "You know how to cut up a rabbit? It's the best meat we have."

Dahyu tilted his head at her, perhaps wondering at her abrupt subject change. "Sure. I mean, it might not be the smoothest, but I don't need my food cut up for me, if that's what you're asking."

"You're our guest, as it were," she said, taking a knife out and twirling it expertly in her fingers. With a flourish, she extended the handle out to Dahyu. "Go ahead and take what you want."

Siler tore off a piece of his squirrel with his teeth. "Don't eat it all. I could use some rabbit too."

Dahyu took the knife from Semra and plucked the rabbit off the fire. Semra and Siler watched him as he cut it into pieces. He had a daintier and less practiced approach, but he had the basics down, and overall Semra was impressed.

Semra was moody that evening, and as the air cooled, the sun set into a chill mist that matched her disposition. Though she listened to the strategy talk and absentmindedly threw out ideas about why this suggestion was ludicrous and that suggestion was more realistic, her mind wandered. *Perhaps your job is death ... but your inclination is life.* Was it true?

The Framatar had always told her she was selfish. If she was hesitant about a mission, she was selfish because good people would suffer for as long as her target was alive. If she withheld information on a colleague's mistakes in the field, she was selfish because she did it not for her colleague, who would only be made stronger after being disciplined, but for herself to make her feel better. If she asked too many questions about a target, she was ungrateful. How could she not trust the Framatar, after all he did for her? Did he really have time to explain the whole life story of every despicable person they would take out?

And yet, it was to life that Semra saved Lesala. It was life that made her leave the mountain to save the prince. Every kill was motivated by bringing a better life to the rest of the world—to leave it a better place than it had been before. Could the same be said of the Framatar?

By now, everyone in the mountain probably thought of her as the very evil they were meant to eliminate. Brens' words rang in Semra's ears. *I am stopping a dangerous traitor ...*

Zezura nosed Semra from behind, wrapping her head around her in a hug as she sat against a tree on the forest floor. A warmth in the mark on her chest translated Zezura's compassion—she'd felt her hurt. Semra felt her eyes begin to well up, and she stood abruptly, only then realizing that Siler and Dahyu had still been speaking about something.

"It's getting dark," she said gruffly. "I'm taking Zezura out. Be back later."

Siler and Dahyu exchanged confused glances, but Semra turned away from them and headed for the edge of the woods by the cliffs, not caring to see their expressions any longer. Zezura followed at a brisk pace, and Semra could feel her excitement mounting the closer they got to the edge. As they pulled away from the camp, Semra felt Zezura's impatience, and she started bounding ahead and circling back, pouncing in front of Semra briefly before taking off again.

Semra couldn't help but laugh at the sight of the fifty-foot dragon gallivanting through the forest. She broke into a run, and as Zezura slowed next to her, Semra swung herself up onto the dragon's back and practiced leveraging her weight and positioning to hold tightly to Zezura as she moved. The dragon let her bright colors fade into shades of the night and pulsed her powerful wings, buffeting the air and lifting them up, up, above the trees, high into the air, where they glided in a wide arc out over the forest and past the cliff.

The Shalladin River twinkled below them in vague reflections of starlight through the mist, and the moon illuminated the silhouette of Shamaran Castle on the hilltop. She could only just make out the outlines of the city of Qalea as it spread out like a blanket beneath the castle. Semra shivered, but whether it was from the cool night air or sheer exhilaration, she couldn't guess.

Zezura swooped to one side, and Semra adjusted her weight, hooking her foot around the spikes on Zezura's sides and bending low over her neck. Semra laughed, and in that moment her stress melted away as they zipped this way and that, up and over and around. Zezura made a chuffing sound that seemed to be a laugh of her own. With a sharp turn, Zezura dropped into a dive, and a tingling thrill ran through Semra's whole body.

Never had she felt such freedom before! Zezura's pleasure mixed with Semra's own, and they were one, leaving every foul intent and menacing threat far behind. Zezura leveled off and swept over the river below the castle, and as they rounded the cliff Semra saw the Dezapi Falls, where the river above spilled over and into the Shalladin. The sound of the rushing water was soothing to her ears, and Semra closed her eyes for a moment to take it all in.

They swept past the falls and climbed back up to the castle keep, where Semra started analyzing its layout. The castle walls were lower on this side where it ran right up to the cliff, and there was room to walk between the walls and the keep itself. The keep was formulated like a "U," with towers at each side of the bend before the straightaways, and the curve set nicely into the natural bend of the bluff.

Semra counted three main floors and two additional floors in the towers, not to mention the spires on top. The first floor stood high above the outer ward between the inner and outer castle walls, with a significant jump to the level below. Semra saw several small windows interspersed along the wall beneath the main floors and assumed they marked guard rooms, cellars, and other servant spaces. In the front, three pointed bastions accented the outer wall behind the main gates and carriage drives up the hill.

When they neared the falls, Semra tapped Zezura on the side of her neck, and the dragon banked right. Semra guided Zezura next to the falls and ran her hand through the water. She couldn't help but smile and ran her hand through it again, but this time, she noticed something—a cleft in the cliff on the other side of the water. Semra tapped Zezura, and Zezura plowed through the waterfall, drenching them both in cold water. They landed, dripping wet, on a shelf beneath the castle and behind the curtain of water.

The cleft sat about halfway between the top of the cliff and the flowing Shalladin below, and, with her head ducked down, Zezura only really fit in the first fifteen feet of it. Semra slid off Zezura's back to explore. It was a small space, perhaps thirty feet wide at the opening and narrowing in as it moved backward. She reached out in the dark, shivering in the night air. Semra felt along the wall around a short bend, out of view from the main opening, until she reached a small narrow door. The wooden door, reinforced with steel, had no door handle on the outside. Semra searched for anywhere to grasp and pull, but found nothing, and pushing against it was equally unsuccessful.

She made note of the place, got back on Zezura, rode out through the waterfall again, and made another sweep around the castle. After committing to memory the locations of as many doors and windows as possible, she turned Zezura back to the wood as the deep darkness of true night settled over the hilltop. They descended through the trees over the campsite, and Scmra slipped off the dragon with a grin.

Her hair was cold and wet, and though the air had dried her off a bit on the ride back, her clothes were still damp. Semra walked over and stood in front of the fire, warming her hands. Dahyu and Siler sat there, holding sticks. One the patch of dirt between them, they'd drawn strategies for getting into the castle.

"Welcome back, sunshine," Siler said, smiling. "Dragon riding certainly seems to be good for your mood."

"It is!" She laughed, still caught up in the evening's adventure.

"What happened?" Dahyu asked. "Zezura dunk you in the river?"

"Waterfall," she answered. "Have you two finalized the plan?"

Siler nodded. "Take a seat. We have a big day tomorrow."

13

Early the next morning, Semra and Siler staggered themselves into the procession of Shamaran Castle servants headed to work. Though some staff lived on the castle's grounds, most lived outside the walls and trekked up the hill every day, passing through the Dragon Gate and trudging back down to Qalea every night. Dahyu had parted ways with them that morning, saying he'd need to get cleaned up and then see what he could find out about security plans for the gala, and a precise attendance list.

Semra and Siler had reconnaissance objectives. They planned to get a layout of the Great Hall where the gala would be held, as well as the whole of the grounds. Siler would be taking the outer wards and towers, and Semra was responsible for the rest of the keep and interior.

"Remember," Siler had said, "They've had months to plan, and we have a single day. Be quick and be thorough, but don't rush ... and don't dawdle."

Great finesse did not pair well with desperate haste. Semra walked with a small bag she'd pinched from Qalea on her way in, holding a roll from the baker's cart she'd passed and the rope they'd used to make a harness for Zezura. After the previous night, Semra felt confident that she didn't need it to fly, and she might have use for it in the castle. If nothing else, it added bulk to her bag, and she needed to have one since no other staff entered without one.

Ahead, Semra saw the huge archway with its heavy gate retracted high over their heads. A dragon with unfurled wings was carved in the stone over the entrance. Above this, a guard paced in the gate tower, overseeing them as they filtered in through the gate. Semra knew there'd be more inside the tower, and she'd noted the narrow vertical slits where archers could be stationed.

Two guards stood at either side of the archway and stopped people to examine their staff identification cards on the way in. Semra pulled hers out and presented it to the guard, holding her breath for a moment, but she needn't have worried. The guard took only a cursory glance and waved her on through.

For a moment she felt claustrophobic as she walked through the Dragon Gate and into the caged tunnel space between the main gate and its twin on the other side of the tower. If enemies assaulted the gates, they'd have to make it through both gates or be trapped between them and picked off one by one in a murder box of sorts. Semra glanced behind her and saw Siler's dark hair underneath a brimmed hat amid the mass of people some forty feet behind her.

"Very admirable, I think it is, don't you?" said a heavyset woman to her friend in front of Semra. "The princess, to deny all the suitors thus far, but consider betrothal to Prince Axis? She's been so terribly picky. Imagine, Belvidore an ally!"

The second woman, slight and beady-eyed, clucked her

tongue. "Princess Avaya hasn't a clue what's in store for her. Ally, my foot! Belvidore has been a shadow on our doorstep for decades, but they've never actually declared war. But I'd rather live with the shadow than lie down with the devil, make no mistake!"

"I think it's perfectly lovely." The first woman sniffed. "Shows the character of the king too." She leaned in close and whispered in her friend's ear, so Semra had to strain to hear, "He abandoned his father's principles and the traditions and responsibilities of monarchy when he married his queen, you know. Slighted Belvidore something terrible, rejecting their offer. Perhaps he's grown and ready to make right!"

"Dear, dear, I wasn't born yesterday! If you're going to gossip, pick something new to gossip about! We already know everything about His Majesty, King Turian. It's none of my business, but I want to know what plans he has if King Arnevon does something pernicious. It's none of my business, you understand, but if he decides to kill us all, why, that would be my business, wouldn't it?"

Semra furrowed her brows and shook her head. Most gossip was just that ... gossip. But it was also a useful tool, and if she kept her ears open, she might just learn something important among the drivel.

They exited the tower tunnel and progressed up a ramp in one of the loops Semra had seen from above with Zezura. The loop arched back into the tower's second level and through to another tunnel inside the southernmost bastion. Here the room opened up, and Semra saw a guardroom to her right and a passage to her left. She hoped Siler would have a good excuse to explore these. A number of staff branched off here, but she followed a smaller group through the main tunnel, up the sloping floor, and out again through a door that led onto the outer ward on top of the bastions and past the outer wall.

To her left, Semra saw where the Nezzi Gate's carriage road spilled out and joined the ward she found herself on. Beyond that, a spacious walkway ran up to the outer wall and wrapped around the castle. No buildings sat around the sides on the outer ward, just a few towers at intervals. To her right, Semra saw the stables, and before her was the tower of the main gate to the inner ward where the courtyard, main gardens, and castle keep lay. The inner wall rose up and around so that the levels looked almost like stair steps leading from the hillside gated entrances to the outer wall, then up to the outer ward, with the inner wall rising from there.

"Honestly, Belon has been in a tizzy all this month, running hither and thither and making everyone frantic," said the larger woman in front of Semra. "I tried to tell her that laundry can only be so clean and linens only so pressed, and it'll all get done so long as she remembers to breathe."

"Well, when an idiot chandlery boy drips wax into a whole vat of fine linen laundry, what can you expect? How does that even happen?" the other answered.

Semra smiled. Excellent. The more frazzled the workers, the more distracted they would be. Her cover as candle staff just got easier. Perhaps she was replacing the poor sap.

The two women bypassed the tower gate of the inner wall, and took a passage to the right inside the wall itself, just before the inner ward. Semra stood in the archway and took in the sight. She'd seen it from above, but it was different from down below, and absolutely beautiful. The impeccably curated lower courtyard had a small pond with Koi fish, a little burbling fountain, and a grassy area dotted with small fruit trees and outdoor seating. A paved walkway surrounded the whole thing, and a path cut directly across the grass. From where Semra stood, several steps led up to the upper courtyard, a paved area closed in on three sides by the castle keep.

At one end of the keep, the first floor had a magnificent floor-to-ceiling, rounded *eibada*, or worship house, for whichever deity or deities the reigning king chose to respect. Dahyu had said there were conference rooms next to it, plus general rooms of state, a large sitting or receiving room, which flowed into an enormous feasting hall, stairs, and then a number of service-related rooms. These would include the kitchen, the cellar, and the pantry beneath that. The opposite side contained guard towers and guard rooms, and a less-formal throne room on the end for day-to-day legislative matters.

Semra stepped back through the tower gate and followed the two women into a long stone hall under the castle. Small windows at the top of the east walls illuminated the hall, but the dank smell and stone passages felt like home. Semra took note of where rooms and corridors branched off, but it seemed an elaborate labyrinth, and she had to make best use of her time and prioritize scoping out the Great Hall, where the gala would be held. She would come back later—after gaining a firm grasp of the main areas—to map out as much of the underground network as she could. Since the chandlery was also on the second floor, her cover as a candle staff member would make that a good place to start.

The two women continued up ahead along the hall, while Semra took the stairs to the right. At the landing for the first floor, Semra smelled rejuvenating spices and heard the distant sound of pots and pans. She peeked out into the central hall. On her left, a tall and beautifully carved door lead to the *eibada* at the end and doors led to rooms off to the sides. To her right, the staff prepared breakfast for the royal family.

Semra continued up the stairs to the second floor and out into the hall. Two serving staff walked past her carrying bed linens, preparing for their royal guests. Dahyu had said that the laundry, storeroom, and chandlery should be to the right. Semra turned right and gasped as she ran straight into a tall, lanky woman with thick eyebrows and a permanent furrow to her brow. Her gaze darted over Semra from head to toe, and she stuck a spindly finger into Semra's chest.

"You ... I don't know you."

Semra raised her eyebrows and stared back in surprise. When she gave no answer, the woman narrowed her eyes and put her hands on her hips.

A voice interrupted from behind her, and Semra breathed a sigh of relief. "Miss Belon, which room needed the sheets pressed again?"

The lanky woman in front of her turned her head. "The one on the end, to the left. Taut and wrinkle-free, or I'm stringing someone up by their ankles!"

"Miss Belon," Semra said, recognizing the name. "I'm new, working in chandlery. So unfortunate what happened with wax in the laundry! It seems Saeb agreed you could use someone less likely to strain your nerves, so close to an important event like this!"

Belon cocked her head. "Saeb liked you?"

"Yes, of course. Why?"

"Saeb doesn't like anyone," Belon answered curtly. "What makes you so special?"

"Nothing. That is, I don't know that she liked me, per se, but she didn't hate me. Said I would do, that's all."

Belon scoffed. "High praise from that witch. Only, don't tell her I said so, or I'll have you strung up too. Very well, come along and don't drag your feet. I can't afford to waste time having another incident, so you'd better have your head on straight."

Semra ducked her head and followed Belon two doors down on the right, where Belon shoved her lightly through the doorway. The room held two workbenches, two large wheels perhaps four feet tall, and, in the center over a furnace, a large cauldron-like pot filled with what Semra assumed to be hot wax. A candle chandelier hung upside down from the ceiling above it, and a middle-aged man stood there adjusting his apron. He glanced up only briefly, then turned back to his work, pulling the chandelier toward him.

"What do you want, Belon?" he asked, annoyance all over his face.

"Don't you take that tone with me," Belon shot back. "Saeb approved this girl to work with you. Get her started, and I'll be out of your hair."

The man glared at Semra. "I don't have time to see if you know what you're doing. And you're hours early for any evening setup."

"I'm sorry, I didn't know," Semra said.

"For heaven's sake, Garbane, just give her something to do," said Belon. "It's not my problem. Don't let her dump any wax in my laundry, and we'll be just fine."

Belon disappeared, leaving Semra standing awkwardly in the doorway while Garbane lowered the chandelier into the wax without a word. Semra folded her arms.

Garbane paused and glowered at her. "You done this sort of thing before?"

"I worked for a chandler in Camar, low-level things. Arranging the shop, prepping wicks, things like that," she answered. "But I can learn just about anything, and my family needs the money."

"Your family must hate you if they sent you to work one door down from that old crone," he muttered, jerking his head in the empty space where Belon had stood. "A day before a momentous event, no less. Maybe they hate me too."

"I'm a hard worker. Why don't I check for candles burned too low throughout the castle and swap them out with new ones?"

Garbane examined her with interest. "You are volunteering to walk the whole castle looking for low candles in its every nook and cranny?"

"Sure. I specialize in crannies, of course, but I suppose I could do nooks as well."

Garbane snorted. "Did they send me a jester or a chandler assistant? Fine, but listen. Candles are expensive, so we aren't going to waste any, however short. Look here—any that are this long or longer"—he held his hands apart to measure the distance—"stay exactly where they are. Any this long"—he moved his hands closer—"get moved to the servants' quarters to finish them off before being switched out. You can skip the Great Hall, Ancestry Hall, and throne room. Those should be done already. There, take that bundle of new candles with you."

Semra picked up the bundle of candles he indicated and dipped her head, but Garbane had already returned to his work and seemed to have tuned out the world. Semra turned on her heel and whisked herself out of the chandlery, past the storeroom and laundry room where Belon was yelling some grievance or other, past the kitchen, and through the door at the end of the hall.

The room beyond was stunning. Intricately carved ceilings rose up to the top of the third floor, and paintings of the

Shamaran kings going back generations lined the walls. A walkway wound around the edges of the top half of the hall, connecting the third-floor, royal-family bedrooms to the rest of the residence. Semra made a mental note to come back later and explore the spiral staircase in the back corner, then she opened the two great double doors that led into the Great Hall and stepped inside.

Semra had seen exquisite villas and expensive apartments, but nothing compared to the Shamaran Castle's Great Hall. Soaring ceilings arched over her head. Six massive chandeliers hung at intervals down its length, and pairs of columns ran down either side, beyond which sat tables and chairs for reclining after dancing or enjoying entertainment. On the left side above these, the walkway from the previous room continued down the length of the room. Someone on the third floor could get across and look down on the guests at the tables on that side, but they'd have only a limited view of the rest of the hall.

Between the sets of columns lay an open expanse of sparkling marble floor, illuminated by huge floor-to-ceiling windows that ran along the wall facing out to the outer ward and the Shalladin River. Mountains could be seen in the distance along with all the expanse of northern Jannemar. In the center of the floor, the symbol of Jannemar shone— royal-blue dragon wings and spear with a gold Nezil Myansara flower glinting in the sunlight.

A pair of knights walked toward her from the other side of the room. Two servants fussed over the drapes on Semra's right, and to the left, a servant wiped down the first table. Semra walked past her to the fourth table and examined the candles in the middle. Garbane was right, they were all exactly the same height and perfect. Semra picked one up as an excuse to be there while she analyzed the room. There were few places to hide, just columns, and two circular alcoves, one on each end of the room facing outward.

Footsteps above drew her attention up to where an elegant lady in her early twenties crossed the walk overhead. Her golden hair fell in ringlets down her back, and the soft rustle of high-end silk followed her as she went. Semra needed to get a look at the room from that walkway. It provided an excellent visual; anyone lying down or crouching from that vantage point would be able to see the whole floor. Tymetin and whichever other assassins were assigned this job would most certainly know the best routes to and from every observation point.

Semra replaced the candle in the middle of the table and walked down the Great Hall, past the circular sitting room to the right, through another set of gilded double doors, and into the library. Books lined the walls from floor to ceiling on both sides of the room, interrupted only by windows and vertical beams. Cushioned sofas and chairs with end tables were aesthetically placed, and Semra tried to imagine Dahyu reading about dragons in this beautiful space. She couldn't.

Semra crossed the floor to the doorway and froze. Two guards entered the anteroom before her from the rooms beyond. The first she didn't recognize, but the second she knew all too well—Radix. She'd been bumped up to his class in the mountain and they'd graduated together, nearly three years prior.

Their eyes met, and Semra stood rooted to the floor.

The first guard stepped through the anteroom, reached for the doorknob to Semra's right, then paused when Radix didn't immediately follow. "Felgan?"

Radix allowed himself a small smile. "Fancy seeing you here."

14

Radix's smile widened, but his eyes were hard. "What are you doing here?"

"I could ask you the same," Semra replied easily, forcing herself to relax.

"I'm a guard. That's the guard tower," he said, gesturing to the door. "Been here for months."

"Felgan, you know her?" the guard asked.

"Yes, yes ... we grew up together. Small world!"

"Ha! Small world indeed! All the way from Pillerae," the guard said.

Radix glanced down at the bundle of candlesticks in Semra's hands. "Chandlery, hmm? Good choice. We should catch up soon, don't you think?"

"Of course," Semra responded. "I have a feeling there's a lot you don't know."

"Not so sure about that. But we'll be in touch," he said, and passed her a threatening glare as he turned to follow the guard into the tower.

Semra stood motionless for a moment. Had he really

been working in the castle for months? *But of course he has. It's far too important a job to do hastily. He'd know schedules, routines, protocols ...*

Semra moved then, fast but not too fast, into the next room, down the stairs, and out to the courtyard. She hurried across and through to the kitchens. Radix could come after her at any time. Where was Tymetin? And where was the prince?

She stepped into the long room to her left and noted the two spiral staircases in the back corners of the room. The one on the right wound upward, and she identified it as the staircase she'd seen from the second floor. But the second staircase—on the left—wound down beneath the castle. She opted for that one, remembering the locked door without a handle in the cleft behind the waterfall. Whatever led down there would be on this side of the castle, and she might need an escape route rather quickly.

Semra knew the first landing wouldn't be deep enough to lead to the shelf on the cliff, so she proceeded down another flight. At the bottom stood two doors. One of them had to lead to the shelf. She reached out and tugged on the handle. Nothing.

The door to her left opened, and Semra's jaw dropped as she saw Manu, one of Siler's class, exit with a ring of keys. Before he could lock the door, she clocked him on the side of his face and leaped at him. Radix had had the other guard around to keep him civil, but Manu had no reason not to kill her here and now.

He gripped her by the hair, yanked her back against the door, hitting her head, and then lifted her up against the door with his hand at her throat. Semra grasped his wrists to take the pressure off her neck and wrapped her legs around his waist for support, while inwardly cursing her skirts for the three extra seconds it took to secure a hold. She released his wrists and buried her thumbs into his eye sockets.

Manu's grip lessened, and an instant was all she needed. Semra sent a jab to the throat and smashed her head into his. He released her, but she held onto him with her legs and slammed her elbow down on his nose. Manu groaned but didn't cry out—a detail that didn't escape her. He didn't want to raise the alarm. *He mustn't be allowed down here.*

Semra jumped to the ground and reached up her long sleeve to rip free the knife she'd bound to the underside of her arm. Manu kicked her in the stomach, and she flew backward, then used the wall to propel herself forward, ducking under his swing and stabbing upward at his torso as she passed under his arm. He went for her again, and she put him in a chokehold from behind, pulling with all her weight.

"He doesn't care about you," Semra hissed in his ear. "You were kidnapped from your village, not saved. It's all a lie."

Manu let out a guttural cry, then flipped her over his head and onto her back. Her breath whooshed from her body, and she desperately tried to suck in air, but her lungs refused to cooperate. Heavy footsteps came down the stairs. Semra rolled away, snatched the keyring from the ground and stashed it in the pocket of her apron.

Two guards materialized from the staircase and stared at Manu, who clutched at the wound in his torso. Semra pushed herself against the wall, curling in on herself, and held her hands out defensively. "Don't hurt me, please! Guards, help, help!"

"What's the meaning of this?" the first guard demanded.

Semra shook her head, catching her breath. "He's been ogling me all day. I don't think he even works here. He dragged me down here and attacked me!"

The first guard grabbed Manu by the arm and hauled him to his feet, and the second examined Semra's head. "You're bleeding," he said.

Semra noticed for the first time that a patch of hair on the side of her head was wet with blood, and a trickle ran down the side of her face. Semra felt okay, but she needed the guard to sympathize with her. She wavered and fell into the guard.

He caught her and stood her on her feet. "We need to get you to medical."

"I'm bleeding too," Manu spat out, "And she's not who she says she is!"

"Sorry excuse for a man," the guard standing with Semra said.

The first guard narrowed his eyes. "How'd you manage to get him so banged up?" he asked Semra.

"I ... shoved him down the stairs, and he dropped his knife. I took it."

The guard's eyes widened.

Semra glanced down and gasped at the bundle of candlesticks, which lay, dirty and broken, on the floor. "Oh, Garbane is going to kill me! *Kill* me! I know where medical is, I'll get there, but let me go make this right first. I haven't finished half my morning's work!"

The first guard snickered. "Garbane really might kill you," he said. "All right, but medical straight after, you hear?"

Semra nodded. "Thank you, thank you for saving me ... and you," she said, turning to Manu. "I really do wish you well. You're more than this."

Manu spat at her, eyes dark. Semra knew he wouldn't understand, but she'd meant what she'd said. She rushed up the two flights of stairs, and was running for the other spiral to the second floor when she heard a crash from down the passage. Guilt filled her, and she hoped the two guards would survive. If he killed them, Manu would need to come up with a good cover that wouldn't raise the alarm within the castle before tomorrow's gala.

She'd lost the knife she'd placed for easy access, and that frustrated her. The others she carried all hid under her cumbersome skirts—she'd have to move one up to her arm as soon as she got the chance. In the stairwell, Semra unwound the strips of cloth from her arm and dabbed at her head. Her dark hair would mask the color there, but not on her skin. She wiped at her face, licked her fingers and wiped again until she was satisfied that at least most of the blood was no longer so visible. A passing glance would get her past most people.

Instead of coming out on the second floor, Semra kept going up to the third floor, but she stopped when she heard voices coming from the top.

"If she's here, so is Siler. I'll take second. You take first."

Radix. But who was he talking to?

Semra's heart pounded as she retraced her steps back to the first floor and turned left down the long hall past the kitchen and servant-access stairway, and through a door that led to several meeting rooms of state. The first, grate-fully, was empty, and Semra moved quickly to the door on her left, hoping to exit out into the outer ward. Voices coming from the other side made her pause at the door.

"Thank you, General," she heard someone say. "Your attention to detail on these matters is invaluable to us."

Semra swore under her breath and turned instead to the far less appealing option of the open courtyard of the inner ward. It was too exposed. She hurried down the steps to the lower courtyard and slipped into the shadows of the fruit trees in the corner. As she did so, she noticed she was not alone. A bearded man no older than forty sat rather dejectedly on a bench in the shadows looking out over the rest of the courtyard, his back against the wall. Though dressed simply, his tunic and shoes were too nice to be a gardener.

Semra shifted her feet, unsure of what to do, and hid the mangled candlesticks behind her back. After a moment, she thought speaking was better than not ... giving a reason for her sudden appearance could remove questions and hope-fully resolve any urge the man had to tell someone of their encounter. If nothing else, it gave her a civilian to complicate matters if Radix found her.

"Excuse me, sir?" Semra asked tentatively. "I'm afraid I'm lost. Where are the catacombs? Someone said the stairs I need are by the catacombs, and I can't find them anywhere."

The man looked up at her, then glanced around himself. "I'm sorry, were you talking to me?"

Semra nodded.

The man parted his lips, then closed them. He smiled. "I'm afraid someone gave you terrible directions. The stairs near the catacombs are on the northeast of the residence, beneath Ancestry Hall ... the one with all the paintings. But few people go to the catacombs for any reason, so I don't see that as a reasonable instruction."

"Ahh. Thank you," Semra said, then fell silent.

The man looked up at her and cocked his head. "Not in a hurry then, I suppose?"

"If it's all the same to you, I think I'd rather wait a moment. I ... seem to have mangled my candlesticks, and I'm a little bit afraid of Garbane." Garbane had turned out more useful than she'd expected. The guard had confirmed his reputation in the castle as a bristly sort, so she doubled down on the strategy. Semra brought the candlesticks out from behind her back, and the man's eyes grew wide.

He laughed. "I see why you may need a moment to gather your courage. Don't let me stop you."

Something about this man felt soothing. He seemed gentle and kind. She wondered what kind of work he did in the castle and how long he'd served.

"What do you think of the king?" She asked softly. Her own question surprised her, but it had stumbled out before she could stop it. Someone working here for a long time might have a sense of the royal family, and Siler's question had come back to her. *What if we only exchange one tyrant for another?*

"The king?" The older man looked up in surprise. "How long have you worked here?"

"Just started."

"And how is it going so far?"

"It's going all right. I don't mind the work, but Saeb is a slave driver! I'll take Garbane any day."

The man laughed. "Is she now! I imagine she puts on a different tone when she serves the royal family. But she's a particular sort. I can't say it surprises me!"

"I am grateful to be here," Semra said slowly. "But my ... uncle always said he was a hard man. The king. He even said once that he was evil, though I'm not sure I believe it."

A shadow passed over the man's face, and he looked to her then like a much older man. Drawn. Worn. "You know," he began, "I think he does the best he can. But he doesn't always know if the best he can is good enough. He makes mistakes, but when others make mistakes, they are forgotten with time. His haunt him."

"Has he tried to make them right?"

"He tried. But I believe his efforts were wasted in youth's

thin promises. He didn't try well enough, and the chance was gone by the time he came to regret it. Even now, he seems faced with an impossible dilemma. Tell me, which is worse: a king letting his kingdom fall, or a father failing his daughter?"

Semra remained quiet. For a moment, all she could hear was the burble of the fountain and a bird call from far away. Something deep inside her resonated with its mournful cry. "I don't know."

The man let out a heavy sigh. "Alas, neither do I."

Realization hit her then like a slug in the gut. "You ... you're the king! Your Majesty!" She dropped to one knee, but he patted her shoulder tenderly and waved her off.

"Yes, yes. But I'm afraid most days there's nothing majestic about it, and no one to really talk to. Everyone has an opinion, and they're either squashing them to boost my ego or pushing their agendas. Is my daughter more important than the daughters of my people? And yet, if I withhold my instinct to protect her, what kind of man am I?"

Surely he spoke of the Princess Avaya's forthcoming betrothal to Prince Axis of Belvidore. Semra wondered what it would be like to have a father like this, protective and worried. She saw then that there was no concern at all of exchanging tyrant for tyrant, and respect for the man before her was born in that moment. Not as a king—she had learned long ago that all men sleep, all men bleed, and all men die, no matter their rank or riches. But here, in the shadow of the fruit trees as she awaited her own doom, she found admiration for a man and a father seeking what was right.

"Well, I must take my leave," said the king, standing. "Thank you, for your listening ear ... and maybe even for not knowing what your king looks like. It's good to be humbled now and then."

Semra curtsied and caught a twinkle in his eye as he squared his shoulders and walked up the steps and across the courtyard. She waited until the king disappeared through the doors, then walked to the tower of the inner wall and slipped into the corridor beneath the castle where she'd found herself that morning on her way in. She had to find Siler.

While weaving her way through the maze of tunnels and corridors under the castle, she found servants' quarters, an armory, guard rooms, a cobbler, and a blacksmith, all with high windows bringing light in from above ground. No one took any notice of her, and as she paused near the blacksmith, she heard several men speaking inside.

"Heard he was in Camar last time," said a voice. "But this time they said he was on a political tour starting in Kinlock."

"He's late this time though," said another. "And I'd wager the king won't send the prince out again so close to an important event like this. It's just so unusual, isn't it, for a prince to spend so much time away?"

"The king's brother certainly spent more time away than this. It bothers him. Maybe he wants to honor his brother's memory or something of that nature."

"Nobody said he was dead, just missing. Anyway, it's not my job to worry about where our little princeling might find himself. If he's late, he'll answer for it, and it's no business of mine!"

Semra mulled the words over. Could she have been wrong about the hit? Maybe they found him and took him out early. Her breathing quickened, and she hurried down the passage, but still found no sign of Siler.

The conservatory. Dahyu had mentioned a conservatory

on the third floor of the castle. A place where plants needed tending would fit his cover, and it was only one room over from the walkway overlooking the Great Hall. By now Radix and whoever he'd spoken to would've long since completed their sweep of the first and second floors of the residence and could be anywhere. Though it was dangerous to return to the keep, she needed to try. Perhaps she could find Dahyu's father, the king's valet, and speak to him directly. *Or maybe I'd just get myself arrested*, she thought dryly. A nice little box to make her assassination easier on Radix.

Semra angled toward the servants' quarters. Rooms lined the right side of a long hall, with small windows opening into the hall, and chairs set in a modest common area held a few bags and belongings. Semra placed her mangled candlesticks in a barrel for trash, then snatched a hair wrap draped over a chair as she walked. She took the keyring out of her apron pocket and pulled her curly hair back and through the ring, using the hair wrap to cover both the blood in her hair and the dangling keys. She tied it snuggly beneath her ponytail, pulled off her apron as she walked past a servant's room, and tossed it through the open window. Even small changes to her appearance were worth making.

Careful to avoid the west side where the guard rooms and armories congregated, Semra made her way back to the servants' staircase on the first floor, then up to the second and straight up to the third. The door at the end of the hall creaked open. Semra slipped further down and across the hall into an open door. She stood on the other side of the door against the wall, and discovered that she'd entered a lavish sitting room with red couches and cushioned chairs.

"And what do you think of him?"

Semra started. The elegant lady from the walkway over the Great Hall that morning sat in one of the oversized cushion chairs, a fur blanket draped over her lap. A lady in waiting perched on the edge of the sofa, and both looked at Semra. It'd been the princess who'd spoken.

"Your Highness?" Semra asked, unsure of what was happening.

"We were just discussing Prince Axis of Belvidore. We've heard he is quite handsome, though perhaps stiff-necked. What do you think?"

Semra opened her mouth, closed it, and swallowed. "I think it's not my job to think, Highness," she said softly, listening as heavy footsteps approached and stopped right outside.

"Your Highness," said a voice not two feet from Semra on the other side of the door. "My apologies for the intrusion. Has one of the chandler girls made it up here? She would be new."

"Sakes alive, Rodoras, have you nothing better to do?" the princess asked, irritation seeping into her tone. "Wax in the laundry, and now this? Is Belon really so short of capable workers that she has you searching the grounds for every useless newcomer?"

"Princess Avaya, I meant no rudeness, only to—"

"Only to do her work for her by interrupting the few moments of solitude I have left? Here I am, retiring to the private royal-family sitting room to contemplate my father's ill-conceived peacemaking and my impending marriage, only to have people continually popping in for this thing or that! I've seen no one, and unless you have juicy gossip or intriguing idle prattle to share, you'd best be off. And tell Belon if she's afraid of Saeb, she should be more afraid of me."

Semra heard the clink of armor as the guard bowed and

made a quick exit. Semra heaved a sigh of relief, and the princess looked on her with renewed interest.

"Any chance *you* are the missing chandler girl?"

"I'm afraid not, Highness," Semra replied. "Though she does seem to be missing. Belon loaned me to Garbane when I finished my morning chores early."

Avaya furrowed an eyebrow. "I see. I admit I was rather hoping you were the missing girl, and I was making Belon a little crazy. No matter. Now, no excuses, I need a distraction. Teriv here heard Axis was a menace, absolutely dreadful, though she made me beg before she told me so. But I have also heard he is fond of women."

"Fondness of women rarely leads to greatness, in my limited experience," Semra replied. "But being stiff-necked could also just mean committed to values the person spreading the rumor didn't like."

Avaya smiled. "I like this one," she said to Teriv, who smiled back. "And what do you think of my father's peace-making? Should a kingdom like Belvidore be trusted? It was in my father's lifetime that they laid waste our southeastern border, all for spite. Surely you know, don't you, how he scorned their offer of allegiance through marriage? My grandparents tried to end the conflict by an arranged marriage between my father and the Belvidorian princess, and my father ruined it. I love my mother, but she wasn't royalty. And now he tries to patch up his own mistakes with me."

Semra paused, unsure what to say. The picture the princess painted was in such stark contrast to the gentle man she'd met in the lower courtyard.

"Oh, you're boring after all, boring!" she proclaimed, after a moment of Semra's silence. "I thought you were fresh and interesting and wouldn't coddle me. But here you are tongue-tied after all. Go, go."

Princess Avaya dismissed Semra with a wave of her hand. Semra curtsied quickly before exiting, then headed quickly down the hall and through the door into the upper half of Ancestry Hall. She glanced over the rail at several staff members passing by below, picked up her pace, and slipped through a tall door onto the Great Hall's walkway, which crossed the width of the hall to a guard tower—the only position from which the entire room could be seen.

Semra's stomach churned at how perfect the trusted guard position would be for Radix. Would he be the lookout or the target operative? With multiple people on the mission, one would be observing, likely from this spot or lying down on the less-visible walkway running the length of the room, with others in the crowd ...

Semra hugged the wall as she followed the path to the end of the long hall, grateful for the columns that provided some limited cover. On the other side, a tall door to her right led to a circular sitting room, and the door in front would open into the conservatory.

As she reached for the handle, Semra heard a shout behind her and turned just in time to see a guard racing down the walkway after her. She whirled around, pushed through the door, and looked about frantically for something with which to bar the door. The lofted glass ceiling above her filled the room with an airy light, and greenery lined the walls and wound around four pillars in the corners. Flowers planted in a built-in compartment holding soil sat in the middle of a round stone table in the center, but none of the trees had sturdy enough branches, and no ceremonial swords hung on the wall to fit in the door's handle. But a glass sliding door led out to a balcony.

Semra threw it open, ran to the edge of the balcony, and looked out. The library would be directly beneath her feet, and though it had windows, none of them opened. Running footsteps slowed just outside the conservatory door. Semra shut the sliding door behind her, grabbed the baluster with both hands and, just as the guard entered, swung herself over the railing to dangle four floors above the outer ward.

15

Semra listened anxiously, her feet swaying beneath her. Footsteps crossed the room above her, and muffled voices drifted through the door. Sweat beaded on her hands, threatening her grip on the baluster. One finger slipped off, and Semra grimaced as she struggled to keep her hold.

The footsteps hurried away down the hall, and for a moment all was quiet. She couldn't keep going like this—it was now or never. She rocked her legs back and forth, aiming to build enough momentum to catch her foot on the balustrade, but her left arm lost its hold. Panic rose in her chest, and she felt a burning in the mark of the dragon's kiss.

Suddenly Semra felt Zezura's distress at feeling her fear, and she knew the dragon would be flying for the castle. Semra willed herself to calm, focusing on sending Zezura the message through her emotions. No, don't come. She wouldn't get there in time, and if she came, any pretense at subtlety would be destroyed.

The fingers of her right hand started to slip, and just as

she reached up to clutch at the balustrade with her left, the sliding door opened and a firm grasp took hold of her wrist. Semra looked up, and saw with relief that Dahyu peered down at her, his strong grip securing her to the balcony. She swung her legs up and caught the balcony with her foot, then pulled herself up on the outside of the railing. A shout rang out from the outer ward far below. She glanced down. A guard stared up at her, then took off around the side of the castle.

Dahyu slipped his arm around her waist and pulled her back over the balcony. "You seem to be having a busy day."

"I could have pulled myself up," she answered, squelching the gratitude she'd felt at seeing his face.

"Sure, sure." He rolled his eyes. "That much was obvious."

"What are you up here for?" she asked, looking him over head to toe. He wore a long-sleeved white tunic under a well-made green vest and black trousers. "Rats and rot, you look like a noble!"

Dahyu grinned. "If I'm going to be rubbing shoulders with the nobility and standing in for the governor, I thought I should look the part. Came up to find my father but haven't had any luck."

Semra nodded. "I've seen two assassins planted in the castle already, one as a guard, another as ... I'm not sure if he had a real cover. The guard, Radix, is going by the name Felgan and is sending the rest of them after me."

Dahyu's eyes widened. "Come on, we have to get you out of here." He grabbed her by the hand and pulled her along behind him into the anteroom.

She tried to shake off his hand, but his grip tightened. "A low-level servant and a noble holding hands, how will that look?" she hissed.

He pulled her through the anteroom and into a circular living room. Windows all around shone light on a beautiful gilded desk, green-velvet seats set against the stone walls, and heavy drapes pulled back on the sides of the windows. A large furnace sat to the left of the door, with the carved profile of some famous ancestor or other set above it. Two-foot-tall bronze statues of guards holding shields embossed with the Jannemar crest stood proudly up high between the windows, surrounded by intricate designs which rose to a vaulted ceiling accented by an elaborate golden chandelier.

Dahyu drew her behind a drape in the small space inset between the curtain and the window as a guard walked by at a brisk pace. He smiled. "Stranger things have happened," he whispered. "After all, you are a beautiful woman, and I am only a man."

Semra's heart quickened as she stared back at him, unsure of herself. It wasn't the hungry look she'd seen in Javed at Governor Mallen's residence, nor was it passive, but she felt at once the tenderness in his eyes and the solidity of his statement. She looked away, distracting herself with the magnificence of the room. "Is this ... are we where I think we are?"

"The king's private living quarters and study."

"We can't stay here."

"Certainly not. We'll go through the bedchamber."

"Are you entirely insane?"

"Hmm. I don't think so. At least, not entirely. But I'm not convinced I would actually know if I were, you know?"

"What if, oh I don't know, the king is in his room?"

"He's not," Dahyu assured her. "And my father's room— the valet, you'll remember—is attached to it. I just checked before stumbling across you, and he's not there either. It will give us some distance from the guards, who won't go in there, and also get us on the other side of the stairs. We just can't go through the queen's chambers, because I do think she's in there. The alarm raised from your balcony stunt will get the guards here in the next minute or two, so we have to move fast. Stay close."

Dahyu led them out a door next to the fireplace and into a lavish bedroom housing a large, canopied bed. Exquisite, golden-inlaid designs decorated the walls, and expansive murals covered the ceilings. A large vanity sat on one side, a desk on the other, and a crystal chandelier hung from the ceiling. Another fireplace sat on the far side of the massive room. Of the two doors, one at either end, one led to the hall and the other straight into the valet's room.

In awe of the extravagant trappings of royalty, Semra stopped. She'd seen great wealth, but nothing like this. But even as she stood, she heard more shouts and feet pounding up the stairs outside.

"No time! Let's go!" Dahyu grabbed her by the arm and tugged her through the door into the much smaller and simpler valet's room. From there they raced into the hall and down past the queen's bedchamber and personal living room.

"So many rooms!" Semra cried in dismay as they pushed through another door at the end.

The room they entered next was a massive hall twice the size of the library and nearly as long as Ancestry Hall.

"Diplomats and fancy people of the court meet here to await the king," Dahyu said as they ran through. "The throne room is just on the other side. Come on!"

Semra ripped her arm free and stopped in her tracks. "Are you crazy? We need to get down! You're going to get us trapped!" She'd seen it from the air. There were no stairs at the end of the throne room, only windows lining the sides and a rounded back end where the throne sat on a dais.

"Do you trust me?"

"Not particularly."

A crash sounded down the hall behind them, and a woman's shocked voice called out, only to be muffled by the clinking sound of multiple men in armor running down the hall. The sound of a sword slithering from its sheath rang out through the wall.

"Well, if you want to live, you're going to have to try. You've run out of options!"

Semra threw her hands up in defeat. The room opened to three large archways. They ran through the middle one and up steps to the main throne room. Gold-inlaid pillars flanked sparkling-white marble floors and meticulous gold designs reached up to the arched ceilings soaring above them. Tall windows lined both sides, and Semra blinked in the bright light as they ran the long length of the empty room to the dais. Two great high-backed golden thrones, set against a rich-blue background, nestled into the rounded curve of the back of the building.

"*This* was your amazing plan?" Semra said. "Get killed, not only for breaking into the castle, but also for getting caught in the throne room itself?"

"Have a little faith." Dahyu grabbed her hand and pulled her up the dais next to the thrones. "I'm not so dim as you might think."

"Well, you aren't looking too bright from where I'm standing."

"That's because you're standing in the wrong spot." He placed his hands on her shoulders, maneuvered her behind the thrones, and reached down underneath the king's seat.

"What are you ... *ahhhhh!*"

Just as the guards poured into the throne room, the floor beneath her feet moved. A small portion of the wall behind the thrones rotated, swiveling her and Dahyu around. He planted his hand over her mouth until they were safely on the other side of the false wall in a three-foot-wide space between two semi-circular walls.

Dahyu reached into a one-inch depression where the floor met the inner wall and pulled a handle. The other half of the floor pulled away, revealing a narrow staircase winding downward. He ushered her forward, and Semra eagerly took the stairs. Once inside, Dahyu released a pulley, sealing them into the staircase in the dark.

"We should be safe in here," he said. "It doesn't open up to any of the other underground areas, and none of the regular guards are aware of it."

"You sneaky little thing!" Semra exclaimed. "Okay, maybe you're smarter than you look."

"Ahh, thank you, thank you. And what exactly, if I may be so bold, do I look like?"

"Nothing, in this darkness. And normally ... um, you look nice." Semra blushed, and something in her stomach suddenly didn't quite agree with her.

"Nice, hmm? I'll take it." She heard a smile in his voice.

They descended slowly in blackness for a moment, accompanied only by the echo of their footsteps, the cold of the stone walls, and a deep dark.

"So, have you decided I'm not so repulsive?" Semra said.

"Repulsive! I can hardly imagine thinking you so."

"Really? Because in the woods, when you found out what I am, you were horrified. Don't say you weren't, because you were; I saw it all over your face."

Dahyu fell silent, and Semra wished she could read his

expression. She waited a beat, two beats, and spoke again. "Not only was I a killer, I was unsportsmanlike."

"I'm sorry."

"That doesn't answer my question."

"Listen, I ... can't pretend it's easy to see how murder is like any other job. You haven't exactly given me much chance to get to know you, your perspective on it, or your experience."

"We haven't had a good opportunity for it. And I don't make friends easily."

"I think that makes sense, given ... given your history. I have thought a lot about it, though, and like I said before, I think your heart may be different from what your occupation suggests. You were forced into it. That must have been terrible."

Now it was Semra's turn to remain silent for a spell. When she spoke, she was slow and deliberate. "It was, and it wasn't. I remember the night the dragon came. A vague flash of my mother, something about dinnertime, all I can remember of her. My ball rolled out the door, and I went outside to get it. I would only be gone for a minute ... " Semra felt a catch in her throat, and tears sprang to her eyes. She was grateful for the darkness.

"What happened?" Dahyu said gently.

"I felt this powerful blast of wind and was suddenly wrenched up off the ground. I screamed and reached down and felt these huge claws around me, and I looked up and saw him—Rotokas—flying above me, outlined against the moon." Semra shuddered. "He brought me into the mountain, and that's when I met Adis and some of the others, and they congratulated me and said I was brave and that they'd saved me from horrible people. That my parents never loved me, that they wanted me to leave them, that they abandoned me. And then they introduced me to the Framatar."

"How old were you?"

"Four."

"Wow. And this Framatar guy, who is he?"

"Nobody knows. Well, I imagine the commander and some of the others know, but everyone just calls him the Framatar. Siler says it means 'lord' or 'dragonlord.'"

"And they train you as assassins when you're a teenager?"

"They start with doctrine, philosophy, basic knife and fighting tactics at age four when you come into the mountain. By six or seven you clean weapons, go to classes, start learning to hunt small game and dress prey. By thirteen and fourteen, kids are assisting and observing missions, then running missions under supervision in practicum at fifteen, and graduating mission ready at sixteen."

"And you're how old?"

"Seventeen."

"So you've been doing ... er, missions, on your own for a year?"

"Two, actually. I graduated a year early."

Dahyu whistled. "That's wild."

Semra shrugged, though she knew he couldn't see it. "It was my normal."

They reached the bottom of the stairs, and Dahyu took her arm and guided her through a maze of turns and straights, sometimes pausing and feeling for openings. Twice they ran straight into walls.

"So why did you leave? Why are you so focused on saving the prince instead of just starting over somewhere?"

"I hate running with a cloud over my head that he'll find me, you know? The Framatar is a very powerful man. So there's that. But I need to expose him for what he's done, to save my friends ... Well, I guess I don't really have friends, exactly, but colleagues at least. And children. Lesala was trying to get back to her family and putting up a big fuss, so they were going to kill her. When I heard that, I knew I couldn't wait any longer.

"Saving the prince is three-fold. One, I keep the Framatar from ripping apart another family. Two, I foil his plans and piss him off. I like that idea. And three, once I piss him off, I'm going to need some help fighting him and his personal syndicate of brainwashed assassins. I figure a king should have the manpower, and I can provide the know-how."

"You've thought this through."

"I'm an assassin. Killing is only ten percent of the job. The rest is thinking."

Silence settled over them as they made their way through passage after passage, listening to their own footsteps as they padded along. Semra wondered how far they were from the residence. It seemed they'd walked for long enough to get beyond the walls.

"What will you do if you can't find the prince?" Dahyu asked at last.

"I'm starting to wonder if they changed their plans, found him, and went ahead and killed him. He was apparently expected to arrive in the castle by now. If I can't find the prince, and I don't see anything shady at the gala, I'll have no leg to stand on as far as evidence goes to get the king on my side. I'm really not sure what I would do, though I'm convinced the king is next on the list."

"How can you protect someone you've never met?"

"It's logistically a bit harder than killing someone you've never met, I admit," she replied. "I hoped to have more time to lay out all the most likely positions, then map out primary and secondary entry and exit routes. Once inside, Siler and I could work together to identify and eliminate the threats, then reveal them to the king, and that evidence would hopefully be enough to get us pardoned for waltzing in uninvited. I assume it would earn us an audience, at least, even if arrested."

"Gutsy. Risky."

"Sure, but in my line of work, that's business as usual. Even getting caught can be okay, as long as it's part of the plan and you have an exit strategy."

"What's your exit strategy for tomorrow?"

"Don't have one."

"And your entry?"

"It's all ruined. I mapped out a good amount of the underground networks, but not nearly thoroughly enough, and I ran into Radix far too early in the day. My cover is blown."

"Maybe the king's security will catch the plot before anything truly terrible happens."

"Dahyu, you don't understand. I ran into two of the Framatar's assassins today, but I didn't see Tymetin, and I know he's assigned to Prince Zephan. The assassins could be on the king's security. There are a few sleepers I'm unaware of, but I know what to look for. And Siler and I are the royal family's only hope of recognizing those that live in the mountain."

"What do you need?"

Semra scoffed. "Need? I need three months of planning, connections, routines, an event schedule, attendance list, and weapons stashed in every corner of the building. I need a cover that will either prevent me from being recognized for a significant portion of time, or be protected and obvious enough that taking me out in the crowd would do more harm than good. And for goodness' sake, I need an entry and exit strategy! More than one."

Dahyu stopped, then turned down a new corridor. "Okay," he said slowly. "You're blown, but I'm not. Your people won't be expecting my connection with you. I'll see what I can do."

"How much farther?" Semra asked.

"Not far."

"Where does it let out?"

"Outskirts of Qalea. Actually, not too far from our rendezvous point."

"Are there any hidden passageways from the second floor?"

"None that I know of, no."

A needling question burned in her brain, and she couldn't hold it in anymore. "How do you know all of this?"

"I ... I've spent a lot of time in the castle."

Semra's blood turned to ice in her veins. Something wasn't right. "Did you now?" She slowly brought her arms up in a defensive posture, the action hidden by the darkness.

"Between assisting the governor and visiting my father, I feel I practically grew up here. My father has served the king for twenty years."

"And how many governors are aware of the tunnels we're in right now?"

Dahyu said nothing.

Semra's heart beat wildly, and she felt a pit in her stomach. *He's not who he says he is, and now he's realized his mistake.*

Dahyu cleared his throat. "None."

Semra's fingers itched; she suddenly wished the knives on her thighs were more easily accessible. If Dahyu wasn't who he said he was, there was no other option, he must be working for the Framatar. Perhaps he was one of the sleepers. And Semra, like a moron, had told him absolutely everything she knew of the plot and all she'd hoped to do about it.

When she spoke, she couldn't hide the edge to her tone.

"How is it, then, that the governor's aide and the son of the king's valet—someone not even on the king's staff and hardly even in his court—would know of secret passageways the guards themselves are not privy to?"

16

Dahyu stopped and Semra, unable to see him in the blackness, ran into him. Tension filled the air until she felt she'd choke on it, but Dahyu finally broke the silence.

"The personal servant to the king is often his closest confidant. My father has been working for the king for longer than he has been king. I'm not a gossip, and I don't easily divulge secrets that aren't mine to share. The only reason you know about it is because I wanted to save your life and saw no better way. I'd appreciate it if you gave your word not to ruin the centuries-old secret that could get my father killed if it got out."

Semra's mind raced like a thousand galloping horses, threatening to run away with her. Anger, guilt, and confusion mixed together in a complicated cauldron of emotion in her chest. Something was off. He was lying—she could feel it in her bones. Still, his explanation made some sense. On the one hand, why would his father break the king's confidence by sharing such a high-security piece of intelli-

gence with his son? On the other hand, perhaps it was difficult to be the confidant of a king with no real confidant of
his own.

Unsure of what to think, Semra decided that playing
along for now would serve her purposes no matter where the
truth lay. "I'm sorry. I just ... I'm not used to trusting people,
and it didn't add up. Forgive me."

"It's okay. Thanks."

Dahyu reached out with his hands and felt along the
wall. "Ah! Here it is. They're hand and footholds. Would you
like to go first, or would you like me to go first?"

The question caught Semra off guard. "You first. Please."

"Very well. Here, I'm reaching for your hand to show you
where the first rung is ... there you go. It should lift up to a
disguised forest floor."

Dahyu climbed a few rungs and Semra pulled herself up
behind him before he pushed up a lid, allowing light to filter
into the tunnel. Dahyu climbed out and reached back down
for Semra. She allowed him to help her out of the tunnel,
which came out right next to a large trunked tree in the
woods. Leaves and other such things covered the lid so that
when placed back in the ground it looked undisturbed.

Dahyu spread more leaves and brush over the edges of
the entrance, turned to Semra, and smiled. "Well, it feels
good not to be chased, doesn't it!"

"I'm still being chased. I just can't see my pursuers
anymore. But yes, it's nice." Semra smiled back.

"Listen. I know today didn't go the way you'd hoped, and
certainly not how I would've wanted either, but we can't give
up on protecting the gala, so I'm headed back to the castle.
I'll meet you tonight, okay? Anything you need?"

Semra shrugged. "Try not to get yourself suspected or
killed. Find out any word on the prince. If someone in the

castle knows where he is, chances are the assassins do too. And if you see Siler, tell him to get out of there."

Dahyu left, leaving Semra with her thoughts as she trudged through the woods back toward the rendezvous point. Though she was in a different part of the forest than they'd used the night before, it was the same patch of woods, and Semra was concerned now that they'd be found. She hoped the buzz in the castle would be distracting enough to keep the assassins from looking for them on the outskirts. The chances of them searching the whole wood successfully was low, particularly considering Siler and Semra's work at concealing the previous night's campsite. Nevertheless, the possibility made her nervous, and as soon as Siler and Dahyu had both returned, Semra would insist they move again.

She'd come out into the woods not far from the outer ward, but further than she'd expected. As she walked, her mind took off again, and she revisited again and again their conversation as he'd helped her navigate the underground network, particularly that squirrelly little pause he'd made when she asked him how a governor's aide could know so much.

What if he was telling the truth? What if he'd saved her life, used sensitive information to get her safely out of the castle, and now she'd insulted him by insinuating he was a liar? Something inside her still whispered like warning bells in her ears. What if he had deceived her? Then she'd really be as stupid as the Framatar would say she was.

For a moment, Semra found herself reliving the escape with Dahyu: the way he'd wrapped his arm around her waist on the balcony, held her hand, called her beautiful as they hid in the king's living room. The tenderness in his eyes. *It's all a lie, Semra. Did you really convince yourself he cared for you?*

How could she have been so stupid? And yet, he said such

strange, thoughtful things that seemed to pull at her very soul. Surprising things. He'd sought to understand her when she explained her history to him. She was never that open with anyone. Why was it so easy to tell him more than she'd intended to? *He's a master manipulator, Semra. He has you right where he wants you. Fool!*

Still, if he worked for the Framatar, he'd be accustomed to killing, but when Semra and Siler had revealed they were assassins, she'd seen genuine surprise in his deep-amber eyes. She thought of how it felt to be in his strong arms on the balcony and behind the curtain ... Semra slapped herself on the cheek. Ridiculous. What was happening to her?

When she reached their designated meeting place beneath a large oak tree, she hiked up her skirts and climbed. Fifteen feet up, she reached into a hollow in the tree, retrieved her pants, and pulled them on under her skirts, then stashed her shoes in the hollow. Finally feeling a bit more herself, she found a perch twenty feet up to wait. Her black pants protected her legs, and she bunched the troublesome skirt of her dress up around her waist. Since it was now only early afternoon, it'd be quite some time before she could expect Siler and Dahyu to return, so she wedged herself against the trunk between two branches, put her head back against the tree, and let herself drift off to sleep.

Early in the evening, a sound startled Semra awake. Snap, crunch. She froze, then eased a hand onto one of the knives on her leg. Someone was walking just below her in the woods. When a low whistle mimicked a bird call, Semra relaxed. She sent out an answering call and craned her neck around the tree trunk to see Siler jump.

He looked up the tree and grinned at her, then climbed up to join her. "Did you miss me?" He laughed, taking in the strange sight of the dress on her upper half and pants protruding out the bottom. "You couldn't stand the skirt, could you?"

Semra shook her head. "I never can! What happened? Did you see Radix?"

Siler nodded. "Yes. But he didn't see me. Have you been back long?"

"Ha! Yes. It was early afternoon when we made it out. Radix saw me and sent the guards on a chase after me. I was cornered and almost didn't make it out. Dahyu found me and got me out."

He raised an eyebrow. "Dahyu?"

"He knew a secret way out. I think he lied about how he knew, but I just ... I just don't know. If he was working for the Framatar, wouldn't he have killed me already?"

"Not necessarily. Maybe they have something else in mind, or maybe you'd be a good fall guy. Where is this entrance?"

"It's a better way out than a way in, I think," she replied. "And if he's working for the Framatar, they'll suspect we'll go in that way and have it watched. If he's not working for the Framatar ... well, it was a secret, and I'd hate to cause more trouble for him if he really is honest."

"Honest! Semra, no one is honest. You're too good, too good for your own good! Where is he now?"

"He went back to the castle to try to get another way in for me tomorrow and some of the reconnaissance I wasn't able to get today."

"Good. We have time to come up with a plan then. We need to keep eyes on him and have something up our sleeves he doesn't know about, just in case."

"I have one thing." Semra untied her hair wrap, pulled her hair down, and removed the key ring, then held it up for Siler.

Siler whistled. "How'd you get this? Where do they go?"

"Manu was down there. He wasn't supposed to be though, so I'm not sure if he had a cover or not. I don't think he did. I found a shelf in the cliff behind the Dezapi Falls when I was flying with Zezura, and there's a door back there that only opens from the inside. I went down the stairs beneath Ancestry Hall trying to find a way to connect down there, and I think it's near the catacombs. There were two doors, both locked, and Manu was coming out the door on the left when I saw him."

Siler's eyes widened. "What did you do?"

Semra explained what had happened. "I'm not sure how bad he's cut, and I don't know which key leads to that door. I'm sorry. I know you two were friends."

"Friend*ly*, yes. I'm not really *friends* with anyone." Siler's steel-gray eyes took on a far-off look, and Semra wondered where his mind had wandered off to. He shook it off, and turned to Semra. "They wouldn't have been expecting that, so whatever he was doing, you've thrown a wrench into that plan. Are you okay? Did you ... is that blood in your hair?"

"What? Oh, probably. I mean, we did fight, after all."

"Not as delicate as you look, hmm?"

"I do not look delicate!"

Siler laughed. "Not easily offended, either I see! Come on, let me look at it."

"It's fine."

"Well then this won't take very long, will it?" Siler hoisted himself up on the branch beside Semra, held onto a neighboring branch with his left hand, and gently tilted her head with the other. Semra pressed her lips together and stared off into the distance while Siler brushed the hair away from her face, took the hair wrap and dabbed carefully at the area.

"No more bleeding, and it doesn't look that bad."

"Told you."

"Does it hurt when I touch it?"

"No," Semra lied. "It's fine."

"Okay, okay. Gee, head injuries make you irritable!"

Semra rolled her eyes but couldn't help but smile.

"Oh no!" Siler gasped in mock surprise. "And your eyes are rolling all over the place! You'll never shoot straight again! All right you, look here for a minute, let me check your pupils."

Semra turned to face him and let her deep-brown eyes settle into Siler's stormy gray ones.

He looked intently at her for several moments before breaking contact. "You know," he said slowly, "once this is all over, and we have to start somewhere new, there are worse people to spend time with than you."

Taken aback, Semra opened her mouth, closed it, then opened it again. "Wh ... I ... " she began, frustrated with herself for the jumbled mess that came out of her mouth.

"Ah, yes. Slurred speech! I'm afraid you're worse off than we thought." He tapped his temple and raised an eyebrow, then settled back on the branch.

Semra ignored his last comment and tried again. "I don't know what I'll do when this is over. We don't even know yet if it will ever be over."

"Of course it will. Either the Framatar and his minions— by which I mean our colleagues, of course—are too strong for us and we die, or we somehow turn the tables and they die. Or at least are thwarted, disbanded, and scattered to the winds."

Semra examined Siler, surprised to find no trace of mockery, just an earnestness and intensity. "If we live, which is a rather sizable 'if' at this point, how would we even begin to start over? What else can we do?"

Siler shrugged. "We could work commission. Selective targets, nasty people only, and employers with deep pockets."

Semra grimaced. "I'm done with this work."

"No problem. With that kind of money, I'll work, and you can hang out in the villa we will inevitably live in, doing whatever you want."

"So now I'm going to be a slob?"

"A slob to keep me company, yes! Or you could go around saving little kids and such, I suppose. Whatever makes you happy."

Semra laughed, but then shook her head. "This is weird to talk about. And I can't live in a house bought with blood, no matter how dark that blood may be."

"You're resourceful, but you don't have any other skills. We could learn something new, maybe, but no one is going to understand you like one of your own. You know how Dahyu looked at us when he found out. He thinks we're monsters, Semra. They'd all think we're monsters if they learned the truth. Think on it."

17

Zezura made her way back early that evening, depositing a freshly killed sheep at the base of Semra's tree. Semra wrinkled her nose. "Um ... thank you?"

Zezura danced her head sideways back and forth and bounced on her giant toes, excitement rolling off her in waves.

Siler laughed. "You aren't going to let free mutton go to waste, are you? Look how proud of herself she is!"

Semra climbed down the tree and examined the sheep. She patted Zezura on the neck and smiled. "Good work, Zezura. Looks like we have ourselves a big meal tonight! I'm cutting around the teeth marks though. I don't know where those daggers have been."

Zezura lay down next to Semra as she went to work cutting up the meat.

Siler set up sticks for a campfire and gestured to Zezura. "Okay, do your thing."

Zezura huffed on the sticks, and they caught aflame.

Siler shook his head. "This is the life! Dragons are handy to have around. Except ... do dragons ever get colds? I don't think I'd want dragons sneezing all over everything."

Semra laughed, and as she removed the prime pieces of meat from the sheep, she turned to Zezura. "All right, go ahead. We won't eat the rest of that."

Zezura pounced on the remains of the sheep, tossed it up in the air, then ripped it to pieces, gulping down large chunks.

Semra winced as she heard a bone snap. "They certainly are noisy eaters."

The sheep roasted nicely, and at dusk, when Siler and Semra were finishing their meal, Dahyu approached from the north.

"This is how I found you last evening!" he said, greeting them with a smile. "Here, I brought you some bread, too. You need something to eat other than roots and squirrels." Dahyu reached into a bag and tossed them each a roll.

"Thanks!" Siler said. "And this is sheep. Courtesy of Zezura. I'm hoping she flew a while to get it and didn't terrorize Qalea."

"There's not been any dragon sightings reported in the castle, so that's a good sign," Dahyu said.

Semra smiled. "Great. So what did you find out?"

"The prince has been in communication with someone in the castle and will attend the gala tomorrow. I think he'll arrive in the morning. Our Belvidorian guests staying in the castle will have their bags sent to their rooms in advance of the gala, and attendees will be announced as they arrive in the Great Hall."

"Wonderful," Semra said. "What's our way in? Locked trunk? Catacombs? Out through the garderobe chute?"

Dahyu wrinkled his nose and drew back. "You want to climb out through the toilet?"

"I want to be undetectable and go places people won't follow."

"If there's any other option, I'll be one of those people who don't follow you there!" Siler said. "Although it is, of course, a strategic option. Which means the Framatar's team has already thought about it. I bet they'll have a man watching the chutes."

Semra shook her head. "They can't have everything watched all the time."

"I applaud your dedication, but that wouldn't work anyway," Dahyu said. "There's a grate inside the chute to prevent any unwanted visitors. I'm not sure anything is less appealing than an attacker coming up from below when you are ... um ... exposed."

Siler chuckled. "All right, then, what have you got? I can't be a gardener again."

"The Belvidorian royal family and nobles are staying on the second floor in the guest apartments. Security will be tighter than usual, but Belvidore will have servants with them, and if you come with the luggage, you should get through without an issue. I know the man who hires supplement staff, so I'll get him to put you on the list of Belvidorian servants also. Once inside, you'll need to change into Jannemar serving staff attire to get access to the third floor and the walkway over the Great Hall, for visibility from above."

Siler raised his eyebrows. "I'm impressed."

"Wonderful," Semra agreed. "What do you have for me? A deep disguise, maybe, something not requiring skirts?"

Dahyu smiled nervously. "Well, remember when you said you needed the attendance list, an event schedule, and some way to make it too gutsy to kill you to be worth their while?"

She groaned. "Tell me you didn't. Tell me I'm not going to be someone people notice and stare at. What am I, part of the entertainment? I don't do performances."

Dahyu shook his head. "Not entertainment. A guest."

"What are you talking about? The attendance list will have been finalized forever ago."

"Yes, but Lady Generiva Swathel will be unable to attend. She is, however, sending a lesser-known noblewoman, Axelia Berinon, in her stead."

Semra's mouth dropped open.

Siler clapped his hands and howled. "An esteemed lady of the court! Ha! Oh, and you thought the servant skirts were bad. You'll love the extravagant, pompous dress of nobility. Maybe you can even wear a train."

Dahyu corrected him. "None of them will be wearing trains. They'll need to be able to dance."

"I can't dance," Semra said flatly.

Siler stroked his chin. "It's not a bad idea actually. It's bold, but it gets you access to everything you need without having to go back and forth to a kitchen or other serving area. You can stay on the floor the whole time, near the royal family, and blend in with all the other fancy-haired women in attendance."

"I can't dance!" Semra repeated. "And I don't have nearly enough money for some precious gown, even if I had time to arrange for it! Do you know how much time ladies of leisure spend primping for events like this?"

The corner of Dahyu's mouth twitched upward. "I do. I have an in with one of the Jannemar guests. She's agreed to help get you in, let you borrow one of her dresses, and get you ready. The dancing part we'll have to take care of tonight."

"An in? Who are you telling our business to exactly?" Siler demanded.

Semra swallowed. "You're teaching me to dance? In one night?"

Dahyu held his hands up. "In my defense, the list of needs was long, and we are short on time. I spoke to the fewest possible people to make the covers the best they could be to keep you both from being murdered. Pardon me for my thoroughness. As for the dancing? Um, yes. We're going to do the best we can."

"How critical is it that I know how to dance?"

"That's a stupid question, Semra," Siler said. "You know your cover requires it, and someone might ask you to dance."

"I could say no."

"Unless it becomes more strategic to accept. Perhaps a dance could help you cross the floor to get somewhere you want to go," Siler reminded her.

Dahyu furrowed his eyebrows and cocked his head. "You'd think I suggested torture, the way you two are going on. It's just a dance. It won't kill you."

"Easy for you to say," Semra muttered. "Is it a big dress? How big are we talking? How will I get to my weapons? There's no time for alterations."

"I'm sure you can wear your knives like you always do," Dahyu replied, offering Semra his hand. "Though certainly not the dagger. But you're resourceful."

Semra eyed him skeptically, but let him pull her to her feet. "Do any of these dresses have a laced bodice or bow or some other unnecessary frill I can unravel quickly?"

"Ah, there's our fine gentlewoman!" Siler laughed.

"Demure damsel, unable to stow daggers in her skirts, preparing instead to strangle people."

Semra sent him a dark glare, but Dahyu smiled as he pulled her toward him with an arm about her waist and the other holding her hand. "I have no doubt you'll figure something out."

He moved her other hand up to his shoulder, slipped his arm back around her waist, and tapped a rhythm against the small of her back. "One and two and three ... "

Semra looked up at him uncertainly, tripping over her own feet as he moved her across the forest floor. He stopped intermittently to explain how to work within the count of the music, where to step, and how to move.

"You'll need to remember the basics and keep time, but also remember two other things. First, not everyone has to be a marvelous dancer. Second, you're a woman. One advantage of being a woman is letting the man lead. Because if he knows what he's doing, you'll look wonderful whether you know what you're doing or not. Although, to be frank, I'm confident you'll look wonderful either way."

Dahyu spun Semra around and brought her whirling back to him into a dip. Semra felt a giddy exhilaration as he moved her along the ground, almost as if she were floating, and a nervousness settled into her middle as they went. He spun her away from him, then back again into a simple lift, stepped back, and bowed.

Siler eyed them darkly as he lounged back against a tree trunk, his mood soured. "I think she gets it. That's good."

Semra glanced at him in surprise. "Since when have you rushed mission prep? Wasn't it you who pointed out I needed to learn it?"

"We still have some footwork to finesse," Dahyu added. "We're almost there."

Siler glowered at them, but said nothing, and Semra turned back to Dahyu. "So what am I doing in this step? I feel all discombobulated."

"Here, stand facing the same direction as me, and I'll do your part with you. Right foot first. Good. Like this."

Semra practiced until her motions were more fluid. Each time she made a mistake, she started over, resetting her feet.

"What do you think of this part, Semra?" Siler asked from the sidelines.

"This part of what?" she asked, trying to focus on the movements.

"The calm before the storm. The last-minute preparations before the mission. Do you have any rituals?"

"Check my gear and equipment? Why? What do you do?"

Siler shrugged. "I eat something. But right before I go out, I take these two fingers"—he held up the index and middle finger of his right hand—"and tap the inside of my wrist like this." He tapped his left wrist. "I know it's sort of weird, but it's a spinoff of Ramas' ritual."

"What does Ramas do?"

"You've never noticed?"

"No. Usually he tells us to do things. He doesn't run the mission himself, so he wouldn't really have occasion to. Was he actually part of the team during missions for your class?"

"Once or twice. He does it before supervising missions too. You know the snake amulet he always wears? He taps it twice and kisses his thumb. I figure I don't need an amulet to protect me. All I have is my training, my own skin and bone, so that's my reminder. I don't need anything else."

"Sort of pretentious, don't you think?" Dahyu put in. "Everyone needs someone."

"Only the weak," Siler replied. "Relying on people often ends poorly. I avoid it when I can."

"That's sad. Trust is not only important in teamwork, but in happiness in life, don't you think? Connection. Relationships."

"I collaborate with skilled people decently enough, and sometimes it's necessary," Semra said. "I'm not sure it's weak to need someone, but it's easier to trust my own ability than to risk dire consequences if my trust is misplaced."

Dahyu stopped the dance practice and turned to her. "What a lonely existence. Even without needing someone you can trust, wouldn't you wish for it? If you always think the worst, if you never risk anything, you'll never know what you could've had."

Semra's stomach turned upside down as he said the words, and somehow, they stung. She swallowed, then looked down.

Siler looked between them, then clapped his hands. "All right then! Dance lessons are over. Speaking of misplaced trust, our would-be father figure has planned to murder these people for months, and we've had less than a day. Let's finalize the logistics, shall we?"

18

A light creaking sound accompanied the footsteps on either side of Semra. She lay in the dark, legs pulled up in front of her in the small space, her back against the side of the trunk, feeling smothered beneath the furs that lay on top of her. A bead of sweat formed on her forehead and rolled down her face and into the single fur lining the trunk beneath her.

It had been Semra's idea to get in using a trunk, though it wasn't the most comfortable of suggestions. Semra and Siler had gone into Qalea that morning to snatch breakfast from the street stalls while Dahyu made the necessary arrangements. There was no feasible way to keep an eye on Dahyu until the gala, where he'd play the role of a noble, elevating his status rather gratuitously from governor's aide. Governor Reza had been invited, before his passing, and Dahyu would go in his stead just as Semra would be standing in for the Belvidorian Lady Generiva Swathel by masquerading as the fictional character Axelia Berinon.

"Just play nice and be ready to either warmly greet or kill

whoever opens the trunk," Siler had told her. "Depending on the circumstance. It could be a trap for all we know."

That morning, Siler had also helped Semra find and steal a small bag, some extra food to carry along, and two sterling silver plates. The plates Semra kept hidden in the bag until Dahyu returned and told her which fur blanket shop had agreed to include a passenger among the merchandise being sent to the castle. The trunk had been left empty for her in the first room she'd entered, with the furs lying neatly folded inside. Semra had lifted them out, laid one inside, climbed in, and covered herself with the remaining furs. She hid the plates between layers of furs, one to the front of the trunk beneath the lock and one above her.

"In case someone decides to impale the trunk," she'd said. "They're more likely to go for the middle than guess which side my head is on. I can't line the whole thing with metal, but it makes me feel better to have something they don't know about, even if it's as small a thing as this."

The trunk swayed with the ox cart as it wound its way up to the Dragon Gate. Semra wondered if Siler was already among the Belvidorian servants, and when he'd be passing through the very same gate. The cart stopped, and the guard asked the driver several questions about who he was and what he was bringing inside. The driver answered that he had purchases for the royal family and the guard let him through the gate. Semra braced herself against the sides of the trunk as the cart lurched forward again.

She could picture the cart pulling up to the carriage yard, and she heard male voices as the trunk was hefted off the cart and carried between two people. After a pause, she heard a door open, and kitchen sounds filtered in from down the hall. The men took the trunk to the stairs and climbed side by side. Dahyu had said he had an in with one of the

Jannemar guests, and Semra wondered whether Jannemar guests would be staying on the second floor with the Belvidorian guests. She could hear Belon yelling something on the second floor, but they passed the landing and proceeded up to the third.

A knot twisted in her stomach. Where were they taking her? Surely noblewomen wouldn't be staying on the third floor with the royal family! The men turned left out of the stairway and down the hall. Semra gripped her knife and brought it close to her chest under the furs, heart pounding in her chest.

The trunk was set down, and Semra heard one of the men knock on a door. A lilting young female voice answered, and one of Semra's bearers responded, "Your purchases from yesterday, Your Highness."

Panic welled up in Semra's chest, and her eyes widened in the darkness of the trunk. Princess Avaya? Semra remembered her eyes from before, when she'd examined Semra and hoped she was the runaway chandler the guards were looking for. Semra shivered. Something about those cold eyes ... Quickly, she stowed the knife back on her leg. If the plan was to get her caught and killed, this was an excellent strategy. She couldn't kill the princess to defend herself, but if she was found unexpectedly inside the trunk, Semra would likely be killed anyway, removing her from interfering with the Framatar's mission at the gala.

The door swung open, and a light and airy, excitable voice greeted them. Too friendly for Semra's memory of Avaya. "Yes! Come in, come in! Set it over there."

Semra felt herself lifted once more and brought into the room, and when the trunk had been set down on the floor, the young voice spoke again. "Thank you very much, that is all. I shall not like to be disturbed today until the gala. Make sure of it."

There was a pause, and Semra imagined the men bowing to their princess, followed by the receding of footsteps and a door closing. For a moment nothing happened. Another bead of sweat ran into Semra's hair as she waited, motionless, under the heavy furs.

The young female voice spoke again, calling out as though to the next room over. "Murin? Have you gone to town on that errand yet?" After a beat of silence, the girl said, "Excellent," under her breath, and Semra heard her kneel in front of the trunk.

"Hello, are you in there?" said the voice. "Dahyu said I should say something before I open the trunk so you know I'm a friend. He said to call you Axelia and to tell you not to be afraid of the dresses. I'm not sure how someone can be afraid of dresses though. They're so delightful, don't you think? Oh dear, I do hope there's someone in there or I'll have been a total buffoon this whole time! Well, I suppose there's only one way to find out. Murin drew my bath, but then I sent her on an errand, so we should have several hours to ourselves."

Semra heard the latch pulled back and the lid creak open. Furs were tugged off her two at a time, and Semra slid the sterling plate to one side and pushed back the last few furs. Above her, a young girl, perhaps fifteen years old, peered down at her with large green eyes filled with a mischievous curiosity. Wavy golden hair spilled over her shoulders. The resemblance to Avaya was unmistakable, but she was several years her junior. Princess Aviama.

Aviama reached into the trunk, grabbed Semra by the hands, and pulled her to her feet. Semra found herself in an extravagant bedroom suite with gilded, embossed designs on the walls, marble floors, and murals of the sky and birds on the lofted ceiling. A bed sat to one side, a vanity and desk on the other, and a partition in the corner next to a large dresser blocked off part of the room. Semra took in the sight, then looked back at Aviama, who stared back at her with equal interest.

Semra bit her lip, unsure of what to say. "Thanks," she finally said, lamely. "I um ... I like the ceiling in here."

Aviama smiled nervously. "Thank you. I wanted the room without any people on the ceiling. It felt weird to have people staring down at me when I sleep, you know? Wouldn't you feel that way? Not that they're not lovely paintings, I just ..." She trailed off, glanced at the floor, and then looked back up at Semra. "Mmm. Do you mind ... I think we should start with the bath and go from there."

Semra suddenly felt self-conscious about the sweat that dampened her forehead and disheveled hair. She smoothed her wrinkled, two-day-old servants' skirts and said, "Highness. If you don't mind. Was that ... part of the deal?"

"Deal! The deal was I get to play dress up with you, and you have to pass for nobility. You're today's project, and ever so much more interesting than it was going to be before, so don't go spoiling it!" Aviama put her hands on her hips. "I take my projects very seriously, and no noblewoman I've ever met smells of ..." she wrinkled her nose. "What *is* that? It's not quite the stables, but it's not exactly the woods."

Semra worked hard not to glare at the prim little princess standing before her. Aviama waved her over behind the partition where a hot bath waited. "I trust you've taken a bath before, yes?" she asked. "Because I must admit that though I sent my servant away for this part, I'm not ready to become a servant myself. I'll just stay over here on this side while you clean yourself up."

"Yes, of course I've taken a bath before." But as Semra stared at the hot water in the large tub with flower petals floating on top and an assortment of soaps, oils, and candles on either side, she wondered if she'd know what to do after all. This seemed somewhat more complicated than a quick soap and dunk in the freezing water in the caves back home.

"Well, go on," Aviama said, seating herself in a chair on the other side of the partition. "I haven't got all day. After all, I have to be ready for the gala too, you know."

Semra hesitantly stepped behind the partition and removed her servant's dress and the pants hiding underneath. She carefully placed the knives inside her clothes to conceal them from view and placed them within arms' reach of the bath. Semra eased into the water—she'd never felt anything so luxurious in all her life.

"So how does a governor's aide bend the ear of a princess?" Semra asked.

"Hmm?"

"How do you know Dahyu? It seems strange for someone in his position to so quickly get in contact with you."

"Oh, yes, of course. Well, his father is well acquainted with my father, you know. He told you so, I know he did, but anyway, I'm close to his father too. Everyone in the residence knows him. And Dahyu has spent enough time around here that we know him too."

Semra picked up the soap. "What has he told you?"

"Oh, that imp! I could hardly get a word out of him. He told me not to ask questions or I'd not know anything at all, but it sounds terribly dangerous and important. Someone evil might be coming tonight, I think. What do you have to do with it? Is it really dangerous? Oh, it sounds like a real adventure! Won't you tell me?"

Semra smiled. This was not what she pictured a princess

would be like. She'd expected someone like Avaya, but Aviama was quite a different type. "You seem fond of him."

"Dahyu? It's hard not to be, don't you think? He's very thoughtful and kind, and I think he's good at just about everything he tries."

Semra smiled. "You're a romantic."

"Romantic! How absurd! Well, I mean, it's true, I *am* a romantic. But not with Dahyu; certainly not. He's like a brother to me. But here I am answering all of your questions, and you haven't answered any of mine! Which one of us is the princess?"

Semra heard a pout in her tone. "Forgive me, Your Highness. This is all very new to me, and I'm curious, that's all. I meant no disrespect. There is someone coming that we're worried about. I want to make sure this person doesn't cause trouble. Call it insurance."

"What kind of person? What are you worried they'll do? Why can't the guards take care of it?"

Semra heard an excitement, an edge, to Aviama's tone and she had a sneaking suspicion the girl had tried to learn this information before. "Did you ask Dahyu these questions?"

There was a pause. "Yes. But he wasn't any help, and I thought that, as a woman, you'd be more understanding. I *need* to know!"

"I'm afraid I can't say more than I already have. You'll have to act like you don't know me tonight." Semra reached for the towel and stood up.

"Oh, fine, if you ... wait, are you done already? You washed and put the perfumed oil on and everything? Goodness, maybe I really am as slow as Murin says!"

Semra glanced around, grabbed the bottle of oil and sniffed it. A pleasant floral aroma filled her nostrils. She quickly dabbed some on, then wrapped the towel around herself and blocked the dragon's kiss on her chest with her hand. "Yes, all done. I thought we were in a hurry. What do I wear?"

Aviama walked around the partition and looked Semra up and down. She nodded her approval. "Okay, now the fun part! Let's get—"

A knock at the door interrupted her.

Aviama folded her arms. "Not now! I said I don't want to be disturbed!"

"Don't be a priss," came a snide voice. "The knock was a courtesy. I'm coming in."

Aviama caught Semra's gaze, and the two stared at each other, eyes wide. Aviama mouthed, "Avaya," and motioned for Semra to stay where she was. Semra crouched behind the tub in her towel, and Aviama stepped around the partition as the door opened.

"Why is Zephan being weird?" Avaya asked. "Have you talked to him?"

"I saw him this morning when he first came in. He always takes a few days to adjust back to the castle."

"No, it's something else. He won't talk about it. You've always been close. Find out what it is."

"Just give him a day to breathe. He'll be fine."

"He doesn't have a day, he has *hours*. King Arnevon and Prince Axis are practically on our doorstep. If our father is going to try to make up for the past twenty years in one night, we can't have it ruined, can we? Belvidorian troops have been mobilizing across the border. They say it's just drills, but Belvidore has always been hotheaded and impulsive—a significant contrast to our peace-loving, overly passive father, wouldn't you say?"

"Avs, how do you know this?"

Avaya started pacing, and Semra ducked down behind the tub to stay out of sight.

"Everyone should know this! Anyone with even the most remote line to the throne should concern themselves with basic matters of state! This is a hugely important night, Aviama. Not just for me. For all of us. For the peace of two kingdoms. Belvidore has always had their eye on the Surion Strip south of Kinlock. An excuse for war is an excuse for expansion. And Zephan is far too like Father. Someone in this family has to be diplomatic."

"And that someone is you?"

"Well, I'm a woman, aren't I? Diplomacy is wasted on women in Jannemar! That's one thing Belvidore has right. The eldest child, no matter their gender, inherits the throne. One day, little sister, you will understand. Royal women will be just as deeply revered as men."

"If I'm so little and such a know-nothing, you can take your venting someplace else," Aviama sniffed.

"One day you'll appreciate what I do for us!" Avaya insisted as she swept out of the room. "Just you wait! And Prince Axis can make it happen."

The door closed and Semra stood tentatively to her feet, still wrapped in the towel. Aviama let out an exasperated sigh and stepped back behind the partition.

"What was that about?" Semra asked. "She's going to do something for women, but she's going to have a man do it for her?"

Aviama rolled her eyes and tossed her hands up. "I don't know; I really don't. She's been on edge for weeks! Now, where were we ... ooooh! Dresses!"

Aviama opened the dresser and rifled through a stunning array of silks and satins. "Oh, this red one would look lovely against your complexion, don't you think?"

"It is beautiful," Semra agreed. "Any chance there is an option that's not such a loud color? What about that gray?"

Aviama put one hand to her forehead and the other to her heart in a dramatic pose. "You hurt me! Never! You need some color in your life. It won't kill you. Besides, that's only part of the dress. I'd never wear an all-gray dress. Even funerals require straight black. Gray is to a dance what soggy bread is to a feast. And I won't have you looking like soggy bread!"

Semra pursed her lips but said nothing. Aviama suddenly gasped and pulled out a light-teal gown with a bronze trim at the hem and long, billowy sleeves. A sparkling, sleeveless piece, in navy embellished with bronze, fit over the dress in a wraparound style. It split below the waist into three triangular pieces. The pointed ends trailed down to the hem on either side and down the back, revealing the teal underneath in the front.

Aviama held it out to her, and Semra reached out and ran her fingers down the fine-chiffon skirt. If she was going to be forced into a dress, this one was certainly exquisite. She hoped there'd be no blood spatter on it by the end of the night, but even so, a dress for the prince's life was a worthwhile trade. She had more important things to worry about.

Semra spent the next hour serving as Aviama's doll as she went about applying powders to her face and painting her eyelids. Aviama assured her that though she had had few occasions to apply the paints to other people, she had watched her lady in waiting, Murin, do it "a thousand times." After several mistakes and corrections, Aviama stepped back to examine her work. "You have a beautiful bone structure. And I have highlighted it quite nicely, if I may say so! Oh, you look gorgeous. I think you wear that dress better than I do."

Semra blushed, though she wasn't entirely sure what made one's bones particularly attractive. She'd always simply determined that bones which did not break under severe pressure were the best ones. As it turned out, hair was not as easily done as it looked. Aviama spent another hour trying to pile Semra's hair high on her head and create elaborate styles, most of which resembled a lopsided bird's nest. Finally, Aviama took down her work, brushed through her hair again, and instead braided her hair into a crown wrapping into a low bun.

"There, that'll do," she said, placing her hands on her hips. "I am more amazing than I thought."

"Your Highness?"

The sound came with a knock at the door, and Semra and Aviama both jumped.

"One moment!"

Semra leaped up and headed back to the trunk to hide, but Aviama grabbed her arm. "Don't you dare," she hissed. "I will not have all my work go to waste. You can hide under the bed, but be careful! Don't mess up your dress or your hair!" Semra slid under the large bed and Aviama shoved the trunk over to the foot of the bed to block the open space visible from the door.

Aviama went to the door and opened it slightly, then widened it for someone to come inside. Semra peeked around the trunk and saw a woman dressed as Avaya's lady in waiting had been the day before.

"Murin! Just in time," Aviama said. "I can't decide how I want my hair for tonight. What do you think?"

"Your Highness, we discussed it just last night. Have you changed your mind?"

"Oh dear … I must just be too excited to remember! Come help me get dressed."

Semra lay anxiously under the bed as Murin dressed Aviama and meticulously styled her hair. Aviama seemed flighty, but Semra hoped it was close enough to her normal state that no one would notice. After spending what Semra felt was a truly inordinate amount of time preparing, Aviama and Murin disappeared down the hall, leaving Semra alone under the princess' bed. They'd been running late, as the water clock on the vanity had alerted them, and guests would begin arriving within the hour. Semra would have to wait until the residence was clear before making her way down to the gala.

Doors opened and closed, and voices came and went. After it had been quiet for twenty minutes, Semra slowly crawled out from underneath the bed, checked her dress and hair in the mirror, and slipped out into the empty hall. She took the servant's stair down to the second floor and came out into the Belvidorian guest hall, which bustled with color and excitement. The highest esteemed ladies and gentlemen of the Belvidorian court spoke in animated voices as they left their guest rooms and filled Ancestry Hall outside the Great Hall.

Semra fell in with the crowd but, rather than admiring the views, found herself scanning the room for strategic positions and nefarious faces from the mountain. A trumpet sounded. The Shamaran royal family must be arriving in the Great Hall from the opposite side.

The announcer called out, "His Majesty the King, King Turian of Jannemar, Sovereign of the Shamaran dynasty … Her Majesty the Queen, Queen Sharsi of Jannemar."

All introductions of the later-arriving Belvidorian guests would be put on hold until the royal family had entered. The huge double doors leading into the Great Hall were open, with guards on either side and the announcer for the Belvidorians standing at the entrance. A sea of people bowed or curtsied at the announcement, and a murmur ran through the crowd.

"Her Royal Highness, Princess Avaya of Jannemar."

Semra's heart pounded as she wormed her way through the crowd toward the double doors.

"His Royal Highness, the Crown Prince Zephan of Jannemar."

Semra tapped the index and middle fingers of her right hand on the inside of her left wrist and took a deep breath to calm her nerves. If anyone could save the prince, it was her.

19

"Her Royal Highness, Princess Aviama of Jannemar."

Semra angled through the crowd until she was close to the double doors. People filled the Great Hall, which she was both grateful for and anxious about. On the one hand, she needed a throng to hide in, but on the other, it took longer for her to get into position. She expected at least two or three assassins to be present—Radix among the guard, Manu or someone to replace him if his role was still needed, and Tymetin to take out the prince. Unless there'd been changes. A hit of this magnitude with Semra and Siler on the loose would certainly make the Framatar concerned.

With the royal family in place, the announcer began again with Belvidorian guests. Semra shifted her weight impatiently as the couple in front of her was announced into the room as a count and countess. Semra looked beyond them to the tables on the far sides of the columns and the sea of people converging in the middle.

"My lady."

Semra startled and looked to the announcer in front of her. "Hmm?"

"Your name."

"My apologies. It's Axelia. Axelia Berinon."

The announcer turned to the room and called out loudly, "Axelia Berinon!"

Semra drew herself up tall and swept into the room. Musicians on her right played a cheerful melody, and she drew underneath the guard's lookout to take stock of the room. Earls and counts and barons of Jannemar and Belvidore alike mingled around the room while servants walked around with plates of drinks and appetizers. Semra identified the Belvidorian royal guests of honor sitting at the far end of the hall next to their Jannemar hosts. The Belvidorian king, a stern-looking man with a deeply furrowed brow, spoke to King Turian next to him.

Semra marveled at King Turian, dressed in resplendent fur-lined attire and a golden gem-studded crown. A confident, powerful ruler talking and making merry with his guests had replaced the humble, somber man she'd met in the courtyard the day before. King Arnevon laughed, and Semra thought Turian must be quite something to crack a smile on such a cheerless man.

Next to them with his back to Semra, Prince Zephan stood in a formal navy jacket and fur-lined cape, talking to Prince Axis and Princess Avaya. Queen Sharsi of Jannemar spoke with a Belvidorian dignitary, and Princess Aviama stood at her mother's side, but seemed distracted by all the excitement around her.

Semra scanned the servants again but saw no one she recognized. The music stopped, and the announcer stated that the King and Queen of Jannemar would open the dance floor. A waltz began, and King Turian extended his arm to Queen Sharsi with a tenderness in his eyes and a warm smile. The queen, stunning in all respects, carried her head high as a dignified leader, yet something in her manner was gentle and warm. Semra thought perhaps they suited one another. The queen returned the king's smile and took his arm as the guests cleared from the center of the hall. He escorted her out to the middle of the room.

The waltz began, and Semra edged through the crowd toward the prince on the other side of the room. She angled her head away from the king and the guard tower overlooking the floor, bypassing murmuring nobles as she made her way slowly down the hall toward the royals. She risked a glance up at the walkway and saw a servant disappear through the door to the conservatory. Had it been Siler?

"The king and queen invite their guests to join them on the dance floor," called the announcer.

People began to move, no longer languidly standing and chatting, as men invited their ladies to the dance floor. Prince Axis offered his arm to Princess Avaya, and she flashed him a winning smile as she took it. Semra felt a tap on the shoulder and spun around.

"My lady, may I have a dance?"

Before her stood an impeccably groomed nobleman taking her in with keen interest. Semra looked back again toward the Belvidorian and Jannemari royal families, and her heart stopped. The prince had disappeared. Panic rose in her chest, and as the king and his wife stepped out of the dance, she saw a familiar broad-shouldered man reach out to grasp the king by the arm in greeting.

The man wore an engraved leather breastplate with gold cords at his shoulders denoting his rank as general. A rich-blue cape draped about his shoulders, and though she'd never seen him bedecked thus, she knew him at once as

General Gresvig. The Framatar's right hand man seemed also to be at the right hand of his enemy. Gresvig leaned in to hear the king whisper something in his ear. Semra's chest burned hot with anger.

"My lady?"

Semra had completely forgotten about the noble. She turned back to him, pursing her lips, suddenly annoyed by his presence, but a second voice cut in:

"I'm afraid this magnificent woman had already promised me her first dance."

Dahyu stood at her side, arm extended. He wore a green velvet tunic edged in golden thread and belted at the waist. Semra opened her mouth, shut it again, and then nodded politely at the noble. "My apologies," she managed, then took Dahyu's arm and allowed him to lead her out to the dance floor.

"Are you enjoying yourself?" he asked.

"There's not much to enjoy," she replied, looking past him to get another look at Gresvig.

"I'm sure your hosts would be saddened to hear it," he commented casually.

"The prince has disappeared, and I'm trying to prevent a disaster," she hissed at him. "Get me toward the far end. Where did he go?"

"He's just about as safe as he could be, I think," Dahyu said. "And nothing horrible has happened yet." His eyes twinkled, but Semra wasn't amused.

"This is not a game. Gresvig is here. I've seen him all my life in the mountain."

Dahyu's smile faded. "General Gresvig? Are you sure?"

Semra nodded. "He's close to the Framatar. I heard him reporting to the Framatar about the prince's location being top secret. It looks like the Framatar has eyes at every level of the Shamaran court."

Semra glanced up at the walkway, but it was empty. She swept her gaze over the guard tower and saw two guards looking out over the Great Hall, but she couldn't make out their faces.

Dahyu danced her across the floor and spoke in a hushed tone. "I think we'll be all right. There have been plenty of opportunities tonight already, and nothing has happened. Semra, look at me."

"I'm working," she replied, glancing at him briefly before casting another look at Gresvig.

"Come now, it's only a moment. People might think you aren't interested in me at all."

"People generally are too busy focusing on themselves to be particularly observant. We are nobodies in a room of royal somebodies. None of the somebodies care about the nobodies enough to watch them closely, and the nobodies only care about getting the attention of the somebodies."

"Semra."

She leveled her gaze into Dahyu's eyes, and the frustration and anxiety in her chest loosened.

His eyes swept over her, and he smiled softly. "Maybe not everything is as bad as it seems."

The song ended, and he pulled her into him, then extended his arm and bowed. Semra curtsied and, as she looked up, saw a juggler's colorful balls make a tall arc over his head and fall in perfect order before sailing through the air once more. The juggler walked by her toward the tables, angled away from Semra, but she caught the smell of garlic.

No servants in the area held trays, and no appetizers being served that evening were primarily garlic. Semra's mind whirred. Arsenic. Arsenic smelled like garlic when it was heated. Heated arsenic caused toxic fumes. Maybe the hit wasn't one person, but the whole guest list! The doors would shut, and any moment now they would all be left to die in this room.

Behind her the queen's musical laugh carried through the room from where she stood next to her husband, General Gresvig, and King Arnevon. Semra left Dahyu on the dance floor, eyes fixed on the juggler as he sent the colorful balls in an impressive swirl behind his back and caught them each in one hand as they fell. Of course! It was the perfect cover. He could meander throughout the room at his own pace, get close to anyone without question, and use his craft as juggler to redirect his audience's attention wherever he wanted it.

Semra stole into the crowd, heart pounding, as she closed the distance between herself and the juggler. In a flash, the juggler's hand shot out and pulled her toward him—yanking her forward and off balance—then released her in time to feign a fall of his own. Juggling balls flew in every direction and screams erupted all around her.

Semra raised her hands instinctively to protect her face and took a slug in the gut. She ripped the candleholder off the center of the nearest table and struck her assailant in the head. To her surprise, his defense was weak, and when she looked up at him he was bleeding from the side of the head.

Tymetin.

His lip curled into an eerie smile meant just for her, and it lasted only a moment before a wounded expression took over his face. Shouts and blood-curdling screams mixed with the clanging of metal in a cacophony of sound that only served to add to Semra's confusion. A flurry of motion had sprung up behind her, but as she turned toward it, pain exploded in her head and she crashed to the marble floor.

Her ears rang, and she pulled her arms up to protect her

head. Guards materialized and formed one solid line of shield bearers, angling in toward four people lying on the floor. Two attendants got up from lying protectively on top of the King and Queen of Jannemar, one helped the king to his feet. The queen didn't move.

"She threw the knife! I saw her, she threw it!" Tymetin yelled.

The guards moved forward and enveloped the queen in their ranks, and from the center of the shoulder-to-shoulder line, six armored men rushed forward. Semra whirled back to Tymetin, but it was too late. Two guards took hold of her arms and dragged her backward, past the queen and toward the library and guard tower on the west side of the castle keep.

A thousand-pound stone seemed to sink in her soul as Semra took in the sight of the beautiful Queen Sharsi of Jannemar, lying on her back in a pool of her own blood. A knife was lodged in the queen's chest, and King Turian shook as he bent over her body. Semra had seen too many corpses to have any question that she was dead. It would've taken less than a minute.

Panic welled up in her throat. Tymetin leaned back against a column, his wry face mocking her. Just before the sea of guards cut off her line of vision, a subtle motion in Tymetin's hands caught Semra's attention. He was laughing at her, rolling a garlic clove in his fingers.

20

"NOOOO!" Semra screamed, as she was dragged out the door. She tried to find Dahyu or Siler in the mass of people, but all she could see were guards struggling to contain the chaos in the room. Semra pulled against the guards on either side of her, but to no avail.

She gathered her feet beneath her and hurried to keep up with the pace of the guards as they swept her out of the Great Hall, through the library and antechamber, and down the stairs past the guard tower. Down they went to the first floor, to the floor beneath the courtyard, down a corridor, and down again, until all natural light had abandoned them.

Semra's mind was on fire, and a burning in her chest threatened to take over her body. She opened her mouth to call out—I didn't do it! You have to believe me—but no sound came. What good would it do her? After all, they didn't have to believe her. And they wouldn't.

Finally they spilled out onto a spacious landing lit by torches. One of the guards grabbed one off the wall as they took her down a short series of steps into the heart of the dungeon. Cells were laid out in a row down the left side of the passage. The guard with the torch opened the barred door to the third cell.

Semra found her voice. She knew it was no use, but she couldn't help herself. "It wasn't me! Please, they're still in danger!"

A third armored man, designated a captain by the red tips of the pauldrons protecting his shoulders, ran down the stairs. "Search her!"

The two guards looked at each other. "Captain, she's in a dress."

"A murderer in a dress does not get a pass," the captain barked.

The guards nodded, and one guard shoved her against the bars while the other patted her down. Semra saw him pause when he hit her thigh, and he slowly lifted the hem of her skirt to reveal the black pants she'd tugged back on underneath Aviama's beautiful borrowed gown. Semra's shoulders sagged. Gresvig had the ear of the king; Radix was established among the guard, and Semra had strapped herself with knives, as always. She would never be allowed to leave the dungeon alive.

The guard confiscated the knives, grabbed her by the arms and threw her into the cell, shutting the door behind her. To break her fall, Semra instinctively rolled with the momentum, then sprang to her feet. The captain raised his eyebrows, and the guards blinked at her.

Shoot. That little stunt hadn't helped her case. Semra rubbed her arms where the guards had gripped her and took a deep breath. Any chance of pleading innocent was long gone by now. Semra still didn't know what had happened, exactly, but she knew she had to change her strategy. The king didn't know there were moles and assassins high in his court.

The captain and the two guards turned to leave, and Semra called out. "Wait."

They kept walking.

"Wait!"

The torchlight flickered as it receded down the passage, and suddenly an anger at being framed and abandoned by the Framatar, left to die in a hole, raged inside of her. They were leaving her. Just as her parents had failed to protect her, leaving her alone in the mountain. Just as the Framatar had always said; without him, she was nothing. No one would save her from this pit. And he wouldn't care when her last breath came.

But she wouldn't go down alone.

Semra stepped slowly to the bars of the door and leaned on a crossbar. She called out again, this time in a soft, high-pitched, sing-song voice that echoed off the cold stone walls. "I know something you don't know."

The footsteps stopped. Silence.

"Death and dying, death and dying, they think that one is done!"

One set of steps came back again, and the captain came into view. His jaw was set, and his eyes were black as onyx. "Fool! Speak your piece, because this is the only chance you get to spout your drivel. And if you don't impress me, I'll make sure you never see the light of day."

Semra leaned forward so her face touched the bars, allowing her eyes to go flat and cold as ice. "Would a fool have been able to steal into the castle and kill the queen under your nose? Such a pity, in this rocky political climate, don't you think? With Belvidore here on good terms, for the first time in—how long has it been?—twenty years."

"State your intent," the captain growled. "Now."

"I'm not alone," Semra whispered. "And the queen wasn't the only target. I'm willing to leverage information in exchange for my life."

"You're hardly in a position to be making demands."

"On the contrary. You're hardly in the position to take me lightly, considering I already killed your queen, and I know who's next. When the next royal falls, are you willing to take the blame? Because their blood will be on your head."

The captain crossed his arms. "Let's say I entertained your insanity. What would you tell me?"

Semra leaned back from the bars and casually seated herself against the stone wall at the back of her cell. "Nothing. I speak only to the king."

"You're out of your mind! You say you killed the queen, and you plan on killing another of the royal family, and you want me to actually let you in range of him?"

Semra shrugged. "I have information that he needs. I speak only to him. What you do with that is on your own conscience."

The captain sent her a long glare, then turned on his heel and marched down the passage and up the stairs, until nothing at all could be heard. Semra sank back against the wall and closed her eyes, willing her breathing to slow and her mind to focus. What had happened?

She'd seen Tymetin from behind, the pouch beneath his tunic, the smell of garlic. She'd thought it was arsenic, but he obviously set her up, using her training against her. Idiot! Semra cursed herself, passing a hand over her eyes. *They baited you, and you took it. Like an amateur.*

Who killed the queen? It had to have been the moment she lunged for Tymetin, which would've diverted attention to their scuffle. Tymetin himself could have done it, or anyone standing right behind him. Semra shut her eyes tight and searched her memory, reliving the scene, searching the faces. She came up empty.

Either way, taking out the queen with a throwing knife had been a smart move. It was the only weapon they could have counted on Semra having on her at the gala, reinforcing the narrative that she'd carried out the hit. With an easy distraction, Semra had been drawn to the right place at the right time, simultaneously removing her interference. The simplicity of it was almost insulting.

But why kill the queen? Had the plan changed? The queen had to have been the intended target. It was a precise hit. Had Semra misunderstood? Perhaps the prince wasn't in danger after all. Semra opened her eyes. What had she overheard Gresvig tell the Framatar?

His location is top secret. Never fear, my lord, no excuse could keep the prince from either the gala or the New Year celebration.

Once the mission is carried out at the gala, King Turian will be so devastated that he will be desperate to keep safe the rest of his family ...

Semra's mouth dropped open as a second memory filtered into her thoughts. Gresvig speaking to Tymetin, right before Semra had gone to let out the drakes:

There are many Turian loves. Use them to your advantage ...

Semra sat bolt upright. She'd been wrong. The mission of the gala was never to kill the prince! The mission of the gala was to emotionally destroy the king by killing his wife and so cloud his judgment. Which meant the Framatar wanted something from the king.

Doubtless the Framatar still planned on killing the prince. What was it he'd said? *I must be the only male Shamaran left after Prince Zephan is dead.* That was why the Framatar had had his uncle murdered. Who was his uncle?

How was the Framatar one of the Shamarans? Yes, Zephan still had to die, but not yet ... he just needed to be found for when the time came, and both the gala and the New Year celebration were perfect opportunities to get a lock on his location.

When was the New Year celebration? Semra tried to remember what day it was. The new year was soon—maybe three weeks away. What did the Framatar want from the king?

Semra's head continued to spin with a thousand possibilities, but though hours passed, she had no certain answers on which to settle. Confessing to the queen's assassination and demanding an audience with King Turian was a bold move, but it was the only card she had left to play. Hopefully, the captain would relay her message. Perhaps if she could just speak to the king, even bound hand and foot, she could warn him.

Escape crossed Semra's mind, but the cell she sat in was a bare, eight-foot-long square stone box. If guards ever patrolled down the corridors or someone brought food with any kind of regularity, perhaps she could come up with something. *Or perhaps the Framatar will send someone to kill you before you get the chance!*

Left in the dark, she examined the bars and the lock mechanism by feel, but she had nothing with which to pick the lock, and the bars were fashioned in a grid of small squares that only her arms could fit through. She was underground, so there was no chance of Zezura reaching her, despite the burning in her chest that told her Zezura was an anxious wreck. Semra hoped Zezura wouldn't get herself killed doing anything particularly stupid.

After much thought, Semra determined that for the time being nothing could be done. She curled up in the corner of her empty cell, spreading her skirts over her feet to keep her as warm as possible. For a long time, she stared into the darkness, listening to her own breathing and the occasional vague sound of guards' voices. She thought of Siler and hoped he'd gotten out safely, and of Dahyu—the strange way he'd looked at her as they'd danced, and the unfamiliar warmth she'd felt as he did. Semra thought of the young, spritely Aviama, whose dress Semra had now completely ruined on the dirty dungeon floor, and imagined the light in her eyes going out when she realized her mother was dead. A single tear ran down her face and into her hair as Semra drifted off into a fitful sleep.

A loud banging woke her with a start, and she lurched forward. General Gresvig sat in a chair on the other side of the bars, repeatedly bashing a helmet against the wall. "You there! Are our accommodations too comfortable for you that you demand an audience and then sleep through it?"

Semra sat up, gathering her feet under her. "Are you planning on adding any spikes to the floor? I think you know I'm used to sleeping in many environments, and spikes are the only thing I can think of to make this one worse."

"And how would I know where you're used to sleeping?" Gresvig asked.

Semra leaned forward and glanced around the door of her cell to see the captain standing to the side holding a torch. They weren't alone, and the captain clearly wasn't one of the Framatar's henchmen.

Gresvig waved her off. "Nevermind, I don't particularly care where criminals sleep. The less comfortable the better in my opinion, and I'll give the spikes some serious consideration. Now. You told my captain you wanted an audience."

"I did."

Gresvig leaned back in his chair. "Well, you're extremely

lucky I gave you a moment's notice before your impending execution. If you have information to share to keep your head on your shoulders, now is the time."

Semra set her jaw and looked back at him darkly. "I thought I made it clear to your captain that I would speak only to the king."

"You will speak with me."

"Your Majesty!" she mocked. "My apologies, I didn't recognize you. It must've been the attire of a general and the presumptuous demeanor."

Gresvig laughed. "Do you know how incredible it is that you sit before the king's right hand? How many people clamor for my ear? I needn't suffer the slights of imbeciles."

"General. Forgive me, but where were you when the queen fell?"

Gresvig drilled Semra with a dark stare. "You are young. When I was young, I thought I knew so much. In time I learned that it's easy to look smart when surrounded by people with less training than myself. It can make a person arrogant. Rash. The game is entirely different when you're not the only expert in the room. My dear, you haven't a clue who you are talking to."

Something in Semra's stomach turned sour. "You remind me of someone. Someone I met once in Mount Hara."

Gresvig stood. "If you are not an imbecile, my next best guess would be lunacy. Mount Hara is the haunt of legendary dragons in stories told to children, and nothing more. You will not speak to the king. Captain, have her flogged for wasting my time."

Semra scrambled to her feet as General Gresvig turned and walked away down the passage, calling back to the captain, "I want you supervising, with five guards standing watch! Report to me when it's done."

Semra's heart leaped into her throat as she heard the captain bark out orders, and in mere moments five sets of footsteps marched down the steps toward her. A loud crack split the air as the first guard came into view, holding a long whip. Radix.

"Why, if it isn't our chandler maid," he sneered, cracking the whip again as the captain unlocked the cell door and swung it open. Radix plunged into the cell and wound his arm back, but though Semra spun to avoid it, the whip still slashed through her back. She let out a shriek and raced to the other side of the cell. Radix blocked the door.

The second blow came, and as it landed, Semra lunged for the whip, coiled its cowhide around her arm, and used it to pull herself toward Radix. He slung a hook at her head, and when her arm came up to block, he kneed her in the gut and threw her to the ground, ripping the whip free and laying into her. Semra cried out and curled into a ball on the floor, wrapping her arms over her head and bracing herself for impact as strike after strike split through the back of her dress and slashed open her flesh.

Her head swam and her vision blurred.

Eventually, the captain called for Radix to cease. "I said flog her, not kill her! Enough!"

Semra flinched at the rhythm of the next blow, but it never fell. Radix pulled back and left her, and as the door of her cell clanged shut, Semra collapsed in a heap on the floor.

21

Two days passed before Semra had any other visitors. Twice a day someone brought her bread and water. They instructed her to sit on the far side of the cell while they set a cup of water and bread wrapped in a napkin on the floor and pushed them through the bars. So when quiet footsteps padded down the passage, Semra picked up her water cup from earlier, set it next to the bars, and receded into the corner.

The steps paused one cell down from her and went quiet. Semra cocked her head in the dark, unsure what make of it. A few more halting steps, and then a whisper. "Semra?"

Semra waited a beat, then answered hesitantly. "Hello? Who's there?"

Torchlight illuminated the front of her cell as the footsteps padded closer.

Semra squinted as her eyes adjusted to the dim light. Hope mingled with concern within her chest as recognition lit her face. "Dahyu?"

Dahyu stepped up to the bars and peered into the cell,

then drew back, wrinkling his nose. "Ugh, it's awful down here. Is that you in there?"

Semra knew it must smell, but her nose had long since stopped passing along that information. She suddenly felt awkward and self-conscious of her destitute state. "I'm living in a box," she replied, as explanation. "What are you doing here?"

"I'm so sorry it took me this long. This was the soonest I could work out a way to get to you." Dahyu crouched on the other side of the cell door, placed the torch on the stone floor, and pulled out a napkin and two bottles. He gestured for her to come toward him.

Semra moved slowly from the corner, inhaling sharply as the wounds on her back complained of the motion.

"Semra? Are you okay?"

"I'm fine. Is that ... do you have water?"

"Yes ... I brought some fruit and pastry, some water, and alcohol for any scrapes or what have you, just in case. I haven't heard much word about you since ... since ..." His voice trailed off, and he looked down.

Semra reached eagerly for the napkin, and he handed it to her.

"This is the best I could do for now."

Semra bit into the fruit and shook her head. "This is amazing," she said with her mouth full. "Thank you. But you shouldn't have come. They'll kill you if they find you."

"I'll take my chances." Dahyu watched her intently as she ate before speaking again. "You weren't honest with me earlier."

Semra glanced up, then winced at the movement. "I didn't kill her. I swear it."

Dahyu shook his head. "No, I mean you said you were

fine, and you're not. You're hurt. Why are you moving so stiff and weird?"

Semra lifted her chin. "I'm not moving weird; I *am* fine, and as much as I appreciate you coming down here, when you leave you need to get out and stay out. Find Siler. Tell him the royal family is still in danger."

"Well, considering they have you in custody and you didn't do it, I would say that's fairly obvious," Dahyu observed. "Turn around. Let me look."

Semra ignored him. She finished the fruit and reached for the water Dahyu held, but he pulled away. "Dahyu, please. I get a cup of water twice a day."

His lips parted in surprise. "That's all?"

"That's all. Please."

A hurt look crossed his face, but then he took a deep breath as if steeling himself and shook his head. "I'm not keeping it from you. You'll get it as soon as you let me see what you're hiding."

Semra sighed and turned slowly so that the flickering light of the torch revealed the crisscross of welts on her back through her shredded dress. Dahyu gasped. "Semra! What happened to you?"

"It's okay; it's fine. Pour the alcohol over it, and that'll be enough for me."

Dahyu shook his head, handing her the water he'd promised. "You need more than alcohol. I have to come back."

"No."

"Hold still." Dahyu uncorked the bottle of alcohol and, reaching through the bars, slowly poured it over her back. Her wounds stung like fire, and she couldn't stop an involuntary flinch and groan. He pursed his lips disapprovingly. "I need more supplies. Hand me back the empty napkin and bottle, and I'll be back as soon as I can."

He pulled away, but Semra's hand shot out to grip his wrist. "Don't get yourself killed on my account. I'm already dead. Get out. Find Siler."

"You of little faith! First of all, I already found Siler. And second, he was right. He told me you are absolutely rotten at receiving help." The corner of his mouth twitched, and he patted her hand gently. "I'll be back."

Semra rocked back on her heels and let out a sigh as he picked up the torch and crept away. On the one hand, chances were excellent that her death was both imminent and unavoidable, and Dahyu's breaking into the dungeons for her could end up with their heads sharing a basket. On the other hand, she wasn't dead yet, and seeing him had given her hope. Semra started exercising in her cell that day, doing anything she could to keep up her strength while avoiding anything that would reopen the wounds on her back.

Semra waited all through the afternoon and evening, and into the night. She assumed it was night, primarily because someone brought her bread and water, and then many hours passed. The darkness never changed except for the torch the servant brought with her sorry excuse for a meal. Dahyu didn't come.

The night dragged on into morning, and still he didn't come. Semra feared he'd been caught. Worse, perhaps he wasn't caught, but decided to take Semra's suggestion and stay away. Perhaps he'd left her.

About midmorning the next day, Semra heard a commotion down the passage and the rustle of metal as guards grabbed their armor and equipment and dashed up the stairs in a flurry. She scooted to the edge of her cell to look down the corridor but couldn't see down to the end. Only thirty minutes or so later, Dahyu rushed down the stairs with a bundle under his left arm and a lit torch in his right. Warmth filled her to see him, and gratitude flooded her heart.

"What's going on?" she asked, as he rushed to her side. *Thank you for coming back for me. I was afraid.*

"It's Zezura," he said as he sank to the floor beside her cell and unwrapped the bundle. "She's made several loops over the castle the last few days, and just now she actually swooped down into the courtyard. One of the guards is injured and being taken to medical."

"What!"

Dahyu nodded. "Siler and I can't get to her without exposing ourselves, and I'm not sure she'd do anything we suggested even if we could. The guards are good men, just trying to do their duty. You need to call her off."

"If you haven't noticed, I'm a little busy doing nothing down here. What do you expect me to do?"

Dahyu handed her a pastry and twirled his finger in a circle, gesturing she turn around. She took the offering and dutifully turned her back to him as he applied salve to her hurts. "You are a dragonlord. She is your dragon." He paused. "She didn't come when you were dangling off a balcony, or in the middle of a gala. Why is she coming now? Can you send her to meet us somewhere?"

Semra thought back to the balcony. She'd felt Zezura's concern and that she'd started flying toward the castle. Semra had calmed her own spirit and sent that calm to Zezura, sending her away. "I don't communicate with her in words. She did start coming to me at the balcony, but I ... sort of willed her away. She wouldn't have gotten to me in time, and if she'd come, any pretense of subtlety would've been lost. At the gala ... hmm. I'm not sure."

Semra grew quiet, lost in thought. Dahyu waited patiently, his hands slow and gentle as he applied the soothing balm. Semra gradually relaxed under his touch, and she finished the pastry. Anxiety churned in her stomach, and she remembered the burning in her chest. "I forgot about the mark. Do you know how anger can feel like heat rising inside? And anxiety gives you that feeling like all your guts are squirming, like they want to be somewhere else? The mark on my chest burns hot when I'm distressed."

"You haven't been distressed until now?" Disbelief colored his tone. It wasn't condemning, but surprised.

"I ... could feel it come and go before. Keep myself in check, let her know I was all right. I think the burning came days ago and hasn't gone away, but my whole mind and body have felt on fire since the gala. I guess I grew sort of numb to it. It's my normal now."

Dahyu was silent. Semra turned to look at him, searching his face. Pain was etched in his features, and slowly a resolution of some kind seemed to wash over it. Semra wondered what it was.

When he spoke, his voice was as soothing to her heart as the balm had been to her physical wounds. "You don't have to be strong all the time, you know."

A lump rose in her throat, and tears sprang to her eyes. She shook her head. "I have been in a hair's breadth from death a thousand times, but just sitting, waiting, with nothing to do but think about ... just waiting in a cage ... " her voice broke and a tear slipped down her cheek. She wiped it away angrily and took in a shaky breath.

An answering tear spilled down Dahyu's face, but he made no move to wipe it away. His eyes were steady as they watched her. Confident but tender, firm, yet somehow safe.

Suddenly a realization hit him, and his face changed. "You would rather be whipped ... than sit here alone."

Semra wept then, her body racked with sobs, and as Dahyu slid his arms through the bars, she curled into his comforting embrace. It was true. She'd often been alone, but to be utterly helpless, trapped in her own dark thoughts ... nothing was worse than this.

Several minutes passed before waves of tears ebbed, and Semra slowly sat up. Dahyu straightened and looked at her.

She wiped her face with her sleeve. "Thank you ... for sitting with me." Semra cast her eyes down at the floor.

"Of course. And for what it's worth, the only new information I learned about you today is that you actually are human."

Semra snorted, then sniffled again. He grinned, and Semra gasped. "Zezura! I forgot all about her!"

"Scourge. So did I."

She took a steadying breath and closed her eyes, focusing on the sensations in her body. She noticed the cold stone beneath her, heard her own breathing, and felt her lungs and ribs expand and contract as she took air in and out, in and out. She drew her attention to her chest, and the burning heat in the mark.

Zezura was anxious, afraid, and confused. Semra settled herself and sent Zezura her calm. She felt the dragon resist the urge to withdraw, ready to fight and claw her way through her own panic, but as Semra continued sending Zezura as much of her own calm as she could manage, she sensed her soothing. The experience had a symbiotic effect. Semra's serenity mitigated Zezura's anxiety, and as Zezura calmed, Semra's own spirit quieted. When Semra opened her eyes again, she felt better than she had in days.

Dahyu watched her in wonder. "Well?"

Semra nodded. "I think she'll pull away now. I just need to keep myself in check and try to let her know that even when I'm distressed, she can't come roaring into the castle like a bull."

"Good. Listen, Siler and I are working on a plan to get you out during the New Year celebration. I'll let you know as soon as I have something more concrete to share."

"That's still almost three weeks away. Is there any kind of investigation into the assassination plot? Why haven't they killed me yet?"

"They have determined that Axelia Belinon was a cover, and that you were hired by Belvidore to ... well, you know." A shadow fell over his face. "The Belvidorians are locked down in the guest suites of the castle while the investigation continues, and they are expected to be released to return to their own country by the end of the week."

"Oh no. What will that do to the alliance? Is the wedding called off?"

"Well, accusing Belvidore of murdering their host queen can't be good for relationship building. It's ... it's bad. But don't worry, we'll get you out of here and come up with a plan from there."

"It was smart to turn it into a frame job. They probably had already planned to, and seamlessly worked me into it."

"It'll be okay. We're going to get you out."

22

Semra held onto that promise all through that day and night, and all through that week. She held onto it when the week ended and held strong when the second week came and went without any word. But when the third week arrived, the cold fingers of hopelessness reached up to strangle any last shred of optimism that dared endure in her dark dungeon.

She tried to concentrate on reaching out to feel for Zezura, and they exchanged a helpless anxiousness that was both validating and paralyzing. Semra wished she could communicate more explicitly with Zezura, have her find Siler and Dahyu, relay messages. She wondered if the Belvidorian guests were still locked in their guest suites, or if they'd been released to their homeland. Was the investigation complete? Why was she still alive? Would they tell her when she had an execution date, or just come get her one day and tell her that day was her last?

The servant who brought her food and water never said anything, and the only sounds she had to keep her company were the occasional, faint shuffling of guards passing by the end of the corridor and the rustling of her own movements in her tattered dress. Semra breathed heavily as she finished a set of pushups, then stood. The wounds on her back were healing, and she could move easier now, though she still felt the aches of her pains if she moved too suddenly. Semra took up an engagement stance and threw a punch toward the wall, coming just short of impact and contracting her muscles at the last possible moment. She didn't want to reopen her wounds, but she couldn't grow soft either.

She retracted her fist and took up her stance again, this time throwing a jab, cross, hook combination. She felt the strength of her imagined hit and nodded to herself. Better. She reset to strike again, but stopped as she heard footsteps coming toward her. She'd already had breakfast, if it could be called that, and it was too soon for the evening meal. Semra turned hopefully to the door. Perhaps Dahyu had come at last, with plans of rescue.

The eerie light of a lantern cast strange shadows on the floor, and a pit formed in Semra's stomach. Dahyu had carried a torch both times, not a lantern. So had the guards. She drew back from the door as a middle-aged man in a hooded cloak stopped outside her cell.

A low, gravelly voice spoke her name, his tone like lethal lace. "Semra."

"Ramas!" Semra recoiled, her throat constricting and her chest tight.

He arched an eyebrow. "No 'commander'?" He set a covered basket on the ground, and Semra eyed it suspiciously.

"You do not command me."

"I should hope not. I've never seen a mission botched so

severely. I would've been ashamed to have such a stain on my record." He crossed his arms.

"Thanks for the feedback."

"Outside of my tutelage, you lose your touch."

Semra felt her heart beat faster. "Are you here to turn me or to kill me?"

Ramas sighed. "You know, I half expected to find you oiling your knives down here. How are you managing your stress without them? You look as despicably dreadful as you smell." He wrinkled his nose and thumbed the emerald-green serpentine amulet on his wrist. "Do you remember the last conversation we had?"

"You didn't answer my question."

"Humor me. After all, if I'm here to turn you, as you say, it would behoove you to maintain a more positive outward relationship with me, and if I'm here to kill you ... well, you have nothing to lose. Any Hatchling class would know I hold the clear upper hand here." He curled his lip in a sneer.

In the space of that sneer, something deep in her core seemed to break. Ramas had been an excellent teacher and had known her better than most in the mountain. Semra took a deep breath. "You told me it was not my place to question the Framatar, and reminded me that discipline creates strength. That Brens' punishment was for her betterment, that being beaten and bruised would better equip her to save the world from evil. Evil like parents abandoning their children. But the children weren't abandoned, were they, Ramas? They were stolen."

Ramas regarded her shrewdly, then straightened and clasped his hands behind his back, slipping into the lecturing mode she knew so well. "Discipline. Discipline to create strength, strength over weakness, good over evil. Weakness is a form of evil, is it not?"

Semra glared at him, but said nothing. It was true, of course—at least in part. Discipline did create strength, and strength was required to eliminate evil.

"Whether the children were abandoned actively or passively, those parents were weak. They *should* have been slaughtered, to rid the earth of their disgraceful torpor. Not all of them were dealt their deserving end."

Fury rose inside Semra. She strode to the cell door to look Ramas in the face. His eyes were darker than she'd ever seen them as her own bored into his. "My parents were not weak!" she spat. "They charged up the mountain after a wyvern for me. They came for me. They died for me."

Ramas blinked, and Semra saw his surprise that she knew so much. Instantly she regretted it. She'd tipped her hand. She was emotionally invested, sensitive ... weak.

A slow smile crept over Ramas' face. "Died, yes. Because not only were they weak, but they were brash fools. Much like their daughter. Brazen, stubborn, and impulsive! You did well in training, sure, after your initial failures. But it wasn't because you were brilliant or calculated. You were unafraid, even when you had reason to be afraid. And just like your parents, your personal connections made you hotheaded enough to believe you could defy the most powerful man in the whole world of Yatzar Hei. It clouded your judgment. Look where it got you."

Semra began to shake. "I thought you were so intelligent. I used to believe you cared about us, that you were ... human." Her lip curled. "You're neither. You're nothing but a lackey for a man with delusions of grandeur."

"Lackey! *Lackey*! I have poured years of my life into a program teaching idiot children my skill set and coddling mommy and daddy issues. I have paid my dues twice over, after a highly esteemed military career lead to my being sought after by multiple heads of state. I am the cornerstone of the Framatar's vision coming to life. Without me, he is nothing.

"And you ... you are less than nothing. You are the nameless, faceless fly on the wall in a moment of time before the new era is ushered in. The Framatar's favorite ... 'keep her going, Ramas. Make her an example of what it means to serve me well,'" he mocked. "Now you will be a new kind of example."

Ramas' hand shot through the bars and gripped Semra's wrist in a vise, pulling her toward him. Semra writhed in his grasp, but it was no use. She tried to pry his fingers back, tried to use her weight against him, but his iron hold would not break. He pressed his face nearly against the bars, and she leaned away from him. "What did you think you could accomplish? Did you think you would save the prince? Please." His eyes flashed, and she winced as his grip tightened. "The prince is dead."

Semra's lips parted, and her breath fled her body. She couldn't speak.

"Belvidore mobilized their armies as soon as they crossed the border, and Turian has sent his own armies out to meet them. The kingdom has been out of control as of late. Governors are falling left and right, opposing the king's directives or encountering ... tragedies, of various kinds. A dragon has been terrorizing the people of Qalea. Turian has not only failed to address any of these issues, but is now plunging the country into war. And who do we have to blame for these mysterious deaths, for the dragon, for the queen's death?"

She felt her mind collapsing in on itself, her chest exploded like fire, and her eyes brimmed with unbidden tears. It couldn't be. The kingdom would be shattered beyond all repair, with Turian left distraught and vulnerable and without an heir to the throne. Because of her.

"That's right. You," Ramas said, echoing her thoughts. "But do you know what the best part of it is? No one will even miss you when you're gone."

He leaned down to the basket, removed the lid, and drew out a long, pitch-black snake with a bright crimson head and hood.

Semra's eyes grew wide, and she yanked on her arm in a wild frenzy. "Ramas! Stop!" she screamed. "Help, someone! Please!"

Ramas flashed her a cruel smile. "If your parents knew who you really were, they never would have come for you. The only thing you were ever good at was killing, and it seems now you can't even do that right. Oh, but don't worry. No one will remember your failings. No one will think of you at all."

Ramas dropped the writhing snake through the bars and over her shoulder. Semra shuddered and froze as the three-foot snake wrapped itself around her torso. *Where is the head? Grab it by the head ...*

Semra looked down and saw the tail and body wrapped around her front, feeling its smooth scaly skin slithering up her back. She reached for the body of the snake with her free hand, but as she pulled lightly, it resisted, tightening itself around her. A chill ran through her, and Semra tried to think of what to do. She could feel the head sliding up and over her left shoulder. She took a deep breath and reached for the head.

Just as the head of the snake slithered around her neck and over her shoulder, Ramas took out a knife and jabbed the snake through the bars. Fangs sank in beneath Semra's collarbone, and she cried out in pain.

Ramas leaned in closer. "I always hated you."

The snake unwrapped itself from around her and dropped to the floor. Semra gasped for air, suddenly finding she could hardly breathe. Her heart rate spiked, and she felt a burning, tingling sensation in her chest. Ramas released her and, feeling lightheaded and weak, she staggered backward and fell to the ground. She heard the rattling sound of a key in a lock, and Ramas swept in to retrieve his weapon.

He picked up the snake and returned it to its basket, then crouched over Semra. She was aware of a faint metallic taste and could only take ragged, shallow breaths. Her vision blurred for a moment and she found she couldn't move. A cage in a cage, paralyzed in her own body.

Ramas leaned over her. "Turian is an impostor. He was never the rightful king, and now the country will see him for who he really is. But there is one who could take the throne and solve all the problems Turian has caused of late. He can restore peace with Belvidore, drive back the rogue dragon, and return stability to the governances. Ah, yes. The irony of saving the royal family, little one, is that the true king is the very same man whom you betrayed. The older brother."

Semra's eyes widened as she fought to breathe. The Framatar was the king? If he really was Turian's older brother, he had a legitimate claim to the throne. How is it he wasn't the king now? Could he not prove he was the first-born? Was he born in secret?

I must be the only male Shamaran left after Prince Zephan is dead. The Framatar's voice rang in her memory. He was removing all obstacles. Even if he couldn't prove that he was older, he would kill everyone else on the list until he rose to the top. He put impossible tension on an already strained relationship with Belvidore, creating problems only he could solve, and used his own personal syndicate of assassins to selectively dispatch governors and amass wealth for his war.

Ramas leaned down to her ear and whispered in a voice sickly sweet, "Turian will die slowly, tortuously, as he grieves the loss of his wife and heir. You could never have saved them, Semra. You're a murderer. That's who you are. This is a death too good for you." He straightened, taking the basket with him.

Semra felt her world spinning. The tightness in her chest would surely kill her.

Ramas looked down at her with derision. "Consider it my final kindness." With that, he turned on his heel and exited the cell, leaving the door open to mock her.

The tightness in her chest transitioned into a white-hot blaze that shot throughout her body. Suddenly the paralysis lifted, and her back arched in a silent scream as the fire intensified to every square inch of her flesh and bone. In a rush of air, her lungs filled at last, and with that first gasp of oxygen, she felt the heat leave her body and be replaced with a stinging sensation in the dragon's kiss on her chest. She reached up with one hand and tentatively felt along its edge. With a shock, she realized that the mark had widened and extended above the cut of her dress toward her collarbone.

In all of Yatzar, Semra thought to herself, *there is nothing so strange as a dragon's kiss! What is happening to me?* She tested her limbs and stood to her feet, feeling strong and refreshed once again. *Zezura, you crazy lizard, you've done it again—and you're not even here!* Not willing to try her luck any further, Semra turned and raced down the dungeon corridor after Ramas.

All the fury of a thousand caged drakes seemed to descend on her small frame in that moment. His words only moments ago filed through her brain at lightning speed. *If your parents knew who you really were, they never would have come for you. I always hated you ... murderer!*

Semra funneled all her rage into launching herself forward and into a kick aimed at the back of Rama's knee, driving downward with her full weight. His knee collapsed, and she landed on the joint as he fell, then gripped him in a headlock from behind, cinching her arm tight. The older man reached up and grasped her wrists, pulling down as hard as he could to regain his airway. Semra fought to maintain pressure on his neck, but he used his bodyweight to sling her into the wall to his left.

Her grip loosened for just a moment, but as she started to fall, she wrapped her legs around his waist and hooked her heels into him, securing her position and cutting off his air supply. He writhed under her grip, and fear struck her when she saw that their struggle had knocked the basket's lid off kilter. A forked tongue slithered in and out to taste the air, then the bright red head appeared at the opening, and the deadly snake slowly glided out of the basket.

Semra seized up for only a moment. In a flash of instinct, she kept her right arm tight around Ramas' trachea while plunging her left hand down and snatching the snake behind the head. She struck Ramas with the snake's head again and again until finally the snake opened its mouth and drove its fangs into his arm. She felt his resistance ebb as his strength left him, and she toppled to one side, snake still held in her hand.

With the other hand, she reached inside the cloak to the dagger at Ramas' waist, drew it, and cut off the snake's head. She tossed the pieces into the basket and leaned over Ramas. "You spout poison, and you die by poison."

His eyes were wide, but he was stiff and still, paralyzed by the snake's venom. Semra looked him over and spied the emerald-green serpent amulet she knew so well. She cut it off his wrist with her dagger, stowed it in her dress, and took off down the passage just as she heard a guard's feet running toward her.

She twirled the dagger in her hand, but just as she thought to kill him with a flick of her wrist, Dahyu's words about the guard Zezura injured came back to her. *The guards are good men, just trying to do their duty.* Ugh. Leaving people alive was so much more work!

Semra grunted and ran forward, deflecting the guard's attack and banging his helmet into the wall with the butt of her dagger. He swung forward, but she ducked and rolled to the other side, parried a second blow with one hand, then sprinted up the stairs and ripped a torch off the wall. Torch in one hand, dagger in the other, Semra turned and delivered a vicious blow to the guard's head with her torch hand. He fell to the side. Semra picked up his shield and continued sprinting up the steps to her right.

Another guard met her as she turned the corner, and she ducked and slung the shield into his knees from below, toppling him over her. She ran past him down the hall, retracing her steps to find the next stair. Shouts came from behind her as she climbed the spiral staircase, winding upward. Three more guards entered the stair in front of her, but the narrow staircase allowed Semra to meet them one after the other, blocking and slashing, parrying, bursting in, and toppling them over each other as she went.

She drove her shield down on the head of the last guard and followed through with a dagger to the guard's sword arm. He drew back, and she adjusted, stabbing straight into the chainmail of his torso. He fell backward. She dropped her shield and plucked the guard's sword from his limp hands, then kicked him down the steps and leaped up the staircase, a sword in one hand and Ramas' dagger in the other.

Semra braced herself for the next round of guards, but none came. She heard sounds behind her, pushing her to the limit as she flew up, up, up to the main level of the castle keep. Why had no one stopped her yet? An unsettled feeling twisted her gut as she continued up the stairs, and as she reached the main-level guard room, she slowed.

Semra didn't know the way from the guard and meeting rooms back into the servants' labyrinth beneath the castle, and knowing she'd never make it across the courtyard, she took a breath before the last bend, trying to think of what to do.

A clanging beneath her reminded her that her pursuers weren't slowing. Taking another breath, she rounded the corner, went up the final steps, and turned right, away from the guard room toward the meeting rooms.

She stopped short, eyes wide. No less than thirty guards stood in the room before her, all armed and waiting. Semra whirled around, but guards at her back seized her. Just as they took hold of her, the guards from down the stair spilled out onto the landing and into the room.

Her heart beat wildly—the game was up. The guards dragged her through a door into a large conference room, and ten more guards fell in behind. The otherwise rectangular room had a semicircle on the right, which highlighted an exquisitely carved armchair standing at the head of a long wooden table. Floor-to-ceiling glass windows allowed light to pour in behind it, and illuminated in the armchair sat the incorrigible General Gresvig.

23

Gresvig lifted a goblet to his lips, set it down, and leaned back in his chair. "So good of you to join us. Please, sit."

The guards dumped her into a chair and stood close on either side. Semra looked around the room and saw three more men of state seated at the table. On the far end of the room, to the left, double doors lead out into the inner courtyard. She was so close! Her heart sank. With this many guards, she'd never make it.

"Gentlemen, you see precisely what I mean," Gresvig said to the other finely dressed men in attendance. "The kingdom is not safe, and I'm afraid His Majesty the King has done little to mitigate the threats. Take this girl here. A child made her way into the castle, into the gala, and murdered the queen! A child! If the king cannot prevent these tragedies, cannot keep even the smallest of threats safely locked away in the dungeons, Jannemar is doomed."

A man with a sharp nose and beady eyes examined Semra from across the table. "We need to overhaul our security. I am prepared to back all the suggestions you made last quarter."

"Thank you, Voldar." Gresvig dipped his head, then turned to Semra. "And what do *you* think of our ... security? Have you managed to murder more of my guards?"

"I have not murdered any guards. It would certainly have been simpler to kill them, but I did my best to slow them down or knock them out instead." Semra felt the burning in her chest, and could sense Zezura's urgency, but as she glanced out the tall windows behind Gresvig, all she saw was blue sky. She lifted her chin and squared her shoulders, returning her gaze to the general.

Gresvig leaned forward on the table and tapped his fingertips together. "Is that so? An assassin with both arrogance and a conscience. Ha! Who has ever heard of such a thing?" His eyes drifted to her upper chest below the collarbone, where the dragon's kiss was now visible above her dress. He lowered his voice so it was almost a whisper. "And where did that pretty thing come from, I wonder?"

"General," said another man at the table, "with all due respect, it seems the issue here is in the training of the guard. Identify how she got out of the dungeon and cull the incompetent among our guard from employment. There is no need to implement curfews on the people or institute a military control over the castle guard. You are overreaching. Have this wretch removed at once and confer with the captain of the guard!"

Voldar shook his head. "General Soldan, we are on the brink of war with Belvidore, and there is a dragon terrorizing Qalea. We're scrambling to get replacement governors up to speed after such a string of tragedies, and the people grow uneasy. A temporary increase in caution and control while we get a handle on the situation is absolutely necessary, or would you have the reign of King Turian known for the riots in the streets?"

Gresvig motioned to the guards, and they grabbed Semra by the arms, pulling her up to stand before Gresvig. "Tell me," he said slowly. "How did you manage to get out? Just long enough to waltz into my rather obvious trap, of course."

Semra's eyes blazed. She opened her mouth to speak, but a huge blue blur crashed through the tall windows behind him, and she threw her hands up to protect her face from the shattering glass. Zezura barreled in, fitting her two front feet and enormous head through the broken window, and swiped Gresvig out of his chair and onto the floor.

The guards fell back, and Semra's heart leaped. She jumped up, ran to Zezura's side, clambered up her neck and out the window onto her back where the dragon hovered over the outer ward. Terrified guards drew their swords, but Zezura spewed a torrent of flame into the room. Gresvig stood, and Semra flashed him a mischievous grin as Zezura beat her wings against the air and tore away from the castle.

For the first time in three weeks, Semra breathed in the fresh air, relishing the wind in her hair, the bright daylight, the freedom of flying. She indulged in the glorious rush of pulling up, up, higher above the castle. But it couldn't last. Zezura colored herself perfectly against the sky, but Semra wasn't invisible. The air was too high profile, especially with Qalea on the lookout for a dragon. With Semra only marginally aware of the arrows falling short of them, Zezura banked left and climbed higher, then dove behind the cliff and flew low along the Shalladin River.

The deeper blue of the river rolled over Zezura's shimmering scales, and her left side mirrored the gray of the rocky cliff. For some time the dragon flew unseen along the cliff, then Semra tapped on her neck, indicating they should find a place to set down. Zezura flew up the cliff face, over open pasture and farmland, and into the wood on the far side of the Dezapi River. She slowed to a walk and lead them to the river where she lowered her head and took in deep draughts of water.

Semra slid off her back and slipped gratefully into the Dezapi's cool, gentle current with a contented sigh. She ducked under the surface, relishing the feeling of freshness after three weeks on a dirty dungeon floor. When she came up for air, Zezura pounced into the river beside her with a huge splash. The dragon tossed her head and flapped her wings, sending gleeful, choppy waves in every direction.

Semra laughed, reached up to Zezura's neck, and held on. The dragon swam deeper into the river and carried her upstream, her body dangling in the water. In the leafy canopy overhead, rays of sunlight played with bright shades of jade and emerald, and springy moss on the forest floor seemed to laugh as the birds hopped around on it. Up ahead and to the left of the river, Semra saw a small cave—perhaps twenty feet tall and fifteen feet wide. A natural door of hanging vines fell over its mouth, grass grew up and over its top, and yellow-petaled flowers welcomed them.

Semra patted Zezura's neck and pushed off into the river. "Is this where you've been hiding?"

Zezura rolled in the water and popped up again with a splash, letting her tongue fall out the side of her mouth.

"It's a great spot," Semra agreed, smiling. "Okay, do you think I can manage to wear pants from here on out? I've been wearing this gown for three weeks, and it's positively disgusting, never mind being ripped up in the back. We'll have to apologize to Princess Aviama someday. At this point, I think it had better be burned!"

Semra pulled herself onto Zezura's back, shrugged out of

her filthy dress, and tossed it on the bank to dry in the afternoon sun, then she dove back into the river and washed the dungeon grime from her skin. The pockets of the black pants she still wore contained only Ramas' serpent amulet. They felt too light with the sheaths built into the pant legs standing empty. Semra thought mournfully of her confiscated knives. Maybe when she figured out what to wear for a shirt, she'd be able to pick up some knives as well.

A rustling in the woods made Semra spin around, immediately on guard for threats. To her relief, Siler walked into view, carrying two felled rabbits and a bow. He wore a white shirt, black pants, and a quiver on his back over his sword. He looked up and saw Zezura, then dropped the rabbits and ran forward. "Semra?"

Though only her head and shoulders appeared above the water, she squealed and ducked down. "Stop! I'm here; I'm fine. I need your shirt. Turn around."

"What? Oh ..." Siler's gaze drifted to the dress on the rocks. He grinned, then turned around, took off his weapons, tunic and shirt, and laid the shirt on the bank close to the water.

Semra made her way to the bank, watching him carefully. She grabbed the shirt and turned around, then glanced back over her shoulder. Siler stood here looking at her, eyes dark. "Siler! I said to turn around." She quickly donned the shirt.

"I was. I just saw your back. Dahyu was right; those scars look gnarly." He set his jaw and took a breath. "Are you okay?"

Semra climbed out onto the bank, but looked away from him, suddenly feeling awkward. "I'm fine."

"Of course you are." Siler sighed. "It's over now. You're safe. You'll be all healed up soon, and we can go."

Semra snapped her head back toward him. "Go? Go where?"

"Anywhere! Anywhere but here."

Semra shook her head. "We can't. He's going to kill again."

Zezura left the water and meandered off toward the cave, and Siler stepped forward and put his hands on Semra's shoulders. "Semra, he's a killer. He kills. That's what he does, and he will continue to kill as long as he has breath. There's nothing you can do."

"I have to try! Ramas says the Framatar is Turian's older brother and the rightful king. Belvidore and Jannemar armies are marching out to meet each other as we speak, and the Framatar has created a slew of problems for Jannemar that he can solve for everyone to establish himself as king. Gresvig is taking over every aspect of security in the castle and the city, using the remaining soldiers under his command. The whole country is under the Framatar's thumb, and the king doesn't even know it." Tears stung Semra's eyes.

Siler pulled her into him and held her. "Shhh. It's okay."

"I don't think it will be," Semra said, sniffling. "The prince is already dead, the king is going to die, and all of Jannemar is doomed."

"That's the spirit." Siler chucked softly against her hair.

Semra pulled away, wiping her face and looking up at him. "Well, it's true."

Siler took a deep breath. "I know it is. I just don't think that perspective is going to be particularly helpful. Wait a minute ... did you say the prince is dead?"

Semra nodded. "Ramas told me."

Siler drew back. "Ramas? When did you see ...? Come on,

I want to hear everything. Dahyu said the prince is still alive, so Ramas must have lied."

Hope sprung to Semra's heart. "Are you sure?"

"Yes. I spoke to him only this morning. Sit with me while I cook these rabbits. I have bread and some other things I snatched from town today too." He leaned down, opened the sack and tossed her a roll.

Semra clutched at the roll and took a huge bite, nearly choking on it in her haste. Siler regarded her with concern and lead her to a makeshift fire pit just inside the cave. She sat down, and Zezura curled up under a low part of the ceiling. The rest of the cave was empty, with only about fifteen feet of unused cave left after Zezura had taken up her place.

"How long have you been here?"

"Not long. Dragons are creatures of habit, and I think she was someplace to the west at first, then she moved here maybe a week ago. I only just found it two days ago after seeing her flying this direction a couple times. But we can't stay. If I found it ..."

Semra nodded. "They won't be far behind."

"Exactly." Siler took out his knife and started skinning one of the rabbits.

Semra gestured toward the knife. "You got any more of those?"

He grinned. "Yeah, sure. You must be going through withdrawals. I can't spare more than one, but here you go." Siler pulled out a second knife and spun the handle toward her.

Semra took it and picked up the other rabbit. "Thanks. So where's Dahyu? He said he'd found you, but that was weeks ago."

Siler took the rabbit from her hands and replaced it with a roll and an apple from his sack. "He should be back sometime this afternoon, I should think. He did find me ... the whole castle went into a lockdown procedure of sorts, with the royal family disappearing down into some secret underground staging area. I pretty much hid out for a couple of days and then caught a glimpse of him the next day. We came up with a meeting place in Qalea, outside that shop where you got in the trunk. Once I got out of the castle, I went by there every evening until he could get some news from inside and let me know what was going on. He said you'd been beaten pretty bad but were alive, and that you'd taken the fall for the hit."

Semra devoured the last of the roll and apple, then reached again for the second rabbit. "Yeah. I didn't have many cards to play, so when I saw they weren't going to let me talk to anyone, I said a plan was in place for another member of the royal family to die, and I would only speak to the king. Gresvig showed up instead."

Siler's eyes widened. "He has a firm control on everything in the castle. It makes sense. Did Dahyu tell you we were working on a plan to get you out? How did you escape? We were going to try to get you out tonight when the New Year festival started. Our plans kept getting muddied, and it took longer than we'd hoped."

"He did, and then weeks went by. I had no means of getting out on my own, but when Ramas came to kill me, I had to try."

Siler paused. "Ramas came to kill you?"

Semra nodded. "With a poisonous snake in a basket. It bit me, and I was paralyzed, and when I was almost dead, he unlocked the door and came in to get the snake and taunt me."

"Wait, what? One of his red-headed kraits? The species he uses kills in minutes. You never would have survived!"

"The dragon's kiss ... it sort of absorbed the venom, I think. The mark is larger than it was before, and then I felt fine. He left the door open so I ran out and killed him." Semra shivered at the memory.

Siler stared at her. "You killed Ramas? You're good, but he's better. How ..."

"I doubt he's used to people coming back to life. I surprised him, got lucky, and managed to use his own snake against him."

Siler furrowed his brows. "And the dragon's kiss ... isn't that a one-time thing? Although, I suppose there aren't many creatures better suited to defend against venom than reptiles. Even really, really big ones, like Zezura. Some kind of dragon magic."

"I don't know." She filled him in on the rest of her escape.

Siler whistled. "How many dead guards now?"

"None, I hope. They're just doing their jobs. Dahyu said Zezura hurt a good man when she came into the courtyard that first day."

"Semra! Didn't they come after you?"

"Yes. I just tried to maim them enough to slow them down."

"You're being irresponsible with your life. If you're caught, you're as good as dead, and none of our rescue plans panned out. Dahyu is making you soft." Siler started the fire and set his skinned rabbit over it. "I don't think you should go back."

Semra glared at him. "I disagree." She wasn't soft ... was she?

"You just spent three weeks rotting in a dungeon and almost died numerous times. You did what you came to do. You got into the castle, you're free of the Framatar. The threat is realized. There's nothing left for you here."

Semra tossed her hands up. "I failed! I played right into their hands. The threat is realized because they made a successful hit on the queen, not because I stopped it. The king doesn't know anything the Framatar doesn't want him to know. I've done absolutely nothing worthwhile since leaving the mountain!"

"You saved Lesala," Siler said, voice soft. "You saved me ... you gave me the courage to leave and showed the rest of them that it's possible to get out. You're a trailblazer, Semra; you always have been. When will you be enough?"

Semra felt a squirming in her gut at his words, but she said nothing.

"This isn't a fight you can win. I want you with me. Please. We can start over."

Semra shook her head.

Siler's shoulders slumped. "I can't sit around waiting for the next suicide mission to take your life. I won't. If you stay, you'll stay alone. Think about it."

Semra stared into the fire with a sullen expression, watching the flames dancing up to lick the rabbit and listening to its crackle. She spitted the rabbit on which she'd worked, cleaned her knife, and wished she had some oil for the blade. Instead, she combed through her tangled mess of hair with her fingers, yanking on the knots and grimacing as she accidentally pulled out some of her hair in the effort. She glanced up at Siler. His face was hard as flint, and he, too, glared into the flames. Zezura slept soundly in the corner, a little wisp of smoke escaping from her nostrils.

"Dress. Still outside," Semra muttered. She slipped the knife into the sheath on her thigh, walked out of the cave, and had just retrieved the gown from the riverbank when approaching hoofbeats called for her attention.

Dahyu rode up on a chestnut mare, and a warm feeling

constricted her stomach into a strangely exciting discomfort. He wore a white, embroidered tunic and brown trousers, and his face lit up when he caught sight of Semra.

"It's true! You're free! How did you find us?" Dahyu asked, slipping off the chestnut and running forward. He reached for her, then stopped short. "How is your back?"

"Much better." Semra smiled awkwardly as Dahyu seized her in a bear hug. When he released her, she said, "Zezura brought me here. I didn't realize you both knew about it until I saw Siler. How are you?"

"Relieved to see you, thanks for asking. It's the best thing that's happened to me since the gala. I wish I could stay longer, but the New Year celebration is tonight, and the royal family wants to keep things business as usual for the people. The nobles are invited, so I'll have to return in a few hours. Are you sure you're okay?"

Semra nodded. "I'm fine."

Dahyu arched an eyebrow. "Would you tell me if you weren't?"

The question caught her off guard, and she paused.

Dahyu gave a knowing grunt and an, "Mhmm, thought so," as she considered the question.

"No. I think I would. A fly on a dragon and a swim in the river really do a person good. And look at all this sunlight!"

Dahyu laughed. "I'm keeping an eye on you. So what happened? How did you get out?"

Semra took a breath and recounted the events of her escape once more, beginning with Ramas and ending with Zezura crashing through the window behind Gresvig and saving her.

Dahyu whistled, and his expression grew grave. "You know, I would appreciate it if you had fewer brushes with death."

"These were entirely unavoidable! I didn't go looking for trouble—"

"Except for confessing to a murder you didn't commit."

"Which was strategic and necessary, thank you very much. And for the record, I consider today's events successful brushes with life."

Dahyu chuckled. "I suppose you can spin just about anything, can't you?"

He walked her up to the mouth of the cave and held back the hanging vines for her, revealing a shirtless Siler sitting moodily by the fire. "Um, hello." Dahyu cocked his head to one side. "Missing something?"

Siler glared up at him. "Nope. I always walk around shirtless. It's the only option for real men."

"Wow, I thought you'd be in better spirits now that Semra's finally free."

Semra rolled her eyes. "He gave me his shirt, and now he's in a mood and refuses to get on board with the plan."

"What plan?" asked Dahyu.

"Exactly," Siler said. "What plan, indeed! No plan. There is no viable plan."

"Ahhh." Dahyu grimaced.

"Siler, you're going to burn the rabbit." Semra plucked the rabbit off the fire and laid it down to cool. "My plan is to not give up and hand over Jannemar and all the children in the mountain to the Framatar."

Siler let out an exasperated sigh. "That's not a plan. That's a daydream."

"How many times have you been faced with almost certain death? And here you are."

"I am alive because of detailed preparation and executing operations where I have an advantage of some sort. Any mission ready knows this. Calculated risk is not the same as suicide."

"I haven't heard you doing much calculating. All I've heard is running away." Semra sent a piercing gaze into Siler that she hoped would shrivel his cowardly soul. Still, a small voice spoke in the back of her mind. What if he's right?

"All I've done is calculate! What do you think we've been doing these three weeks? Spinning our wheels and burning our useless brainpower, because none of it was enough. Nothing worked. If Ramas hadn't tried to kill you, the door never would have been left open, and you would've rotted in the dungeon. If the dragon's kiss didn't contain some extra dose of mystery magic, you would have died. If you hadn't killed Ramas, you would have died. Even with all those lucky strokes, if Gresvig's trap hadn't ended in an above-ground room with huge windows facing the outside, and Zezura hadn't come when she did, guess what? Again, you would've died. Just because you haven't seen me going crazy doesn't mean I haven't been. And I have been."

Semra swallowed, the fire within her softening at Siler's desperate tone and wild storm-gray eyes. He looked down at the floor as she stared back at him, and he started cutting up the rabbit with sharp, harsh strokes.

Dahyu glanced between them but said nothing.

Not yet willing to relinquish the embers in her heart, Semra cleared her throat. "I ... appreciate what you've been through. And I know I've been lucky. I just ... it doesn't hurt to try. What did you think about so far?"

Siler stayed quiet, pouring his energies into the cooked rabbit. Dahyu waited a beat, then spoke. "Honestly, most of our ideas haven't been realistic. We did think the New Year celebration could be helpful to us, since everyone will be wearing white and carrying lanterns to celebrate late into the night. Blending into the crowds of Qalea should be easy, but beyond that, we hit a wall. I can still get into the castle, but I might not easily get back out until tomorrow at the earliest."

Semra nodded as she picked up a piece of meat. "Okay, so the two of you already got white shirts—except, now I'm wearing Siler's, so he still needs one. We can start there. And we can't stay here much longer or the assassins of the mountain will track Zezura and find us. At this point the only thing we can hope for is an audience with the king, without Gresvig or Voldar there. We can stage a kidnapping for all I care, but it's a last ditch effort."

"That'll be tricky. The royal family is under extreme surveillance. I barely got out."

"Well, you're not royal family, so naturally it will be harder to get close to the Shamarans," Semra said. "But you have access. If you could tell the king directly, tell him you have sensitive information that requires a private meeting, it could work."

Dahyu shook his head. "He's never isolated enough. I've tried to get him alone, but he's swarmed by his generals and other important figures of court at all times. Whenever he has a moment, he locks himself in his living quarters, with guards everywhere."

"But you know Aviama. Use her and your father's connections to get the message across. There has to be a way."

"With the celebration tonight, I don't know how it will be possible, but I'll certainly try."

"We could wait in Qalea for some sort of signal, and meet you behind the Dezapi Falls, or on the roof of the castle with Zezura once it's night."

"We've talked this round and round already," Siler said.

"It won't work. Not with the number of spies the Framatar has in the castle, and not with so many of his minions unaccounted for."

Semra ripped off a piece of rabbit with her teeth and swallowed. "Dahyu and I are going to town to get you a white shirt and finalize a plan. We'll come back, clear out of here, and wait somewhere new for night to fall. I'm doing this. While we're gone, think up some new ideas and get your head in the game."

24

"What if someone sees me?" Dahyu asked, staring past Semra to the rack of clothes drying in the afternoon sun outside a stone house on the outskirts of Qalea. From their cover at the edge of the woods, they couldn't see anyone.

"Ignore them. Be confident, and they'll assume it's yours."

"What if whoever sees me owns the house?"

Semra shrugged. "Come up with something. Just play it off and get out of there."

Dahyu shook his head. "I can't do that."

"What's so hard about it? Nobody ever died from having one less shirt. They have a whole basket of clothes! They'll be fine."

"I know, but it's just the principle of it. It's not ours to take. They bought it with their own money or made it with their own hands. What if it's sentimental?"

"Dahyu! It's a shirt! Siler needs a shirt, and you're going to steal one for him. If we don't all die tonight, we can pay them back later."

"Well, excuse me if theft doesn't come naturally! I haven't spent my life killing and pillaging to fuel the whims of a madman."

Semra drew back, Dahyu's words hitting her like a slap in the face. Her lips parted, and she pressed them together again in a hard line. "Fine. Stay here in your fancy, pressed, embroidered shirt while I go steal one for our friend who gave up his for me. Haven't you any sense of loyalty? Don't sit too tall on your high horse or someone will see you."

Semra slipped off the back of the chestnut, leaving Dahyu in the saddle, and headed for the house. She heard Dahyu hiss her name as she left the cover of the woods, but she ignored it. Siler would never have cared about snatching a single shirt. A woman wearing pants in Qalea was more memorable than a man, especially with her hair looking like a frizzy bird's nest. He would've been happy to do it, and he probably would've grabbed an extra just in case.

But he's spent his whole life 'killing and pillaging' too, Semra thought darkly to herself. *In Dahyu's eyes, he's just as evil as you are.* Trying to shake off the thoughts, she strode forward with all the confidence of royalty. Three houses down and to her left, a woman called to her children from the kitchen window, and to her right, a teenage boy transported firewood in a wheelbarrow. Semra shook her head. *Siler is the only one who understands you, and he's going to leave you. Dahyu can't understand you, so he'll leave you soon enough.*

She walked up to the drying rack and plucked one white shirt and one dark one off the rungs. Aware of the teenager wheeling his firewood along the street, she turned her back to him, then tossed the shirts over her shoulder and made a fuss of straightening the remaining clothes on the rungs. A clanging sounded from the house. Semra edged closer to the wall next to an open window and peeked inside. Through an interior doorway, she saw a woman sweeping. A hairbrush and comb sat on an end table in arms' reach of Semra at the window, and a white dress lay on the bed.

Semra eyed the comb. Dahyu wouldn't like it. But who was Dahyu to dictate what she could and couldn't do? *If he thinks he's so much better than me, he can save the world himself.* Surely the woman didn't need both a brush and a comb. They didn't serve exactly the same function, but the brush would suffice for the woman in a pinch. Something was better than nothing, and Semra had nothing.

She waited for the wheelbarrow to pass out of view, glanced behind her, and reached through the window to grab the comb. After folding it inside one of the shirts, she walked two houses over, then turned and headed for the trees.

Semra arrived back in the woods without incident, and Dahyu met her on horseback. Something tightened in her gut, and a guilty feeling made her lower her gaze. Suddenly angry at herself for caring, she looked up and glared at Dahyu, who stared at her with open consternation.

"What?" she demanded, stalking into the forest. "If you have something to say, say it."

"I thought all you needed was a shirt." There was a woundedness in his tone that Semra tried hard not to care about.

"Yeah, well, I changed my mind. Siler might need a darker clothing option later on, and my hair is totally out of control. I don't fight as well with crazy hair."

"That's ridiculous. You can't stand skirts, but your hair has to be perfect?"

"Perfect? Perfect? I've been in a dungeon for three weeks without adequate food or water, without a garderobe chute or chamber pot, nothing but my own filth to keep me company, and mere hours into my freedom, you're going to chastise me for wanting untangled hair?"

Dahyu held his hands up. "Okay, okay, I'm sorry. Look, I know you've had it hard, but the people of Qalea don't always have it easy either. Especially those living on the outskirts here. You've been edgy lately."

Semra shot him a flat look. "Again, might I remind you of the dungeon scenario."

"I don't think it's just that. What's bothering you?"

Semra stared past him, letting her thoughts race each other for prominence. Jannemar is doomed. I've done nothing right since leaving the mountain. Everyone I've ever known will kill or be killed until none are left. The Framatar will win. Siler is right. The mission is suicide. Semra snapped her head toward Dahyu. "Is that really all you think of me? Killer and a thief, fueling the 'whims of a madman,' is that it?"

"Wait, hold on. No!"

Semra put her hands on her hips. "That's what you said."

"I didn't mean it like that."

"And what exactly did you mean? When you said I spent my life killing and pillaging?"

"Well ... I mean, you have. Strictly speaking, that's correct to say. But that doesn't mean you have to be like him. The dragonlord."

Semra's mouth dropped open and she stepped back. "You think I'm like him!"

"I think ..." Dahyu paused.

Semra gathered everything she needed to know in the space of that pause. She clenched her fists, set her jaw, and whirled around and stomped into the woods without a word.

Dahyu rode up behind her. "Stop! You didn't let me finish!"

She turned to face him. "I didn't need to. You think I'm like the dragonlord. I grew up killing; I'm a rotten person; I'll never be anything else."

"That's not what I said! The dragonlord does whatever he wants without regard for anyone else. And you just stole three things when at most you only needed one. Maybe you picked up a thing or two, that's all."

Semra's eyes blazed with anger. "That's all? *That's all?* Maybe I've got some things in common with the murderous dictator who slaughtered my parents. Well, you know what? Maybe you have something in common with the rich elitists who strut around in their marble-floored houses, having more money than their people could ever dream of having, yet still wanting nothing more than to have more and more. Maybe your image is more important to you than anything else, and maybe you can't stand to be seen with me because it would damage your reputation."

"You're not listening!"

"I heard you loud and clear."

"You're being self-centered."

Semra felt tears prick her eyes, and she turned on her heel and walked off into the forest, yelling back at him as she went. "If I'm being so self-centered, warn the king yourself. You're probably the best shot he has anyway. And don't follow me!"

Self-centered? *Self-centered?* She left the mountain for Lesala and Brens, not for herself. She came to stop the Framatar and save Jannemar, to save the royal family, not herself. Siler wanted to run away, and she'd said no, because staying and fighting was the right thing to do. How could he think her selfish?

Tears fell freely now, running down her face and into the blurred sea of leaves she crushed underfoot as she went. Angrily she wiped them away, but steady hoofbeats sounded behind her, making them fall afresh. She screamed back at Dahyu, "Don't follow me!"

The hoofbeats stopped, and part of her hurt not to hear them, though she knew she'd also have been upset had they continued. She was right, anyway. Dahyu had connections in the castle and was the best chance of warning the king. Maybe Siler was right. She'd done all she could; she'd never be enough, and Jannemar was on its own.

Semra broke into a run, replaying Dahyu's words over and over. *Well, excuse me if theft doesn't come naturally! I haven't spent my life killing and pillaging ...*

The dragonlord does whatever he wants without regard for anyone else ... Maybe you picked up a thing or two.

You're being self-centered.

She crashed through the brush, feet pounding into the earth, heart racing. Siler's voice filtered in through the chaos.

Dahyu is making you soft.

You're being irresponsible with your life.

This isn't a fight you can win.

You did what you came to do. You got into the castle, you're free of the Framatar. The threat is realized. There's nothing left for you here.

She wiped her face with her sleeve and finally slowed to a walk, yanking the comb through the tangles of her hair as she went.

You saved Lesala. You saved me ... you gave me the courage to leave. You're a trailblazer, Semra, you always have been. When will you be enough?

How could he know who she really was, and still see her in such light? Siler knew she was a killer. He knew she couldn't escape her identity. And her skill made him respect her, not hate her.

I want you with me.

Could Dahyu say the same? Semra thought back to Siler catching her coming from the drakes' cages, carrying Lesala on his back on the mountain plateaus, and distracting the dragon wranglers while Semra made her escape. He had resources from skimming off the top of his missions, and he wanted her with him.

What will you do when it's all over?

I don't know. Maybe I'll get a house.

A house? You want a house? *Our kind can't stay in houses ...*

Their conversation in the forest outside the Shamaran Castle came back to her clear as crystal. He was right, of course. Who did she think she was to be able to settle down in some cottage sweeping floors and doing laundry, cooped up in four small walls with small-minded idiots who'd never done anything in their whole lives? Maybe going with Siler wouldn't be the end of the world. It might even be the best option she had.

But if running away from Jannemar's problems to live in some villa with Siler was the best option she had, why did her stomach still turn when she thought of it? Regret swept through her, and she jerked the comb through a particularly stubborn tangle, so hard that the knot broke off in her hand.

"Ow!" Semra yelped, looking down at the gnarled knot of hair in her hand. She dropped it and continued marching onward. Dahyu's face filled her mind, and a lump rose in her throat as she replayed their last conversation. She hadn't meant to hurt him. He wasn't really a pompous elitist, was he? Dahyu had been shocked when he'd learned of her roots as a child assassin, but he'd also been kind and understanding when he heard her story. He'd insisted she was more than an assassin, that death was her job but her inclination was life.

Semra found the shallow place in the river that Dahyu's horse had waded through earlier, and crossed to the other side. She clambered up the bank and made her way back to the small cave Zezura had been calling home. Semra knew she hadn't left things well with Siler by telling him to get his head in the game while she and Dahyu traipsed off to get him a shirt. It was an excuse to be away from him and a refusal to accept his decision not to watch her kill herself in some impossible savior complex. A reasonable decision on his part, really. She would apologize, make things right.

Semra stopped just outside the mouth of the cave, taking a deep breath to steady her nerves. He would forgive her. Wouldn't he? She shook off the thought. Of course he would forgive her. After one more steadying breath, she pulled back the hanging vines and stepped into the cave.

It was empty. All traces of the fire that had been there only shortly before were gone, and the hollowness of that space echoed in her soul. Her stomach dropped, and her legs felt filled with lead. Her voice trembled as she sent it out into the small cave. "Siler?"

Nothing. He'd left her? Even Zezura was gone. Could her dragon be angry with her too, angry enough to fly away from the one place Semra knew to return to?

"Siler!"

The nothingness mocked her, reminding her with a cold dose of reality that she too belonged to that nothingness. She had done nothing, was worth nothing, had nothing. And nobody cared.

Anybody who had cared, she'd effectively driven away. Siler had followed her dutifully, a constant companion and comfort, ever since the mountain, and finally he'd had enough, had told her so, and she'd ignored him. Dahyu had tried to follow her even after she insulted him, and she'd screamed accusations at him and run him off.

Semra sank to her knees, heart aching, hands trembling. Neither of them deserved such treatment. She didn't always agree with Siler, but in this he was right. There was no hope of success and dying for an impossible cause wouldn't do any good. Dahyu didn't always understand her, but he seemed to believe in Semra in a way she couldn't believe in herself.

Even tears had abandoned her—nothing to relieve the pressure building in her chest. Sapped of energy, she shut her eyes against the torrent of thoughts swirling about her, and out of the chaos came the voice of her childhood, the dragonlord.

My dear, my dear ... you know I am the only one who has never left you.

Semra took in a ragged breath and shut her eyes tighter, shaking her head.

I taught you to be strong, to take care of yourself so no one could mistreat you or see you as weak again! I gave you a place here, a purpose, a name. And what is your name?

Bandaka. Semra Bandaka.

She thought of Adis comforting her as a child, of the Framatar at the naming ceremony, officially blessing her with the name of Bandaka that she had so joyfully accepted. She had turned her back on the only family she ever had.

Ramas' voice whispered from a corner of her mind.

I always hated you.

If your parents knew who you really were, they never would've come for you.

I always hated you.

The Framatar's soft, threatening voice and insistent gaze

caught up with her again, the melody of his sound weaving in between the hurt, stricken expressions she'd last seen on Siler and Dahyu's faces.

My dear, my dear ... you know I am the only one who has never left you.

I always hated you.

Killing and pillaging ...

There's nothing left for you here.

Maybe you picked up a thing or two ...

You're a murderer, Semra. It's who you are.

Semra opened her eyes, scanning the empty little cave and its monotonous black and gray. Its dull, lifeless colors highlighted the emotions she felt within herself. She drew the one knife she had, the one Siler had given her, and stared at it. It could use a polish, but it still reflected her red, puffy eyes in its blade.

Weakness!

Semra let out a blood-curdling shriek, lifted the knife above her head and held it there as all the tension, grief and anger built up in her shoulders and arms, then she brought it plunging down into the dirt floor with all the might she could muster. The sound of her own scream reverberated in her ears as her shoulders heaved from exertion. She ripped the knife out and absentmindedly wiped it on her pants, staring off into the nothingness of the cave, and of her life, and her soul.

A small crinkle of leaves sounded behind her, and an instant later, her head exploded with pain and she sprawled onto the ground. Semra rolled to one side and gathered her feet under her, turning to face her assailant. Not one, but three assassins stood in the opening. Pinji, a dark-haired, wiry young man from Siler's class, stood in the center holding a club. Isra, a broad-shouldered lout who'd graduated with Semra, stood behind him to one side. But it was the third assassin that caught Semra's attention. Small nose, thin lips pulled back in a snarl, and piercing brown eyes she'd know anywhere ...

Brens.

25

Pinji bent his knees, preparing to spring into action, and Isra and Brens crept forward. Semra twirled the knife in her hands and felt the burning in her chest as she sent out a distress signal to Zezura. She felt nothing in return.

"I didn't think I'd find the traitor sniveling in a hole," Pinji sneered. "And to think, you were always teacher's pet."

"Pinji, you don't understand. Serving the Framatar was my life. Purging the world of evil has always been my life's work, as it has been yours."

"Right up until the time you betrayed us all," Brens bit back.

Semra nearly choked on the bitterness rolling off her in waves. "No! I'm committed to our purpose now more than ever! Brens, please. You have to understand, I was trying to protect you. The Framatar has lied to you, to all of us. Our parents didn't abandon us. The Framatar commanded Rotokas to kidnap us from our families, and they didn't know what to do or even that we were still alive."

"You're lying!" Isra spat. "He said she'd do this," he said to the others. "She always has excuses."

"And if I were telling the truth, what exactly would he have you believe?" Semra demanded. "He's created an army. He'll do anything to keep it from turning against him!"

Pinji lunged forward and swung the club, but Semra danced out of range and back to one side of the cave, refusing to be cornered in the back.

"Why should we believe you?" Isra asked, as Pinji leaped at her again.

Semra redirected the club with the bony portion of her forearm. "I heard Ramas talking with the Framatar. Ramas admitted it to me himself just this morning! Please, let's move out in the open. I don't want to kill anyone, but if you corner me, you'll force my hand."

They ignored her request, and as Semra and Pinji circled one another, Isra and Brens watched with interest from the sidelines.

Isra spoke again. "So if I were to press Ramas, he could confirm this?"

Semra snorted, danced in to nick Pinji's neck, and danced back out. "No, but there are a lot of reasons for that."

"Such as?" Brens pressed.

"First of all, none of you are stupid enough to believe he would tell you the truth if I'm right. Second, he only told me because he was confident I'd be dead within minutes. And third, because I killed him this morning."

Brens' jaw dropped. "You did not."

"She's lying, morons," Pinji said as he juked left and shoved her up against the rock wall, pinning her. "Why don't I dispatch her now?"

Semra's breathing came quickly, and she glared back at

Pinji, but his weight was too much for her to move. Doubt flickered across Brens' face.

"Wait," Isra said. "How in Yatzar could we believe you?"

Semra nodded toward her pants' leg. "My pocket. Reach in."

Isra eyed her cautiously but gestured toward Brens.

She walked forward, dug into Semra's pocket and retrieved Ramas' emerald serpentine amulet. Brens gasped. "You ... you killed him!"

"Only once I knew he was evil! He came for me with one of his poisonous snakes, and what was I to do but survive? We've all lived a great lie!"

"She may have killed him, but if she did, she deserves a long and painful death all the more," Pinji snarled.

"No, we don't have time. Kill her and be done with it," Isra said.

"Haven't you ever wondered why we never knew more about our targets?" Semra asked. "Haven't you ever wondered whether children should be beaten for a misstep? Search your memories! Do you have any clear memory of your families? Are they evil? Or are the bad memories foggy, as if planted there by years of suggestion?"

"Enough!" Isra yelled. "Kill her!"

Pinji kneed her in the gut, but as Semra doubled over in pain, she used the proximity she gained to stab him in the stomach. Isra stripped the knife away from her in one smooth motion, and Brens caught her arms from behind. Semra pushed off the ground with her feet and wrapped her legs around Pinji's throat as he sank to the ground, cinching tightly around his neck.

Brens fought for control of Semra's writhing arms, and Isra drew his sword and put it to Semra's neck. "Enough of that," he hissed. "Let him go."

"Why should I?" Semra tightened her grip around Pinji's throat. "I'm dead anyway."

"Sure, but if you let him go now, I won't hack off your legs first."

"Is that really necessary?" Brens asked.

"Are you getting sensitive on me?" Isra challenged her. "Do as you're told. Don't make me tell the Framatar it was a mistake to send you."

Semra felt an answering burn in her chest, an anxious hurriedness as Zezura zoomed from wherever she was to find her. She wasn't close enough. Semra's own fear spiked in response—she'd be dead before Zezura could reach her.

"All right!" Semra cried. "All right. I'll let him go; I'll run myself through and save you the trouble, whatever you want … but first, tell me one unique memory you have of your family. A single memory, one that neither Brens nor Pinji has."

Isra paused, and the pressure against Semra's neck lessened for a moment. Pinji reached out and grabbed Isra by the leg. Isra looked down at him, and the moment of hesitation was gone, replaced by a deep-seated hatred. Isra drew back his sword. Semra screwed her eyes shut against the fatal blow, but suddenly she felt herself drop to the floor, and metal met metal.

Her eyes flew open, and shock flooded her at the sight of Brens holding a dagger to Isra's blade, inches from her nose. Semra leaped to her feet, and Isra jumped back, sweeping his sword after her, but she rolled out of reach just in time, then sprang up and positioned herself behind Brens as Brens backed out of the cave. Pinji rubbed his neck and glared up at them, and Isra pointed his sword at Brens. Semra lifted Brens' bow off her back, snatched an arrow from her quiver, notched it to the string, and pulled her elbow back.

"What do you think you're doing?" Isra said. "You'll die for this."

"I can't think of a memory," Brens answered. "Can you?"

"Moron!" Pinji exclaimed. "They're mind games. We were children. No wonder there are no memories."

"I have a memory." Semra looked down the shaft of the arrow to Isra's chest. A lump rose in her chest, but she forced it down. "My mother. She was gentle, she said something about ... about dinnertime. My ball ran out the door, and I went to retrieve it. I never came back. Rotokas took me the moment I stepped away from the house."

"You've got pluck, I'll give you that." Isra stalked closer, and Brens adjusted her footing. "Why do you care about the Shamarans?"

"My parents came up the mountain to find me, and the Framatar had them murdered before they made it to the top. He was going to kill a new induction for remembering her family and causing too much trouble trying to get home. I had to save her. And he was going to destroy another family, a whole family, by killing the prince. I heard them planning it. All our recent hits have been about giving him money and taking out political opposition."

"The girl?" Brens asked, not moving her eyes off Isra.

"Yes, when you found me fleeing the mountain, that was her," Semra answered. "She's safe, as far as I know."

"You were trying to save the prince?" Pinji laughed.

"Rotokas picked him up from the woods not an hour ago," Brens said. "Wasn't he with you?"

"W-what?" Semra stammered. "With me? No, I've never even met him!"

Isra chuckled. "The game is up. You sent a pretty strong message when you danced with him at the gala. Trying to stake your claim, eh? How'd that work out for you?"

Semra's mind reeled. She hadn't danced with the prince. She saw only his back, in a navy jacket and fur-lined coat. The noble who asked her to dance most certainly was not the prince, and she'd rejected his offer. The only person she'd actually danced with at the gala was Dahyu.

She froze. He'd known the guard at the obscure gate around the bend of the cliff. He knew the best covers to use. He knew about a secret door in the throne room that not even the regular castle guards were aware of, much less the underground labyrinth attached to it. Dahyu ... the governor's aide, who knew everything about the inner workings of the castle, because he wasn't an aide. The prince was missing for months at a time ... for a strange apprenticeship to healers on the outskirts of Jannemar.

"Ha! She didn't know," Isra chortled. "How is it possible you spent all this time trying to save a man, danced with him, went on forest strolls with him, and still you were oblivious to his identity? And to think, you graduated early!"

Semra stepped back, and Isra lunged forward, tackling Brens to the ground. Semra no longer had a clear shot at Isra and instead fired at Pinji, but a figure dropped on top of her from the grass growing over the cave, and her arrow flew uselessly into the branches overhead.

Semra grunted on impact as she hit the ground. She clawed at her assailant and sent a right hook to his face. "Vix!" she exclaimed. "You're alive!"

"No comfort to you, I'm sure," he growled, pinning her to the ground.

"I never wanted you hurt, and it was the dragon that tossed you around," Semra answered, struggling in his grasp. She hooked his leg with her foot and bucked her hips upward to throw him off balance, but he anticipated the move and rolled over her just in time. Semra gathered her feet and they squared off. "We were just trying to survive. For you."

"Ha! For me?"

"Yes, for you! Nobody wants to be saved when they think they're in a good place. I had to expose him. He's using us!"

"What do I care? I get what I need, and I'm good at what I do. And those of us who remember loyalty are about to be rich."

Semra glanced to the side and saw Brens struggling with Isra. Isra had the upper hand, and Pinji was running forward with his club. Semra lunged for Pinji, but Vix was faster, tackling her to the ground. He pummeled her with his fists, and instinctively Semra brought her arms up to protect her face. She heard a sword ring free from its sheath, but Vix didn't let up. She shifted her arms to look up and saw Manu leering at her over Vix's shoulder, fury in his eyes.

She was a magnificent fighter, but taking on ten castle guards was easier than two of the dragonlord's assassins. Semra heard Brens crash to the ground beside her, and Semra lunged forward, catching Vix's head in a vise between her arms and pulling herself up toward him. Manu struck her on the side of the face with the butt of his sword, and she fell. Manu pulled Vix off her and swung his sword down, missing her by a hair as she dodged the blow.

Just then Semra felt a knife handle set into her palm. She looked over and saw Brens give her a short nod before grunting, rolling to grab an arrow from the quiver on her back, and plunging it into Pinji's neck as he reached to grip her by the throat. Semra's fingers closed around the knife handle, and with a guttural snarl, she slashed up Manu's torso, lodging it in his armpit. Manu crumpled, and Vix leaped forward.

Semra rolled away, scooping up Manu's sword and pulling Brens to her feet. They stood back to back, Semra holding a sword in one hand and knife in the other, and Brens empty-handed as they faced off against Isra and Vix. Semra passed the sword back to Brens, who swept it in a wide arc.

"What is this, charity?" Brens said with a laugh. "You think I can't handle myself with a knife?"

Brens struck after Isra and their swords met.

Semra smiled. "No, I'm being selfish. You know I've always been a knife girl. You're the one who saved me today." She threw up a block as Vix sent an uppercut and a right hook.

"And don't you forget it!"

Isra and Brens' swords met at the same moment Semra and Vix exchanged blows. Just then a shout from behind them called Semra's attention. She knew that voice! Siler sprinted around the bend, sword in hand, and Semra's heart leaped. He rushed Vix, knocking him to the ground and placing his sword on his throat. Semra struck him in the gut and drove her elbow into Vix' chest before placing her own knife at his throat.

"I've got him! Help Brens!"

Siler nodded and wheeled around to engage Isra. Together Siler and Brens drove Isra back, but Isra refused to be cornered back into the cave. Siler lunged in, nicking Isra's side, and Brens disarmed him with one smooth circular motion of her sword.

The air shook as a roar filled the air, and a stream of fire shot out from over the top of the cave. Zezura landed with a rumble, then looked back and forth between Semra and Vix, Siler, Brens, and Isra.

"Yeah, that's right," Semra said. "You were slow! Siler got here before you did, and he only has two legs!"

Zezura huffed and dropped to the forest floor, flaring

bright blue, purple, and then settling into her natural colors. She circled Semra and Vix. Vix' eyes grew wide.

Semra turned to Siler. "Thanks for coming back."

"I wasn't going to," he said. "But then I saw Rotokas headed to the castle with Dahyu in his claws, and I figured there was trouble."

"Did you know he was the prince?"

"I wondered as much, but only over the past couple of days. When Rotokas grabbed him, it confirmed it in my mind."

"Tell me, Siler," said Isra. "Are you a snake or are you gullible?"

"What are you talking about?" Siler lifted his arm and pressed the point of his blade into Isra's neck. Isra lifted his hands in surrender, but Siler shook his head. "Arms down, fool. And if I see them move toward my sword again, I'll have Semra *sic* the dragon on you."

Isra glared at him, but slowly lowered his hands. "The way I see it, there are only two options. You are either a traitor or an idiot. I wouldn't have pegged you to fall for a sob story about our parents. Most of us are immune to such things by now." He sent a sideways glare at Brens. She blanched, but said nothing.

Siler smirked. "You mean to tell me you believe everything the Framatar has ever said, without question? By what evidence? And you call me the gullible idiot. Inconceivable. I've known the Framatar was a liar for six years now, and I've seen him murder those of us that don't show the same brainless devotion you do. Remember Koran and Xiffin?"

Isra shrugged. "Sure. Died in the field."

"Nope. Koran died the illustrious death of being a snack for Rotokas, after challenging the Framatar's methods and threatening to tell students he was a fraud. Xiffin technically did die in the field, but the Framatar sent him to a sleeper's location, and the sleeper killed him. Xiffin found out the Framatar's targets served a personal agenda rather than purifying the world from evil."

"How do you know this?" Isra asked.

Siler leaned forward. "I've kept my eyes and ears open. Did some digging of my own, without being as stupid as Koran or Xiffin were. I saw Rotokas devour Koran myself."

Isra's eyes narrowed. "You're lying."

"Spoken like a true hoodwinked moron."

"Is that true?" Brens asked, looking at Siler.

"Listen, if you didn't already know Isra's a moron, there's not much I can do to help you," Siler said.

"No, not that. About the Framatar."

Siler nodded. "Every word."

Semra slid a knife out of Vix's belt, then stood and gestured to Zezura. "Keep an eye on Vix, Zezura," she said, then climbed on Zezura's back. "Siler, we have to go."

"Is there a reason we shouldn't kill them both?"

"Yes. Because Ramas and the Framatar think we are nothing but killing machines, and we're better than that."

"You killed Pinji and Manu," Vix said.

Semra swept her gaze over the two bodies on the ground, and sadness weighed heavily on her heart. "True, but I consider those relatively unavoidable. I was serious when I said I wanted to save you too. All the children of the mountain. Brens, are you coming with us?"

Brens' eyes grew bright. "If you'll have me."

"Are you sure that's a good idea?" Siler asked.

Semra nodded. "Brens is half the reason I left in the first place. She didn't deserve to be beaten up and beaten down. Besides, if we leave her here, Vix and Isra will kill her."

"Unless we kill them first ..."

"No, Siler. Leave them be."

Brens took the sword sheath off Manu's body and buckled it around her own waist, then sheathed her sword. She turned, approached Zezura and reached out, then paused. The dragon cocked her head curiously. "Is it ... safe?" Brens asked tentatively, retracting her hand.

Semra smiled. "As long as you're with me. Use the spikes on her side there as footholds and take my hand." Semra reached down, and Brens followed her instructions, clasping her hand around a spike and pulling herself up. Siler slowly backed away, then turned and clambered up behind Brens.

Zezura beat the air with her wings, and Brens put her arms around Semra.

"I know where they're keeping the prince."

26

"The Framatar has taken the castle," Brens said as Siler settled in behind them. "He's there now, with Gresvig in charge of any remaining soldiers not sent with the army to meet Belvidore. He intends to force the king to publicly hand over the kingdom, using the prince as leverage."

"And his daughters?"

"Locked in their rooms. He'll probably use them for alliances later, if he doesn't end up killing them tonight, but they can't inherit the crown like Turian's only son."

Zezura lifted off and pulled away.

"You'll pay for this!" Vix screamed from the ground.

"Tell you what," Siler called back. "We'll race you to the castle, and if you win, we'll turn ourselves over!"

Brens raised her voice against the wind as Zezura rose above the tree line. "They'll be in the upper rooms—the king's chambers, the throne room. I'm not sure where they're going to make the announcement from."

Semra nodded. "Have they gone in through the cata-combs?" But the wind carried her voice away as Zezura picked up speed.

She tried to think. If Voldar had been successful in assisting Gresvig in placing military control over the castle guard, Gresvig would now be at the head of every armed man in the Shamaran Castle. If the Framatar really had taken control of the castle, it would be nearly impossible to get in. Household staff would go out for the evening but wouldn't be allowed to return, and the gates would be locked down. But tonight was the celebration of the new year. Some staff would be working late, and there would be dancing in the streets until the wee hours of the morning.

Dahyu is the prince. She hadn't had time to process it before. How could it be? Why would a prince spend time in a poor village? Why had he played along with her and Siler, and if he was the prince, what had he done when he went into the castle to talk to his father?

To talk to his father. Semra shook her head. Not the king's valet, but the king himself. What had he asked him? He'd talked about the dragon's kiss, and how he learned about it from reading in the royal library ... the family didn't mind, he'd said. Ha! Of course not. He *was* the family.

My father works in the castle.

Well, it wasn't an outright lie. His father *did* work in the castle. But not as the king's attendant, and Dahyu didn't work as the governor's aide, so those were blatant decep-tions. But why lie?

Semra rolled her eyes at herself. Whatever he was doing in the outskirts was secretive in nature. And Semra herself had told him at the beginning that the only thing protecting him was agents of the mountain being unaware of his location, banking on finding him at the gala and New Year celebration. Even so, once he learned she was a safe person, he should have told her! What had kept him from it?

Dahyu! The thought of him brought a flutter to her stomach, and she shivered. Memories filed in at his name, and a warmth filled her.

Dancing in the woods. Finding her on the balcony and pulling her against him behind the drapes in the king's private living quarters, speaking softly to her in the dark as they navigated that underground maze. Touching her gently as he attended to her wounds in the dungeon. Holding her while she cried.

He'd not held her tears against her as weakness or accused her of being too sensitive. *For what it's worth,* he'd said, *the only new information I learned about you today is that you actually are human.* Semra sniffled, fighting the tears welling in her eyes. It was worth quite a lot.

Something about Dahyu was different. A difference she'd never understand if he died. *Perhaps your job, as you call it, is death … but your inclination is life.* He didn't see her as a killer. The killing and pillaging bit, he'd spoken out of anger. He saw her as something more than she'd seen of herself. Suddenly Semra was terrified that if Dahyu died, she'd never know whether he was right—or if Prince Zephan died.

Why had he lied about who he was?

Evening was falling, and the cool breeze off Zezura's wings rifled through Semra's hair. Semra guided her away from Qalea, over the Dezapi, and down over the cliff, retracing the path Zezura had taken when she saved Semra from Gresvig only that morning. Had it been only twelve hours ago? It felt like a lifetime had passed since then.

Zezura drew beneath the shelf in the cliff and climbed

slowly up to it. Her tongue slithered out to taste the air, and then, apparently satisfied, she passed through the veil of water cascading from above them and landed in the cleft. Semra gasped and wiped her face as they passed through the cold water. She climbed off the dragon, ducking beneath one of Zezura's wings to protect herself from the mist of the falls, even so, goosebumps cropped up on her arms.

Siler and Brens slid down next, and Brens let out a low whistle. "Whoa, look at this."

Semra snatched Brens' wrist and shook her head, motioning her silence. The Framatar and his team surely knew of the exit she'd seen when first scouting the place with Zezura. If they had forced their way in, perhaps the door would be damaged enough to allow them through, but if it was, could they trust it to be safe?

Her heart pounded as she released Brens and crept to the back of the shelf to examine the door without a handle. Wooden door, reinforced with steel. Untouched.

Semra sighed. She kept her voice low when she spoke. "I'm not sure what to do. Even if we could get in through here, should we go together and increase our chances of making it through the catacombs, or split up and cover more ground? Zezura is too visible, especially with Rotokas inside. She's an advantage to us, but she doesn't remotely level the playing field with the kind of numbers they have. I never even got to map these rooms."

"I don't know them fully, but I have a general idea of the layout," Brens said. "They've been keeping a close eye on me, but Isra left one of the maps out once, and I caught a glimpse before he stuffed it away. There are catacombs on one side, leading here, and a large cellar on the other, leading to a spiral staircase."

"Yes, that's where I ran into Manu."

Brens nodded. "Exactly. Through the cellar, though, is a passage into the emergency living spaces the royal family occupied after the queen's death and during the investigation. It served as a base of operations for a time, though by now it may be clearing out somewhat. There are only a couple of keys that lead to the cellar, though, and I don't have any."

Siler reached into his pants pocket and retrieved a ring of keys. "How about these?"

Brens' eyes widened. "Where did you get those?"

"Semra lifted them off Manu and gave them to me. I didn't get the chance to use them before, but I've kept them ever since."

Semra turned to Brens. "Do you know where they all go?"

She shook her head, examining the keys. "No, but this long brass one is probably the catacombs, and this one might be the cellar."

"We still can't get inside. The door won't budge."

"Are you telling me," Siler said, "that the great Semra Bandaka, brilliant-kid, teacher's pet who graduated early, can't figure out how to open a door?"

Semra rolled her eyes. "A locked door reinforced with steel. Without a handle. And no keyhole."

Siler clucked his tongue. "Such a shame. I would've thought you were more resourceful."

"Do you have a suggestion to share?"

"We need something quiet," Brens added.

Semra caught a twinkle in Siler's eye. "You don't need muscle for this one. Just brains. And I'm known for my exquisite cognitive abilities, of course. If I get us through this door in the next sixty seconds, will you concede that I'm the brightest of the three of us?"

Semra folded her arms. "Certainly not. Even if you get us on the other side, we might die the moment after."

"Aha! Very well. I propose a competition. Two points for getting us inside, and one point for surviving the moment after. Anybody who calls attention to themselves loses a point."

Semra grinned. "Okay, sure. But why is it two points for getting in the door and only one point for surviving the moment after?"

"Because we've been standing here for several minutes already and neither of you have any good ideas for getting in. I would start you both off in the negatives, but that just sounds depressing. After that, we'll all be working on the fly."

"Fine," Brens said. "How much do we get for taking people out?"

"Two points for killing, one point for maiming," Siler answered.

"No, that's not right," Semra said. "If we don't absolutely have to kill, we shouldn't. If you have to, do it. And only circumstances can tell if it would be easier to kill or to maim ... sometimes killing is easier."

Siler rolled his eyes. "Soft, I tell you. Soft. Have it your way ... two points for maiming, one point for killing."

"What if we get caught?" Brens asked.

"Oh, definite deduction of points. Minus five points."

Semra nodded. "So once we're inside, providing you can get us in like you say, what's our plan?"

"Another point for me for doing the planning! Man, I am really doing the heavy lifting here. We'll have to split up to find the prince on the third floor. Semra, you'll need to stay close to towers or windows as best you can, so Zezura can get to you whenever we need our getaway."

"Two taps to signal to come to where you are, three for danger and to stay away," Brens added.

Zezura huffed a hot spiral of smoke from her nostrils, as if displeased to have been left out of the conversation.

Semra smiled and gave her a pat. "Are we really doing this?"

"At this point, I have no choice!" Siler said. "I'm already ahead on points and have to defend my position as number one."

"As I recall, you only have one point for planning, and Brens should get one too," Semra pointed out. "You haven't gotten us inside yet."

"Quite right." Siler walked to the back of the shelf and examined the door. He pushed against it, but it didn't move. Brens put her hands on her hips, but Siler winked at Semra. "One has to utilize all the resources at one's disposal in order to avoid doing any real work, you see." He stood back, lifted his hands dramatically toward the door, and paused. "Zezura, would you be so kind ...?"

Zezura jerked her head up and huffed, then pranced her enormous weight over to the corner and let out a stream of flame that forced Siler to hug the wall and Brens and Semra to stand well away from it. Fire engulfed the door, and all four of them stared at it as the heat slowly softened the wood.

"Sort of anticlimactic, wasn't it?" Brens commented.

Zezura shook her head and plunged forward to ram the door. With a crack, the side bent in and pulled away from its hinges.

"Nicely done!" Siler praised her. "Although the noise lost you a point for possibly drawing attention. But then, you gain a point for helping me gain two points by getting us through the door ..."

Semra hugged Zezura around the neck and stroked her head. "Great job, Zezura. Stay close. Stay safe. And stay out of trouble."

Zezura nudged Semra warmly with her nose, and Semra gave her another squeeze before bending down to follow Brens and Siler. She stepped through the narrow opening between the remains of the flaming door and the rocky wall, and walked down a short hallway into a large room with pillars every six feet and arched doorways into dark recesses. Six-foot-long stone coffins with carvings of great men and women of the Shamaran family stood at intervals throughout. The dim light from the fire behind them pooled at their feet but didn't carry far enough into the room to see the end of it.

Semra took a deep breath and listened, hand resting on the handle of one of her knives, but heard nothing. Adrenaline coursed through her veins, and she tapped the handle restlessly. This was home. Standing in the dark, underground space with a knife at hand and Bandaka colleagues on either side. Children of the mountain, purging the land of evil ... except this time, the evil was the father figure they'd grown up admiring, fearing, even loving. A man blessed by the gods, they'd been told. Beyond reproach of any kind.

"How long is a moment?" Siler whispered. "I think it's been a moment. Which means I have four points already."

Brens snorted. "That one seemed a little cheap. We haven't done anything yet, we just got lucky nobody seems to have heard the door. Come on, I know the way out ... and I'll take a point for leading you, thank you very much."

Semra grinned. "I think you swiped one of Zezura's points, Siler. She took care of the door."

"Call it a supervisory fee," Siler said, waving her off. "It was my idea."

"She's my dragon. I could charge a lending fee."

"Fine, whatever, you get one point. I'm still ahead."

Brens rolled her eyes. "Shall we? We have almost certain death to look forward to."

She stepped forward, Semra touching her shoulder as they headed into the darkness beyond. Siler tapped his left wrist twice with two fingers of his right hand, and reached up to touch Semra's shoulder in a three-person train as the orange firelight from behind them dropped away, leaving them in blackness. Semra focused on her breathing, one hand on Brens and one on the handle of her knife sitting securely in its sheath on her thigh.

Brens lead them through the large room, their progression slow in the darkness, their quiet footfalls sending hollow echoes off the walls. The trio passed through a series of smaller rooms and came to a stop in front of a wooden door. Semra listened and heard a light scuffling through the wall to her right.

"Key," Brens said softly, placing one hand on top of Semra's.

Siler found Semra's hand and placed the keyring in it, and Semra passed it to Brens. She found the correct key and fumbled with the lock to open the door.

It opened just a crack, a sliver of dim light falling through the narrow opening. Brens peered out, then reached back and tapped Semra twice on the shoulder. Come.

Semra turned and repeated the tap on Siler's shoulder behind her, then crept out the door after Brens. They entered the bottom of the spiral stair where Semra had encountered and fought Manu. Scuffling footsteps and low voices came from a mostly-closed door to their right. Brens started up the stairs. Semra waited a few beats, then followed.

She crept up the stairs on the balls of her feet, hugging the wall, listening intently. Her heart pounded, and she let her mind go blank, letting go of every worry aside from this moment. The sound of three light taps came from up ahead. Semra froze. Danger. Stay away.

Brens must be at the top of the stair leading out onto the first floor. Semra waited, straining to hear anything of importance. Something behind her moved, and Semra nearly jumped out of her skin. She whirled, but saw only Siler and glared at him. He clutched his chest dramatically as if startled, then relaxed. Semra shook her head, but the corner of her mouth twitched.

Two taps. All clear.

Semra slipped up the stairs, paused to listen, and crossed quickly to the other spiral staircase on the other side of the room. She stepped inside the staircase just as two guards rounded the corner and walked through. There was no sign of Brens, but Semra figured she'd gone ahead and it was time to split up. Semra would make her way up to the third floor by the spiral staircase, and Brens would take the service stair further down. Not everyone would know she'd turned, but they would also expect her to be far from the castle in the woods with Pinji, Isra, Manu, and Vix.

The king's chambers were on the other side of the castle, but so were the primary guard towers, and Semra had no interest of getting caught there again. On the other hand, the walkway over the Great Hall was an easy place to get cornered. She'd need more than two knives to get by.

She'd start with the prince's quarters and go from there. After she ruled out the prince and princess's rooms, she would have to come up with a better way to make it to the other side of the castle. Semra had reached the top of the second flight of stairs and started up the third when she noticed a guard standing at the opening. She grimaced, retraced her steps soundlessly to the second level, and peeked around the corner.

She'd found herself in Ancestry Hall, and as her eyes swept over the magnificent paintings rising above her, she noticed a family portrait of the Shamaran family: King Turian, Queen Sharsi, Princess Avaya, Princess Aviama ... and Prince Zephan. Semra cursed herself for not noticing it before. She could recognize Dahyu's face anywhere, and there it was, staring serenely back at her, mocking her. She wondered what would happen to him if she didn't get there fast enough.

You know what will happen, her thoughts berated her. *The only thing you don't know is how fast they'll kill him.* Would it be slow and tortuous? Would he be thrown to Rotokas? *The only thing you know for sure is it'll be a horrible death.*

She needed to get to the third floor.

Semra glanced to her right and saw two guards stationed on either side of the Great Hall, but to her left, the way was clear, leading into the kitchen, laundry, and chandlery rooms. Semra took a deep breath and watched the guards. When their heads swiveled back toward the Great Hall for a moment, she dashed across the open space into the kitchen.

Once bustling with serving staff, now only two women remained. They fussed over the garnishes on a line of plates of food, their backs to Semra.

"Presentation is everything," said the older, broad-shouldered woman with graying hair tied back in a bun. Arms folded across her chest, she examined the younger girl's work. "In times like these, terrible times, we must provide all the hope we can. And food is hope."

Semra ducked out of the room and leaned against the wall, listening.

"Saeb, we're not being let out until morning. What if we're never let out at all?"

"It's New Year's Eve, darling, it's a long night for all of us. Now with the nobles and royal family to feed all at once, guards everywhere, well ... listen, I don't know anything, you don't know anything, and that's safest, you understand. But that sallow fellow, I'll poison his steak before he eats the king's best!"

"You'll be killed!"

"Hush now, and I'll make sure you don't see the light of morning if you say anything else about it. Unless you carry poison in your skirts, you've nothing to squabble about ... did you hear something?"

Saeb strode to the door. Semra stepped deftly into the next door down and found herself face to face with Garbane, who held a long pole with multiple wicks dangling off it over a vat. The older man looked up and swept his gaze over her tunic and pants, and the two knives strapped to her legs.

He grunted. "You never worked for a chandler."

Semra shook her head. "No."

His expression was stoic, but his shoulders slumped ever so slightly. "Are you here to kill me?"

"And spoil all that quality time you get with Belon? I would never." Semra smiled.

But Garbane wasn't impressed. He dipped the wicks, holding them in the wax for several seconds, then raised them up again. "What do you want?"

"I didn't do it. I didn't kill the queen, and I'm not one of them."

"Could have fooled me."

Heat flushed her face. Semra stepped forward and spoke

softly, urgently. "I was one once. I wasn't given a choice. I came to try and stop them."

Garbane dipped the wicks again, held them for several seconds, then lifted them up. Semra waited anxiously, shifting her weight. He dipped the wicks again.

"Well?" Semra said.

"Well, what?" He didn't look up.

"Do you believe me? Are you going to raise an alarm? What's going on in that head of yours?"

Garbane lifted the wicks, examined the thickening wax, and placed the pole on an open-framed table without a top, so that the candles hung suspended from the center. He glanced up at her. "What does it matter?"

"I could use your help."

Garbane grunted. "I have a bum leg, and I don't carry weapons. Wouldn't know what to do with them if I did. Won't be much help. I'm not raising any alarm, because the alarm would only go to the loon that seems to have taken over. I serve the king." His chin lifted ever so slightly. "Whoever you are, an enemy of my enemy is hard to come by today."

Semra dipped her head. "Thank you."

Garbane raised an eyebrow. "Never thank a man for refusing to take action. We're a lazy lot."

"I doubt that very much. You don't have a lazy bone in your body."

The corner of his mouth twitched.

"You don't like skirting around issues. I don't either. I need to get to the third floor in the dumbwaiter."

Garbane straightened and folded his arms. "And you need Saeb not to cause a ruckus."

Semra nodded.

"Ha! To what end?"

"I need to find out where they're holding the prince before they kill him and the king."

"There are nobles locked in the guest rooms, and the princesses are locked in their rooms. I insisted on finishing my work but now I'm not permitted to leave this hall. The king must be somewhere on the west wing."

"And the prince?"

Garbane shook his head. "I've heard nothing of the prince."

Semra chewed her lip. "Nothing? What about a black dragon?"

"There have been reports of a blue dragon flying over the castle and Qalea the past month, and just today Belon said she saw a black dragon in the courtyard. I thought she was telling stories."

"Hey!" a loud voice yelled from the doorway behind her. Semra spun around to see a large woman holding a rolling pin like a club. "What do you think you're doing?"

Semra's lips parted, and her stomach lurched.

Garbane passed a hand over his eyes. "Saeb, so good of you to join us. Pipe down, will you? You're giving me a headache."

"You're such an old bat, Garbane. You'd let them do anything! You there, what did you hear?"

Semra raised an eyebrow. "Threats to poison people, for one. It wouldn't work though. Who's to say the Framatar wouldn't make the king taste test?"

Saeb's face went white. "May the king live forever! And whoever the other man is ... him too! What's a Framatar?"

"He calls himself dragonlord—that's what Framatar means. I'm not with him. I need your help. And maybe any extra weapons you have lying around ... something a little more effective than that rolling pin."

Saeb swallowed, looking uncertainly from Semra to Garbane and back again.

Garbane smiled. "Come now, Saeb, you're not as sneaky as you think you are. I heard you talking from here, so you're lucky the guards are stationed in Ancestry Hall! Now shut your trap for once and listen. I have an idea."

27

Semra pulled her knees in tight to her chest inside the dumbwaiter as Saeb and the other servant girl picked up two trays of food and headed for the service stairs. Garbane gave her a short nod, shut the dumbwaiter, and she felt herself lurching upward inside the walls. Semra's breathing quickened in the small space. She wondered if Brens and Siler had made any headway.

The dumbwaiter stopped, and Semra slid open the door and squeezed through the opening into the empty kitchen on the third floor. She lowered the dumbwaiter back to the second floor and heard a soft clattering sound as Garbane set the tray inside next and sent it up to her. Semra took out the tray of meat, vegetables, and soup bowl and stepped to the doorway, pausing to listen for Saeb.

"Dinner for Princesses Avaya and Aviama," she heard the older woman say to someone. "I was told to bring it, and here I am, so please open the doors."

There was a pause, and the guard down the hall said something imperceptible.

"Yes, of course you will! It won't very well fit under a door, now, will it? Can you imagine, cutting everything that thin? I'm not paid enough. Not paid enough for that nonsense, do you hear me? Now, whatever your boss wants with their Highnesses, they seem safe enough in their rooms, and they need something to eat! Have you ever dealt with Her Royal Highness Princess Avaya when she hasn't eaten anything? I certainly hope you never shall."

Semra smiled at Saeb's pluck and slipped out the door and into the walkway above Ancestry Hall, balancing the tray on one hand and plucking the dinner knife off it with the other. A guard step out of the tower toward her, but Semra never stopped moving. Without hesitation, she flicked her wrist and sent the knife into his throat. He gagged and fell to the ground. Semra stepped gingerly over his body and onto the walkway over the Great Hall. She paused there. Garbane was next, and she could hear him talking to the guards below her already. With one guard down, she didn't have much time.

"If the wick is not the right size, it will not have the proper burn. If the wax is not the proper mixture—"

"You're not listening," a guard answered. "We couldn't possibly care less about this. Just use what you have or wait until we get word to release staff from the castle."

"Use what I have? *Use what I have?* Ha! This coming from a man who doesn't know the difference between beeswax and soy wax! And no, soy is not a type of bee, if you were wondering. But you weren't wondering, were you? Because there's nothing between those ears but air!"

"Now you listen here," the second guard said, "you can't speak to him that way. We are just doing our—"

"Jobs? Were you about to say you're doing your jobs?"

Semra heard a crash and took it as a sign the guards were

sufficiently distracted. She smiled to herself at Garbane's commitment, took the tray, and headed across the walkway as Garbane continued berating the guards.

"Your job is to protect the king, his castle, and its operations! I am part of its operations, and you are not allowing me to do my job, so why is your poorly executed job more important than mine?"

Another crash sounded behind her, and Semra picked up her pace. She recognized three dragon wranglers and three supporting assassins standing watch by the tall windows below her. With Brigg and Behruz dead, and Vix still in the woods to the east, these three were the last trained dragon wranglers. *Smart*, Semra thought to herself. *They're keeping watch for Zezura in case she crashes through the tall windows.* The wranglers glanced at the commotion Garbane caused, and Semra approached the other side unseen, mostly obscured by the height of the walkway and the row of columns. She reached the other side, but a guard in the tower to her right called out to her.

"You there! Stop!"

"I have orders to bring a meal," Semra answered evenly, eyes drilling into the guard.

"No you don't." He reached for the hilt of his sword, and Semra tossed the hot soup bowl—filled with wax, courtesy of Garbane—at his face. He screamed and clawed at his eyes, and Semra lunged forward and bashed his head into the wall. He stumbled back, and Semra took off through the doors to the conservatory.

Panic welled up inside her, and she fought to keep the burning in her chest at bay. Zezura would only expose herself if she came now. Semra burst through the conservatory, into the anteroom, and down the hall past the king's circular living room, drawing a knife into each hand as she ran.

Shouts erupted and heavy footsteps pounded down the hall toward her. Semra opened the door to the king's bedroom and saw a chair knocked over and a goblet on the floor, but the room was empty. She closed the door behind her, ran through the valet's bedroom, through the queen's chambermaid's room, queen's room, and then took the door back into the hall on the other side of the guard tower.

Doors slammed as the guards split up to go through the bedrooms and down the hall after her. Six guards charged after her from her left, and she took off toward the throne room just as two more emerged from the queen's room. Semra felt a light tug on her tunic. One of the guards had swiped at her and missed by an inch.

She ducked low and spun, bringing her knife up into the guard's gut. She twirled him round with her knife still in his torso, using him as a shield against the guard behind before removing her knife and thrusting the first guard into the second. The second guard jumped back, and Semra threw her knife into his neck, snatched the first guard's sword, and reached for the double doors of the throne room.

They swung open of their own accord, and a soldier appeared in the opening. Semra thrust her sword forward and met the soldier in combat just as the six guards reached them. The first of the six suddenly fell to the ground with a knife sunken under his arm. Semra jerked her head up to see Brens engaged with a second soldier.

Semra feigned an attack up high, slashed his exposed abdomen when he moved to block, then sprinted across the room. She ran by Brens and sliced the back of her attacker's neck, and together they bounded past the columns and up the stairs into the main throne room with five guards and the remaining soldier hot on their heels.

On the far side of the throne room, the Framatar sat on

one of the two golden thrones. King Turian knelt, chained, on the floor before him. Four assassins stood nearby, two behind the king and two behind another form lying on the ground to the right. The figure on the ground twisted toward the commotion, and Semra's heart leaped into her throat as her eyes met the familiar warm amber ones of the man she knew as Dahyu. Prince Zephan.

She saw pain in those eyes, and it seemed to deepen when he recognized her. He was bleeding. She noted that one of the assassins behind him held a club. Tymetin. He raised his gaze to Semra and smiled wickedly.

Two more assassins stood on either side of the entrance to the throne room, but even as they descended on Brens and Semra, she didn't care. Semra felt a rage build up in her like never before. It consumed her chest like fire and fueled her with an energy and power she'd never before known. The first assassin reached Semra, a young woman she recognized as Tav. Semra snarled as she parried the sword blow and burst in close. In a smooth motion she caught Tav's head in a vise and broke her neck.

Tav's body crashed to the ground, and Semra surged across the throne room. Brens continued fighting off her adversary, and five guards and a soldier ran up the throne room stairs after Semra. Nothing existed in that moment but her feet slapping on the pristine marble floor, her breath as it came in—*two, three, four*—went out—*two, three, four*. The Framatar stood and shouted something. Three of the assassins with him drew swords, and the fourth pulled out a bow and notched an arrow to the string.

Breath in—*two, three four*—out —*two, three, four*.

The arrow left the string. Semra rolled to one side and heard the *chink* of the arrowhead hitting the pillar behind her. She turned with sword upraised to block a downstroke from a soldier who'd caught up to her, then, letting out a guttural cry, she knocked him off balance. He fell on top of her, and she skewered him through and shoved him to one side, her sword still embedded in his trunk.

She stood, but four guards swarmed around her and knocked her to the ground again. She had only moments before they'd pin her arms and take her. Semra sliced the ankle tendon of one of the guards, and as he fell, she gained just enough space to send her knife flying across the throne room toward the Framatar. He moved his head slightly, and the knife struck the back of the throne and clattered to the floor.

The guards seized Semra and hauled her to her feet. A huge shattering of glass sounded at the end of the throne room, and Semra jerked her head toward it. She could feel Zezura flying, but she wasn't that close.

Rotokas landed on the marble floor and swung his massive serpentine head toward his master. He let out a roar that shook the air, and goosebumps sprang up on Semra's arms. She felt the guards tremble and step back, but they didn't release their grip. Rotokas' talons clicked on the marble floor as he ambled up the Great Hall and settled himself next to the Framatar.

Semra fought the heat in her chest to keep Zezura at bay. If she came now, Semra would be killed before she had the chance to get free and Zezura would have to contend with Rotokas. Perhaps if she waited, a solution would present itself.

"Welcome, Rotokas," the Framatar cooed, placing a hand on the wyvern's nose. "You will shortly be of great assistance to me." He turned to Semra. "If you wanted so badly to join us, you could have just asked. Come closer."

The guards pushed her forward so that she stood ten feet

from the Framatar. Five feet to her left, guards held Brens. King Turian knelt next to her, and Prince Zephan lay only four feet to Semra's right. She chanced a glance at him, and his eyes pierced her through. Soft, caring, concerned. For her.

Semra bounced her gaze away, remaining any longer would only place him in further danger. The Framatar caught the glance and smiled. Semra glared back at him, lifting her chin.

"A little slow, aren't we, Radix?" he called to someone behind Semra.

She turned her head to see Radix striding toward them, carrying shackles and a ring of keys.

"Did you get lost?"

The corners of Radix' mouth turned down in a frown. "No."

"No? Because if you had, you could have followed the trail of bodies. And if you'd been here sooner, perhaps there would be less cleanup." The Framatar nodded at Semra, and Radix stepped forward to shackle her wrists and ankles.

"Should I get another pair for Brens, my lord?"

The Framatar shook his head. "No, no, that won't be necessary."

Brens looked as though she'd been slapped in the face. Another insult.

The Framatar turned back to the king. "Turian, do excuse me. I'm afraid I need just a moment to sort out my affairs. Not all of my children are as dedicated or grateful ... or intelligent ... as Tymetin here."

"Azi, stop this!" the king said. "If you relent now, I will see to it no harm befalls you. This is madness!"

It occurred to Semra then for the first time that she'd never heard the Framatar's name.

Azi curled his lip. "No harm? *No harm?* You would lock me in a cage, and you know it. Wouldn't your father be proud?"

"*Our* father."

"No! *Your* father! The man who allowed our mother to carry out her crazy experiment, and then punished me for it, choosing you when I was the clear choice. *My* father was a coward who betrayed me. *Your* father was doting and coddled you."

"Ramas said you were the older brother," Semra said. "If that's true, why weren't you named heir to the throne at birth?"

"Fraternal twins," Zephan responded, pulling himself to his knees. Tymetin gripped his shoulder to keep him from standing. "My grandmother refused to tell my grandfather which was older, and demanded they determine fitness for the throne by merit. One was to be raised in the castle, and the other raised among the people."

Azi glared at Zephan but chose to ignore his explanation and turned to Semra. His eyes narrowed. "Ramas told you I was older, you say?"

"Ramas," she said, nodding. "He also said you were nothing without him. He sends his regards."

Azi scoffed. "He said nothing of the kind."

"Oh, but he did. Of course, he also told me the prince was dead, so what do I know? You are both well-practiced liars. A shame what happened to him … did you hear?"

Azi stepped closer and placed his head inches from hers. She turned her head away, but he leaned in. She could feel his breath tickle her ear as he whispered, "You will beg me for death before the end."

A chill ran up Semra's spine.

"Radix." It was Brens' voice. "He has lied to us ever since we were brought to the mountain. We were kidnapped, and he kills whoever defies him. Koran and Xiffin didn't die in the field. He murdered them. Siler saw it himself."

"Siler!" Radix sneered. "Worthless traitors, all of you."

The Framatar turned to Brens. "What gave you the impression you were allowed to speak? You show your gullible, moronic nature when you open your mouth." He glanced back at Semra. "I told you you were too sensitive. And this is what you team up with? You choose her? The weakest link."

"She's not weak."

"You would have had me keep her weak, wouldn't you? To spare her my sensible discipline? And now you, too, are weak. Weak! Weakness is worthless. Weakness must be purged. And if it cannot be purged ... eliminated." The Framatar clasped his hands behind his back and nodded at the assassin holding Brens. Without a sound, he slashed her throat and she fell to the ground.

28

"**N**OOOOO!!!!"
Blood poured from Brens' throat, and she made a choking, gagging motion before her eyes glazed over and she moved no more. Semra's throat grew tight, cutting off her own scream, and tears sprang to her eyes, pouring in rivers down her face. Bren's blood seeped across the marble floor, soaking the king's trousers as he knelt there. The king hovered over her, shaking, reminding Semra of the scene when the king knelt over his murdered wife at the gala.

"What have you become, Azi?" he cried.

"Weakness!" Azi called out. "Your pathetic kingdom is rife with it! We must prune away the weak so Jannemar can be strong once again. Let this be a lesson to you all!" He whirled to face Semra.

Her eyes wild, frozen in shock, she stared at Brens' body on the floor.

"You! So you were stolen, were you? Coerced into this

life? Look at you, away from me for a month and already reduced to a sniveling worm. What is your name?"

Semra stared at Brens, unable to tear her gaze away, Azi's words coming to her as though from a dream. They felt so distant to her now. Life was such a fleeting thing. Is this how they were to die?

Azi struck her in the face, and she buckled beneath the blow, but the guards held her up. He nodded to them, and they released her, just in time for Azi to hit her again. She sprawled on the ground, and Zephan lurched forward, but Tymetin held him fast.

"What is your name?" Azi demanded, standing over her. "You chose it! We chose you, and at the naming ceremony, you chose us in return! You knew what you were signing up for, and you wanted it. Loved it. *What. Is. Your. Name?*"

"No!" Semra screamed. "Four-year-olds do not choose to be ripped from their families! Indoctrinated children cannot agree to a lifetime of killing. Killing for your coffers."

"Let her go!" Zephan yelled. "She has nothing to do with this."

"You're a fool," Azi said, waving him off. "Of all the pawns in this room, you are the least significant. Your father has a duty to fulfill, and he will be alive until he fulfills it or convinces me of his uselessness. You are here as an instrument to determine whether or not your father loves you enough to do what he needs to do. You matter not an iota to me. This insolent child, however, is my own. My own to teach, train, punish, kill. She is mine."

Azi turned back to Semra, crouching over her, twirling a knife blade between his fingers. "What is your name, little girl?"

Semra looked up at him with a level stare. "I have no name," she hissed.

Azi straightened. "The name of Bandaka was not so detestable to Brens when she crawled back to me with those bruises you gave her, turning you in when you fled my mountain. She wasn't good enough to hold you off. She was punished for that, for you ... and now she is dead. Because of you."

Turian lifted his head. "Bandaka? Bondservant?"

Azi slapped him in the face. "I wasn't speaking to you."

"Do they not know what it means?" Turian raised his eyes to Tymetin, Radix, and the other assassins. "He mocks you, and yet you serve him."

Azi locked eyes with Radix and snapped his head at Turian. "Silence him. Below the face."

Radix took the club from Tymetin's hands and slugged the king in the stomach. He fell to the ground.

"Stop!" Zephan screamed.

"Where was I?" Azi said, stroking his chin. "Ah, yes. I need my dear brother to make a pronouncement before the nobles that I am the rightful king. My wretched princeling nephew is here to secure my brother's cooperation, or die in the effort. And by a stroke of luck, the princeling cares for my traitorous daughter. Yet no daughter of mine was ever so ruled by her emotions."

"Certainly none of them lived," Semra muttered.

Somewhere Zezura was in a frenzy trying to get into the castle, unsure of exactly where Semra was. Her heart sank. She was likely headed for the Great Hall where the dragon wranglers would be waiting.

"You are a coward," Azi said, advancing toward her. "And now, after your failure to save the queen, the king will lose his son as well as his wife, and if he does not comply, his daughters will be left as orphans. Oh, but don't worry. I'll take great care of them in his absence." He grinned wickedly.

Zephan and King Turian shouted something, but Semra couldn't hear them. Her breathing came quickly, her eyes fixed on Azi.

"Worthless whining baby, ever since Rotokas dragged you, a miserable, helpless excuse for a child up from Kalma. Take a child out of Kalma, but you ... well, I suppose we couldn't beat the Kalma out of you."

Semra pulled her hands up over her face, and Azi snapped his fingers. Rotokas stalked behind Azi and lowered his huge head over Azi's shoulder. "Your little dragon pet sounds like a nice treat for Rotokas. Do bring her by for a play date. Rotokas, be a dear and remind our little Semra what her name is."

Rotokas bobbed his head up and down and dropped his head to Semra's level on the floor. His black eyes gleamed with pleasure, and Semra felt panic welling up inside as she pictured Rotokas devouring the man in the mountain, burning Brens, and snatching Semra up from the ground as a child. Rotokas drew his head back and opened his mouth. She could smell the musky, rotten smell of death on his breath, saw the flame glow as it rose from the back of his throat.

Semra screamed and rolled to avoid the torrent of fire Rotokas unleashed across the marble floor. One of the guards standing behind her shrieked as the fire enveloped him, but the wail ended and the smell of burning flesh filled her nostrils before she saw the smoking, disfigured body hit the ground. Semra unwittingly rolled on top of Zephan, and he caught her.

Her eyes turned wildly to meet his, and in them she found a settled resolve that gave her strength. As Rotokas turned, Zephan shoved Semra behind him and shielded her with his own body. Tymetin ducked out of the way. Rotokas let out a short huff of fire. Zephan's muscles stiffened around Semra and he groaned in pain.

Zephan was ripped off her, and she turned to see Rotokas pulling him away with the claws at the joint of one wing. Azi laughed. "He knows his targets, this one. But perhaps incineration is too quick a death. Tell me, who whipped you last time?"

Semra stared after Zephan, now crawling toward his father on the floor.

Radix stepped forward proudly. "I did, my lord."

"Ah yes. And an excellent job you did too. She still moves like lightning. Tymetin, show Radix how to properly give someone a whipping. Rotokas, keep our royal friends company, would you?"

Semra staggered to her feet. Rotokas snagged Zephan's tunic with his claw, dragged him backward and, while letting out a roar, encircled him with his long, spiked tail. Semra lifted her chained wrists to wipe her face, and wearily raised her eyes to Tymetin, who produced a whip and snickered.

She lifted her hands in pleading. "Tymetin, please. Not for me. For Koran and Xiffin. For your parents, whom you've no memories of. No memories uniquely yours. Please, he's using you."

"I remember my parents," Tymetin said, cracking the whip in the air. "And they were exactly the kind of evil that deserve to be stricken from the earth!"

Semra tried to roll away as the first stroke fell, but she couldn't escape it. She cried out as the whip ripped at her flesh.

"Unwanted," Azi crooned. "Unloved, unworthy, and now you die as a failure and a disappointment both to me and your newfound friends." He clucked his tongue. "Such a shame, such a shame."

The whip cracked again, and Semra collapsed under the heavy blow.

"Oh, Semra. Too smart to be a pawn, too sensitive to be an assassin, too reckless to save ... well, anyone, really. What have you accomplished exactly, to make all this trouble worthwhile, hmm?"

Semra moaned as the whip hit her again. She could only bring herself to worm away from Tymetin, but he only stepped closer.

"You'll have to speak up, dearest. I'm afraid I didn't catch that."

"Leave her alone!" Zephan screamed. "Take me instead!"

"Azi, if you're going to kill me, get on with it!" Turian called.

"Oh, but you see, I only plan to kill you if you prove unhelpful to me," Azi said. "And if you prove unhelpful, I will have Rotokas tear your son to pieces before your eyes. Perhaps I'll let him watch as his friend Semra is torn apart first. After all, they seem to have a fling going, so it's only right they be together in the end. If you wanted to speed things along, you would agree to name me your successor and the rightful king of Jannemar."

Turian shook his head. "Impossible. The people would never stand for it, and the nobles would never believe you."

Tymetin struck Semra again with the whip, and her flesh burned as if on fire. She cried out again and curled into a tight ball on the ground, strength waning. She heard Turian and Azi talking but struggled to focus on anything but the next blow.

"The people?" Azi said. "Ha! The people will beg for me. What has your rule brought them as of late? Dragons terrorize Qalea. Governors are dropping like flies, and governances are left in chaos. Your impulsivity in marriage to Sharsi, an imprudent union spurning the alliance of a strong nation, is only highlighted now by starting a needless war with Belvidore. It won't be long before everyone knows Belvidore is not responsible for your wife's death. Your reign will be characterized by forsaking tradition, failing to control the provinces, and instigating a time of bloodshed. When I take the throne, all these problems will be solved."

"You ... *you* killed her!" Turian struggled to his feet and lunged at Azi with his hands still tied behind him. "You killed my wife!"

"Now how will that look, brother? The rightful heir returns to the kingdom, and the jealous younger brother kills him?"

"You loved her too. You *loved* her."

Azi waved him off. "She wouldn't have me. Now no one will have her."

Tears trailed the king's face. "No one knows which of us is older. Mother refused to tell Father. You have contrived something."

"On the contrary, our governess was with our mother when we were born. And she lives."

Semra's limbs felt limp, and she could hardly hold up her head, much less anything else. Tymetin increased his strokes, and she screamed in agony until her throat refused to continue, and the sound choked off. Her vision swam; her muscles spasmed, and misery laced her body.

It was a beautifully executed plan, and he'd won. Four guards, six assassins, the wyvern, and the dragonlord himself all testified to the fact. Azi held up his hand and Tymetin paused. Semra gasped for air, crumpling on the floor in grateful respite.

"Semra, I have good news. I've changed my mind." Azi strolled to Rotokas and stroked the great beast's head. "I think ... perhaps you will die second. My brother wants to move things along, and I'm inclined to acquiesce. As a favor. For family, of course. And you know how I feel about family, Semra."

Semra closed her eyes, trying to shut him out. Just a few more strokes, and it would all be over. Blackness, her sweet friend, would bring relief in death.

"Rotokas will kill the prince first. And there really is no reason for Tymetin to fully wear himself out. Look at you, Semra. A puddle could put up more of a fight."

Semra's eyes snapped open, and she took in a ragged breath. She raised herself up on her elbows, pain exploding in her joints with each movement, and lifted her eyes to Zephan's. He stood, encircled by the fifty-foot-long black wyvern, fists balled at his sides, eyes searching hers.

Semra's mind whirred for any solutions, but she found none. None that would get them all to freedom. She scanned her body for any ounce of strength left. Even if she had the fortitude to fight, she could only take one action before the assassins would cut her down.

Zezura called to her heart, homing in on her location. She was freeing herself from a fight with the wranglers, but even if she survived distracting Rotokas, the throne room contained too many trained assassins for Semra to take out with wrist and ankle shackles. She cleared her throat, and opened her mouth to speak, but only a hoarse squawk came out.

She tried again. "Azi."

Azi turned slowly toward her and arched an eyebrow. His lip curled in a menacing snarl. "What did you call me?"

Semra raised her hands defensively. "My ... lord. Please,

before you kill me. Tell me. Your operations are so perfect. Is this how my parents died ... by Rotokas? How did you do it without making a scene in the mountain or in Kalma?"

Azi snapped his fingers, and Rotokas uncoiled his great length, unfurled his great wings—nearly the length of the hall—and let out an ear-splitting roar. Azi laughed. "Lord of the mountain, lord of dragons! You think I have ascended this high without getting blood on my own hands? It was a pleasure to exterminate them myself. Rotokas, kill the boy."

Semra glanced to the side and saw Radix struggling to contain the emotion leaking into his expression. He'd heard the truth. Looking at Tymetin, she saw no such conflict, and the other four assassins were difficult to read.

Semra gathered what shreds of strength remained and, in a burst of energy, she hooked Tymetin's leg, yanked him to the ground, snatched the whip, and slung it to strike Rotokas' impenetrable hide. "Rotokas, you worm, doesn't he let you play anymore? All business now, isn't he?"

The beast swung its head toward her, and Zephan ran to her side.

"What are you doing?" he demanded.

"Shhh, just stay behind me," Semra answered softly, so only he could hear. "And don't stiffen up. You'll land better that way."

"What? Land where? Semra, we're three flights up on one side and four flights up on the other."

Semra ignored him and raised her voice toward the wyvern. "I've learned a thing or two about dragons. You understand more than he lets on. I don't know how he could possibly have saved your life, a creature as great as you are. You return the favor with lifelong devotion, and he gives you a short leash."

Rotokas rumbled in his throat, but eyed Zephan behind

her. He was still locked onto his target, and if he chose to incinerate them both, they would be dead in an instant.

"Won't you ask him if you can come play?" Semra taunted.

Rotokas tilted his head toward his master, and Azi waved a hand. Rotokas huffed in pleasure, and his forked tongue slithered out to taste the air. The remaining guards inched their way down the throne room toward the doors, and the assassins watched from a distance.

Semra cracked the whip. "Cat and mouse."

"Semra, no," Zephan said, shaking his head. He took her hand. "Stop."

Semra gripped his hand hard and pushed him back behind her, toward the shower of glass on the marble floor, while walking backward, never turning from Rotokas. Night had descended on the castle, and a chill breeze swept through the air. The coolness felt good on her open wounds.

"Cut her off!" Azi called out. "Don't let her by the open window!"

It was too late. Semra glanced through the massive hole where windows had once been, then released Zephan's hand and shoved him toward the opening.

He clung to her arm. "If we're going to face death, we'll face it together," he hissed. "Why won't you let me help you?"

Semra gazed into his earnest face and softened. Rotokas let out a burst of fire, and Semra and Zephan fell together to the side to escape its blast, then staggered to their feet once more. Resolve hardened in her heart as she looked up at Rotokas and saw Azi and the six assassins crossing the empty space toward them.

Semra hooked her arms over Zephan's head from behind him so the chains between her wrists cut across his throat.

"If you die, the hope of a nation dies with you. If I die," she said into his ear, "nothing happens. No one mourns. No one cares. You are important."

Zephan gripped the chains at his throat with one hand and brought his hand down hard to hit her in the gut with the other. She grunted and buckled forward, and he took the opportunity to duck under the chains and twist out of her grasp. He snatched a fallen sword from the ground and turned to face Rotokas.

"You're important to *me*." He lunged at Rotokas, but Semra leaped forward, gripped him around the waist, and with a guttural cry flung him through the open window.

She landed hard on the shattered glass, her torso hanging over the edge of the castle above four stories of darkness. A shadow of wings swept underneath her as Zephan fell.

"Get him somewhere safe," Semra whispered, closing her eyes as she sent the message as best she could.

Her body lurched into the air as Rotokas picked her up with a taloned back foot and slung her across the room and away from the windows. He roared a torrent of fire, and the gold inlay of the ornate ceiling shimmered to liquid and dripped onto the floor around her. Semra snatched one of Brens' fallen knives and slid it into place on her thigh, then picked up the fallen whip again.

"Enough!" Azi bellowed. "End her!"

An arrow notched to a string behind her, and knives were raised, but as Rotokas struck out toward her again, she rolled underneath him, slung the whip around his neck, and grasped it from the other side so that it served as a rope holding her to him. Semra swung her legs up and caught the chain between her ankles in his teeth.

Rotokas reared up, sliding her up the underside of his

spiked neck, and clacked his teeth together to free them of the annoyance. With a *chink* the chains broke, and Semra wrapped her legs around the thick scaled neck. Rotokas shook his head and beat his wings, twisting to see her clinging to him. Semra hooked her legs between the spikes and pulled herself around to sit at the back of his neck, right behind his head.

Grab a snake by the head, she said to herself.

An arrow whizzed by her ear, and Rotokas shook his head again, letting out a stream of fire in a wild arc that forced the assassins back. At that moment a commotion of running feet sounded from the stair, and Siler emerged with a dozen soldiers behind him.

"To the king!" he cried, and the soldiers raised their swords and ran forward to engage the six assassins. Siler looked up at Semra, and his eyes widened. "I see you found the high ground! I'm at ten points so far, plus one for finding a troop of General Soldan's unsullied soldiers."

"Great, great, now get Rotokas to focus on you instead of me!"

"It'll cost you another point, I'm afraid. Just know that if he kills me, I earn a thousand points for my sacrifice! You'll never catch up."

Semra smiled but braced herself to hold on as Siler danced around Rotokas' feet, in and out, dodging talons and flames as Rotokas turned his attention on him.

"I need his head down!" Semra yelled, holding tight to both ends of the whip to secure her position.

Siler slashed at Rotokas' underbelly, but his sword left no mark on the thick hide. "Any other demands for the little guy on the ground trying to control a massive dragon?"

"Oh, never mind! I'll do it myself!" Semra clamped her legs as tightly as she could, held the whip with one hand,

and drew her knife with the other. Rotokas lunged for Siler, and just as Semra began to topple forward she buried her knife into the wyvern's eye.

Rotokas let out a hideous screech and took off through the huge open windows and into the night, Semra holding on for dear life. She gasped as the cold air hit her, less pleasant than the breeze had been, and her vision blurred for a moment as her eyes watered against the wind. Rotokas took her for a tailspin down, down, and pulled up again.

Semra had hardly caught her breath when Rotokas drove forward and raked her against the side of the castle, crushing her against the stone. Semra screamed and lost her grip, and Rotokas pulled away as Semra plummeted to the outer ward below. The ground raced toward her, but in the last moment a large shadow flung itself under her and she found herself landed on Zezura behind Zephan.

Zezura took a wide arc over the castle, and Semra saw soldiers clashing in the courtyard under torchlight. Semra slowed Zezura so she could speak.

"What are they fighting for?"

"General Gresvig's soldiers are fighting Soldan's," Zephan replied. "Soldan seems to have been kept in the dark, but it looks like he's found out Gresvig's schemes."

"They're all under the king!"

"Yes, but they don't realize what they're fighting about. Too many stories are going around. Also, thanks for the ride ... but I don't appreciate being tossed from my own castle."

"It was for your own good."

"Says you. I know I'm no assassin, but I'm not worthless in a fight, and I deserve to defend my father, my home, and my country."

"Sorry."

"Don't be sorry. Just stop making my decisions for me.

Zezura, take us to the forest. Semra will be safe there while I finish out the battle."

"Look who's making decisions for who now!" Semra said, anger rising in her chest.

"Semra. You were half killed back there, twice over. I'm not exactly sure how you're still here. You need to rest."

"I'll do nothing of the sort! And luckily I'm the one with the dragon's kiss, so I'll be doing the commanding of the dragon. Zezura, we're going back to the throne room."

"Together?"

"Together."

29

Zezura's wings rhythmically beat the air as she accelerated, and then she set them into a glide back to the throne room. Semra tried to focus on her breathing, on the feeling of her lungs expanding and contracting. She closed her eyes, centering herself in a moment of calm before being thrown back into the storm. In this instant of serenity, she could—

Wham!

Semra jolted out of her reverie as Zezura veered hard left, her shriek slicing through the air like a knife. Rotokas had crashed into them, forcing them off course. Semra and Zephan ducked under Rotokas' wing as it cut above them. The wyvern turned and came at them again. Zezura dropped altitude, then banked up and let out a flood of fire, but Rotokas would not be deterred. The two beasts smashed into one another and barreled into the throne room's walls and windows in one massive ball of flame. The windows burst and the wall cracked and crumbled under the pressure. Zephan and Semra pitched forward into the room through the bashed-in window and the cloud of dust rising up from the wreckage of the wall.

Siler looked up, spun away from Tymetin, scooped two swords from the floor and tossed them in their direction. "Two points for dramatic entrance!" he called. "Minus one for leaving the fight!"

"I don't think I had much choice in the matter," Semra yelled back as she and Zephan each caught a sword.

A swarm of soldiers and assassins had converged on the throne room in Semra's absence, and Semra and Zephan fought their way to the king, who, despite the chains, was fighting Radix with expert form.

"The king is phenomenal!" Semra said as she blocked and countered against her adversary.

"Who do you think taught me?" Zephan answered with a laugh, artfully making a stroke against his opponent, then spinning behind Semra's and slicing him through.

Semra arched her eyebrows. "Aren't kings supposed to be busy ruling and stuff?" She ducked under a sword swing as another assassin came after her.

"I had lessons from several people, but he still took the time to work with me himself." Zephan danced forward and backward as steel met steel again and again.

Semra slipped a knife from the belt of the fallen assassin and threw it into the neck of Zephan's opponent, with just enough time to meet her own assailant's next attack. She made a swift downward stroke to disarm, slit her adversary's throat, and kicked him backward. Zephan and Semra closed the gap between them and the king, and the three of them stood back to back.

All three ducked as a huge black wing coursed over them, and Rotokas and Zezura rolled across half the length of the massive hall. Spurts of fire went up at intervals, and fighters on both sides dove out of the way. Siler continued to engage with Tymetin, but they were evenly matched, neither gaining nor losing any ground.

"Semra, I don't think we've formally been introduced," the king said, deftly returning Radix's blow.

"I do wish it were under more favorable circumstances," Semra answered as she parried a dragon wrangler's stroke. "How do people who already know each other's names introduce themselves?"

"Excellent question. I may have to think on it."

"Father, meet the bravest woman in Jannemar." Zephan lunged at his attacker.

"Am I interrupting a reunion?" Radix demanded, as he met the king steel to steel once more.

"It certainly seems so," Semra agreed. "If you would be so kind as to lay off, we could all meet more properly."

"I'm afraid I would need assurances of full immunity. As it is, I'll live with a handsome reward if the Framatar wins and be killed or imprisoned if he loses."

"You certainly couldn't expect a reward for turning sides only when it suited you," the king responded. "I can't say you've earned many points for trust."

"I'm no man's lapdog. If my cause is no longer a cause, perhaps I would be better suited to contract work."

"I can't say I'm impressed by your moral compass," the king said.

"Some of us had it beaten out of us, but Radix never had one," Siler called back, as he stepped up the dais and launched off the throne itself.

"Because you're such a saint!" Radix snorted, parrying again.

"If your efforts assist in turning the tide, I'll see to it your deeds earn you leniency," the king answered. "But if you merely jump ship to whichever side claims victory at the end, you will receive no such grace. The time to decide is now."

Semra looked up and saw Azi striding toward them, his jeweled collar glittering in the torchlight and dragon flame, his dark attire blending him into the night. Semra shoved her assailant aside and stepped forward as Zezura and Rotokas made another pass at each other and took off through the rubble of glass and stone along the east wall. Azi swept confidently over the marble floor, swinging his sword in a flourish. The opal dragon's kiss at his temple glimmered as his long dark hair rippled away from his face in the night breeze. Semra thought his eyes were chiseled of stone, and if ever he were blessed by the gods, even the gods might fear him now.

She adjusted her grip on her sword and swallowed. Zephan had moved down to fight with Siler against Tymetin, and Semra stood next to Radix and the king as they continued their duel. She walked forward, placing herself between the dragonlord and the king. Her tired muscles were tense, but her mind was more awake than it had ever been. She listened to the distant sounds of wind, steel, and exertion, and let her senses center themselves around the Framatar. He would swing one-handed with his right hand first. He would step as he moved.

She moved forward to meet him further from the king. The Framatar reached her and swung with his right hand. She spun behind his outstretched arm and attacked from the side, but in a flash, he defended with a powerful ring of steel. Azi struck forward, and Semra nicked his wrist in a slicing motion, but he followed through and made a shallow scrape across her throat before they danced apart.

Semra danced in, feinted, and drove forward to the left. Azi anticipated the feint and pushed her back. She tried again, and again, but Azi forced her back each time, further and further back toward the king. She glanced around her for bodies to strip, her frustration building.

"Looking for one of these?" he taunted, producing a knife in one hand. "Don't worry, I'll get rid of it. Fair fight and all." Azi threw the knife, but not at Semra. To her surprise, it went flying past her—toward the king.

In the last moment, Radix blocked the knife with his blade and spun round. He had chosen a side.

Azi snarled, and Semra took advantage of the moment to surge forward in a vicious attack that drove him back at last. Azi swore under his breath as they fought, again and again meeting blade on blade, but this time Semra refused to give way. A blue ball of fury rolled in through the ruins and unfurled behind Semra. Zezura reared her huge head up to the lofted ceiling and peered down at Azi.

Rotokas tore in after her and positioned himself behind Azi, the two dragonlords and their great beasts facing off. Rotokas released a torrent of flame, but Zezura met it in equal force, two pillars of fire from the dragons' throats meeting in the center. Azi and Semra battled beneath the inferno, embers sifting down around them and glinting off the sparkling oval on Semra's chest and Azi's temple.

Semra grimaced as she locked blades with Azi, leaning into one another, their faces mere inches apart.

Azi licked his lips and smiled. "I've had the pleasure of killing a lot of people in my life," he hissed. "But you I shall truly treasure."

Semra glanced down and saw the hilt of a knife strapped to his left thigh. She looked back at him. "How does it feel," she said, "To have spent the last twenty years of your life on this moment, taking the throne from your brother, only to fail now?"

Azi roared in anger and pushed forward. Semra pretended to stumble, stripped the knife from his thigh as she fell onto her back, blocked his follow through with the sword, and stabbed upward into his thigh. Ripping the knife free, she pushed away from him, flicked her wrist and embedded the knife in his side. Rotokas turned his one good eye to his master, and Zezura pounced on him, rolling across the room once more and striking his wings with her taloned forelegs.

From the arched entryway, General Gresvig ran in with three squads of fresh soldiers. "Arrest this impostor, Turian!" he yelled. "Your duty is to protect your king, and there he is, Azi Shamaran!" Gresvig gestured to the Framatar, but his face fell when he saw his supposed king kneeling in pain, a knife protruding from his side.

General Soldan took the stairs three at a time with squads of his own and bellowed for all to hear, "General Gresvig is hereby relieved of his command." Soldan nodded at his soldiers and four of them stepped forward to take hold of Gresvig. The soldiers behind Gresvig looked between their generals, down the hall at the Framatar, and caught sight of their king as Turian, Radix, and Zephan teamed up to push Tymetin backward. The soldiers saluted General Soldan and he jerked his head up the throne room.

"Protect your king—King Turian—and obliterate all opposing."

Semra circled the Framatar, and Siler appeared at her side. Azi stood slowly, bearing nearly all his weight on his good leg, and raised his sword. Siler stepped forward and thrust his blade, but Azi blocked it. Siler struck again, and again Azi parried the blow, but his face was growing pale, and his strength was waning.

Semra scanned the throne room. The assassins were

depleted, some dead on the floor, but a number of them seemed to have mysteriously disappeared. A rope tied around one of the columns and running over the edge of the wall of rubble provided some insight. Tymetin slipped down it to the outer ward before Radix, the king, or Zephan could apprehend him or cut through the rope.

The soldiers rounded up only three assassins and brought them before General Soldan and King Turian, who stood together at the foot of the dais in front of the two golden thrones. One of the soldiers fetched a set of keys and quickly unshackled the king's wrists. He rubbed them gratefully. Turian's face looked drawn, his fine clothes soaked in sweat and blood, but he kept his shoulders back and his chin high.

Siler knocked the Framatar to his knees and wrested his sword from his grasp. Additional soldiers filed into a semicircle behind him, weapons drawn. Semra held her sword in both hands, wrists still shackled with one foot of loose chain between them. She shifted her sword to one hand and dug into her pocket with the other. Zephan spoke with his father, and both walked toward Semra and Azi, while the dragonlord's beady eyes examined every move.

Semra pulled out Ramas' emerald snake amulet and tossed it on the ground before Azi. He glanced at it and back up at her, eyes turning flat and lip curling ever so slightly. Semra waved her sword in a flourish and took a short bow. "Sentiment. It is weakness, no?"

She couldn't help but smile to herself, but as the adrenaline in her system settled, her movements reminded her of the tremendous beating her body had taken that day. Semra winced and straightened slowly. Zezura flew back in through the open space, a satisfied expression on her face, and circled behind Semra. There was no sign of Rotokas. Semra reached up to stroke Zezura's face, and the dragon flushed bright blue at her touch. After a moment Zezura pulled back, eyeing Semra's chains and cocking her head.

"You're right," Semra said. "It's been long enough." She extended her arms, and Zezura bit down on the chain, creating a furnace in her closed mouth until the chains gave way. A trail of smoke floated up from her nostrils.

"Semra."

She turned.

The king approached her with Zephan at his side.

She bowed. "Your Majesty."

King Turian raised her to her feet and grasped her forearm in respectful greeting. "Your name seems too short to give you appropriate credit for all you have done for my family. My son has filled me in somewhat, though I gather it will take more than a few minutes to regale me with the full tale. I look forward to hearing it."

Semra's glance flickered to Zephan with a quizzical look, but his bright, laughing eyes just twinkled back at her. She smiled at him, wondering how much he'd shared, and returned her gaze to the king. "Semra is good enough for me. I have no surname."

Turian nodded. "I remember. It shall be a name of high honor. Without your efforts, I fear my family, my line, and my kingdom would have been lost."

"I do wish I ... that I could have ... stopped things sooner."

"So do we all. So do we all."

Siler cleared his throat. "Your Majesty. Sire. If I may be so bold, this man"—he gestured to Azi—"has brought great tragedy on us all, and none more than your own family and kingdom, as you have said. I can see no reason to allow him live, and as such, I would be most joyfully obliged to purge this evil from among us."

"Purge this evil ..." Semra shook her head, smiling. "The noble pursuit of our childhoods, hmm?"

Siler nodded. "Naturally."

Zephan reached for Semra's hand and squeezed it. Siler's expression soured.

"What is your name?" Turian asked.

"Siler, Your Majesty."

"I presume you don't know your surname either?"

"'Semra' is good enough for Semra, and 'Siler' will be good enough for me."

"Very well, Siler. Your efforts will be rewarded, as my son has also told me of your hand in recent events. You are an admirable young man, Siler. As for my brother ... no, I think it has been too long since he lived in the house of his fathers. He will enjoy the hospitality of our dungeons, and I do hope he finds his stay every bit as unpleasant as Semra's was to her."

"You have always thought yourself so much better than me," Avi spat. "Look at you! Defended by ignorant children in your own territory. What does that say about you?"

"I would think it says very little about me," Turian responded. "First, it says something about these young people—their skill, fortitude, and resilience in the face of your vitriolic abuse overseeing their childhoods. Second, it says something about you, that these ignorant children, as you call them, were able to dismantle your miserable life's work targeting your own flesh and blood. Perhaps with that knife in your side, you will learn some empathy. Until that time, however, we will keep your poisonous existence away from society."

Azi locked eyes with Semra, and Zezura clacked her teeth together in warning. "I murdered your parents with my bare hands," he hissed. "I wanted to slow it down, savor it, feel the crack of their bones, taste their blood. You came to me crying, missing them, that very night. I comforted you with their blood fresh on my hands."

Tears sprang unbidden to Semra's eyes, even knowing he was trying to goad her. She set her jaw and clenched her fists, but said nothing. Suddenly she realized Zephan's hand was still in hers, and she was crushing it. She tried to release him, but he held onto her. *I am not fragile,* he seemed to say.

Azi scanned her face and turned to Siler. "Whatever morality you think Semra has, you've never been so hindered. You know what you want to do. You are stronger than she is. Do it! You are a free man, aren't you? You have no king!"

Siler leveled his gaze back at him, then turned to Turian. "Your Majesty, this man deserves to die. But I have to admit, he may want me to kill him even more than I do, and the idea of his fear being caged might even be enough to stay my hand."

"Wretch!" Azi screamed. "Fool!" He reached for the knife in his side, tore it free, and reared his arm back to hurl it, but Siler and two soldiers rushed forward to force him face down onto the marble floor.

"Get him out of here!" Turian bellowed. "I want a dozen soldiers escorting him to the dungeons and shackling him to the bars with a short leash. Go!"

The soldiers hauled Azi to his feet, leaving a smear of blood as they brought him up and half dragged, half carried him down the hall and out of sight, his insults and curses dwindling away as he disappeared through the double doors.

Turian sighed and turned back to them. "Where were we?"

"Semra still has shackles on," Zephan said, squeezing her

hand again before letting her go. "And she needs medical attention. Also, Avaya, Aviama, and the nobles are all still locked in their rooms."

"Gracious, I nearly forgot!" Turian called for the soldier with the keys, and he ran forward to release Semra from the shackles. She'd already managed to break free of the chains restricting the movement of her arms and legs, but the shackles themselves had remained. Semra rubbed her wrists and nodded thankfully at the soldier. A rush of lightheadedness went to her head, then passed.

Turian turned to the remaining soldiers. "Captain Firfell, see to it my daughters and the nobles are released, and check on any servants that were trapped here but live outside the castle. Offer them servants' quarters if they wish to stay the night, or see them safely out the gates if they choose to go home."

"Father, Voldar is one of Azi's sympathizers," Zephan put in.

Turian took a deep breath and let it out, shaking his head. "Firfell, when you release the nobles, make sure Voldar is taken directly to the dungeons to accompany his puppeteer."

The captain nodded and turned from the room, followed by eight men. Turian faced General Soldan, and eyed General Gresvig, still held fast by Soldan's soldiers. "General Gresvig. Your egregious overreach in military power over the guard was concerning enough, but I now have no choice but to charge you with treason and strip you of your rank. Sentencing will be forthcoming." Turian gestured at the soldiers. "Take him away."

"General Soldan. Your quick action and the trust you have built with the men under you is a testament to your caliber as a man, as a warrior, and as an esteemed member of military. There are few men I trust implicitly, and even fewer after today. I am unwilling to give you up as general of my armies, but I would like to offer you a concurrent dukedom over Dulnor. It will be a lot on your plate, but I have full faith in your success."

Soldan bowed. "Your Majesty! I am honored!"

"I am honored by your acceptance, duke. Unfortunately my first order to you now is as general. Our armies are marching on Belvidore as we speak. Send urgent word to the front lines to recall the troops and arrange a meet with King Arnevon before it is too late. We cannot afford to start a needless war. My own twin brother, Azi Shamaran, murdered my wife. Belvidore is hereby acquitted."

Soldan bowed again. "Right away, Your Majesty."

Soldan took his exit, and Turian suddenly straightened, looking to his left and right. "Where ... where did that surly fellow go, the one impersonating one of my guards?"

Semra blinked. She only now realized Radix was missing, and she hadn't seen him since well before Azi was removed. Her vision blurred, and she rubbed her eyes.

Siler laughed. "Your Majesty, I believe he's in the wind."

"I suppose I should have expected nothing less. As for you, Siler, you are welcome to stay as our guest for as long as you desire."

Semra wavered, and Zezura let out a concerned moan as she started to fall. Siler and Zephan each reached out to grab one of her arms, steadying her on either side. Semra groaned as the pain of the whip wounds, the myriad of hurts from Rotokas crushing her against the castle, and from fighting in the subsequent battle caught up with her at last.

"We need to get her to bed."

"She needs a healer."

"I'm a healer."

"You're an apprentice."

The words swirled around her, and Semra struggled to keep her eyes open as the burning pains mixed with the aching pains and threatened to take her over.

"Call the castle healer at once. I want her fully examined before he examines me, and I want a report the instant he has one to give. Zephan, go with her to get her settled and then meet me in my chambers. Make sure Saeb has two fresh rooms prepared for our guests."

30

Morning light filtered in through the window of the second-floor guest room, a wistful breeze playing gently against the panes. Semra squinted as she opened her eyes and found herself lying on her stomach in soft linens on a tall, luxurious bed. The spacious room had a vanity and wardrobe on one side and a desk on the other.

A knock sounded at the door, and an excitable young voice piped up. "Semra! Are you awake? Are you decent? Avaya's being a grouch, and I need to get off the third floor."

"If she wasn't awake before, she certainly will be now," Saeb's voice scolded from the hall. "Leave her be. She'll come out when she's ready."

"Semra?"

Semra grunted and sat up gingerly, careful to avoid injury to her back. It had been a week since she'd battled Azi, and her injuries were beginning to heal thanks to the efforts of Coanor the healer. Zephan had appointed himself as apprentice under Coanor and often came along with him. Still, she moved stiffly and cautiously, as every twist or bend of her striped back reminded her of Tymetin's whipping.

The door opened, and Aviama bounced into the room in a light-pink dress, her golden hair flowing freely about her shoulders. "Good morning! How long have you been awake? Why haven't you come out yet? Isn't it so beautiful outside today?"

Semra raised an eyebrow. "Did I invite you in and just not remember?"

"I knocked on the door and you answered."

"I grunted. With those just-waking-up noises people make when they aren't prepared yet for real words." Semra smiled despite herself. Aviama had been a ray of sunshine in her recovery, and in all honesty Semra was grateful for her positive attitude.

Aviama shrugged. "Close enough. Isn't it stuffy in here? It's so pretty outside. You know, if you had taken Father's offer to let a servant help you, they could have already opened the windows."

"I don't want any servants. Plenty come in to fix the bed and such as it is, and I'm afraid I wouldn't have any idea what to do with them. I can dress myself."

Aviama looked her up and down and stepped around Semra to see her back. The corner of her mouth twitched. "But you can't seem to keep any clothes we give you in one piece."

"Not true. I wear the same thing to bed so that I don't have to destroy more than one," Semra said proudly. "If it felt good to throw all kinds of layers on my back, I would do it, but it doesn't, so, you know ... I needed to air out."

"Mhmm. By ripping the back of your tunic."

"It's not scandalous or anything. And I'm only sleeping in it, anyway."

"Have you considered wearing a dress today? We can pick silk or something gentle on your skin."

"Oh, no ... no, I haven't."

"Come on! You've been here a week and you haven't worn one once!"

"The last time you gave me a fancy gown to wear, it was destroyed beyond all recognition."

Aviama made a face. "I'm confident you will have no reason to fight anybody today, and you won't end up in any dungeons either."

"You never know! Best to be prepared."

"Well, you have to put something on for breakfast. What do you suggest?"

"A tunic and pants?"

Aviama wrinkled her nose. "Have you always dressed like a farm boy?"

"It's very practical attire."

Aviama folded her arms. "I am going to burn everything in that wardrobe except for dresses."

"Well, that would be silly, since everything in there was stocked by castle staff. Who would be destroying things then?"

"Hmph." Aviama walked to the wardrobe and rifled through it, then pulled out a floor-length violet dress with gold stitching at the arm and a draping belt about the waist. "Okay, look. This one is comfortable and flowy, reminds you that you are in fact a woman, but isn't too tight. I'm not leaving until you put it on. You can pretend you are Axelia Belinon."

Semra frowned, sizing up her young friend, who jutted out her chin and held out the dress. She wasn't bluffing.

Semra might indeed sit in this room all day before Aviama let her leave wearing anything else. "Fine. But I want my old trousers back by the end of the day. Belon promised to bring them back to me when they were washed, but that was six days ago, and I haven't seen them since!"

Aviama grinned. "My fault. I told her to keep them from you until I got you into a dress. Put this on, and I'll make sure they reappear by nightfall."

Semra shook her head. "You trickster! Hand me that gauze, and I'll be ready to get dressed."

Aviama handed her the gauze, Semra carefully wrapped her torso to protect her wounds from rubbing and replaced the shredded tunic with the dress. Semra stepped around the partition, and Aviama clapped her hands.

"Yes! A woman! I'm so proud of you. Come on, we have to show you off." Aviama grabbed her hand and tugged her into the hall.

"I don't need to be shown off. I need breakfast!"

"My father is meeting with Siler and Zephan right now in the east meeting rooms, and if you'd been awake, you would've been there too. They'll have food there."

Semra allowed herself to be dragged down the hall, and she looked longingly into the quiet of Garbane's chandlery as Aviama whisked her passed the chandlery, laundry, and kitchen and into Ancestry Hall. They took the stairs down to the first floor, passing two guards that paused to stare at them as they passed, and exited out into the courtyard.

"Do they hate me?" Semra asked as soon as they were outside.

"Who?"

"The guards. They all stare at me, and I did kill some of them."

"From what I heard, there were a few unfortunate losses

from people who followed orders of a general to go against their king. Any guards further away from the throne room didn't know what was really going on and why the castle was in lockdown, and they're probably in awe of you for singlehandedly dismantling a plot they themselves had nothing to do with. Also, your mark looks pretty cool. And you have a dragon."

Semra glanced down at the dragon's kiss glistening on her upper chest and blushed. She looked up at the throne room to her upper right and saw Zezura's silhouette through the windows. Materials for repairs had been ordered, but in the meantime Zezura was allowed to stage herself in the only room the castle had to offer large enough to house her and allow her to come and go as she chose. In an instant, the blue dragon flew through the gaping hole on the other side of the building and descended onto the courtyard to greet them.

Aviama held back, watching Zezura carefully as Semra stepped forward to greet her. The young princess was a firecracker, but even she was nervous around a fifty-foot dragon. The whole courtyard seemed to have shrunk significantly.

"Um, can we ... get you to breakfast?" she asked tentatively.

Semra placed her forehead against the huge serpent's nose and breathed in deep. Rain or shine, forest floor or castle, Zezura had become a comforting constant. Semra straightened and patted Zezura once more before turning back to Aviama.

"Just saying good morning. We can go."

They walked down the courtyard and through a door near the end on the left, straight into a conference room. King Turian sat at the head of a long table, with Prince Zephan to his right, General Soldan to his left, and Siler next to him. To Semra's surprise, Isra stood with two guards to the right.

Isra raised an eyebrow. "You clean up okay."

"Doesn't she?" Aviama cooed, seemingly oblivious to the strange meeting before her. "I told her she had no choice but to put on something feminine today, now that she's moving around better, and it's been a whole week without a single dress! Doesn't she look gorgeous? Can you even believe she has been in frumpy farm-boy clothes this whole time?"

Zephan and Siler stared at her in wonder.

Aviama tapped her foot impatiently. "Well?"

Zephan cleared his throat. "She does look beautiful."

King Turian glanced between Semra and his son, and Semra flushed deep red and stared at the floor. She pinched her fingers nervously. If only the magic of the dragon's kiss could also make her invisible!

"Axelia, was it?" Siler said, pulling himself together.

Semra grinned, grateful for the levity, and King Turian waved her to take a seat.

"Come join us, Semra. We could use your insights. Thank you, Aviama. Would you give us the room?"

A platter of fruit and pastries sat in the center of the table, and Semra eyed it hungrily as she rounded the table to the left and seated herself next to Siler. Siler bumped her leg with his knee as she sat down, and she casually edged away and reached for a pastry. She winced at the motion, but her pain was forgotten as she bit into the sweet.

"You seem to be moving better," Turian observed as Aviama left the room.

"Much improved, thank you. Has our friend Isra decided not to try and kill us, or did he already try, and get caught?"

Siler grinned. "It's not generally considered wise to stroll up to the murder boxes of a castle as a known assassin."

Semra's eyes widened. "You went to the front gate?"

Isra nodded. "I did. What you and Siler said about the Framatar ... I couldn't shake it. I want to be free of him, free of his lies, and start somewhere fresh. I didn't know where else to go."

"Certainly gutsy. How can we believe you?" Zephan asked skeptically.

Isra turned to Semra and Siler. "I remember Koran's disappearance. It was suspicious at best, and I remember thinking something didn't add up with the explanation they gave, but I shook it off. And the memories ... the only unique memory I have of my family is a good one. All the others are memories we all seem to have, scenarios we all heard since we were brought into the mountain. Imposed memories. That's how I knew you were telling the truth."

"How many people were in the mountain?" General Soldan asked, breaking his silence.

"About one hundred and fifty," Siler responded. "But those are mostly children going through the program, between the ages of four and fifteen."

"One hundred and fifty!" Turian exclaimed.

"Roughly ninety children before mission-support levels," Isra agreed, nodding.

"What are mission-support levels?" Zephan asked.

"Saber class encompasses ages thirteen and fourteen, in which students engage in mission support for getaway, distraction supply drops, and a practicum of twenty missions observed from planning stages through execution," Semra explained. "By age fifteen, students are expected to take lead on missions, under observation, and by age sixteen, students graduate to 'mission-ready' status and solo missions."

"Unless you're Semra, and you graduate early," Siler added.

Semra shrugged. "Yes."

The king raised his eyebrows and let out a deep sigh. "And how many older children?"

"Twelve children are taken in per class," Isra stated. "Sometimes a few are lost in missions gone wrong, especially for young students just getting their feet wet with real missions. Each class has a doctrine leader and apprentice, and each category has a captain, all overseen by Colonel Nepraunik."

"Until mission readies, which were under Ramas—until Semra dispatched him." Siler grinned.

"So how many of these mission readies, would you say?" Turian asked.

Semra took a moment to calculate the answer in her head. "There were ... what, around twenty? Not including the few sleepers he has hidden somewhere. Not all the students continued on the mission-ready track. Others were repurposed to other jobs such as doctrine, cooking, hunting, things like that."

Siler rubbed his forehead. "With seven about to graduate. Actually, they would've graduated with the new year— class of year 5000." He looked at Soldan. "How many are dead, and how many are in the wind? Are any captured?"

"Three are in the dungeon with Azi, Gresvig, and Voldar," Soldan replied.

"All of them could easily have been involved," Zephan said. "Eight bodies in the castle weren't members of our guard or military."

"Plus Manu and Pinji, who died in the forest east of the Dezapi, which brings the body count to ten." Semra turned to Isra. "Where is Vix?"

"He ... didn't want to come," Isra said. "He assumed he'd

be killed on the spot or thrown in the dungeon. I decided to take my chances."

"So Vix, Tymetin, and Radix are all in the wind," Siler said. "With Isra, Semra, and me here, that's ten dead, three in the dungeon, three in this room, and seven missing, not counting the graduating class of seven, the hundred and twenty or so children younger than them and maybe twenty other staff positions."

"And five sleepers," Semra reminded them. "In summary, there are nine experienced assassins out there, seven trained but not yet graduated to solo missions, and children and staff."

Turian passed a hand over his eyes. "And our army is still beyond our borders. We need them back *now* to send some to save the children in the mountain if any are still there."

"We have not yet heard word back from Belvidore that it is safe for us to completely remove our forces, Your Majesty," Soldan reminded him. "And we will also need some sort of task force to mitigate the damage these rogue assassins could cause."

A knock came at the door, and King Turian called for the visitor to enter. Captain Firfell appeared in the doorway. "Your Majesty. General. I'm afraid I have news that cannot wait."

"Out with it, man," Soldan said.

"It is ... rather sensitive," Firfell responded, gaze flickering to the three assassins in the room.

"It's all right," the king said. "Speak."

"Belvidore refuses to accept your gifts, your apology, and your request for a meeting. Our forces drew back at your command, but King Arnevon has officially declared war on Jannemar."

The solemn news seemed to suck the life out of the room.

Silence fell. Time seemed to drag on, and Semra shifted in her chair. Even defeated, Azi had managed to taint the peaceful rule of his brother and throw the Shamaran family and Jannemar kingdom into chaos.

"He won't give up until he claims the Surion Strip," Zephan said at last. "We've accused him of murder, embarrassed and insulted him, and the alliance through Axis and Avaya's would-be marriage is broken."

"I'm afraid you are right," Turian responded. He leaned back in his chair, stroking his beard. It seemed to Semra that he grew older in the space of that minute, as he contemplated the inevitable loss of life to his men and the strain on his people. When he looked up, his eyes had hardened with resolve and a confidence settled on his shoulders. "Firfell, alert the highest members of my court that I will speak to them on an urgent matter this evening. Soldan, hold a military strategy meeting immediately and provide me with reasonable options before that time.

"Soldan is right. We are spread thin, and we need a task force to resolve questions regarding children and staff still living in Mount Hara, as well as locating the missing assassins. Siler, Isra, I would like you to be on this task force and reach out to Vix if you can to see if he would be willing to assist in exchange for immunity. Young, expert killers with splintered loyalties are a serious threat, and the three of you have unique firsthand knowledge that will be indispensable. Zephan will split his time between military strategy at war with Belvidore, and overseeing the task force.

"Semra ... you have given much already, and you are not yet fully healed, but the advantage of having a dragonlord on my side who is both knowledgeable and compassionate is not lost on me. Skill that is refined by character is not easy to find, and I believe I see that in you. I would like to place you in a senior position on this task force."

Semra felt a strange warmth mingle with the apprehension in her chest at the king's words. Her skills could still be used, this time for good. She would be protecting children like Lesala, purging the world of evil that could not be turned, and for the first time in a week some deep part of her felt at home.

She bowed her head. "Your Majesty, I would be honored."

BOOK #2: BROKEN BONDS

Continue the adventure with Broken Bonds...

Bloodlust: the one thing she's good at. The one thing she must fight against.

With rogue assassins in the wind and a restless dragon on her hands, Semra accepts a final mission to solve a kidnapping – as the neighboring king's paranoia threatens war.

THANK YOU FOR READING!

Thank you so much for reading *Dragon's Kiss,* book 1 of *The Blood and Flame Saga*! I hope you enjoyed reading it as much as I enjoyed writing it.

If you did, would you be willing to leave a review? Reviews help enable authors to continue doing what they do, and help other readers to find books best suited to them.

If you'd like to leave a review on Amazon, **click here.**

ABOUT THE AUTHOR

Author of *The Forgotten Stone* and the *Blood and Flame Saga*, E.A. Winters loves pouring herself a cup of hot chocolate with a mountain of marshmallows and delving into creating epic fantasy worlds for you to enjoy.

Erin lives in Virginia with her husband and two boys. When she's not writing, Erin is spending her time with her family. She loves playing board games and reading, whenever the elusive "free time" opportunity arises.

ALSO BY E.A. WINTERS

BLOOD & FLAME SAGA

Book 1: Dragon's Kiss

Book 2: Broken Bonds

Book 3: Noble Claims

Book 4: Crimson Queen

STAND ALONES

The Forgotten Stone